HUNGRY WOLF

Suddenly, there was a change in the air. It was the same thing that made cats arch their backs and swish their tails; the same thing that put dogs on snarling alert. My hackles went up, adrenaline boiling my blood. I licked my lips, the saline taste of danger in my saliva.

I heard the growl, first.

It was a low, predatory rumble. Earthy and primitive, like nothing I've heard before.

Except I did hear it before. Once.

My feet were rooted to the ground, but I turned my head slowly. The rumble was low enough that I couldn't hear which direction it came from. But it called to me, and I knew where it was.

"Lawson." I heard Alex call behind me and I slowly held up a hand, silently willing him to understand, to stay put.

And when I turned again I saw it. A wolf, in the narrow, darkened corridor between two houses. I could make out nothing but his eyes and his teeth as the black rim of his lip curled up into a fearsome snarl . . .

Books by Hannah Jayne

UNDER WRAPS

UNDER ATTACK

UNDER SUSPICION

UNDER THE GUN

Published by Kensington Publishing Corporation

UNDER THE GUN

The Underworld Detection Agency Chronicles

❖━━◆━━❖

HANNAH JAYNE

KENSINGTON PUBLISHING CORP.
http://www.kensingtonbooks.com

KENSINGTON BOOKS are published by

Kensington Publishing Corp.
119 West 40th Street
New York, NY 10018

All Kensington Titles, Imprints, and Distributed Lines are
available at special quantity discounts for bulk purchases for
sales promotions, premiums, fund-raising, and educational
or institutional use. Special book excerpts or customized
printings can also be created to fit specific needs. For details,
write or phone the office of the Kensington special sales
manager: Kensington Publishing Corp., 119 West 40th Street,
New York, NY 10018, attn: Special Sales Department, Phone:
1-800-221-2647.

Kensington and the K logo Reg. U.S. Pat & TM Off.

ISBN-13: 978-0-7582-8110-4
ISBN-10: 0-7582-8110-2

First Mass Market Printing: February 2013

10 9 8 7 6 5 4 3 2 1

Printed in the United States of America

To Sandra McIsaac,
who told me she'd let me pass algebra
if I dedicated a book to her one day.
Our debt is settled. And thanks.

Acknowledgments

A book never truly has one author, and though an idea can be hatched alone, it takes a team of incredible friends and colleagues to create a story. Thank you to my editor, John Scognamiglio, who had the wherewithal to send me a politely worded e-mail that boiled down to "seriously?" To Amberly Finarelli, who will always be my agent and friend, even as she's tending to the cries of the Twinarellis rather than the cries of errant authors. To Vida, Justine, and Alex, the best Kensington cheerleaders a girl could have. To my parents who support and encourage, even though having an adult daughter obsessed with made-up creatures probably wasn't what they expected. To my brother, Trevor, because when people ask, "what happened in your childhood to make you write such gruesome stuff?" I can quietly point to you and fifteen beheaded Barbies. As always, tremendous thanks to Shirley, Penne, Kristin, Gary, Nadine, Marilyn, and everyone else at Club One for giving me an outlet. To the Rogue Writers Group, thanks for the constant encouragement. To my readers and fans—ohmigosh! I have readers and fans! I'm going to bake each and every one of you cupcakes. To Joan, John, and Oscar for always being there with a cocktail, toilet paper, and Diet Coke—the writer's triumvirate. To Vicki, Robert, Katherine, Katie, Anna, and everyone else who worked on the UDA production—thank you for bringing my story to life! And last but nowhere near least, to my fellow Moustachteer Authors, Marina Adair and Britt Bury—I can't wait until we're old and gray, when we've earned our glaucoma, RA, and shoulder pain, and we live in our cozy little cottage with jars of money buried out front, talking about the good ol' days—which is everyday we're together. Love you guys. And don't call me Shirley.

Chapter One

You might think that after a visit from my dead grandmother, a run-in with my dead sister, and a rent-controlled apartment shared with an undead vampire fashionista, a visit from the undead wouldn't be so un-expected.

But you'd be wrong.

Which was why I was frowning while he stood in my doorway looking remarkably comfortable, without the faintest glow of otherworldly aura or the oozing, fetid sores I had come to expect on those who returned from the dead.

"Sophie."

He said my name and my hackles went up; I was all at once intrigued, delighted, and horrified.

I opened my mouth and then closed it again, willing the words that tumbled through my brain to form some coherent, cohesive thought, something great and all-encompassing enough to explain what I was feeling.

"I see dead people," I mumbled.

Without conscious thought, I snapped my arm back and slammed the door shut. I ran backward into my apartment, falling over the arm of the couch and landing with a thump on the pillows, ending in an inelegant heap on the carpet. My puppy, ChaCha, trotted over to me, sniffed, and walked away. *It's happening, it's happening, it's happening. . . .*

I was shaking, the mantra rolling through my head as I curled in on my chest, rocking gently. I'd known it was only a matter of time before I developed some sort of mystical powers—red hair and an insatiable appetite for chocolate or anything in a take-out box couldn't be the only things I'd inherited from my mother and grandmother who both had been powerful mystics with the ability to tell the future.

"I'm getting my powers." I licked my lips, terror and joy bounding through me.

That was it.

This was my power.

"I see dead people."

I felt the words in my mouth, the exhilaration of finally belonging, and finally feeling a connection to my paranormal family and office mates chipping away at the terror that sat like an iceberg at the bottom of my gut.

The jiggling of the ancient hardware on my front door brought me crashing back to the reality of the doorknob turning in front of me. I stared at it as it moved horror-movie slow and my blood pounded in my ears. The person on the other side of the door knocked again. This time it was a quick warning rap, and when he pressed the door open, the air that I had gulped in a greedy, terrified frenzy whooshed out.

"What are you doing here?"

He grinned. "I thought you'd be happier to see me."

I rolled over onto my back and pushed myself up, my eyes still trained on the man—*the apparition?*—who stood in my foyer, smile wide, welcoming, and corporeal looking.

"Mr. Sampson?" His name was a breathy whisper that

made my bottom lip quiver. "You need me to help you cross over," I said.

I took a tentative step toward the man whom I had known so well—who had been more like a trusted confidante than a boss to me for so many years, who had given me my start at the Underworld Detection Agency. The man whom I had watched being tortured until he finally disappeared, news of his death reaching me months later.

I reached out in front of me, fingers shaking and outstretched, willing myself to touch him, knowing that all I would feel would be a cold burst of nothingness of the displaced molecules that should have been a living, breathing human form.

I stuck my index finger in his right nostril, my thumb brushing his bottom lip.

"Oh, gross!"

"Sophie! What the hell?" he snapped.

My hand recoiled back in near-boogered terror. "Oh my God! Mr. Sampson! You're alive!"

My heart slammed against my rib cage and every fiber of my being seemed to expand with joy. I crushed myself against Pete Sampson, feeling his wonderful heart thudding against my chest, relishing the human feeling of his tender, warm skin against my own.

He shrugged me off—gently—and held me at arm's length. "You look wonderful."

"You're alive. . . . You're alive." I mumbled it dumbly again and again until my eyes could focus on the stiff reality under my fingers. I massaged Mr. Sampson's arms, feeling the ropey muscles flinch underneath his soft flannel shirt, my fingertips working down his forearms until I found his bare skin, his pulse point. I paused, counted.

"You're not dead at all. You're really, really alive."

A smile cut across Sampson's face—a smile that went up

to his milk-chocolate eyes that crinkled at the corners and warmed me from tip to tail. I stiffened, shook his hands off, and slapped him across his chest, anger and betrayal walloping me.

"How are you alive? You're dead. You *were* dead! I mourned for you! And Alex," I huffed, a sob choking in my throat, "and Will." I sniffed. "And I'm the Vessel. . . ." Tears flooded over my cheeks, dripped from my chin as I hiccupped and quaked. "Will's my Guardian."

Sympathy, with just the slightest tinge of amusement, flitted across Mr. Sampson's face as he took me by the wrist and offered me a stiffly starched hankie. I held it in my hand, my fingers working the burgundy stitching—the letters P and S embroidered elegantly against the white cloth.

"You look so different," I whispered.

The Mr. Sampson whom I had known was always freshly shaven and dressed impeccably in tailored suits that highlighted his powerful build. He kept his sandy brown hair close-cropped and slicked back. This man sported a three-day beard peppered with gray stubble and looked unkempt and disheveled in a wrinkled flannel shirt that was unbuttoned over a plain white T-shirt. His hair was beginning to thin, but still slightly shaggy. He wore a pair of jeans that were a combination of broken-in and over-worn, but as I held the handkerchief to my nose I smelled the faint scent of the Mr. Sampson I used to know—a scent that was spicy, familiar, with just the slightest hint of salt and pine.

Sampson pulled me to the couch and I sat down next to him, leaving just enough space to let him know that despite his heavenly return from death, all was not forgiven.

"What happened to you?" I managed to say.

It was then that I noticed the easy laugh lines that had sat like commas on either side of Sampson's mouth were hard etched now; it was only then that I noticed the latticework of worry lines between his eyes, the thick frown line that cut across his dark brow. A thin streak of gray sprouted at his hairline, peppering his too-long hair with a washed-out sheen.

"I'm sorry I never contacted you." Sampson shook his head and stared at his hands in his lap. "I wanted to; the last thing I wanted was to have you—you and everyone else at the UDA—worry about me. But if you knew I was alive, that's what would have happened. You would have worried."

He offered me what I assumed was supposed to be his appeasing smile, but it only served to stir up a hot seed of anger in my belly.

"You could have let us decide whether or not we worried about you," I spat. "I thought that the chief killed you. That's what Alex said—"

I stopped, the words going heavy and bitter in my mouth. Alex.

Alex was the fallen angel who had the annoying habit of popping into my life at inopportune moments (think bathtub) and the even more annoying habit of making my knees weak and my nether regions wanting, bathtub or no. He was fallen, but good; wickedly sexy, but moral.

And now I knew that he had spent the last year lying to me about one of the most important people—and the most intensely painful situations—in my life.

I felt my eyes narrow, and knew that I was holding my mouth in a hard snarl. "Did Alex know? Did he know this whole time?"

Sampson pushed himself off the couch, avoiding my gaze. "Sophie, Alex—"

I launched myself up then, too, hands on hips. "Alex knew this whole time, didn't he?"

"Not the whole time, Sophie. I had to hide. I had to make it look like I was dead or they would keep coming after me and no one at the Agency would be safe. I wasn't going to do that to the Underworld, Sophie. I needed to know when it would be safe to come back again. And the only way I could do that—the only way I could do that and still even have the slightest hope of coming back—was to have eyes out here."

"Alex's."

"He helped me, Sophie."

I thought of Alex, of his ice-blue eyes and that cocky half smile, of the two-inch scars above each shoulder blade that had grown silvery with age after years of wandering the earth without his wings.

Alex may have been fallen, but he swore he was determined to do good, to one day be restored back to grace. He had been my protector, my lover, my friend.

And he had been lying to me.

"Does he know you're back now?" I wanted to know.

"No." The stern look in Sampson's eyes convinced me he was telling the truth. "And you can't tell him. You can't tell anyone I'm here. You can't tell anyone I'm alive."

I swallowed hard, the weight of knowing crushing against my chest, squeezing out the air. "No one?"

Sampson shook his head. "You have to promise me."

I felt myself nod, mute, while the wheels spun in my head. Finally, "If you don't want anyone to know you're alive, why'd you come back from—where were you?"

Sampson cocked his head. "Everywhere. Nowhere. After that night—"

An involuntary shudder wracked my body. The memory of being chained with Sampson in an underground basement while a madman sharpened the sword he was going to use to pierce my flesh was still as cold and as fresh in my mind as it was a year ago. Sampson slid a comforting arm across my shoulders and I slumped against him, my body relying on muscle memory because my brain was still calculating, figuring, trying to make sense of Pete Sampson, alive, in my living room.

"I was rescued—or so I thought—from that damn little kennel."

Sampson clapped a hand over his chin and rubbed where the salt-and-pepper stubble littered the firm set of his clenched jaw. He looked at me and I could see the smallest flitter of embarrassment cross his face; his shoulders seemed to sag under the weight, under the memory of being chained, being beaten—being treated like an animal by a man whom he had once considered a friend.

"There were people—they said they knew about the Underworld. I didn't have a choice. I got in the car and immediately passed out. I must have been drugged. Then I was crated, moved. I woke up in a shipping yard, somewhere. I knew it was woodsy, or forested, but that's all I knew. Nothing was familiar."

"They dropped you in the woods? In the middle of nowhere? That's awful!"

Sampson wagged his head, the hand that was stroking his chin now raking across his ragged curls and over eyes that were tired, heavy. "I was starving, naked, in the middle of nowhere, and by the time I fully came to, so did they."

I gulped, the sour state of my own saliva catching in my throat. "Who were they?"

"The werewolf hunters." He licked his lips. "Trackers. It's an ancient calling. . . ."

I nodded. "I know what trackers are, Sampson."

I knew all too well. It had only been a couple of weeks since Will—Will, the man charged with keeping me and all my Vessel of Souls–filled self safe—had had a run-in with Xian and Feng Du, Werewolf Hunters. And although werewolf hunters sound incredibly elegant and

Van Helsing-esque, you should know that werewolf hunters have come out of the silver-bullet-forging days of ancient, dusty castles and now taken up residence in more urban environments—like in the back of a retro delicatessen in San Francisco's Chinatown.

You should also know that werewolves are not the drooling, shirtless mongrels changing each time the moon becomes full that modern cinema would like us to believe. First of all, it's not just the moon that brings on the hairy changes in werewolves. If it was, I might have never gotten my first job at the Underworld Detection Agency under Pete Sampson. What edged out the other applicants—a fairly well-put-together zombie woman with melon-shaped boobs and a vampire so newly formed that his fangs were still short—was my ability to chain up a grown man in thirty-four seconds flat. That grown man was Pete Sampson.

I licked my lips, choosing my words carefully. "So why now? Why did you come back now?"

Sampson swallowed slowly, his eyes flicking quickly over mine, then working hard to avoid my questioning stare.

"Hey, who's this?" He patted ChaCha, who popped up on her popsicle-stick back legs and danced around like the ferocious three-pound ball of fur that she was. I snatched her from under his hand and held her to me.

"Why now?" I asked again.

"I couldn't run anymore." Sampson's lips were set in a hard, thin line. "I would have to spend my whole life running. The trackers weren't—aren't—going to back down."

"How do you know that?"

"They sent me a message."

He paused and I sucked in an anxious breath.

"There was a den—about six of us, werewolves that had been driven from our previous lives. We were living off the grid in a nothing town north of Anchorage. The townspeople were good to us, didn't ask questions, but"—he cocked his head—"they knew."

I put ChaCha down, hugged my elbows. "What happened?"

"A few of us went out, decided to check in with one of the satellite UDA offices. When we got back"—Sampson swallowed slowly, his Adam's apple bobbing with the effort—"the whole den had been slaughtered."

"That's awful."

Sampson nodded. "They didn't stop there. The town had been ravaged, too."

I felt myself recoil, felt the ice water race through my veins. "They went after the townspeople? I thought the trackers were only after werewolves."

Sampson looked at me, his warm eyes full and wide. "It used to be that way. But this new breed of trackers . . ." He looked away, breathing out a sigh that seemed to dwarf his shoulders, seemed to carry the weight of the years in it. "They're relentless. They attack werewolves . . . and anyone who helps us."

I looked over my shoulder, the hair on my arms standing on end. Sampson reached out to touch my knee, then seemed to think better of it, his arm falling listlessly to his side. "I don't want to put you in any danger, Sophie. I'm only here to warn you. I couldn't stand it if I knew that this"—Sampson turned his hands palms up—"that I, was responsible for anything bad happening to you. I think I'm going to leave tonight. I just needed you to be aware."

"You can't keep running. You said so yourself. They're just going to keep coming after you."

Sampson shrugged. "It's nothing I'm not used to."

"No." I clamped my hand around Sampson's arm. "I want to help you." I paused. "I'm going to help you. Me and Alex—and Will, and Nina—"

Sampson's jaw clenched, fire blazing in his eyes. "I told you. No one can know I'm here. It's my fight."

"You said they were coming after the Underworld. It's our fight now, too."

"You don't understand, Sophie. It's bad out there." He gestured absently over his shoulder, toward the San Francisco Bay or the entire world, I couldn't be sure.

I sucked in a breath and forced a smile. "I'm okay with bad. I mean, how bad is bad? Werewolf hunters. Silver bullets, right? Heh, that's nothing. I was almost blown up. And I was kidnapped. Held hostage in a restroom. A *public restroom*." I raised my eyebrows in *Beat that!* style.

"After they attacked our den, they decapitated all the townspeople."

My stomach lurched and bile tickled the back of my throat. "That's nothing," I whispered hoarsely, my smile painted on.

"So it's settled. You'll stay here." I looked around my apartment, feeling suddenly hopeful. "Yeah. Yeah, you could stay here. They wouldn't come looking for you here, no one would."

"And what about Nina? You think she won't notice a big hairy wolf on her couch? Or smell me?"

"First of all, it's *our* couch. And you're right. Nina smells all my friends." I cringed. I wasn't sure what was worse: the need to hide someone I cared about deeply from someone else I cared about deeply, or the fact that I cared deeply about someone who had the tendency to smell all my visitors.

I snapped my fingers. "I've got it! I read on the Internet—work is slow, I've had some time to read—that drug dealers pack dryer sheets with their pot so dogs won't be able to smell it. We could do that."

Sampson's smile was staid. "Well that's . . . offensive."

"I could make it work."

Suddenly Sampson's smile was gone.

His hands closed around my forearms, his eyes wide and dark. He shook his head. "No, Sophie. You can't tell anyone I'm here. And I don't want to put you out."

"But—"

"No one. Please. Please tell me I can trust you to keep my secret."

I nodded, and the relief was visible on Sampson's face.

"Wait—where are you going to go?" I asked. "Where are you going to stay?"

Sampson's hands dropped to his sides and the deep look of exhaustion haunted his eyes again. He sighed. "I'll find somewhere."

"But where? And, how will I be able to find you? I'm going to help."

"Sophie, I don't want you to get involved."

I crossed my arms in front of my chest, feeling indignant. "It's a little late for that, isn't it?"

Nina and I sat in my car, silent save for the nattering of the morning DJs on the radio.

"I didn't mean to overhear," she said finally.

"Oh, I know," I said, lightly pushing the gas.

While I was flopping over the couch and narrating an M. Night Shyamalan film, Nina had been in her bedroom finishing off a Zumba DVD.

For a vampire who could eat all the fat guys she wanted and never gain an ounce, I had to admire her pluck.

"So what are you going to do?"

I shook my head, gnawing on my bottom lip. "I don't know. But I can't just let him go on running. What kind of life is that? Always looking over your shoulder, never getting close to anyone." A little prick of pride poked at me.

"I'm going to help him, Neens. After all he's done for me? I owe him that. I can totally help him."

Nina didn't even bother to hide her skepticism. "You're going to help him *not be* a werewolf?"

"I'll figure something out."

My sudden bravado was stemming from the new leaf I had been considering turning over. In my life, I did a lot of crying. And sniveling. And falling down. For a girl whose CONTACTS list was loaded with the undead, the overpowering, and the often stinky, I didn't have a heck of a whole lot going for myself other than my near infallible ability to screw things up.

That stopped now.

"Yeah," I muttered to the windshield, my super-hero grin widening. "I'm going to save Sampson."

Nina eyed me, then squirmed in her seat. She folded her shoulders in and put on a pair of sunglasses that covered up the majority of her flawless pale face. "Sure."

"What are you doing?"

"It's hot." She rolled down the window and tucked one of the many pieces of discarded clothing-slash-garbage that I kept in my car just for situations such as these—or just because I'm lazy—in the window. "Didn't anyone tell the sun that this is summer in San Francisco? You're off for the season!" she yelled out the window.

While summer in San Francisco usually consisted of hoodies and hot chocolate, this year the temperatures were unseasonably warm. I loved the opportunity to bare skin that spent the majority of time cuddled in fleece; Nina hated it. I suppose I would, too, if every ray of sunshine made me sizzle and smoke.

Vampires have sun-free immortality; we breathers have flip-flops, tank tops, and skin cancer.

When the morning DJs rattled off a string of hotter-than-usual temperatures for the rest of the week, Nina's lip curled and her nostrils flared.

"God, I hate global warming."

As we inched closer to the police station, my heartbeat started to speed up. Once we pulled into the lot, I was fairly certain my spasming heart would bolt right out of my throat. I swallowed hard and tried my most ordinary grin on Nina.

"Did you put your jeans in the dryer again?" She cocked a quizzical eyebrow then hovered one perfectly manicured fingernail in front of my perma-grin. "You're looking a little pinched in the face area."

I dialed down the grin and killed the engine.

Though the Underworld Detection Agency is firmly hidden beneath thirty-five floors of earth and concrete, the very idea of it—and of me, walking through a place that catered to a magical, mind-reading clientele with a secret the size of the *Titanic*—made my heart pound and my palms sweat.

Some days I wished I had stuck with my childhood dream of becoming an Avon lady or a pony.

I closed my eyes and chanted to myself: *I'm good at keeping secrets, I'm good at keeping secrets. . . .*

And I am.

I've kept the lid on the entire existence of the demon Underworld, the fact that my roommate is a vampire, and once, when I was on a plane from New York, the winner of *American Idol*. But walking through an office staffed with the undead, the unearthly, and the unable to keep their noses out of my 100-percent-normal, breather mind, is a different story entirely.

I felt the surge of pain before I heard her voice. "Jesus crap, Nina, what the hell did you do that for?" I rubbed at the rapid bruise I was sure was forming on my rib cage where Nina had zinged me with her index finger.

"You were doing your weird, freight-train breathing again. Are you okay?"

"It's called relaxation breathing, and I'm just trying to center myself." My eyes darted to the police station's double doors. "I need to act calm and normal or people are going to suspect something's up."

Nina leaned over and pulled the biggest hat I've ever seen out of her shoulder bag, then worked to arrange it on her head. Finally she turned to me and smiled. "Soph, if you walk into the Underworld Detection Agency acting either calm or normal, everyone is going to *know* something is up."

Touché.

Like I said, the Underworld Detection Agency is housed in the same building as the San Francisco Police Department, but nestled a cool thirty-five floors below. The thin veil that separates the "breathers" (anyone with a beating heart and the breath of life) and the Underworld inhabitants allows our elevators to go straight on down, while theirs sticks to Lower Lobby and above. Hence, the San Francisco Police Department doesn't even know we're here.

But not many breathers do.

My hand closed around the door handle and a shiver went through me—this one had nothing to do with Sampson, nothing to do with my promise. This one was all about Alex Grace.

His face flashed in my mind: that cocky half smile, those sweet cherry lips—the surprised look on his face when I walked out of another man's apartment clad in little more than an oversized soccer jersey and a handful of last night's clothing.

We're not together; we had "the talk," I reminded myself. *I didn't do anything wrong.*

But deep down in my gut, I was sure that I had.

I prayed that Alex would already be in his back office, head down, working away—oblivious to the fact that I, Sophie Lawson, traitorous woman, walked among him and his law-and-order associates.

Nina and I slipped into the police station vestibule and I kept my eyes firmly focused on the prehistoric linoleum in front of me. I counted the cracks and the curled edges, tapping my foot and willing the elevator to move at a slightly more acceptable pace.

"I can hear your blood rushing from here," Nina said. "Calm down."

When the big steel doors opened and I was still undiscovered, my heart did a joyful double beat and I sent out a blanket thank-you to the universe and the Otis elevator people.

I stepped inside the elevator, a myriad of feeling pummeling me. I was hoping for another quiet day lining up Post-It notes and changing my outgoing message—"Hi, you've reached Sophie Lawson, director of the Fallen Angel Division of the Underworld Detection Agency. If you would like this message to continue in English, please press one." I didn't speak any other languages so the message generally ended there.

Thankfully, the UDA waiting room seemed to be in full-swing, business-as-usual mode. A few ex-clients of mine—my client list had quickly dwindled once I found my first dead dragon—looked over their shoulders at me, then looked at the floor suddenly, as if nappy industrial grade carpet were the most fascinating thing in the underworld.

Nina linked her arm through mine, her cool, bare arms making gooseflesh rise up on mine immediately. "Don't worry about it, Soph. Everything is going to go back to normal soon enough, and you'll be swimming in intake forms and slobber like the rest of us."

She smiled, her small fangs even more visible in the overhead light, and though I was up to my ears in nervous twitters, I had to smile back. Nina is my best friend, my roommate, and by far the wisest person I know.

I was convinced that coming back from the dead must make you super smart.

She is tall and lanky to my short and square, with perennially perfect black hair that swims over her shoulders and nips at her tiny waist. I like to believe that I have the same lustrous hair just in a deep, radiant auburn. I also like to believe that I look like a kick-ass warrior woman in black leather pants and skimpy tops that crisscross my stair-step abs. But in actuality, my curls have a mind of their own, auburn equals a red not found in nature, and the one and only time I wore leather pants they chafed so badly I had to see a doctor. I do have a decent chest—not remarkable, but passable, especially compared to Nina's—and strong arms, generally from carrying around loads of Granny-inspired cantaloupe (long story). Nina has a padded bra and jaws that can rip a grown man's throat out, so I guess she wins again.

She was born (the first time 'round) in nineteenth-century France and still holds on to the poised countenance of a noblewoman. While I tend to be on the loud and falling-down-a-lot side, Nina tends to glide, to bat her mile-long lashes and purse her heart-shape lips and the world's population falls at her feet. And if they don't, she'll bite them. Luckily for you, centuries of roaming the Earth and a signed-and-sealed contract with the Underworld Detection Agency mean that Nina kept her fangs to herself and breathers like us never have to worry about becoming a vamp snack.

That's mainly what we do here—file paperwork, keep

demons in line, keep tabs on anyone and anything just passing through. But before you think we work in a dark, dank cave and wield stakes and swords to vanquish and behead, I should tell you that the UDA office pretty much mirrors the humanoid DMV, and the only thing I've wielded down here are Swingline staplers and Scotch tape notes. I vanquished a fallen angel with a trident once, but that was strictly on private time.

The old-school maroon velvet line dividers were up and the waiting room was teeming with all manner of demon and demon offspring, half-breeds, the dead, the undead and the . . . other. The line was zombie heavy again today and I narrowed my eyes at a grayish newbie standing far too close to the announcements board, what remained of her jaw moving in a steady arc as she ate a notice about a missing dog. I considering interrupting, but it was fairly useless with zombies. Once they were chewing they followed through until the item was gone or their teeth fell out. Or both. We lost a lot of pushpins and other clients that way. I just shrugged and made a mental note to update my zombie apocalypse survival kit.

The waiting room hummed and ticked and although the clientele kept our waiting room at a chilly sixty degrees or so, I felt the sweat starting at my hairline, felt the undeniable anxious heat of keeping information under wraps start to prick at my skin. I felt like everyone was staring at me, taunting me, waiting for me to spill. Suddenly, my body was wracked with those unstoppable titter giggles that blink like an I'VE GOT A SECRET neon sign.

I focused hard on the carpet and cut through the waiting room as quickly as I dared, when I heard Kale yip, "Hey, Sophie!" as I edged my way past the equine part of a centaur.

I smiled genuinely when I saw Kale—it was her third

day back after a stint in the hospital from a hit-and-run that I still felt partly responsible for.

"Hey, Kale—you look great."

Kale grinned and then her eyebrows shot up. "Oh! I almost forgot!" She dipped under the front desk. "I brought your jacket back."

She shoved it over to me and bit her bottom lip. "Lorraine tried to get the tire tread out of it."

I gingerly took the coat, unable to look at it. The last time I had seen the thing, it was wrapped around Kale's crushed body, out of place and sadly limp in an intersection while tires screeched away. Just the memory made my stomach ache. "I'm just glad you're okay."

Kale gave me a "no big" shoulder shrug. I tucked the jacket under my arm and tried to step around her, but she stayed rooted in front of me, her Manic Monday lips a brilliant shade of purple and pushed up in a smile that went to her eyebrows.

"Is there something else?" I asked her.

Kale's eyes zipped to the vase full of blood-red blooms on her desk and then back to me, expectantly.

"Wow," I breathed. "Those are gorgeous."

Kale beamed, but didn't move. "Ask who they're from," she whispered.

I moved my speed-bump coat to my hip and played along. "And who might these be from?"

"Vlad!" His name practically burst through every pore in her tiny Gestalt witch body; her hair shook and the wattage of her smile could've lit homes from here to Tampa. "Can you believe it? He sent me flowers! Again! Almost for no reason this time!"

"*Almost* for no reason?"

Kale flapped her hand. "Well, you know, I got hit by the car and all. But look—they're beautiful, right?"

Ah, young love.

I would never understand it.

I zipped into the back office, doing my best to project an air of nonchalant confidence and supreme normalcy. Which isn't easy to do when the path to your office is lined with a team of angry pixies, a steaming hole in the ground from a wizard who blew himself up (seriously, when was someone going to fix that?), and a new succubus intern who made me want to take my pants off at every turn.

It was business as usual for them. *They* were the norm. I was not.

As usual, there was a small congregation of fairies at the water cooler. Their melodic chatter stopped cold as I approached and they turned, glittery wings scraping the linoleum floor as they glared at me. It wasn't me they were mad at—it's just that fairies are notoriously private. And mean. Thanks to Walt Disney, fairies are depicted as pixie-nosed, spirited sprites that smell of sugar cookies and long to be liked by lithe human boys. Down here, there are no facades: fairies are the Mean Girls of the Underworld. Best to avert your eyes and leave them alone. And I was doing just that when I ran smack into Louis "Vlad" LaShay.

I thunked back from Vlad's hard marble chest and he looked down his nose at me. "Soph."

I narrowed my eyes, mirroring his sneer. "Vlad."

Vlad is Nina's sixteen-year-old nephew and our permanent couch surfer. He's surly, cranky, and pathologically unable to throw away an empty blood bag or clean up after himself. But, because he's chronologically well over a hundred years old and the new head of the UDA has a thing for vampire nepotism, Vlad is also my boss.

Even if he does dress like Bela Lugosi.

At home I've come to love him like my own obnoxious little brother. On occasion I even helped make a protest sign or two for the organization Vlad championed, the Vampire Empowerment and Restoration Movement. It was a group of like-minded vampires who protested the sparkly, soft-fanged portrayals of vampires in the media, and incited all of the organization's adherents to bring the modern vampire back to the glory days of graveyard dirt and frilly ascots. They were wholly against vampire/demon mixing and sought to restore ultimate power back to the vampire. Adherents were expected to dress in the classic garb (more Nosferatu, less Edward Cullen) and do vampy things like brood and pace. While their up-with-fangs agenda might sound fearsome, the whole movement was basically the equivalent of an orthodontically gifted group of Dungeons & Dragons players.

And I was having a hard time getting used to Dungeon Master Count Chocula facilitating my yearly reviews.

"Nice weather we're having, huh?" I said with a wide, eager grin.

Vlad quirked an eyebrow. "I prefer the fog."

"Fog's nice, too. Anyway—" I stepped back and poked at my wrist. "Time is money and my boss is a slave driver. Heh." Before Vlad had the opportunity to break into my babble, I was in my office, seated at my desk, my heart doing a spastic patter. I grabbed a felt-tipped marker and scrawled the word *VACATION-slash-HEART ATTACK* over the entire next month in my calendar. Some days working with a Small World collection of the mythical, mystical, and undead is a wonderful, stimulating experience. Sometimes it's a huge pain in the ass.

I was eventually able to calm myself down with three cups of Splenda-laced herbal tea and one and a half apple fritters, but every time someone passed by my office door or my phone rang, I was challenging my kegel muscles and trying to keep my heart from exploding through my chest. I hunkered down at my desk, and smiled at my clients, doing my best to avoid letting on that I knew anything more than anyone else in the world—like that the hunted, haunted, and left-for-dead werewolf Pete Sampson was currently at my house, stretched out on my hand-me-down chintz couch.

But every time a client cocked his head at me, or looked at me with a questioning eye (or three), I found myself doused in paranoia and re-convinced that someone was reading my mind, or was monitoring my spastic heartbeat, or had found out in some other way that I was hiding one hell of a hairy secret.

Even when I wasn't saying anything, I couldn't help but feel like my lies exuded out of my every pore. So when I ran into Lorraine in the bathroom, I tried my best to seem nonchalant and unaffected.

"Hey, Soph," she said, strolling in.

I forced myself to smile, and the image reflected in the bank of mirrors was me, grinning like an idiot. "Hi, Lorraine. How are things? What are you doing? Is everything good?"

Some people have tells when they lie—tiny eye twitches, averted eyes, a blank expression. I went for babbling idiot.

"Nothing's going on with me. Just washing my hands."

Lorraine nodded slowly, her amber-colored eyes studying me. "Are you okay?"

My mind raced and I forced myself to clear it—or to focus on something banal. The last four episodes of *Lost* flashed in my mind.

Among Lorraine's many talents—general witchcraft, home Tupperware saleslady of the month (although I don't think it's entirely kosher to threaten to turn non-buyers into squid), and finance—was also mind dipping. It was an art that not many witches were able to master—Kale, Lorraine's protégé, was still trying, though I think her issue is the mind she most often tried to dip into was focused wholly on video games and vampire porn (Vlad—the flowers, remember?). Theoretically, her mind dipping can't be used on me. Besides being the breathing, blood-filled darling of the Underworld Detection Agency's Fallen Angel Division and one hundred percent magic free, I am also impervious to other people's magic. Theoretically. Or . . . generally.

I may have the preternatural ability to walk amongst the demon Underworld, to easily see through the veil that keeps the breather population blissfully unaware of the demon one, and to recite all fifty states in alphabetical order, but the one thing I didn't have, was grace.

So when Lorraine cocked her head, her eyes unfocused and unblinking, a zing of heat ran up my spine and bloomed red in my cheeks. "I think I'm going to be sick."

I kicked open the nearest stall door and dry heaved, staring at the toilet water through misty eyes.

"Oh," I heard Lorraine say, "Sophie, I'm so sorry."

I heaved again and heard Lorraine turn on the faucet. She stuck her arm into my stall and waved a damp paper towel at me. "I would stay and help you, but I'm a sympathetic vomiter."

I nodded and opened my mouth, growling as though I were birthing a dinosaur. "That's okay, Lorraine," I choked. "I'm sorry you had to see this."

Once Lorraine hightailed it out of the bathroom I turned around, sitting on the toilet, head in hands.

Keeping this secret was going to be harder than I thought.

"Sophie! Soph, are you okay?" Nina pushed in through the bathroom door next and I groaned.

"Can't a woman get a little privacy?"

Nina crossed her arms in front of her chest, jutting out one hip and taking me in. "Not if you're going to keep the door open while you sit on the toilet. What's going on? Lorraine said you had the plague."

I looked over Nina's shoulder and grimaced at my red-rimmed eyes, the banana-pudding hue of my face. Strands of hair were already starting to shoot out around my head like intelligence-seeking antennae, and I frowned at my best friend, my eyes scanning her.

"Sounds about right," I said, trying in earnest to make my wrinkled, pilling twinset look passable.

In addition to using the immense years of her afterlife to brush up on history, name-calling, and general trivia, Nina had also spent her time collecting an incredible array of vintage couture to support her massive fashion habit. She stood before me today in a corset I know she nabbed from a French noblewoman (premaking her a tasty tidbit), a great little blazer, and a pair of jeans so skinny I had mistaken them for a scarf and worn them around my neck all last winter. I had long ago given up the contention that my fashion habits only paled in comparison to *hers*, as she spun in a drop-dead pair of sparkling silver Louboutins; I knew that my Target shoes and my surprising-as-mushroom-soup wardrobe never stood a chance.

"So," Nina said, dark eyes raking over me, "should I call in the dead collectors?"

I blew out a sigh and stood up, turning on the tap and splashing cold water onto my burning cheeks. "No. I'm not really sick. I faked it."

"That's usually my line."

I rolled my eyes. "My problem, remember?"

"Right." Nina leaned against the sink and checked out her impeccable manicure. "So, what exactly is your problem today?"

"Don't say it like that. I don't have a problem every day!"

Nina raised her eyebrows and I was out of supporting information. "It's Sampson," I said, my voice hushed. "I don't know how I'm going to be able to keep his coming back a secret. I don't know if I'm going to be able to keep a lid on everything until it all gets sorted out."

"First of all, as he's lying on our couch, he's *our* problem. And second of all, it's not a problem we're going to have for very long."

I patted my face with a paper towel. "Why do you say that?"

Nina leaned in conspiratorially. "Well, he needs to no longer be hunted, right? You know, all returned to glory and stuff?"

I wasn't sure I knew where she was going. "I'm hoping to find out who's after him so he can stop running."

"Potato, po-tah-to. You know who the werewolf hunter is. It's that Fang, right?"

"Feng."

"That's what I said." Nina bared hers in the mirror. "So, you just go to this Fang person and let her know that you've got everything under control. That she can call off the attack of this particular werewolf."

Nina looked supremely proud of her plan, and even as I remembered the warm and friendly way Feng had welcomed me into her office the first time I met her—by closing her fingers around my neck—it was hard not to be infected by Nina's grinning self-assurance.

"I guess I could do that. But"—I frowned—"the Du family's whole existence is based on werewolf hunting. I don't think she's going to let one go just because I ask her to. She doesn't exactly seem the favor-granting type."

Nina shrugged and whipped a lipstick out of her bra. She puckered her lips. "It's worth a shot, isn't it? Besides,

Sampson's been here a whole night and it's not like the city has gone to rabid dog hell."

I raised an eyebrow and Nina rolled her eyes. "That's a compliment." She frowned. "Okay, wait. Sampson was running the UDA all on the up-and-up or, you know, down-and-Underworld-y for ages. Why weren't the Sisters Grimm after him then?"

I frowned myself. "I don't know exactly. Maybe he was just off their radar?"

"Well, there you go. Either you convince this Feng that Sampson is not the threat she thinks he is, or we make sure to, once again, get him off their radar." Nina was proud, but I couldn't even begin to hide my skepticism.

"Fine," Nina said, wrinkling her nose. "Option number three? You can't do a job that's already been done. Tell Feng that Sampson's already dead."

I sucked in a shaky breath. For some reason, I felt as though he already was.

I left the bathroom with the damp paper towel clasped against the back of my neck and little droplets of cool water dripping down my blouse. *I'm in the clear*, I told myself as I zigzagged my way through the Underworld Detection Agency's hallways. They were crowded with the mid-afternoon rush, buzzing with hushed conversations, and it may have been my imagination, but every conversation seem to get more hushed or stop completely when I walked by. People turned to stare at me, their eyes dark and accusing. I should have been used to being stared at this way, because as far as blending in with my co-workers and surroundings? Well, that always got a big, fat "needs improvement" on the monthly reviews.

Secrets or not, my breath made me suspect to some of

the purist Underworld inhabitants. The fact that demons and people tended to drop like flies whenever I was around turned some off and wreaked havoc on my Match.com profile. And surely the fact that I was practically running down the hall, doing my best to look nonchalant, was killing what remained of my minuscule ability to fit in.

My body was humming with nerves, a beacon letting every Underworld demon know that that was something going on and that something was big. My blood pulsed and a few of Vlad's VERM cronies turned to me. Slate-grey eyes looked through me. I heard nothing but the thunder of my heart, the rush of blood as it coursed through my veins. I walked in slow motion and the VERMers blinked at me. One slowly licked his lips. I knew it was involuntary, the way I salivate over a newly opened package of chocolate marshmallow pinwheels. The sound of blood, the pulse of my heart in its heightened state, was appealing to them. Though eating humans—even the slightest nibble—is strictly against UDA policy, it still skeeved me out to know that at any given time (especially times like this), any number of my coworkers was imagining me on a plate with a parsley garnish.

I needed to get out of the office.

By the time I made it to the elevator my nerves had begun to settle and I realized that I was overreacting, that no one was staring at me or licking their lips. The piped-in Kenny G ballad that struggled to cover the sounds of the aged, groaning elevator was even soothing and I breathed deeply. I was perfectly calm, my heartbeat at a normal pace as the elevator whisked me upward. I swayed a little bit. I whistled along with Kenny G. I was going to bail Sampson out. Everything would be okay. I was going to be the hero for once.

I smiled a little bit, imagining what my superhero costume

would look like. Maybe something with flames and that super-shaping spandex. Nothing too showy. I wondered if Spanx made capes?

The elevator dinged and the big steel doors slid open, revealing the fluorescent glow of the San Francisco Police Department vestibule and perfectly framing Alex Grace.

And just like that, my calm, cool countenance turned to quivering jelly.

I really could have used that super-shaping spandex.

I chewed on my bottom lip, trying to pull up some of the cool nonchalance that had been sliding off me all afternoon. But regardless of my intellect or my personal soliloquies, my body tended to have the uncanny ability to spring to hormone-pulsing life whenever Alex Grace was around. Maybe it was his piercing, ice-blue eyes. Maybe it was the chocolate curls that lolled on his perfect head and licked the top of his completely kissable ears. Maybe it was the dual scars just under his shoulder blades—perfect, silver-fleshed reminders of the wings that had once been there.

I fisted my hands, tried to call up my own personal *Rocky* theme song as I faced down the most perfect specimen of man or angel ever expelled from the heavens.

His eyes flicked over me and he edged his chin in the universally sexy-man way of saying, *Hey*. Then his voice came out, sinfully smooth. "Hey, Lawson, haven't seen you in a while."

My mouth instantly went Mojave dry, my every muscle sucking in on itself. I felt my eyes dart, looking for some tiny wormhole through which I could escape.

It wasn't that I wanted to avoid Alex per se; I had every intention of talking to him the second I was ready. I just was hoping to be able to select that second of readiness myself, ideally after some lengthy therapy, or at least when the memory of me stepping out of Will's apartment in the early morning and running into Alex, his face creased with shock and dismay while we stood in an oppressive, awkward silence that seemed to last the span of several lifetimes, was less distinct and raw.

I sucked in a shaky breath and tried to will the hot coil in my stomach to disappear, tried to shake off the guilty prickle that climbed up the back of my neck. *Alex and I are broken up,* I tried to remind myself. *I'm a grown woman, and I can spend the night with whomever I want.* I might love Alex, but I'm certainly not in love with him.

Right?

Suddenly, my tryst with Will was feeling less like a lapse in judgment and more like a mammoth mistake.

His grin deepened. "Cat got your tongue?"

Alex Grace was an angel—of the fallen variety. And sometimes I was sure that I had crashed right along with him.

I pasted on my friendliest smile. "Hey," I roared back.

His eyes widened and my cheeks flushed again in what I was certain was a candy-apple red. Adorable on a bouncy brunette. Positively lobster-ish on a pale-fleshed redhead like myself. "Sorry," I said, lowering my voice.

There was a beat of awkward silence before Alex put his hand on the elevator door and raised his eyebrows.

"What?" I asked.

"You coming out or were you just taking this puppy for a ride?"

"Right. I was just heading out." I pointed to the door, in case he was questioning my mode of exit.

"Me, too," he said.

"But you were waiting for the elevator."

"Checking up on me?" he said, falling into step beside me.

Maybe he isn't upset with me, I said, my body suddenly feeling light. *Maybe he's going to ignore what happened and we can go back to being friends! Maybe everything can go back to normal.*

Before we hit the glass double doors, a voice called out. The chief of police had tired basset hound eyes that zeroed in on Alex, then flicked quickly to me. "Grace! Oh, hey, Lawson. Hey, man, we just got a call. Sutro Point. Double homicide. Looks pretty bad."

Oh, yeah. Things were definitely going to be back to normal.

Chapter Two

Alex gave me a gentle push forward.

"See you later, Lawson."

I flattened myself against the wall as officers surrounded Alex, giving him the lowdown as their shoulder radios squawked and beeped. Alex's shoulders stiffened, his eyes on the officer in front of me. I took a few tentative steps closer, my head cocked as I tried to listen. My stomach dropped.

". . . bloodbath," said one of the officers.

"Double homicide," another one finished as he shrugged into his coat.

"The area is destroyed. Looks like a tornado hit it."

The officers filed out into squad cars, kicking on lights and revving engines. Alex went out the door toward his car and I followed, yanking on his arm.

"What's going on?" I wanted to know.

"None of your business." He didn't meet my eyes, but I noticed how the color had drained from his face. His jaw was set hard and that same muscle—the one that said he wasn't telling me the whole truth—jumped. I flipped on my heel.

"I'm coming with you." I had the car door open when Alex turned the engine over.

"No, you're not." He kicked the car in reverse and I did a double hop, surprising myself when I flopped down into his passenger's seat, yanking the door shut behind me. There was a faint smile on Alex's lips as he looked over his shoulder, backing us out at warp speed and throwing on the flashing lights.

"You really don't understand the word no, do you?"

I shrugged, hoping he couldn't hear the wild thump of my heart. "Seems like kind of a waste to learn now. What's going on, Alex?"

He pinned me with a hard glare. "Why don't you tell me, Lawson?"

Heat surged over me once again and I jammed my hands under my thighs. "I mean right now. This case."

He swung back to stare out the windshield, negotiating the midafternoon traffic like the SUV was a pinball. "Double homicide out by Sutro."

"I thought they said bloodbath."

Alex's eyes flashed. "You were listening."

I nodded. "The place was destroyed? Like a tornado?"

Alex's eyes stayed fixed on the road in front of us, but I could tell he was thinking, considering how much to tell me. His grip on the wheel, his white knuckles, told me there was a lot to consider. "It's police business."

I narrowed my eyes, shooting him a steely glare. I was surprised when my hard look softened him a touch. "Fine. As far as I know, right now it doesn't look supernatural, but it does look bad. Real bad. Which means you're going to sit your pretty little ass right here in this car while I go take a look."

I was happy to have my ass acknowledged and happier still that it was preceded with "pretty" and "little." But it didn't stop me from crossing my arms in front of my chest and hitching my chin. "How do you know it's not supernatural?"

He blew out a sigh. "Look, if I find any unicorn hooves, I'll call you, okay? If I weren't in such a hurry I would have tossed you out of the car."

"You still could have."

"Before or after your *Dukes of Hazard* stunt?"

I thrummed my fingers on my thighs as Alex slowed for a light. "Hey, about the other day." I kept my eyes fixed on the dashboard. "When I ran into you in the hallway? I was leaving Will's apartment and it looked bad, but . . ."

I mustered up my courage to look Alex in the eye—or in the right ear, as he was staring out the windshield—when he stepped on the gas and we blew through the intersection, sirens echoing off the sky-high buildings all around us. I was pressed against the leather seat with my heart firmly lodged in my throat and clawing toward the dashboard to right myself when I heard the cackle and scratch of the dispatch radio.

"We're almost there," Alex barked into it.

He made no motion to acknowledge my speech—or my presence—as he banked a corner that sent me sliding into the center console, the seat belt cutting against my chest.

I cleared my throat as the car and my heartbeat slowed. "As I was saying . . ."

"Oh, Christ." Alex raked a hand through his ragged curls and snatched the radio with the other. "I thought they were keeping this one under wraps."

"We did our best," the broken voice answered him. "But you know how it is. People smell blood on the air and they come running."

We pulled into the cracked parking lot that sat above Sutro Point, our tires crunching against the gravel. I saw

Alex's jaw harden as he maneuvered the car through the crowd of cop cars and emergency vehicles parked at angles. Civilian cars dotted the lot, too, and every other inch of space was taken up by enormous news vans setting up makeshift stations, their coifed and ready anchors stepping in front of cameras and painting on suitably concerned faces as they launched into their monologues. A handful of on-lookers circled the anchorpeople and vied for their chance to wave on film; another cluster was gripping the metal police barricades and craning their necks to peer through the trees. The air was charged with palpable electricity; I couldn't tell if it stemmed from the fear or excitement of the onlookers but every inch seemed solid and static-filled. A tense murmur cut through the crackling of police radios and the detritus of the news teams; I hadn't even left the car and I could feel the electricity pulsing through me, the collective disquiet pushing painfully against my chest.

I glanced at Alex as he kicked open his car door and swung his legs out—the leg of his jeans rode up over his ankle and I saw his gun holstered there. It gave me a little shock but a weird sense of security. I scrambled out after him. He shot a look over his left shoulder at me and cocked a brow, but seemed to think better of telling me to get back in the car.

"Grace, Lawson."

Officer Romero was standing on the other side of the yellow crime scene tape, beckoning us with his blue, latex-gloved hands. Alex grabbed my elbow and yanked me through the crowd.

"What's going on?"

Romero stood just a few inches shorter than Alex, and where Alex filled out his black T-shirt and jeans mercilessly with muscle that begged to be touched, Romero's uniform bulged with jelly donuts and dimples over his elbows. He wagged his head, then stroked his scraggly black goatee.

"I'm not going to lie, Grace, it looks bad." Romero lifted his chin toward me. "I don't think you're going to want to go down there, Sophie. It's just—" He looked at me, his heavy shoulders shimmying under a small shudder. "It's really messy."

"She's not going in. She's going to stay here with you. Up here." Alex's eyes raked over Romero, daring him to challenge, but Romero just broke into a grin.

"Good. I could use another set of eyes. Make sure them over there"—he jerked a thumb toward a group of civilians pressing hard against the police tape—"stay back."

"Can't." I shook my head and snatched a pair of gloves from Romero's chest pocket. "I'm going in."

Alex turned and I followed him down the trail. "I don't even know why I try," I heard him mutter.

"So fill me in," I said, yanking on the gloves. "Tell me everything you know about this case."

Alex turned. "You know as much as I know. And I'll let you take a look at this crime scene, but that's it. No more nosing into my business."

There was real annoyance in Alex's tone. I hadn't expected it to cut me so deeply, but it did and I felt a pang of sadness stab at my gut. I wanted to answer him, but I was afraid to open my mouth and set forth a slew of blubbering explanations, apologies, and pent-up frustration so I just nodded and followed him, my gloved hands raised, doctor style.

There was a clearing in the brush where the trail veered off sharply, nosediving toward the cliffs. The grass here was matted down and the vegetation was broken; the smell of the foliage was heavy with something else, too, something overpowering and metallic. I felt bile rise in my throat.

"Blood," I whispered.

It hung heavy in the air, giving the usually calming stretch of forest an ominous, sharp feeling. It stuck out against the crisp, refreshing air of the forest.

We wound through the trees and popped out in a clearing; the foliage was heavy but shorter here, and I was able to spot slivers of the roaring ocean through the trees. The scene would have been picturesque had it not been for the police officers, the men in their white-lettered FORENSICS jackets, and the two sheeted bodies laid out on the dirt. I sucked in a breath and steadied myself.

"Something came through here like a tornado." Detective Campbell was standing with his back to us, staring out over the ocean and speaking to no one in particular. He was built like a fireplug with a basketball-shaped head that seemed to bleed into his shoulders, into his thin white button-down shirt. He jammed his hands into his pockets and spun around, shaking his head and clucking his tongue like we were dealing with an errant teenager rather than a heinous crime scene.

My eyes followed his to the half circle of redwood trees that surrounded the clearing. The bark was torn clean from one of them, and it looked as if someone had taken an ax to the trunk, leaving four clean slice marks across it. The lower branches on the surrounding trees and the suckers around that were mashed down and broken; the soft pine underbrush was kicked up and scratched into two deep grooves.

"Grace!" Campbell's face broke into a wide smile when he noticed Alex, and I snapped to attention.

Alex shook Detective Campbell's hand. "What happened?"

The smiled dropped from the detective's face and he led Alex by the shoulder, stepping cleanly over one of the sheeted bodies. My stomach twisted and the backs of my eyelids pricked; someone was underneath that sheet and the detective *stepped over him*. Suddenly, strangely, I was overcome with sadness and I crouched down to brush off the bits of pine needle and dust that Detective Campbell's shoe had rained over the body. My hand stopped, frozen, when I saw the bubble of blood seeping from beneath the sheet. It moved in a slow river at first, picking up bits of debris from the forest floor, then moving faster, pooling.

I felt the acid churning in my stomach and burning the back of my throat. My brain commanded me to stand, to move, to run, but I was rooted to that spot and now everywhere I looked was marred by blood—in smears and in pools, congealing, dirty, splattered. The smell was overwhelming and my head felt heavy, my knees weak. I saw the forest roll upward and the blue of the sky before Alex grabbed me. His hands were rough—one around my waist and one on my upper arm—and I tried to right myself, but his lips were on my ear.

"I told you to stay in the car."

I shook him off and swallowed hard, willing my stomach to settle. "Wha—what happened to them?" I asked.

Alex shook his head, waiting until I stood on my own before turning toward the detective.

"Any word—murder weapons, wounds, anything?" Alex nudged his chin toward the bodies and Detective Campbell nodded, flipping open his black leather notebook.

"We don't have positive IDs yet. So far, we're fairly certain it's two females, late teens early twenties, maybe."

"You're 'fairly certain' they're females?" I asked.

It was then I noticed the chalky bits of spit gathered at the corners of Detective Campbell's mouth. His skin was ashy. "It's that bad."

Alex put his hands on his hips, dropping into cop mode. "What are you thinking?"

"Wild animal, maybe. Never seen anything like it before. Not out here at least."

Without warning, the detective leaned down and pinched one corner of the sheet, pulling it up. I felt my eyes grow and every muscle in my body tightened, curled in on itself, crushed my breath from my lungs. When Alex pressed a palm to the back of my neck I leaned into it, loving the cool feel of his skin on mine. A breeze kicked up and sent a shiver through me; I realized that my whole body had broken out into a bitter sweat and I clamped my eyes shut instinctually, bent over at the waist.

"You okay?" Alex's voice was a throaty whisper and I let him help me upright.

I cleared my throat, but my voice was still hoarse. "What happened to her?"

The detective dropped the corner of the sheet, but the image of the woman—decimated, torn—was seared into my mind. Her skin looked like it had once been a flawless, pale porcelain but was shredded into snarled ribbons now; what remained of her clothes and stringy blond hair was blood soaked and caked with mud and pine needles. I gagged when I realized that she hadn't been placed so much as dumped—limbs next to torso, torso next to head—and none of the limbs were attached.

I turned around and gagged, not caring who saw me vomit. I tried to keep my eyes open because every time I pinched them shut, the girl—what remained of the girl—was burned into my eyelids and I gagged again.

Alex rested his hand on the small of my back. "Are you okay, Lawson?"

I used the back of my hand to swipe at my eyes and nose, then spat on the ground and used the bottom of my shirt to wipe my mouth. I nodded, still bent over, hands still on my knees. "Yeah."

When I straightened up I saw that Alex's face was pale and his eyes were glassy. He had been a detective for a long time and the crime scenes he was privy to were some of the most gruesome, but this destruction was overwhelming.

"You don't have to stay out here," he said, shaking his head. "There's nothing UDA about this."

"So you think this was, what? A mountain lion, black bear?"

Alex put his hands on his hips and looked at Detective Campbell, who shrugged, his meaty shoulders brushing his earlobes. "We don't have many details. A runner found them." He nodded toward a thin man in papery-looking running shorts, the goose bumps visible on his legs. The man had his hands clasped behind his back and was fidgeting or shivering—I couldn't tell which—as he gave a statement to two officers.

"The guy runs here every morning, usually heads out about five, five-thirty a.m."

"He runs the Sutro trail?" Alex asked.

The detective nodded.

"What's he doing here now?" I wondered. "It's almost four."

Detective Campbell sucked on his teeth. "Guy said he missed his run this morning, so he came out on his lunch hour. Put a call into his office and his story checks out. He was working this morning and checked out around eleven-forty."

"Okay, so he heads off for a run." Alex turned, his cornflower-blue eyes scanning the trail we had just come from. "He would have been up there. Why did he cut off the trail? What made him come down here?"

I looked up toward the top of the ridge where the trail

cut in. The tops of the heads of the onlookers and officers barricading them could just barely be seen. "He probably couldn't have seen much if he was on the trail. Especially if he was running."

"The guy said he heard something."

"Heard something?"

"A rustle, something. He didn't really say, other than something distracted him from his course.

"He wasn't wearing earphones, an iPod, anything?"

Detective Campbell shrugged again. "Nah. He's a real nature type. Says he likes to run first thing in the morning because it's quiet or just before the lunch rush. He likes the peace."

I wasn't a runner—far from it, often considering my other options even when something is chasing me—but something seemed wrong about the runner's story.

"Excuse me for a second." Detective Campbell slipped away from us and toward another officer who was chatting comfortably with a newscaster.

I put my hands on my hips, biting my bottom lip. "This smells fishy to me."

Alex scanned the horizon. "Yeah, well, we are surrounded by the ocean."

I rolled my eyes. "Who goes running at five a.m.? It's still dark. And then running at noon? Was he going to go back to work all sweaty?"

Alex wasn't looking at me. "I don't know, Lawson."

"Like I said, fishy. I think this guy is searching for an alibi."

"Going running is a pretty weak one."

"Right. And who goes running without an iPod?"

"Someone smart, who knows that he may be relatively alone on this trail, so it's best to listen to his surroundings rather than the Spice Girls."

"So sue me for liking classic pop." I tapped my foot, still unsettled, until it hit me. I spun to face Alex and leaned in close. "Okay, then. You don't listen to music so you can listen for cars, ax murderers, amphibians, sea-creatures, or whatever. That means the guy takes precautions, right?"

"Lawson, I told you. This is pretty clean," he gulped, his eyes flitting over the rapidly soiling sheet. "A relatively cut and dry murder case."

I looked back at Alex, flicked my gaze over the bodies. "It's anything but cut and dry. Did you see those bodies, Alex?"

His eyes flashed and I practically growled. "Don't you dare tell me this was probably gangbangers."

"It's not your jurisdiction, Lawson."

"Just tell me this, Alex. What kind of guy takes precautions and runs *toward* a rustle in the bushes?"

Alex paused, but still didn't look at me.

"Look at him, Alex. The guy is practically naked."

Alex glanced over to the runner—his legs were bare, his shorts covering little more than his rear and the tops of his thighs. They were so tight that I could make out a key ring with a single key on it and something small and rectangular—a cell phone or a wallet—pressed into the zipped back pocket. He wore a long-sleeved shirt that was fitted against his thin torso, and sneakers and no socks.

"He's got no protection and he's running into the bushes on a practically deserted trail? Explain that."

"I can't. But I can tell you that the blood is pretty fresh on these bodies and whoever did—did what they did to them—has to be completely covered in it. That guy's clean."

I raised a challenging eyebrow and Alex's inner groan was almost audible. "I'm going to go ask him a few questions anyway."

I moved to take a step toward Alex and he put a hand on

my chest, effectively holding me in place. "You've got two choices. Go sit in the car or wait here. This is a police investigation."

"Don't patronize me, Alex Grace," I hissed.

"You're not a cop, Lawson." Alex's eyes had changed from that warm, inviting cobalt to a steely grey that rivaled the unsettling rage of the ocean. "I don't need you here."

Alex walked away from me and suddenly the hiss of the sea-soaked wind was biting. I pulled my jacket against it, but the icy fingers still slid down the back of my collar, whipped up my pant legs, and stung my cheeks. I was left in the clearing with the two sheeted bodies—dead bodies, I sadly reminded myself—while the police, paramedics, crime scene investigators, and finally, the coroner, buzzed around taking statements and photographs or poking through the foliage carefully collecting evidence. I watched while a younger guy, his black jacket slick with mist, bent down and collected a few strands of hair with a pair of industrial-sized tweezers.

I squinted at the find when he did—a small bunch, possibly ten or twelve—of brown hair, about six inches long. I filed it in my mental database when he zipped it in his evidence bag. He took a careful step and I found myself doing the same thing, gingerly picking my way through the shrubs and the broken remainders of puzzle bark suckers. I don't know how long I wandered, but when I looked up the crime scene and its surrounding task force were just a few inches tall, the chatter and squawk of the police radios and onlookers strangled by the sound of the crashing waves below me. The grass and shrubs were broken here, too, tramped down and spattered with something tarry and black. I poked at it with the tip of my finger and recoiled, the blood dripping down to my palm. "Oh, god!" I rubbed my palm against my thigh until it burned.

I did my best to pick around the broken grass and splattered blood, but in my zeal to be delicate and light-footed, I hooked my toe over the top of a jutting rock and vaulted forward, landing hard on my chest in the grass. My head bobbed forward and a starburst of pain shot across my forehead, blinding me. I tried to blink away the blob of darkness that started in my right eye, but when I looked up, everything was a watery blur and fuzzy black spots shot across my field of vision. I tried hard to focus on what was right in front of me: first a few blades of grass. The rock that sprouted an offensive trickle of my blood. The trees swaying in the breeze fifty feet in front of me. The shadowy figure that stood there.

Terror overtook the pain and I shoved myself up, feeling the soft earth digging itself into the tears in my palms. I knew the wind was blowing, slapping my hair against my cheek and neck; it matted into the blood at my temple, but I couldn't hear anything, couldn't feel anything. I tried to yell, but the wind snapped by and snatched the scream right out of my mouth.

"Lawson!"

Alex was at the bluff running toward me. I had pushed myself onto my butt and was shivering, my teeth chattering. I tried to tell him, tried to warn him, but all I could do was point. Two women had been torn limb from limb twenty feet from me and there, in the trees, their killer lurked.

"What?" Alex turned, eyes squinted, looking toward the trees.

"There's a person there!" It was barely a croak, barely audible.

Alex stood up to his full six-foot height, still staring toward the trees. "I don't see anything. Are you sure?"

I pumped my head—then stopped. Was I sure? I gingerly touched my forehead. The cut was sticky and throbbing.

"I hit my head."

"Yeah." Alex turned to me, slid an arm under my shoulders to help me up. "Looks like you banged it pretty hard. Can you stand on your own?"

I strained to look over Alex's shoulder while he supported me. "Did you see him? Did he get away?"

"Lawson, there's no one there. You hit your head." He went to touch it but recoiled. "You really did a number on it."

I tried to squirm out of Alex's arms but he held me firm. "So you're saying I'm seeing things?"

"No," Alex said, pushing me farther up the bank, "I'm saying you fell and hit your head and that there is nothing over there now, okay? Don't make this bigger than it is."

"There was someone there, I'm sure of it. He was watching me. Watching the crime scene."

I looked at Alex hard and his eyes softened as he relented. "Okay. Can we get a medic over here?" he called. "Romero, Tibbs—Lawson thinks she saw someone."

I pointed. "There. About fifty feet down."

The guys took off running and I sunk down on the back of the ambulance tailgate. *Thank you*, I mouthed to Alex. He nodded.

The paramedic began cleaning my wound and I tried not to wince, tried not to squirm away, but I wanted to turn and stare in the direction the officers ran. "Do you think it was the killer?"

"Do I think who was the killer?" Alex asked, not looking up from his iPhone.

"The guy that I just saw!" I huffed.

He shrugged. "I don't know, Lawson."

I frowned, my eyes sweeping the bluff, then looking back at Alex, at the grizzly crime scene behind him. My stomach went to liquid as I tried not to look toward the coroner gathering up the ruined remains of the second body. My muscles tightened involuntarily; probably in a show of solitary gladness that they were still attached to my limbs.

"I hope it wasn't him." I rambled on, "But who else would it be? Don't psychopaths enjoy injecting themselves into an active investigation? Or returning to the scene of the crime to re-experience the joy or whatever?"

Alex cocked a half smile before looking away from me. "Glad to see you're still a TV junkie."

"Hey. I probably watch as much Discovery Channel as I do *The Bachelor*, okay? There's real learning there. Cut me a little slack."

I would keep the fact that the Discovery Channel had just come out with another version of *Hoarders* my personal secret.

Alex and I both snapped to attention when Romero and Tibbs came lumbering through the grasses. "We couldn't find a thing," one of them muttered. "There was nothing out there."

Heat washed over my cheeks. "He was there, I swear. I know I saw something."

Alex looked down at me, his eyes fierce. "Are you sure you checked everywhere, guys?"

Ever since a brush with my half-sister—a fallen angel called Ophelia who was hell-bent on ruining my life, in a very serious way—I've been a little sensitive to the idea of my seeing things. Mainly because she had the unfortunate (for me) ability to *make* me see things—horrible things, like maggots and blood-bathed murder weapons. It wasn't so much the images that bothered me, however; it was the idea of those images making me feel one-hundred-percent, grade-A, bat-shit crazy.

"I know I didn't imagine it."

"We checked everything. There weren't even any trails in

the grass. Sorry, Sophie, but maybe you just saw a shadow or something."

A shadow? I clenched my teeth and tried my hardest to focus, but the pain in my head was like a humming, buzzing swarm of bees, making it incessantly hard to concentrate. *A standard murder,* I told myself, *not my jurisdiction.*

I gingerly touched the bandage the paramedic had just finished winding around my head. "Any nausea or dizziness?" he asked me.

I gazed back toward the bodies, caught sight of the river of spilled blood. "Nothing unexpected," I murmured. I watched Alex as he stepped away from me, leaning in toward Romero and Tibbs as they talked, each cutting the other off, flailing their arms and pointing toward either the crime scene or the crest of forest they had just searched. I bobbed away from my paramedic as I tried to listen in on the officers' conversation.

"Desecration," I heard. "Wild animal."

The paramedic turned my palms facing up and began swabbing. "Hold still," he said without looking at me.

"Who called an ambulance? I mean, those girls were already . . ." I let my voice trail off, unable to say the word.

The paramedic, whose name badge said N. Torres, glanced through his lowered lashes at me. "I guess someone was hoping."

I wanted to be professional—stone-faced, matter-of-fact. But I knew that somewhere, someone was hoping that the police report was wrong, that the body under the sheet wasn't their daughter, wasn't their girlfriend, that she wasn't dead. I swallowed back a tortured sob.

"One sick fuck," I heard the chief say. "Can't possibly be human."

Alex turned slightly and caught me staring at him from

* * *

I generally have two complexion colors: impossibly pale or lobster red. But as I drove home from the Underworld Detection Agency—and the heinous crime scene on the bluff—I realized there was a new hue to add when I checked myself in the rearview mirror: ashen. It was the complexion equivalent of the way that I felt. Murder, I was sadly getting used to. Ditto with crime scenes. But lying—scratch that—lying to *Alex*, was a different thing entirely.

I trudged up the stairs and brightened when I stepped into my apartment and ChaCha, in a bout of spastically happy yips, tossed herself at my ankles. I scooped her up and she gave me a comforting nuzzle.

"Wow, Soph," Sampson said, stepping out of the bathroom. "You don't look so well. Everything okay?"

I pinched my bottom lip, trying to think of a better greeting than, "I saw the gnarled remains of a pair of college coeds on the Point; what did you do today?"

"I need chocolate" was my kindly response.

In a matter of moments I was stationed at the kitchen table wearing a stack of chocolate marshmallow pinwheels on my index finger. I was eating them like candied apples and dumping the remains of a chilly chardonnay in my *Carrie for Prom Queen* coffee mug.

"It was awful," I said to Sampson, shuddering so that a spray of chocolate fell into my cleavage. "The destruction was . . . complete."

"Did Alex have any leads? Did anyone?"

I frowned, shaking my head. "Nothing. But . . ." I let my word trail off as I bit into my cookie, hoping the chocolate-marshmallow goodness would dull the ache of those sightless eyes.

"But what?"

"Well, I wandered away a little bit—and ended up sliding in the—in the blood."

Sampson gestured to my turban of gauze. "I was wondering when you were going to mention that."

"I just hit my head. But before that, I'm almost certain I saw something. A figure or something in the bushes."

"Something or someone?"

I looked at Sampson and was taken aback by the intensity of his gaze. "I'm not sure. It was hard to tell."

He nodded and there was something unreadable in his expression. It was almost heartwarming, the way he focused on me, on my wound, on my story.

I gulped my mug of wine. "It may have been after I fell. But I felt it watching me. I felt it—or him—watching the whole crime scene."

Sampson bristled. "Does Alex know about this?"

I nodded, bit into another cookie ring. "I told him, but I think that he thinks—" I paused, picked at a chunk of chocolate on the table. "I think that he thinks I was seeing things."

I saw the question in Sampson's eyes, and I immediately changed the subject. "No leads. They found some hair, but I'm not sure what came of it."

"Hair?" Sampson's brows went up. "Victim or perp?"

I grinned. "You sound like a real detective!"

"Well, I did spend the afternoon watching *Law & Order*."

"Same detective school I graduated from," I said, glugging the remains of my wine. I stood up. "If you'll excuse me, I need to scrape the crime scene from me, now that I've been fortified. Oh—" I paused, turning slowly to face Sampson. "There was one thing that was weird though."

Sampson was gathering up my cookie crumbs with a napkin. "Oh yeah? What's that?"

"Feng was there."

Sampson stiffened and I saw the tremble go through his body. He tried to hide it, tried to brush it off, but I noticed the crumbs he had just palmed were sprinkled back on the table. "Feng? The werewolf hunter?"

I nodded.

"Sophie, why didn't you tell me this sooner?"

I looked from Sampson's pinched expression to my empty wine mug. "I—I only thought it was weird—not important."

Sampson let out a long sigh and lowered himself to the dining chair. I could see the cogs turning in his head.

"She doesn't know you're here, Sampson. She was at the crime scene—miles from here."

"You said that they found hair?"

"Yeah," I stumbled, confused, "one of the officers was bagging it."

"Do you know anything about it? Were they planning on running it for DNA?"

I smiled. "You must have caught a couple of *CSI* episodes, too."

Sampson avoided my gaze. "I'm not joking."

I was taken aback. There was nothing overtly angry in his statement, but the way he kept his eyes averted from me let me know that, suddenly, a wall was up between us.

I gripped the back of the dining chair.

"She's looking for us, Sophie."

I straightened. "She saw me. She didn't try to talk to me. I really don't think she knows you're here. And if she did—I know her, Sampson. Why don't you just let me talk to her? I can tell her about you, explain that you're not a threat to her. Or to anyone else."

"No!" Sampson's eyes flashed with a rage that was buried in fear. My breath caught and I saw his expression immediately shift from surprise to sadness. He reached out and patted my hand, used his other hand to rake his sand-colored hair back from his forehead. "I'm sorry; I didn't mean to startle you. I just—please, don't contact Feng. Don't say anything to her until I can figure out what we're going to do."

I nodded, but unease thrummed through my body. I was comforted that Sampson referred to *us*; I wanted to do everything I could to help him. But as I looked at the exhaustion in his eyes, the way he worried his bottom lip, I wondered if everything I could do was going to be nearly enough.

Chapter Three

I'd thought it was a physiological impossibility for a good-looking man to snore.

And if it isn't, it should be.

"Is he dying?" Nina wanted to know.

I gnawed on my bottom lip. "No, unfortunately not."

Nina's eye's flashed, part shock, part careful consideration. "Sophie Lawson!"

I rubbed my temples and moaned softly. "Maybe I was wrong. Maybe he doesn't turn into a werewolf. Maybe he turns into a Boston terrier."

We were standing in our living room, tiny slivers of yellow-grey San Francisco morning light-slash-fog poking in through the blinds. I was pajama clad and bed-headed, Nina was Audrey Hepburn chic complete with signature boat-necked black dress and broached chignon. All that was missing were the elbow-length gloves and one of those long, elegant cigarettes.

"What do we do about it?"

"It" was Sampson. He was a beautiful specimen of a man, indeed—his sandy brown hair was peppered with steely grey and it made him look distinguished, sexy. He had one of those incredible Roman noses and full lips that fell apart just a quarter inch in his slumber, letting out the most raucous, brain-shattering snores.

Maybe it was a paranormal thing.

He had a nice chiseled chest and well-muscled arms, but after three nights being serenaded by the nose symphony, I couldn't see straight, let alone appreciate anything other than a man who slept in beautiful silence.

And Sampson was not that man.

Seriously, I was about to consider snuggling up with Vlad, if only for the blessed silence of a breathless vampire.

"I don't think we can do anything about it, Neens. The man's been on the run for over a year. He said he's always had to look over his shoulder, to question his safety. This is the first time he's felt safe since—since the incident."

The night Pete Sampson went missing and I was nearly bled to death by a Snuggie-wearing maniac had become known as the night of "the incident." It was easier to explain, and for me and Sampson to remember it, that way. For me it was simply traumatic, my first (and, unfortunately, not my last) run-in with someone who thought this world would be far better without me in it. For Sampson, it was the night his life had gone from simply complicated to in desperate danger.

As I looked over the peaceful, rhythmic rise and fall of Sampson's chest, I couldn't help but feel a glowing sense of pride. I hadn't necessarily had anything to do with saving his life and had been a very good part of the reason Sir Snuggie almost ended his, but protecting him here on my couch seemed like the least I could do.

And then his mouth dropped open again, breathing in a rush of air that came out again, rattling our picture frames and my brain more than any of our native earthquakes ever did.

Nina looked at me, her perfect, coal-black eyes actually seeming to show a bit of purple-tinged exhaustion. "We have to find out who's hunting him so we can get him out of here."

I nodded. "ASAP."

In the eight blessed seconds of Sampson-breathing-in silence, our front door opened, and Vlad poked his head in.

"It's bad enough I have to smell him, now I have to hear him, too?" he growled.

I looked from Nina to Vlad; the family resemblance was undeniable now as both of them glared at me, fangs at the ready. I held up a hand, slight panic rushing through me.

"Okay. Nobody eats anyone. I'm going to take ChaCha for a walk and clear my head. Then I'll get this sorted out and get Mr. Sampson on his way as soon as possible."

Sampson, still dead to the world but as loud as a freight train, snored his agreement.

I clicked ChaCha's leash around her tiny neck and stepped into the hallway. I was going to lock the door behind me, but I figured with a werewolf on the couch and a two silence-deprived vampires, our collection of Ikea furniture and Burger King china would be safe from looters.

"Whoa, love." Will Sherman, standing in his open doorway across the hall, stepped back, the expression on his face one of sheer shock, quickly covered by something that was supposed to resemble—I guessed—nonchalance.

"What happened to you? Been out hunting the nutters and whatnot?"

Though I like to think I'm not one of those women who go all quivery-jelly around good-looking men or who feel the need to slap on pearls and lipstick to impress the hairier sex, I still felt my hand fly up to my bedhead nest of orange fuzz and my cheeks burn a little.

Will shook his head, clucking his tongue. "You look a sight."

I tried to narrow my eyes, but lack of sleep disallowed their free movement. I wanted to look hard and angry, but that was impossible with my spastic pup, ChaCha, doing her love-starved dance at the end of her leash, throwing her entire eight pounds against Will's calves, rolling over like the pet-slut she was to show off her rubbable dog belly.

Will grinned, leaned over, and scooped ChaCha into his arms.

"I thought I wasn't allowed to do any hunting without my Guardian in tow." It wasn't meant to be a compliment, but Will took it as such.

"Ah, a Guardian's work . . ."

I shifted from foot to foot, still stupidly holding ChaCha's pink, camouflage leash while Will nuzzled ChaCha, who threw her head back in ecstasy, little dog legs kicking at the air.

Will Sherman is my Guardian. And no, I'm not under eighteen—far from it. I'm also not a trust fund baby à la Athina Onassis or Paris Hilton (pre–sex tape/pantiless partying/jail time). I'm simply the Vessel of Souls and Will is, simply, my Guardian.

Yeah, I really thought I could get that one past you.

I didn't always know—nor was I always, I guess—this otherworldly Vessel for all human souls as they cross from the human plane to the either angelic or *other* plane. It's not like the souls are inside me—no, that's actually more like a steady stomach of chocolate-marshmallow pinwheels and anything that ends with the phrase "on a stick." And it's not as though I could burp up the soul of say, Bea Arthur, at any moment. I prefer to think of myself as more of a gateway rather than a gag gift from some ancient congress of angels who thought it would be a real gas to hide the one thing that both the angelic and demonic plane want more than anything—me, the Vessel of Souls—in plain sight. Yeah, plain sight. Me.

So even if I wanted to describe myself as a rare, exotic beauty the likes of which you only see in storybooks or in the *Sports Illustrated* Swimsuit Edition, I couldn't, as I am supernaturally bound to be this "plain" thing.

At least that's what I keep telling myself when I stare into the mirror and find that my has-a-mind-of-its-own red hair has decided to curl in its own circus clown fashion, whipping and swooping into my lime Jell-O-green eyes. Plain, yes. Regular? Not so much.

As I was saying, Will Sherman is my Guardian, bound by all things holy and un to throw himself in front of me in desperate, pointy situations, lest I fall into the wrong hands and get gutted, clubbed, or locked in a public restroom with nothing but hand soap as an escape method.

Yeah, he's not great at his job.

I blinked at Will. "I'm having a hard time sleeping."

"That explains why you're up at a decent hour."

"We've got a houseguest and he"—I considered my words, as a simple "snore" didn't seem to capture the gravity of the situation—"rocks the city as a whole."

Will cocked an eyebrow and stopped nuzzling ChaCha. She whined.

"He snores. Loudly. I can't believe you can't hear it from your place."

Will grinned and looked over his shoulder, his hazel-flecked eyes going from sparkling and friendly to sensual and fierce.

"You could have always come across the hall. There's room in my bed."

I swallowed heavily and my stomach began a raucous flutter.

Any other woman would have swooned to get an offer like this from Will. He is nothing short of gorgeous with his always-mussed gold blond hair, hazel eyes that sparkled with bits of mischievous gold, and a body that was carved from a soccer god.

And then there was the accent.

Will is English and has that lilting, melodic voice that makes anything sound wildly intelligent and sexy. He uses words like "nappies" and "loo," which I know mean diapers and bathroom, but when he says them, they tend to be nothing short of panty melting.

But I had already gotten myself into that situation once and due to the werewolf snoring on my couch, I was still in the midst of processing my tryst with Will, whether or not it had been a mistake made out of need or something more, and whether or not I had ruined everything with Alex Grace.

My body hummed with a nervous energy as Will's eyes flashed over mine, almost daring me to respond.

I wanted to say something very Carrie Bradshaw, very kitten-with-a-whip.

"ChaCha needs to go to the potty."

Hey, I'm the Vessel of Souls. I can't expected to be a sexy linguist, too, right?

I took ChaCha downstairs and once her little legs hit the sidewalk, she beamed like only a dog can and pranced in front of me, wagging her tail and her tongue at everyone we met, peeing on everything static or everyone who moved slowly enough to allow her hindquarters adequate aim.

We walked over to Huntington Park, a luxurious little patch of green not far from our neighborhood where ChaCha could sniff until her little heart was content, and I could find a free park bench on which to lay down.

With lack of sleep, comes lack of shame.

I slipped the loop of her leash around my wrist and closed my eyes, letting the rare shard of sunlight wash over me, relishing the delightful feeling of warmth bathing over my shoulders, my cheeks.

In my uber-relaxed state I could hear the sharp barks of dogs overwhelmed at the abundance of new things to pee on and the steady hum of traffic as it ambled up California Street. I liked to imagine that I was lying on the beach and every whooshing Metro bus was a wave crashing against a coconut-scented white sand beach. In my imagination, I was wearing a tiny turquoise bikini and showing off the six-pack that currently lived somewhere underneath my hibernation flab. In actuality I was laying spread eagle on a park bench with my mouth partly open and my hand dangling in the grass. ChaCha must have seen the opportunity in my dozing because halfway through my fictitious daiquiri, she gave the leash a yank, slipping the loop off my wrist, then took off yipping and yapping across the lolling green hills of the park, her little dog eyes glued to the jaunty butt of a brindle terrier. The little jerk on my wrist sent me sputtering and coughing and sitting up, feeling lost, confused, and blinking into the sunlight.

"Oh, crap!" I saw ChaCha's pink leash slithering through the grass and I launched myself off the bench, running after her. "ChaCha! ChaCha, stop!"

The little dog didn't abide and seemed to just get faster, and within seconds she had zigzagged through a tight congregation of boxwood bushes, barking as though she were a Doberman or a wooly mammoth. I was sucking in my stomach, following her, getting angrier by the second.

"ChaCha! You better stop this right now or Mama is going to be—"

It was nothing overt. Call it a feeling, a whisper on the

wind, but something rushed by me and made my blood run cold. I stopped short, my hackles up. I felt the hot prickle of someone's laser gaze on me and gooseflesh bubbled on my arms. "ChaCha?"

I heard the crush of tanbark, the crinkle of leaves.

Low, ragged breath.

The air suddenly smelled salty with a weird mix of earth and sweat. I whirled all around me, seeing dogs running with wide, toothy dog-smiles, tongues wagging, their owners chanting, clapping. The noise of the park and the animals blurred into one solid cacophony and I couldn't make out another sound.

The footsteps crushing the tanbark; the low breath—had I imagined them?

"ChaCha?" My heart slammed against my rib cage. My saliva went sour, my voice starting to quiver. "Come here, girl."

I felt it before I heard it, and then I was on the ground. My forehead thunked against the tanbark, my teeth smacked together. All the breath left my body and I opened my mouth and sucked uselessly at the air, trying to get something into my failed lungs. My ribs screamed. My wrists ached. There was a burning swath across the back of my calves where something—or someone—had swept my legs out from under me.

I dug my palms into the tanbark, ignoring the bits of wood that embedded themselves into my skin. I tried to push myself up, but then I felt hands on my shoulders grabbing fistfuls of my shirt and yanking me up. I kicked uselessly at the air. I tried to squirm to see my attacker, but he must have seen me first because he dropped me, fast, another rib-crushing belly-flop to the earth. I heard his footsteps as he stumbled backward.

I knew I should move. I knew I should get up, should

run, should find help. But everything ached and my whole body felt as if it was made of lead. I heard footsteps and everything tightened, waiting for another blow. But none came. The footsteps disappeared and the raucous crunching of leaves and twigs and tanbark was gone, replaced by a breezy silence, punctuated by the occasional dog bark, the occasional belch of a Muni bus.

"ChaCha," I was finally able to croak, feeling the sting of tears at the edges of my eyes.

I pressed myself up onto my haunches and my little pup came barreling toward me, yipping as though someone had just released her. I curled her into my chest and stood, holding what little breath I had and listening to the silence. I felt at the bandage on my forehead, then glanced back at the tiny tears and splinters on my palms, an unabashed fear washing over me. First the Sutro Point murders and the person watching me there. Now I'm manhandled by— what? I looked around me, my stomach going sour. I wasn't sure I wanted to know what had knocked me down.

There was definitely something going on in San Francisco and as usual, I had succeeded in getting into the middle of it.

By the time ChaCha and I returned to my apartment, the luscious smell of coffee had permeated the whole third floor. I didn't have the vampire sense of smell that Nina and Vlad had, but I was almost one-hundred percent sure I smelled donuts, too. The kind with sprinkles.

"Hey!" Sampson turned when I walked in the door and I had to grin. He was dressed in *GQ* pressed jeans with a dark wash, and a viciously starched button-down shirt. The thin red stripes of the shirt were kept clean by a frilly apron with kitschy cherries all over it that I had purchased in a fit of Donna Reed-dom (thankfully, that particular fit was fleeting).

I was grinning at Sampson, but his smile fell when he saw me.

"Sophie, what happened?" He rushed out of the kitchen, and I set ChaCha down and shrugged my shoulders.

"Dog fight?"

Sampson pulled a mammoth hunk of tanbark from my hair. "Someone attacked you." He began untying his apron. "I knew this would happen. I knew my being here was a bad idea."

"No!" I leapt forward, wincing, putting my hand on Sampson's forearm. "This had nothing to do with you."

Sampson's face was hard. "I come to town, you get attacked, and it's just a coincidence?"

I waved a scratched-up hand. "You wouldn't believe how often I get attacked. This city is really going to hell."

Or hell is coming to the city.

Sampson went hands on hips. "Who did this to you, Sophie?"

I unhooked ChaCha's leash and hung it on the hook. "I don't know," I said honestly.

"Sophie—"

"You said yourself that the people who were after you *beheaded* and slaughtered the people in Anchorage. I just got a little roughed up." I forced a smile, not entirely sure how the words "beheaded" and "slaughtered" fit into a pep talk. "Is that bacon?"

Sampson finally relented, shaking his head. "Yeah. Coffee, first of all," he said, pouring me a cup, "then eggs, bacon and—"

"I thought I smelled—"

Sampson flopped the oven door open, exposing a grease-stained pink bakery box. "Donuts."

I slid the box out of the oven and selected a donut.

"You made these? Box and everything?" I asked with my mouth full.

"I'm sorry. I didn't realize you had company."

I turned at the sound of Will's voice behind me. "Uh," I started. "Uhhhhhh . . ."

Sampson brightened immediately, giving Will a curt nod. "I'm Joe. Sophie's uncle."

"Right," I said, nodding spastically and oozing relief. "Joe is my uncle. Joe, this is my friend, Will."

Sampson stuck out a hand, but Will hung back, studying Sampson and me. He stepped forward then and without moving his lips muttered, "If you're here against your will, say spatula."

"Spatula?" I didn't have time to blink or to think about the fact that I had spat out what Will defined as a safety word because Will was on Sampson, and ChaCha darted from her dog bed, yapping at the rolling cacophony of elbows and arms. Will grabbed Sampson in a headlock and eggs went flying. ChaCha stopped her yapping to lap them up and I threw myself in the middle of Sampson and Will— groans, growls, and me screaming, "Wait, no! Stop! I didn't mean spatula! I didn't mean it!"

There was a throaty growl and then everything stopped: Will's eyes were huge, his cheeks ruddy and carpet burned. His elbow was firmly clasped around Sampson's throat and Sampson's eyes were truly wild—a look I had never seen and that was all at once chilling and mesmerizing. White bubbles of spittle bubbled at the corner of Sampson's mouth and a glistening sheen of sweat beaded on Will's upper lip as Sampson's arm clamped down hard around Will. I was kneeling on the floor, yanking on Will's arm, palming Sampson's forehead.

"Stop it! Stop it!"

"But I thought—"

"I don't need your help," I spat at Will. "Sampson, let him go."

There was huffing and grunting as Sampson and Will untangled themselves from one another. I stood in the middle, pushing them apart.

"Sampson?" Will said, sandy eyebrows raised.

My heart, which was already doing a thunderous double-thump, dropped firmly into my knees.

"Isn't Sampson your old boss?"

Sampson pierced me with a glare. His lips were set firm, nostrils flaring. "Sophie . . ."

"No, Sampson," I said, grabbing him by the shirtfront. "This is Will. My Guardian."

The two men evaluated each other much the same way cage fighters evaluate each other before going for the jugular. "He lives across the hall and enjoys the heady, albeit rare, scent of bacon. And Will, this is Mr. Sampson. You're right; he used to be my boss at the UDA."

"Didn't he also used to be dead?"

"Theoretically." I turned to Sampson, watching as uncertainty flitted across his face. I grabbed his shoulder and shook it lightly. "Don't worry; Will's a good guy."

Will spread his legs slightly and crossed his arms in front of his chest. His brows were drawn, his eyes laser focused on Sampson. "So is Sampson."

There was a momentary retreat to corners until Sampson pulled out the plate that had been keeping warm in the microwave. "Bacon?"

We sat down with bacon as the universal peacemaker. As Sampson heaped the table with breakfast, Will jutted his chin toward me.

"What's all this about?"

My hands immediately went to my hair and I shook out

a leaf. In all the commotion I had forgotten about my blitz attack. "No biggie. Someone attacked me at the park."

Will crossed to me and circled my body, examining, gently poking at my scratched skin. "Who attacked you?"

I shook my head. "I don't know. I didn't see him."

"The park is wide open, love. And last I checked the sun is working overtime. How did you not see him?"

"Blitz." Sampson said. "Got her from behind."

I pushed away from Will's probing fingers. "I'm fine."

"I'm not. Who do you think did this? Fallen angel?"

I crossed my arms in front of my chest, winced at the starburst of pain in my ribs, then put my hands on my hips. "You're asking *me* if it was a fallen angel? What am I paying you for?"

"With all due respect, love, you're not paying me at all."

I poked the donut in his hand. "Consider that payment. And no, I don't think it was a fallen angel."

Will quirked an unconvinced eyebrow and I groaned.

"Fallen angels don't jump their prey at a dog park. They light stuff on fire, make you eat bugs, and accuse you of murder."

Sampson raised his eyebrows.

"It's been a challenging year," I told him.

"But—"

I held up my hand, effectively silencing Will. "I know you're concerned about my safety and I appreciate that. But you realize there are donuts to be had."

Sampson handed me a donut. "Same old Sophie."

It wasn't that I wasn't concerned about the dog park jumping. I was. But a little bit of tanbark up my nose quickly paled in comparison to everything else going on in my life. And also, there were donuts.

I was polishing off my second (third) donut and mowing

down a heap of cheese-flecked scrambled eggs while Sampson gave the basic overview of his story to Will.

Will nodded, listening intently, and when Sampson finished, Will wiped his hands on a napkin. I stopped him before he could talk.

"So, Will, when Alex and I were at the crime scene, we saw a werewolf hunter."

Will frowned. "You didn't tell me there was a crime scene."

I shrugged. "This is the first time I've seen you."

He cocked his head. "You've seen me."

I couldn't tell if his sentence was an innocent statement, or a cheek-reddening reminder that I *had*, in fact, seen him—naked. I said nothing until Will rambled on.

"What kind of crime? Real blokes or some of your gobblygooks?"

"I'm pretty sure that's offensive. And it was a double homicide." I grabbed another piece of bacon and stuck it in my mouth, relishing the oozy, salty flavor. The fact that I could eat and talk homicide said volumes about how far I'd come in the investigative world—or in the culinary one.

Sampson pushed his plate away and folded his arms on the table, his eyes fixed on me, lips pressed in a hard thin line. "Her name is Feng. Her family—"

"Feng!" Will put in. "The bird who tried to strangle you. I'd almost forgotten. How is the old gal?"

"Fine, I guess."

"Did you have a nice chat?"

"No. She just kind of glared at Alex and me."

Will's shoulders flexed, the movement tiny, almost imperceptible. "You were with Alex?"

"Yeah, it was a crime scene." I suddenly felt an odd surge of embarrassment. "Kind of his jurisdiction. If something was on fire, I would have called you."

When Will wasn't nicking free food from me or making my nipples stand at unfortunate attention, he was a San Francisco firefighter, red hat, rubber boots, and all.

"If Feng the werewolf hunter was around, isn't it kind of your jurisdiction?"

"No." I swung my head. "The crime was not supernatural. Although it was pretty gruesome. They did kind of toss out the killing could have been done by some sort of animal."

I saw Sampson blanch slightly.

"Don't worry," I said, putting my hand on his arm. "I didn't say a word about you to Alex."

"Why's that?" Will said, snaking a piece of toast. "Alex think one of your wolf guys is responsible?"

Now it was my turn to blanch. "No, of course not. It was probably . . . gangbangers. Anyway, he doesn't know about you, Sampson, I promise." I looked imploringly at him. "You have to know I didn't say anything to anyone about you being here."

Will cleared his throat, looked down at his plate.

"That was different. You barged in. You have no respect for privacy." I glared at him.

"So why was Feng at the crime scene?" Will asked, bringing us right back to the crime scene.

"I don't know."

Sampson looked as though he was working very hard to keep himself under control. "Why did Alex think she was there?"

I shook my head slowly. "He didn't say. I don't think he thought anything about it. A lot of people were there." Even as I babbled, I could feel the heat rising in my cheeks. "There were a lot of people trying to see what happened. People always want to . . ."

Sampson stood up quickly, his fork clattering to his

plate. "I have to get out of here. I knew it was a mistake to come back. I'm putting you in danger."

"No!" I stood up, too, a shower of sprinkles and pink icing dropping from my lap. "No, you're safe here. If I were in any danger, Feng would have taken me out right then and there. She was just hanging out. It had nothing to do with you—or with me. I'm sure of it." I wagged my arms, physically trying to get my point across. "And the last time I met her she choked me, just like Will said."

"She's a charmer, that one."

"If I was in any real danger, she would have killed me on the spot. But she didn't." My lack of death should have been a victory, but somehow, it didn't quite feel like it. "And you're safe, too. She left. She didn't find you. She wasn't looking for you."

"She was at a crime scene."

"Maybe she's taken to hunting actual criminals now," I offered hopefully.

Sampson sucked in a breath. "Do you know how werewolf hunters work, Sophie?"

"Yeah." I nodded, my eyes going to Will. "Feng gave us a little bit of the lowdown on our . . . visit."

"She has a sister," Sampson said.

Will grinned. "Right! Sailor Moon!"

"Xian," Sampson corrected.

Feng's twin sister—identical, except for their fashion choices—spent every moment she wasn't tracking werewolves dressed up as a wide-eyed, short-skirted anime character, while Feng chose to dress like G.I. Jane.

"Xian is the tracker," I said slowly.

"And if Feng was out there, Xian told her to be. Xian sensed something."

"That's perfect!" Relief washed over me in cool waves and I grinned. "Xian's sensor is off then. Obviously! It was a regular crime scene. Double homicide, nothing special. Far from here."

"What happened to the victims?"

My cool sense of relief left as easily as it came. "They were murdered."

"Gunshot? Knife wounds? One of those eggy gang initiations?" Will asked.

"It was graphic. Lots of destruction. Looks like it was a team, if not a gang." I focused on Sampson. "But there was nothing supernatural about it. There is no reason to think that Feng was there for any other reason than any of the other onlookers were there. She's a looky-loo. Her business is slow. She said it herself."

Will nodded agreeably. "She did say that she and the sis were rather good at their jobs. All but put themselves out of work."

"That's reassuring," Sampson said. "Either way, it's not safe here." He began clearing plates. "I'm leaving as soon as I get this cleaned up."

I crossed the living room and put my hand on Sampson's forearm, taking the plates in my other hand. "No, you're not. You're safe here. You've got me and Vlad and Nina and Will. Will is right across the hall and he can fight. He can fight if Feng comes after us, or if anyone else does. And he has a car named Nigella."

Will grinned, pride washing over him. "She's a beauty."

"See? You can finally stop running. Like I told you before, we're going to help you. We'll figure this out, Sampson."

Will crinkled his nose, shifted his weight uncomfortably. "Actually, love, that's what I came here to talk to you about."

I sighed and did my best to shoot *Really? Right now?* daggers at Will. "I thought you came here because you smelled bacon."

"Well, that was an added bonus. But I was hoping you

could help me out. I'm leaving for London tomorrow morning." He turned to Sampson. "Going to go visit Mum. She's getting on and having some trouble moving around the flat."

I felt myself gape. "You're leaving? Now? And what do you want me to do? Fill in as my own Guardian while you're gone?"

"With all due respect, love, you've spent a good deal of time telling me how lousy I am at my job and how much you don't need me. I mean, you are a crack shot with a Glock, right?" Will smiled, and his humor stabbed at me. My cheeks must have gone beet red because Sampson looked momentarily alarmed.

"She shot a guy in the arse."

Sampson smiled, looking impressed. "You've come a long way."

I blew out a sigh that came out an audible groan. There had been a time, once, when I was afraid of guns. It pretty much extended from the first time I shot a gun (I cried) until . . . right now. Yes, I'd shot a guy in the butt. But I'd been aiming for his head. And it'd been a matter of life or death and the backfire had still terrified me and made me pee a little bit when it happened. But before that, in another life-or-death situation (you know? I really need a vacation), I'd aimed my gun, steadied it . . . and thrown it at the red-eyed creature that broke into my apartment. So sue me; I was terrified. But it was true, I'd come a long way since then.

Well, at least I was able to hold on to my gun.

And the ass thing? Lucky shot.

"So you're coming over here to let me know you're out?"

"No. I was coming over here to ask you if you could water my fern."

"You have a fern? You don't even have a couch and you have a fern?"

"She's called Esther. And she likes to listen to the football game in the late afternoon. Helps her get all bushy and all."

Sampson nodded as if this were the most normal thing in the world.

"Fine. I'll water your fern." I pointed to Sampson. "But that doesn't mean you're any less protected and that we're not going to get out of this being-hunted situation."

Will clapped a hand over his chest and cocked his head. "Oh, I feel honored that my leaving takes nothing from the situation."

I smiled sweetly. "Your leaving will take nothing from this situation right now, so why don't you get to it?"

Will turned to Sampson. "How do you feel about ferns?"

"That's perfect. Sampson could stay at your place while you're gone. Esther gets hydrated, Sampson gets a little breathing room." I nodded at Will. "You *are* good for something."

Will raised fawn-colored eyebrows. "She always been this feisty?"

Sampson nodded. "Pretty much. And thanks for letting me stay at your place."

I crossed my arms in front of my chest and adopted a kick-ass stance. Will seemed to get the message because he left without saying anything and once again my insides roiled, tortured and confused.

Sampson glanced at me. "Nice fellow."

I nodded, my teeth digging into my bottom lip. "Sure."

Sampson paused for a beat, then held me with a serious look. "I'm not going to put you in danger, Sophie."

"You mean—about Will?"

"About everything."

"You keep saying that and I keep telling you: you're not,"

I said, putting my plate on top and taking the whole stack to the sink. I looked over my shoulder. "Besides, it's been a long time since you've been around. I can take care of myself pretty well now." I itched the back of my calf with the toe of my shoe. "Totally."

And it wasn't a total lie.

In my last couple of years as sole breather in the underworld, Vessel of Souls, and undefeated holder of the Most Likely to Bleed and/or Get Socked by a Bad Guy title, I learned a few things. One being that when it came to taking care of myself beyond the basic eating/sleeping/breathing essentials, I really couldn't be trusted. The other was if there was bad to be found, I would run headlong into it (metaphorically), waving my arms and screaming like a maniac so that said bad didn't miss me. This wouldn't be terrible if I were some kind of supernatural ass kicker or even just a butch chick with a penchant for black leather, weapons, and wanting to kill a man just to watch him die. I wasn't, but after the last couple of ass-whoopings and blubber-fests, I decided it was about time I put my big-girl panties on and learn some technique.

I signed up for a Krav Maga class at the Fillmore Community Center. I hadn't gone yet, but it was all about baby steps. I rented three self-defense DVDs from the San Francisco Library and Netflixed the entire first season of *Alias*, kicking and jabbing in the living room. And I had even talked Vlad into giving me the occasional vamp-approved hand-to-hand combat course.

I wasn't a black belt yet, but I was totally inching above complete imbecile.

* * *

"I need to head off to work," I said, sweeping a rag over the counter. "Do you have plans? Maybe we could meet for lunch?"

Sampson smiled and for the first time since he showed up, he looked like his old, relaxed self. "This isn't a vacation, Sophie. I've got to talk to some people, see what I can find out about the contract, about Feng and Xian."

"What contract?"

"There's a contract out on my life."

I felt myself gape. "So we're not only dealing with Xian and Feng, we've got the mob after you, too?"

"The contract is Xian and Feng's."

I crumpled up my rag and tossed it in my to-be-washed mountain. "I think Xian and Feng were pretty much kill-at-will."

"They like people to believe that. But, technically, under UDA bylaws they have to be contracted or they're considered rogue and enemies."

I sat down hard. "Wait. You're telling me UDA governs the Du family, too? What the hell?"

Sampson shrugged. "The Underworld is complicated."

"Well yeah, obviously. But can't the UDA just override Feng and Xian? Don't you—or Dixon, or just the bylaws—override a stupid contract?"

"I appreciate your enthusiasm, but it's not that easy. I'm just one man and the contract only pertains to me, to my life."

"This has to enrage other demons, Sampson. Someone can just contract someone else and your life is over? That's a travesty. It's absolute crap. It's un-American. We should protest. Or sue." I thought of the late-night attorneys on TV, urging people to join their class-action lawsuits against asbestos poisoning and "vaginal mesh slings"— whatever those were—and even though I wanted to do

everything I could to save this man, to make things right—
I had a hard time imagining the same crooked lawyers im-
ploring demons to call out the people who tried to kill
them. "Or something."

Sampson was already shaking his head, but I rattled on.
"Can we just ask them to stop? We can tear up the contract!" I imagined myself then, leather clad, because anytime I imagine myself doing kick-ass things like tearing
paper, I'm clad in leather, haughtily tearing and crumbling,
throwing teensy-tiny nullified contract crumbs up into the
air. Then I'd drink a scotch. "What do you think?"

The look on Sampson's face was one of those sweet, sad
ones a father gives his elementary school daughter when
she says she's going to marry SpongeBob when she grows
up. "I wish it were that easy. These contracts aren't paper
bound and they aren't as simple as pen and ink."

I've been in the Underworld a long time, and although
the Detection Agency runs on what seems like thousand-
year old Word documents, I'd yet to see any contract come
through that wasn't "paper bound" or "pen-and-ink." I licked
my lips. "Like, written in the stars? In blood? On big stone
tablets? We can still get it, ruin it, jackhammer it if we have
to." I'd skirted enough hard-hatted workers to have a pretty
good idea what jackhammering entailed, but that sweet,
sympathetic look in Sampson's brown eyes said that even
power tools were out of the question for this.

"The contract is bound by blood and flesh."

I felt my own flesh crawl and my mouth quirked into an
involuntary grimace. "Flesh?"

Sampson nodded solemnly and I considered a hunk of
demon buttock squirreled away in some file cabinet somewhere. "How is that even possible?"

"You know that things in the Underworld don't work the
same way that things in the over world do."

"But"—I pantomimed dumping a hunk of flesh on the table—"I don't get it." I was silent for a minute, considering. Then, with a slight brightening, "Should we just be looking for someone missing a hunk of flesh? Where do they take it from? Would he have, like, a hook for a hand, or one of those prosthetic limbs? Or"—that grimace again—"is that where the vaginal mesh sling comes in?"

Sampson cocked an eyebrow, his brow wrinkling. "Excuse me?"

It may have been a matter of afterlife or death, but I couldn't believe I had just spewed the words "vaginal mesh sling" in front of my boss. A hot redness bloomed in my cheeks. "So, where does the flesh come from?" I asked again.

"It's mine."

"Yours?" My eyes immediately slipped over the length of Mr. Sampson, taking in every chiseled inch. His face and neck certainly weren't missing any flesh and his button-up shirt didn't seem to bow over any fleshless gaps. I tried not to look any lower.

"It was cut from me when I was in my werewolf form. In order for the contract—the hunters—to consider the contract bound, it must include flesh from the"—Sampson swallowed slowly, his Adam's apple bobbing—"*animal,* and blood from the contractee."

God, I felt bad for their file clerk.

"So, in order for us to end this thing, we have to . . ." I felt my lip curl in a disgusted grimace. "Get your pound of flesh back?"

"It's not a pound of flesh. It's a piece of flesh."

"So, to end the contract . . ."

"We need to destroy the contract, the contract holder, or the hunters."

"Who's the contract holder?"

Sampson shrugged. "I have no idea."

"Well, it has to be someone who knows you—maybe someone who's holding a grudge? Someone you met through work?"

"I don't know. It was all I thought about up north."

"Okay, well. How about the contract? Hunk of flesh and blood notwithstanding, the contract is, like paper, right? I mean, it's not tattooed on the back of an ogre or burned into the side of a volcano or something, is it?"

"The binding part is written on the flesh."

I fought the urge to heave while my stomach lodged firmly in my shoes. "So we're looking for some wordy flesh."

"No, we're not. You've done enough for now." He glanced at the clock on the microwave. "I know I'm not your boss anymore, but aren't you about to be late for work?"

"Did I mention how nice it was to have you back?" I socked Sampson in the arm and pulled a healthy lunch—a Fresca and two Pop-Tarts—out of the fridge, then yelled for Nina and Vlad to get their undead asses moving. While I waited, I yanked open the blackout drapes in the living room and let the beams of glorious, rare San Francisco sunlight wash over me. I was marveling at the way our Ikea furniture sprung to glistening life in the natural light when Nina tore out of her room, like a tiny, raven-haired cyclone dressed in a painted silk kimono robe.

"What are you trying to do?" she screamed. "Kill me?"

Sampson raised his eyebrows and I set down my Fresca. "What are you talking about? And where's Vlad?"

Nina turned to gape at me. Or at least I think she did, because she was wearing her enormous dark sunglasses. "Have you not seen the weather?"

Sampson and I exchanged uncertain glances. "We live in California, Neens. We don't have weather."

Nina wagged her head. "It must be so easy to live a life with so few consequences."

Sampson hid his smile behind his coffee mug and I rolled my eyes, about to remind her that I had been hung up by my ankles and accosted by a lunatic with a gunshot in his ass (courtesy of me, but still), when she went on, slapping her arms and raving. "I'm practically burnt to a crisp thanks to your obsession with opening the blinds."

I blinked at the blue-white of her forearms. "Sorry. But if you were burnt to a crisp you'd be, well, burnt. To a crisp."

She narrowed her eyes. "We're talking life-or-death situation here, Sophie. You'll have to let Dixon know that I can't come in today." She shrugged her tiny shoulders and flopped down on the couch in pure Scarlett O'Hara fashion. "I can't risk it."

"If you can't be out in the sun to get to work, what makes you think Dixon will?" Dixon Andrade, a vampire (and former Nina boy-toy) took over the UDA after Sampson's "disappearance."

Nina waved her hand, the reflection catching in her Jackie O glasses. "Just let him know I'll be working from home today."

"Holy crap!" The front door slammed open and I coughed, covering my mouth and nose over the plume of smoke that came racing in. A man was hunched, an ugly, military-looking blanket pulled over his head. The whole thing—the man, blanket and all—was smoking.

"Vlad!" Nina sprung to her feet and began smacking smoking Vlad with a rolled-up *US Weekly*.

"Oh my gosh!"

Vlad dropped the blanket and raised an eyebrow at me, nostrils flared. "I'm on fire."

I tried to think of something soothing to say, but came up blank. "Sorry," I muttered.

"Did you see the news?" Vlad asked.

Did you see the news? should be a basic, non-sweat-inducing question. And for most people, it is. But for me, it is nothing less than ominous and I had the sudden desire to jump in my Tae Bo fighting stance, or at the very least call Jennifer Garner as Sydney Bristow in for backup. I swallowed, finding my mouth immensely dry. "Did something happen?"

"Uh, yeah. The weather! The sun?" He gaped at me when my reaction wasn't a mortified as his. "This heat wave is supposed to last all week! It's supposed to be *sunny in San Francisco*. For a whole week!"

"All week?" Nina groaned, then flopped back on the couch, fainting goat style. Sampson edged away from her.

"What are we supposed to do cooped up in this house all week?"

"It won't be so bad, guys," I said. "We're well stocked with blood bags and we've got cable and"—I rummaged through our junk drawer—"almost an entire deck of Uno cards! It'll be like summer camp!"

Vlad and Nina glared at me, now both shoulder to shoulder on the couch, Sampson wedged at the end.

"Fun!" I said, injecting as much joy into my voice as I could.

No one moved.

"Okay," I said on a sigh, "I've got to get to work, so . . . call me if you need anything."

Nina reached out and clamped a frozen hand around my wrist. She looked up at me, her eyes an impossible black, wide and mournful. "Tell the world I said hi please."

I blinked. "Um, okay."

Chapter Four

Nina and Vlad weren't the only ones upset by our recent weather pattern. As I pulled out from the underground parking garage, it was obvious that confusion riddled the streets. People walked aimlessly around, faces upturned, brows furrowed. I poked my head out of the car and spotted some teenagers sporting bare arms and naked bellies. They zipped past on bicycles, hooting and hollering and loving the sun. Generally, I feared ax murderers and the zombie apocalypse way more than good weather, but for me and my fellow townspeople who were used to seeing spontaneous drag parades, roadside preachers, and trees that spoke, heat was an uncomfortable anomaly and I wasn't entirely sure what to do with myself. After a few lights I began enjoying the natural warmth so I rolled down all the windows and played "Walking on Sunshine" on an endless loop.

It's going to be a good day, I told myself.

I was still hopped up on vitamin D and walking on Katrina and the Waves' special brand of sun-kissed pop perkiness when I skipped into the police station vestibule, and Alex made a beeline for me. He had a wad of file folders pushed under one arm and an expression on his face that killed any hope for a big musical number.

"I've been waiting for you. I need to talk to you about the Sutro homicides."

As I knew Katrina and the Waves never sang about homicide, the music in my heart came to a slamming stop. "What, exactly, about them?"

It was then I noticed the heavy bags under Alex's eyes; that the glistening blue of his irises had dulled with lack of sleep. "Is everything okay?"

"Sophie!"

Will's accented voice pinged through my head as I blinked at Alex, trying to make sense of what had just happened—Alex in front of me, Will's voice behind? I blinked and Alex stiffened; I felt Will's hand on my shoulder. I spun and gaped at him.

"Where did you come from?"

Will grinned and jutted a thumb over one shoulder. "Lift. I thought you'd be at work by now."

I looked from Will to Alex and back again, while the heat seemed to ratchet up at least sixty degrees. I felt the sweat bead on my upper lip and at my hairline, could feel my carefully straightened curls begin to spring back into place.

I don't belong to either of them, I told myself. *I'm walking on sunshine. . . .*

Uh-oh.

Nothing was said between the two men. There were no overt dirty looks or scowls, but even without taking a single step, Alex and Will seemed to be doing that menacing staring circle that dogs about to sink incisors in do. I should have felt glorious to be the prize that they growled over, but all I felt was an awkward, both-of-these-men-have-seen-me-naked tension. The ex-boyfriend, the almost-boyfriend—and me, not knowing which was which.

I licked my lips and forced a bared-teeth smile, patting Alex on the forearm. "Alex, you remember Will."

Alex's ice-blue eyes were fixed on Will's hazel ones. "You don't usually forget the guy who stabbed you," he said evenly.

"Right, mate, sorry 'bout that. Misunderstanding with the whole Vessel–Fallen Angel thing." He shot out a hand. "We good?"

I tried to read Alex's expression as his gaze scraped over Will's outstretched hand. I tried to decipher the nuance in Will's stance, the inflection in his voice.

"Yeah," Alex finally said, giving Will's hand a quick, dismissive shake. "We're good."

"Great!"

Will clapped his hands, looking expectantly from Alex to me. "So, what are we Sherlocking this week?"

I shot him a tight-lipped, keep-your-stupid-English-trap-shut look. He just kept grinning.

"We"—Alex pointed to me and then back to himself—"are working on a homicide. Multiple. Nothing that would interest you. No fires, nothing about guarding the universe or whatever."

Will, firefighter by day, Vessel Guardian by later that day, narrowed his eyes. "I don't guard the universe. I guard Sophie from the big baddies in the universe. You know, fallen angels and such."

Alex's bristle was physical. "I've seen Lawson in action. She can take care of herself."

I jumped in between the two men, who somehow seemed to have gotten closer by the puffing of chests alone. "Um, thank you, Will, for your guardianship. And Alex's services are excellent, too, and he's not a bad angel."

There was a juvenile flash of triumph in Alex's eyes and

just-as-juvenile indignance in Will's expression. "Your services are great, too, Will."

I immediately dropped into a bout of lobster-red embarrassment. Because if you want to keep your romantic trysts under wraps, the best thing you could possibly do is thank a man for his *services*.

"Good Guardian," I clarified, clapping Will on the shoulder. "You're a good Guardian and you're a good angel."

There was a beat of dead awkward silence that I'm fairly sure lasted just under a millennium. Of all the times the earth couldn't break open and swallow me whole.

"So," I said, breaking the trance, "Will, what did you—?"

"What do you want, Will?" Alex broke in. "Lawson and I have a case to get through. Some of us like to protect the population from actual danger."

There was a slight flare in Will's nostril, then an equally as slight upturn of his lips. He raised his hand to eye level, a silver key on an Arsenal keychain pinched between thumb and forefinger. "I just needed to give you my key, love," he said, his eyes focused hard on mine. I felt my mouth drop open as he looked over my head at Alex, then grinned supremely.

I spun. "I'm looking in on his bush. His plant. His house. Will's going out of town and I'm watering his plant and thank you very much for coming all this way to bring me your key even though you live across the hall and could have very easily slipped it under the door." I sucked in a huge breath.

"I know," Will said calmly. "I meant to give it to you this morning at breakfast, but it slipped my mind." He cut his eyes to Alex, then they flitted back to me.

"Headed out of town, huh, Will? Didn't know Guardians got vacation. What are you taking—two weeks? Three?"

Will looked at Alex and back at me, then brushed a

finger under my chin. "I'll just be gone a bit. You're a cop, right? I trust you to take care of my girl."

I felt myself gape. "Your girl?"

Then I felt Alex's arm as he slung it around me, the edge of his chin brushing the top of my head sweetly. "I always take care of my girl."

Now I spun, fairly certain that one more gasp would send me into cardiac arrest. "Your girl?"

Neither seemed to hear me—or see me—as they held each other in steely glares. I was apoplectic, uncertain as to whether I would be in the middle of a massive fistfight or cuddle fest. I snatched Will's key and mashed the down button on the elevator, then spun to point first at Will and then at Alex. "You're an ass and you're an ass," I yelled, jumping in the elevator once the doors opened.

"Can you believe those idiots?" I screamed into my phone as I paced a bald spot in my office carpet.

"Yes," Nina said. "What size do you wear?"

"Eight . . . ish. Ugh! I mean, neither Alex nor Will even raise an eyebrow and suddenly—"

"To be fair, Soph, both of them raised more than eyebrows. Or maybe it was you who raised their—"

"Not helping!" I snapped.

"Sorry. Are you more of a heather blue or a heather gray kind of girl?"

"I don't know, gray, I guess. What the—are you even listening to me? They were acting like animals! One more minute, and one of them would have peed on me."

"I'm listening, I'm all ears. I am. Have you ever actually watched the Home Shopping Channel? They have some pretty good stuff."

"Neens!"

"Right. The guys peeing on you."

I pinched the bridge of my nose, hoping to quell the ache that had started before it became a full-blown migraine. "It's just that for like, my whole life, I couldn't get a date. Not one!"

"I set you up with that one guy."

"He was part goat, Nina."

She harrumphed. "I've seen you eat. You might be half-goat yourself."

"Remind me to drive a stake through your heart when I get home."

"I wouldn't fight you. This heat is killing me."

"Nina?"

"Okay, I'm sorry. But Sophie, can you really blame two guys for fighting over you? Two incredibly hot, save-the-world guys? I mean, in the last couple of months, you've gone from sad and wimpy to uber-confident and gun toting. I mean, ask anyone. That's hot."

Even though I had just been called sad and wimpy, my toothy best friend spoke the God's honest truth and it warmed me.

"Aw, Neens."

"And you're also just a little bit slutty."

"Ms. Lawson?"

I was eyebrows up at "just a little bit slutty" when Dixon knocked on my door and poked his head in.

"Gotta go," I murmured to Nina. "Dixon, hi. I was just . . . giving Nina her assignments."

Dixon nodded. "She's staying out of the light?"

"Yeah. Um, sit down, please. Can I help you with something?"

Dixon pulled the door to a soft close behind him and I felt my spine immediately stiffen. When he turned to look at me there was something in his eyes—in his stance—that was awkward, uncomfortable. In all the time I had known him, I had never seen Dixon misstep or misspeak; he was a pinnacle of confidence and surety, and this air of uncertainty made me nervous.

"Is everything okay?"

Dixon sat, and produced a folded newspaper from his breast pocket. "Do you know about this?" he asked, handing the paper over.

I gave it a cursory scan, my eyes sticking the second they saw the word "murder." The story was detailing the incident as Sutro Point and the familiar sick feeling in my stomach bubbled.

I nodded. "I know about it." I pushed the paper aside. "I was there."

Dixon's eyebrows went up. "You and Alex?"

I nodded again and Dixon pulled the paper toward him, unfolded it one more time, and slid it back. He stood over me now, and pressed a finger against the page. "Do you know anything about this?"

It was a tiny article buried amongst the blowout sales and freeway closures—a single emboldened headline: MARINA WOMAN SEES CREATURE.

I chuckled as I scanned the small story.

> Eleanor Holt of Marina Green called police to report the sighting of a "creature" running through her backyard on Tuesday night. "It ran on two legs like a man, and then on four, like a dog." Holt said the creature was "about the size of a bear" and covered in fur; it "snarled and growled" like a dog and frightened Holt's own animals; she said it

was after her rabbit hutch. Police searched
the premises and found nothing. Holt
maintains that she heard howling and crying
throughout the night, that her animals
remained on edge, and the creature "was
probably Bigfoot."

I looked up at Dixon. "Is there an article about Bat Boy
in here, too?"

Apparently Dixon and I didn't share the same sense of
humor. He blinked at me and I refolded the paper and
cleared my throat, folding my hands in front of me.

"No, I hadn't seen that article, nor did I know that Bigfoot lived in the Marina. Must be making good money; I
know I can't afford a place down there." I grinned.

"So, you've not heard of any sightings from any clients
or any of your"—Dixon's eyes went up the ceiling—"other
friends?"

"No, Dixon, I haven't. And you know as well as I do that
Bigfoot is a myth."

Dixon quirked an eyebrow and I sighed. "An actual
myth."

Finally, Dixon's shoulders slumped a quarter inch and he
eyed me. "I ask because there was another killing."

I stiffened. "There was?"

"It was before the Sutro Point homicide and it was one
of our own."

I swallowed hard, my mental Rolodex scanning through
UDA employees, staff members I hadn't seen lately. "Oh
my God, who was it?"

"Octavia."

"Octavia Aronson? But she's a—" I held a hand out, gesturing toward Dixon, finding myself strangely unable to say,
But she's a vampire.

"Yes, she was a vampire."

"But you're immortal."

Dixon laughed, a mirthless, short bark. "No one is truly immortal, Ms. Lawson."

"Right, but . . ."

"Whoever attacked Octavia Aronson was able to kill her."

I leaned back in my chair, sighing. While the Underworld Detection Agency is the only agency tasked with keeping tabs on underworld inhabitants, the occasional over-world "protection" agency has been known to spring up. Usually a host of Buffy-slash-Blade type vampire killer wannabes or the intermittent Van Helsing throwbacks. They were rarely successful and generally fell out of their chosen paths when a new superhero took favor or Comic-Con ended, but now and again there was enough hubris to cause my clients harm.

"I don't see what Bigfoot has to do with a vampire slayer."

Dixon laced his fingers together and pursed his pale lips. "I think whatever Ms. Holt saw was what attacked Octavia. And we both know it wasn't Bigfoot."

"She wasn't staked?"

"She was beheaded."

Ice water shot through my veins. "Beheaded?"

"Torn apart, actually."

Though Dixon's voice was steady and held his usual air of nonchalance, he seemed paler than usual and was still having a hard time getting comfortable.

He was actually upset.

"Why are you telling me this? And why—" I gestured to the newspaper.

He cleared his throat into his fisted hand. "I know that you and Mr. Grace—"

"Alex," I corrected.

"I know that you and Alex tend to look into certain police cases that—" Dixon cleared his throat again and looked away. "That may pertain to supernatural assailants. And, frankly, I'd like to ask your assistance."

I felt my eyes bug unnaturally. "You want to ask me for help?"

Finally, Dixon met my gaze. "I'm not certain, but I think we might be dealing with a rogue demon."

I nodded, unsurprisingly used to the hypothesis.

"I think the demon we're looking at is a werewolf."

I sat in silence after Dixon left, my hand hovering over my cell phone. I began to dial Sampson and then hung up before the call connected.

Do I ask him if he's beheaded any vampires lately?

I almost lost my lunch when the phone rang on its own.

"Sophie Lawson?" I asked into the receiver.

"I'm bored," Nina whined on her end.

"Well, play a board game or something. What's Sampson doing?"

"He's not here."

"Well, where did he go?"

I heard Nina blow out an annoyed sigh. "I don't know, Soph. He wouldn't take his leash. Can't you come home?"

"Nina, I'm working."

"What am I supposed to do here?" She stretched out every word to emphasize her all-encompassing boredom.

"Go for a walk," I said.

"I'll die!"

"Risk it."

I hung up and tried my best to focus on the work in front of me, but my thoughts kept creeping back to Sampson, to Alex, to the mercury gradually rising on my Internet weather tracker. A bead of sweat rolled from between my breasts to my belly button and I sighed, making a mental note to check property rates in Antarctica.

By 1 PM I had highlighted the same papers over and over, and my olfactory senses closed in on themselves when Steve, a troll, appeared in my doorway. At barely three feet tall Steve has the ego of a much taller man and the stench of a rancid hunk of blue cheese smeared on a decomposing cow.

And also, he's in love with me.

"Steve needed to check in on his woman," Steve told me, his little troll legs bobbing two feet from the ground.

"I'm not your woman, Steve."

"Sophie will be Steve's woman," Steve reported, undeterred. "It is very hot outside. Sophie makes Steve's temperature rise." He waggled his bushy caterpillar eyebrows, grinning at me with a mouth full of yellow snaggleteeth.

"What do you want, Steve?"

"Steve has some information that Sophie might find useful."

I stiffened and surreptitiously moved my scented candle closer to my face. "Oh yeah, what's that?"

"Might Sophie enjoy a cold drink?" Steve waved an icy bottle of water in front of me, his grey hand gripping it tightly.

"What's the information, Steve?"

"Drink?"

I pinched the bridge of my nose. "Sure."

Steve unscrewed the cap and pressed the bottle to his mouth. I watched his lips part and his narrow knife of a tongue dip into the water. He took a long drink, then held the bottle out to me. "Lovers share everything."

"So share."

"Steve saw you at the crime scene."

My ears pricked. "On Sutro Point?"

He nodded.

"And?"

"And Steve saw the werewolf hunter."

I crossed my arms, growing annoyed. "So did I. So did Alex."

Steve thumbed his own chest. "Steve knows why she was there. Steve and Feng made small talk."

I cocked my head. "You and Feng made small talk? She doesn't seem the warm and fuzzy, sharing-small-talk type."

He grinned, supremely satisfied, then looked alarmed. "Don't worry! Steve likes it rough sometime, but Steve will always return to his beloved." He licked his lips and my stomach lurched.

"So why was Feng at the crime scene?"

Steve launched himself out of the chair and stuck his arms out. "The clue is in Steve's pocket."

"Get out of here, Steve."

He waggled his left hip at me. "It's in this pocket right here. Does Sophie want the clue?"

I folded my arms and raised an annoyed, stench-soaked eyebrow. "Sophie doesn't want anything that badly."

Steve shrugged and dropped his arms to the side. "Okay then, Sophie will never know what Feng was doing at the crime scene." He turned on the stacked heel of his cowboy boot and I bit my lip.

"Fine, Steve. What's the clue?"

He turned around, grinned, his eyes going toward his pocket. I held my breath, crouched down, and dug a single finger into the pocket of Steve's track pants. A low, approving rumble emanated from his chest while bile rose in mine.

"There's nothing in here!"

"Oh." Steve frowned, then jutted out the other hip. "Must be this pocket then. Innocent mistake."

I groaned, dug into the pocket, and extracted a single silver bullet.

The heft was familiar. The construction was impeccable. It was one of Feng's.

"Where did you get his?"

"Steve told you: at the crime scene."

"And what did Feng say?"

"Feng told Steve that her sister Xian knows there's a werewolf in town. New scent. Old blood. Feng knows who this werewolf is. So does Steve."

Heat, like a live wire, raced up my spine. *Feng knows that Sampson is here*? I pushed myself up and began to pace.

"Who else knows, Steve?"

Steve mimicked zipping his lips. "No one else knows. Steve's good at keeping secrets."

"Good. Let's keep it that way."

"Zip my lips?"

I nodded. "Yeah, right."

"Seal them?"

"Sure."

Steve's zipped lips rolled into a salacious smile. "With a kiss?"

My allegiance to Sampson was huge, but I wasn't crazy. "Not a chance."

Steve shrugged and kicked the leg of my visitor's chair. "Sophie's love will come in time," he said before disappearing in a blue-cheese-scented huff.

I rolled the bullet around in my palm, thinking of the tragic crime scene—the bodies destroyed, lives cut short—and then of Sampson.

"No," I said to my empty office. "I know Sampson had

nothing to do with this." I slipped the bullet into my purse.
"And I'm going to prove it."

I was able to slip out of the UDA without much problem.
The heat had thinned out the clientele and was slowing
down the employees, and Steve's odor knocked out everyone else. With each floor the elevator climbed, my confidence grew. I was going to talk to Feng and Xian. Let them
know their wires were crossed. Pete Sampson had nothing
to do with this murder. Maybe it was another werewolf.
Maybe it was a marauding band of horrible humans. Either
way, I would get the werewolf hunters to lay off. I felt
myself smiling, even.

"Well, don't you look like the cat that swallowed the
canary." Alex grinned at me from the police station vestibule.
It was a smile that went to his eyes, that made their deep blue
sparkle with a kind of sexy mischief that cut right through
me and did things to my nether regions. Bad things.

Focus, focus, focus.

"Hey," I said, using my best attempt at nonchalance.
"What are you doing out here?"

"Actually, I was heading down to see you."

Another zing, this one starting at my belly button. "You
were?"

Alex nodded and held up a stuffed manila envelope. "I
was hoping we could go over some of these pictures from
Sutro Point."

And just like that, the delicious zing of angelic sex was
vanquished.

I bit my lip. "I'm actually on my way out. Later?"

"Yeah, sure. Where you headed?"

I looked over my shoulder at the sunbaked parking lot.
Think, I commanded my brain, *think!* I had the introductory
paragraph of my Krav Maga class and three whole seasons

of *Criminal Minds* under my belt. I was practically a special agent.

"I'm going for a pap smear."

Yes. I was *Sophie Lawson: Special (Ed) Agent.*

I was closing in on Chinatown when I had the over-whelming feeling of being followed. But unless my pursuers were a Vanagon full of photo-snapping German tourists, my intuition was way off—which wouldn't be totally un-heard of for me. I nabbed a space right along Stockton Street and was skipping through Grant's Gate before the full weight of what I was about to do—and who I was about to see—hit me.

The last time I'd met Feng on her turf, she'd greeted me with a chokehold. I could still feel her fingers, like steel bars, closing in on my windpipe. I hightailed it back to the car, popped the trunk, and shook the knife out of a plastic Big 5 bag.

To answer your question, yes, I have a gun. But the last time I'd used it, I was forced to shoot a *person*—a sweaty, bat-shit-crazy, murderous person—but still. He screamed. He bled a heavy river of bright-red blood. And although I only shot him in his plentiful ass, the idea that I could have killed this *human being*—ended his life—was rough on me. So, I bought a knife. Not so much with the intent to gut and fillet; more with the hopeful idea that my brandishing such a weapon would incite a fearful retreat by whomever was ready to pounce.

I was tucking my new weapon into my shoulder bag when the hairs on the back of my neck shot up. I cocked my head, trying to decipher the sound of footsteps, of heavy breathing from the huffing grunt of the Muni buses and the general clatter of downtown.

I was definitely being watched.

"I have a weapon," I murmured without turning around. "And we're in a very public place."

"I have a weapon, too," he murmured back.

I turned around, groaning. "Alex! What the hell are you doing here? Were you following me?"

He was looking at me with that stupid, sexy half smile, one eyebrow cocked. "Who says I was following you? Maybe I was in the mood for some chow fun."

I slammed my trunk down hard and crossed my arms in front of my chest. "Are you in the mood for some chow fun?"

"Are you asking me out?"

I felt the unattractive flare of my nostrils and Alex broke into a gale of laughter. "Okay, fine. Sorry," he said.

I eyed him.

"I was following you."

"I told you I was going to get a pap smear and you follow me? Man, you've got some weird sexual fetishes. No wonder they kicked you out of Heaven."

Alex rolled his eyes. "So you're honestly telling me you go to a gynecologist in Chinatown?"

I hitched up my chin. "Dr. Kwan does good work. And I get a free egg roll afterward."

"You're a nut."

"And you almost got yourself gutted," I spat.

"Is that so?"

"Why are you following me?"

Alex fell in step with me. "Because you didn't tell me where you were going."

I opened my mouth and put up my hand to answer—as I had, in fact, told him where I was headed—but Alex grabbed it, pushed it down by my side. "You lied. That much I knew."

"Since when do I have to tell you where I'm going?"

"Since when do you lie to me?"

I jammed my hands in my pockets but didn't answer him.

"So, where are we headed?"

"If you must know," I said, slipping around a heap of tourists posing for pictures at Grant's Gate, "I'm visiting a friend. And no, you can't come."

Alex looked almost hurt and I was surprised to feel a pang of sadness. I sighed. "Okay, you can come, but you can't come inside. She and I need to talk." I caught his questioning gaze. "Girl stuff."

I had some questions to ask Feng, and if I was going to keep Sampson's secret safe, the less people who heard, the better.

Alex just shrugged. "Sounds fair," he said. "But do I get to know who you're visiting? Wait." He splayed his hands. "Let me take a guess. Can I take a guess?"

I rolled my eyes and jutted my chin in the universal sign for *Get on with it*.

"You're going to visit the famous werewolf hunter."

I stopped dead in my tracks. "How did you know that?"

He slung an arm over my shoulder. "I'm an angel. I know all sorts of things." He pointed to a bakery. "Pineapple bun? You know there's not actually any pineapple in them, right?"

"I don't want a pineapple bun."

"Well, I do want to talk to the werewolf hunter myself. She was at the crime scene, right?"

"Yeah on the crime scene, still no on the pineapple bun. Come on."

We walked in companionable silence, huffing our way up two hills and zigzagging through tourists and pop-up sundries shops while doing our best to avoid the wilting, fetid stench of vegetables left to rot in alleyways. I stopped when I saw it and sucked in a sharp-edged sigh: Feng's workshop.

"That's it? They set up shop in a Chinatown delicatessen?" Alex asked, skepticism all over his face.

The Du family factory—or at least where Feng and Xian did their tracking and hammering out of silver bullets—was creatively disguised as a Chinese delicatessen. According to its peeling, fading sign, the place was called CHINESE/AMERICAN FOOD DIM SUM FREE WI-FI RESTROOM FOR CUSTOMERS ONLY.

At least some of their wares were transparent.

I shrugged. "Great location. Best dim sum in town."

"Because that's what everyone wants right after they meet up with their local werewolf hunters."

Alex went to grab the handle of the door, but I put my hand on his, stopping him. "I think I should go in alone."

"I don't think so. It doesn't look safe."

I'm not exactly sure how he could surmise whether or not the place was safe as every single inch of the floor-to-ceiling windows was pasted over with sun-faded Chinese calendars from the years before I was born and curl-edged posters of pretty Asian girls hocking everything from videos to glazed crockery with cute, fuzzy kittens poking out of them.

"I know what I'm doing, Alex. And besides, I have a weapon."

Surprise registered on Alex's face. "You do? Are you carrying your gun? Weren't you the one who told me that of all the weapons one of us breathers could have, a gun would be right up there with a teaspoon in terms of effectiveness?"

"I believe I said a gun would be about as effective as a ladle, but yes. And that's why I have this." I dug into my shoulder bag and whipped out my brand-spanking-new Big 5 knife.

I'd expected Alex's eyes to go wide or at the very least, go slightly hooded and bedroomy (what was sexier than a chick with a knife?). I hadn't expected him to clap a hand over his mouth and break down into near-snort-worthy guffaws.

"What's so damn funny?"

Alex, shoulders shaking as he tried to control his torrent of laughter, said nothing. He just pointed at my knife.

"You're really going to sit there laughing like an idiot while a woman brandishes a weapon at you?" I unsheathed the blade, hoping to scare the piss—or at least the giggles— out of him.

He just laughed harder, tears slipping down his cheeks.

"What the hell is so funny? Don't think I won't use this on you!"

Alex's eyes shot down the length of the blade. "To do what? Gut me?"

I narrowed my eyes. "Maybe."

"You know what this is for, don't you?"

I looked down at the blade in my hand. It did suddenly seem slightly less menacing, but it was a blade nonetheless, and blades were made for gutting people.

"It's for scaling fish," he said.

Or for scaling fish.

"What?" I looked at the damn thing in my hand again, squinting at the tiny bass imprinted on the side. "It's a bass knife."

"For fish."

So I thought it was a bass-style knife. As in, "Bass! The serial killer fish of the lakes!"

Alex took the knife out of my hand, his finger going over the portion of the blade that carved upward.

"You hook the fish right here. Then you pull it down and

fillet it with this part." He flopped the knife over. "This is how you descale it."

I snatched it out of his hand. "Well, that might be what it's for in your world. But in the Underworld, things aren't always what they seem."

Alex looked unconvinced. "So you're telling me Big 5 sells magic bass knives?"

"How'd you know this was a Big 5 knife?"

"Do me a favor," Alex said, effectively ignoring me and going for the door again. "Leave the weaponry to me. Unless, of course, we run into a giant bass monster in the next twenty minutes."

I shoved my knife back into my purse and glowered at him. *Note to self,* I thought, *once this whole werewolf incident is over, prove to Alex that a fish-scaler can double as a fallen angel gutter. . . .*

"I'm going in alone."

"No. You're not."

"I know what I'm doing, Alex. And besides, I have a—"

"Fish scaler."

I put my hands on my hips. "I was going to say a plan, jackass. I have a plan."

"And that is?"

I blew out a sigh. "Well, if you must know, I was going to march in there, paste on my friendliest and most innocent smile, and ask to speak to Feng."

"Isn't that kind of what you did the last time? You know, the time you nearly got choked to death?"

"That wasn't my friendly smile."

"Well, get used to having company because I'm coming in with you."

I shrugged. "Fine. But I talk to Feng on my own."

Alex nodded, considering. "We'll see."

"But be prepared for total animation domination."

I yanked open the door and smiled when Alex's jaw dropped.

"What the hell?"

Though the sign on the outside of the building advertised CHINESE/AMERICAN FOOD, FREE WI-FI and BATHROOMS FOR CUSTOMERS ONLY, the inside was bright and cheery and looked like a scene out of an episode of *Sailor Moon*. Brightly colored Formica tables covered every bit of the available floor space and crammed at each table was a selection of glossy-haired people in various states of cheery Anime dress. There were schoolgirls in knee socks and over-the-shoulder nunchucks, sailor girls with wide eyes, argyle socks, and plastic swords, and the occasional guy staring out under extra-long bangs and guyliner.

Alex leaned close to me, his lips tickling my earlobe. "These are the terrifying werewolf hunters who nearly choked the life out of you?"

"Shh," I hissed.

One of the animaniacs stood up with a sweet grin on her face. She was dressed in a crisp navy and white sailor suit with a kicky red tie. Her red and white striped knee socks were tucked into the hooker version of little-girl Mary Jane shoes and her glossy waist-length hair was pulled into two adorable ponytails that framed her deep set, almond-shaped eyes.

Eyes that immediately clouded over when she recognized me.

"I remember you," she said, her voice preschool-kid sweet while her eyes shot daggers. "You were here before." She circled an index finger a half-inch from my chest and then her eyes—and her pointing finger—went to Alex. "You were not."

"It's Xian, right? I'm Sophie. I'm not sure we actually were introduced the first time." I paused, my mouth still hanging dumbly open as I followed the lines of heat that went from Xian to Alex. Her cherry-red lips were pursed, her finger still hovering just in front of Alex's chest. I watched in horrifying slow motion as Xian's lips parted ever so slightly. The tip of her tongue darted out and slid across her lips, leaving a glossy sheen around her cupid's bow.

"So anyway," I went on, somehow thinking that if I spoke louder, the sex spell would be broken, "this is my friend." I wrapped my hands around his upper arm. "My dear friend, Alex."

Alex was stiff, either locked in Xian's steamy gaze or completely terrified of being pummeled by the sexy sailor. I gave him a rather hard—yet friendly—shake. "I'd like to see Feng." I spun on my heel, my fingers digging into Alex's flesh. "Is her office still back here?"

I felt Xian's tiny hand on my shoulder; she dragged me back with the strength of a linebacker. "Why do you need Feng?"

I stumbled backward, nearly falling against Alex. He steadied me and I quickly learned the daggers that Xian was shooting at me earlier were her kind, fluffy daggers. Her entire countenance changed and I was pretty sure that I was about to be gutted by a life-sized cartoon character and her band of merry ani-men. I straightened and looked Xian in the eye.

"What do you two want with Feng?"

"Actually, Xian, it's just me." I put my hand on my chest and smiled slyly, rubbing my tongue over my bottom lip and dropping my voice. "I want to talk to Feng. If you don't mind, Alex would like to stay out here with you. He's a huge fan of anime."

Xian brightened, and I was suddenly off her radar. She grabbed Alex by the hand. "Come with me."

I saw the terrified look on Alex's face as I zipped down the back hall.

Take that, angel.

Chapter Five

I quickly navigated the narrow hall, picked my way through the grease-and-soot-covered kitchen, and stopped just before pushing open the ancient screen door. I expected Feng to be in her workshop shaving some kind of metal or killing baby bunnies or something, but she was in the alleyway, slouched against the brick wall, head thrown back. Her eyes were closed and a single shard of sunlight made its way through the surrounding buildings and washed over Feng's throat.

I laid my hand on the screen door's latch. The sound was miniscule, the latch scratching under the weight of my palm, but Feng's eyes flew open, her whole body going into a rigid fighting stance. She narrowed her eyes, practically snarling when she saw me through the matted screen.

"What are you doing here?"

Fear, like a lead weight, sunk low in my belly. It pressed against my bladder, made my knees feel weak and made every other limb feel loose. Feng was a trained assassin. I was an idiot with a bass knife. What was I thinking?

I held both of my hands up surrender-style. "It's me,

Sophie Lawson. We met before. I was here with my friend Will, and then we—I saw you—at Sutro Point?"

Feng's hard face registered no emotion, no indication that she remembered me or had even heard me speak. Finally, she said, "I know who you are. What do you want?"

I gently pushed open the screen door and stepped into the alley. The heat here was moist and oppressive, the stench of rotted vegetables, leftover food, and deep fat fryers making it feel heavy and slick.

I knew that Feng and Xian were twins and though their faces—the almond-shaped eyes, the high sleek jawbones, and hard mouths—were identical physically, that was where the similarities ended. Where Xian's eyes were rounded out with coal eyeliner and big, waggly lashes, Feng's were tight, narrow slits, always on the verge of shifting, glaring. Her mouth was set hard, her lips pressed blade thin. She was as tall and willowy as her sister, but Feng kept her shoulders rounded. Her belly was concave and her hips were straight and angular, two inches of smooth olive skin visible in the spot where her baggy camouflage pants came up to meet her fraying black baby tee.

"I need to talk to you."

"About what?"

I looked over my shoulder, my eyes sweeping the dank kitchen behind me. Assured no one was lurking or listening, I dug the silver bullet out of my pocket and held it up to her. "Business."

Feng's eyes zeroed in on the bullet. No one else in the city—in the world, likely—made silver bullets like these, but I spun it around anyway so Feng could inspect the tiny Chinese symbol carved on the shaft. The Du family was known not only for their werewolf hunting prowess but for their "artistry." Each bullet was carved with a symbol that indicated the season in which it was forged. A nice sentiment for an instrument of death, I guessed, but disconcerting nonetheless.

"It's one of yours," I assured.

"Fine."

Feng shrugged and I followed her into her "office." It was a big, empty room that looked as though it were carved out of concrete, with a uniformly bland gray paint job. Bare bulbs screwed into dented aluminum sockets hung from the ceiling, the yellow light casting weird shadows in corners and against walls. There were no windows, no phone lines, no computers. Floors blended into walls blended into ceiling, giving the whole place the unpleasant feeling of a solid steel block, while flimsy tables that looked like they were discarded from the restaurant hinted at more of an inescapable sweatshop. The Du family emblem was painted on the wall behind Feng—the surname *Du* intertwined with the American spelling, a stylized painting of a wounded werewolf dying behind the heavy black print. Nausea roiled in my stomach.

I hugged my arms around me, then slyly dipped one hand into my purse, letting my fingertips rest on the sheathed blade of my bass knife. Feng may not be a fish, but I was ready to gut her just the same if it came to it.

At least I hoped I would.

I looked around, trying to quell the nervous heat that prickled around my hairline. *If Feng was going to kill me,* I whispered in my head, *she would have done it by now.*

Feng settled herself behind an enormous hunk of mahogany wood—part desk, part work station—and pushed aside a mammoth toolbox that I knew housed bullet samples, spent shells, and tools.

My palms went damp when Feng stared up at me, her eyes like flat stones, but her lips quirked up at one end in a kind of wry, challenging smile.

"So what kind of business do you want to talk about?" Feng wanted to know.

I licked my lips and perched on the end of the folding metal chair set up across from Feng. My throat was closing, but I did my best to control angst in my voice, forcing my words to come out smooth and natural. "Can I ask you a question first?"

Feng pursed her lips, but gave an almost imperceptible shrug.

My heart slammed itself against my rib cage and my mouth suddenly felt impossibly dry. I rubbed my palms on my jeans and when my voice came out it was low, breathy. "What's it like?"

A single cocked eyebrow. "What is what like?"

I looked around the shadowed room, taking in the sparse furnishing, the cold existence. "Your job. I mean—I work in an office. I stamp papers and give people"—I almost choked on the word—"info sessions to get them acquainted with their new insurance policies and positions."

It wasn't a complete lie. There were papers and stamps and even insurance policies. But my "people" were generally dead and their new position was generally an afterlife one. And most of my life insurance policies were collectable once the holder died and then came back to life.

But I wasn't going to tell Feng that. Or that the whole of my employable existence consisted of trying not to be killed by my clients.

Currently, I run the Fallen Angel Division of the Underworld Detection Agency. Fallen angels are everywhere, but my clients are few and far in between, I suppose the consensus on that one being, "If I'm bad enough to get ejected from Heaven, I'm bad enough to avoid some UDA paperwork." Not a lot of them come in to register. So, I do a lot of Internet searches, determining if certain weird news "events" could have been caused by one of the fallen rather than just your garden-variety sociopath. Sometimes I hit. Sometimes I get hit. More often I miss.

But that's beside the point.

"I mean, my job is pretty boring, pretty run of the mill." It is, if your office fridge is stocked with blood bags and your bathroom has three normal stalls and one tiny one with very high walls for pixies.

Pixies are notoriously, dangerously private.

Feng shifted her weight, resting her elbows on her desk. She looked like she was considering my question, thinking of what she wanted to tell me—and what she didn't.

There was a moment of stiff, uncomfortable silence and I briefly wondered if Feng had triggered some sort of silent alarm, if maybe the Anime Army wasn't strapping on bubbly pink shields and climbing astride unicorns to come kill me. I only hoped that Alex would be able to sweet-talk Xian enough to at least get her to leave the nunchucks behind.

Feng's eyes sliced back to me, part scrutinizing, part studying. My heartbeat sped up and I readied myself for the soliloquy where she told me that she was born into the family legacy of a werewolf hunting and she did it so as not to disappoint her overbearing father, but she really wanted to be a ballerina or an accountant.

"It's incredible," Feng said instead. I watched her lick her lips as if just the very idea of hunting was delicious. Her eyes were fixed but dreamy, and her shoulders tensed under her faded black baby tee. She pushed a lock of her glossy black hair over one shoulder and leaned into me, chin resting on her hands.

"It's best at night, when the moon is full. There's this silvery glow over everything and you just—you just know when they're near. There's this deathly quiet first. It feels like there's no one alive in the world—it's just you and it."

"It?"

"The beast. The dog." She bit her words off hard and I felt a stripe of terror run down my spine.

"Go on."

"You close in on it." Feng stiffened now, her whole body reacting to her words. "You step closer and you can hear your own breath. Your heart is—it's like, thundering in your ears. You can hear your own blood rushing. And then"—her eyes flashed—"You hear it."

I swallowed hard, horrified but rapt.

"Its breathing is hard. Once the dog knows he's cornered, his fear is everywhere. You can smell it. It layers your skin; it's practically—"

"Palpable," I said with a shaking voice.

Feng nodded her head rapidly, her dark hair bouncing over her shoulders. "You can almost taste it. Once you get it in your sight—" She slowly cocked her head to the right, her ear near her shoulder. She closed her left eye, and pantomimed holding a gun, her right arm pulling back, her left steadying the barrel.

I felt myself leaning closer to Feng, my heart pounding, my eye closing, trying to get her sight.

"Then boom!" Her voice was so loud and booming I squelched a startled yelp.

"You blow the fucker's head off. Nothing but brains and fur on the back wall." Feng was grinning and splaying her hands, heinous, psychopathic jazz-hand style. She giggled and bile clawed at the back of my throat.

I thought of Sampson and her words reverberated in my head—*His fear is everywhere . . . brains and fur on the back wall. . . .*

And then she *giggled.*

My stomach roiled when she looked at me, the grin going all the way up to her eyes. "It's the most amazing feeling in the world, man."

"The killing?" I could barely get the words past my teeth, knowing the hunted, the "it" she could be looking for was within seven square miles of Feng's rage, and someone who was so close to me.

"No," Feng shrugged. "That's just a fringe benefit. The real good feeling comes from knowing that you're keeping San Francisco safe from another one of those salivating tree-pee-ers."

"Really?"

"No." Feng wagged her head, her grin not faltering at all. "I really like the killing."

I tried to mirror Feng's overjoyed grin, but I'm pretty sure mine came out as wildly uncomfortable as I felt. I shifted in my chair, trying to take the immense weight off my suddenly full bladder. "At least you enjoy your work," I managed.

Feng frowned, looking off in the distance again. "Yeah, but, a lot of it is just busy work now. At least that's the way it feels. Don't get me wrong; I like making the bullets."

"They're like art," I mumbled absently, repeating what I had heard her say, had heard Dixon say, had heard Will say.

Feng pumped her head, her lips rolling up into an agreeable half smile. "Yeah, they are. I like doing it—and not just because I know what their final destination is." She mimed shooting a gun once more, and once more my stomach threatened to escape through my mouth.

"It's just that there's not a lot to do lately. Not a lot of active duty. We're pretty clear. Except . . ."

I leaned forward, the angst and sickness in my stomach flip-flopping to heart-palpitating anxiety. "Except?"

Feng leaned back, all the spunk and joy going out of her

face as a suspicious expression masked it. "What did you say you wanted again?"

"Um," I stuttered, digging in my pocket for the silver bullet. "This. This bullet. It's yours."

"Uh-huh."

I sucked in a shaky breath. "I found it at a crime scene."

Feng looked at me blankly, her expression giving nothing away.

"At Sutro Point."

Finally, she nodded. Whether it was in agreement or understanding I couldn't be sure. "You were there." We locked eyes and I straightened, feeling slightly bolstered. "Why were you there?"

Feng crossed her arms in front of her chest looking relaxed, but guarded. "Same reason you were there, I suspect."

"I came with a police detective. We were processing the crime scene."

She raked a hand through her hair, looking away. "Same here."

"It was a homicide. Two humans were murdered by another human being."

Another cocked eyebrow, another hint of that wry smile. "I disagree. Actually, my sister Xian disagrees." She leaned over and plucked the bullet from my hand. "And I don't shoot just to shoot."

"So you saw—you saw the perpetrator?"

Feng didn't answer, didn't even look at me. She dropped the bullet on the desk and spun it with a finger. I watched the glistening silver blur as it spun.

"So, you were at the crime scene . . . because Xian sensed something?" Xian was the tracker, and Feng was the shooter. That much was pretty clear.

Feng looked at me as if alarmed. "How did you know that?"

I felt my mouth drop open, felt the words sticking in my throat. "Uh . . . uh . . . I just assumed."

Her eyes flashed as if she was considering my answer. "A werewolf was responsible for those deaths."

I swallowed hard. "You think?"

"I know. Xian sensed a new wolf in town and twenty-four hours later, two people are torn apart. It's not rocket science, Pippi Longstocking."

I bristled.

Feng sighed and crossed her arms. "Why exactly did you come here?"

"I know you're hunting werewolves. I know you know there is a new wolf in the city."

Feng's face remained hard, but I could see her façade crack, just a tiny bit. "And?"

My breath felt short and shallow, and I could feel the damp heat on my palms. "And I need a favor. I need you to call off the hunt."

Feng's lips cracked into an amused smile and she waved her hand around her. "You know what we do here, right?"

I slowly snaked my arms in front of me, crossing them at my chest while I kept my eyes firm on Feng's. "I know exactly what it is you do here, Feng. You're werewolf hunters. That's not in question. Now I'm asking you for a favor. I need you to lay off this particular wolf, this particular hunt."

"Why?" She looked me up and down, her expression making it obvious that she wasn't all that impressed by what she was seeing. "Does Pippi Werewolf Hunter wanna take a shot?"

I cocked my head, a lock of my red hair tumbling over my shoulder as if on cue. "I'm not screwing with you, Feng. You need to stop hunting this wolf. He's not one of them."

Feng's brows went up. "He's not a wolf?"

"He is a wolf. . . ."

She shrugged. "Then he's one of them."

"You don't understand. He's not—he's not bad. He's one of the good guys."

Feng picked up one of her own handmade silver bullets and spun it in her hand. "I think those two women on the trail would beg to differ."

I sucked in a breath and clenched my teeth. "He had nothing to do with them."

"Cuz he's one of the good guys, huh? So, what? Were-wolf vegetarian? Is that like a vampire with a soul or with a movie deal?"

"He didn't do it," I said again.

"Then who did?"

"It could have been anyone. Serial killer. Psycho. Jealous boyfriend, angry Justin Bieber fan, Satanic ritual—"

Feng's voice was low, steady, and her eyes were fixed hard on mine. "Did you see those women, Pippi?"

I opened my mouth to answer Feng, but she shook her head and held up a silencing hand. "Not women," she said. "There wasn't enough left of them for anyone to know that they were human, let alone women."

My saliva soured and I willed myself to think of something other than the desecrated bodies.

"Their blood was muddy. There was more of it on the ground—mixed into the dirt, ground into the grass—than there was on the corpses. One of them—it looked like she may have been blond—was missing an eye."

My stomach bubbled and I felt myself step back as if trying to get away from Feng's disturbing description.

"It had been ripped clean out of her head. Her eye, half her cheek."

I bit down hard on my bottom lip, feeling the hot, metallic taste of my own blood filling my mouth.

"Tell me how something human could do something like that."

I shook my head. "People do heinous things." My voice was a bare, unconvinced whisper and the thought—so brief—flitted through my mind: *Who am I trying to convince?*

"Sometimes people do. But people don't have the kind of strength it took to pull this kind of torture off."

"But a gang—"

Feng's barking laugh echoed through the room. "Tell yourself whatever you want. I've seen firsthand what a werewolf will do." She looked sad for a fleeting moment, her eyes going glassy and losing their focus on me.

"But not all of them."

"I'm not about to take any chances finding out. They're all capable of this kind of violence. It's what a werewolf was bred for. Sooner or later, they'll all come to this."

"No." I shook my head, a sudden burst of strange confidence surging through me. "No, not this one. Maybe others but not this one. The werewolf you're looking for has been like a father to me. His name is—"

"His name is Pete Sampson. Six foot two inches tall. Turned in 1989 by Addison Brown of San Francisco, California." Feng licked her lips. "Since deceased. Interested in learning anything else?" Feng flashed the paper toward me and I was able to catch a few snippets of the information printed there: home address, driver's license and license plate numbers, car and make.

I shuddered to think what else was contained on that paper.

I wet my lips. "Can I see that?"

Feng cocked her head but didn't hand it over.

I was astonished, but did my best to keep my focus. "If

you know so much about him, then you know he's not a threat."

Feng stood up and leaned across the table. "Look, Pippi, I don't know if you noticed—and frankly, I don't care whether or not you did—but we're not in the business here of threat estimation. We do the threatening. So I don't really care if your canine buddy there is a flesh-eating werewolf or a tutu-wearing lap dog when he's changed. I have a contract. I have a wolf. I will finish both off." She blinked. "And I don't fail."

I felt my stomach churning, the bile rising in the back of my throat, but I worked hard to keep my stance. "What do you mean, a contract?"

Feng looked at me on a sigh, doing nothing to hide her obvious annoyance. "We hunt dogs. All of them. And sometimes, someone hires us to put a certain pup on the top of our list."

"Someone hired you to get Sampson? Who? Who would do that?"

Feng stared at me for one second longer than was comfortable before sitting back in her chair and pulling a ledger and a pencil toward her. "We're done here," she said without looking up. "Go away. And I'm sorry in advance for the loss of your friend."

I opened my mouth to respond to Feng, but my head was in such a fog that all I could do was close my mouth dumbly, then let myself out of her office. I stumbled into the alley where the heat had gone oppressive and sticky in the short time I had been inside. It pressed against my chest and stole my breath, and the stench of sun-rotted vegetables was everywhere; I felt it on my skin, in my hair.

When I walked into the delicatessen, each of the anime-clad clientele whipped their heads to look at me. Alex's eyes were narrowed and angry at first, but upon seeing mine, they went wide and concerned.

"I've got to go," I heard him say, his voice sounding a million miles away. "This has been . . . fun."

I watched Xian get up and grasp his hand. She batted her eyelashes and kicked the stacked toes of her enormous Mary Jane shoes against the scuffed linoleum. "Can't you stay just a little bit longer?" she asked, cherry red bottom lip pushed out.

"We have to go now." My voice cut out through the din of anime conversation, broke over the whining hum of an overworked air conditioner.

Alex shrugged his shoulders and broke away from Xian, following me out the door.

"You couldn't have done that, like, twenty minutes ago?"

I pressed my index fingers against my temples and rubbed tiny circles.

"I was just kidding, Lawson. It wasn't that bad. If I go LARP with them this weekend, Xian said I could be the Pirate Prince of Pettigrew. Whoever that is." He pressed his lips together in a sweet smile, then cocked his head, his blue eyes clouding.

I was blinking furiously.

"Lawson?"

I wasn't going to cry. I hated crying.

It was one of the things I was known best for.

"I take it Feng wasn't amenable to giving you any intel?"

I sniffled. "No. Not at all."

Alex didn't look totally shocked and that annoyed me.

I crossed my arms in front of my chest and Alex fell in step beside me. "You didn't think she would?"

"First if all, it's not that I don't trust your powers of investigation. But Lawson, they're werewolf hunters. Generations old or whatever. Did you really think she was just going to let you in on her plan? No offense, but you and your job? Kind of diametrically opposed to her and her job. She probably doesn't think you're on her side with this one."

"On her side?" I spat. "I'll never be on her side."

"Weren't we trying to make sure that if a wolf was the perpetrator of the homicides, he gets taken care of?" Alex asked. He paused for a beat, then licked his bottom lip and shifted his weight. "We're on the same side, right?" He had the gall to look apologetic and that burned an angry hole in my gut. I seethed silently until Alex sighed.

"Did she at least let you know if she was working that day at Sutro? Is she actually tracking a werewolf?"

I gritted my teeth and fisted my hands. "Not anymore," I said, shooting down the sidewalk.

I situated myself in the car while Alex got himself inside and fiddled with the radio until he found a Giants game. He cheered when the fans cheered and then looked at me quizzically.

"Really? You take me to my first game and you don't even care that we're creaming the Rockies?"

"Huh? Oh." I shook my head. "Is there any new information?"

Alex's eyebrows raised and pinched together. "It's a live game, Lawson."

I blew out a larger than necessary huff and clicked the radio off. "Not the game. The crime scene. Anything new?"

Alex flicked on his blinker and hung a sharp right, his black SUV veering toward the police department. "We can check. Can I ask you something, though?"

"Sure."

"Why are you so interested in this case?"

I put on my super-cool-Sophie face. "What are you talking about? I care about all of our cases."

Alex didn't hide his amusement, but he didn't look at me either. "Our cases?"

I rolled my eyes. "Fine. *Your* cases. Cases that affect the city in which I live. Cases that involve rabid maniacs tearing unsuspecting women apart limb from limb. But they are *your* cases. Happy now?"

I felt the car lurch forward as Alex leaned on the gas. "It was just a question."

I was still unnerved and uncomfortable by the time I got into my car. Feng was going after Sampson and she wouldn't let up. *If I could at least find out who sponsored the contract, maybe I could buy Sampson some time,* I thought.

But time for what?

I wanted to help Sampson. I didn't want him to run anymore. But with Feng and Xian and the entire Anime Army, did he even have a chance? Did we?

I clicked on my earpiece and dialed Sampson's cell phone, listening to ring after ring until it went to voice mail. I groaned and clicked off the phone, then cranked up the radio, hoping the latest pop star du jour would take my mind off the images seared into my brain, the images that Feng recalled so readily.

My heart was doing a spastic *I've ruined everything* pump by the time I pulled into my underground parking space, pop princess cooing about young love and butterflies notwithstanding. My eyes were wet and I took the stairs two at a time, huffing by the time I got to the third-floor landing, my heart threatening to bulge through my eyes, my blouse sticking to my sweat-damp bra.

I rapped on Will's door, crossed myself, swore that I

would lay off the pinwheels and lay on the treadmill, and tried to chase away the I'm-responsible-for-almost-killing-everyone-I-know vibe. By the time I was able to talk myself off the proverbial ledge and out of my pity party hat, I realized that I was standing in front of Will's door, still knocking, door still tightly closed.

I dropped my arm, flexing my now-bruised knuckles and pressed my ear to the cool wood, holding my breath, listening.

Nothing.

"Sampson?" I hissed against the door hinge, hoping my throaty whisper would sail through the miniscule crack and directly to Sampson's canine ears. "Sampson, are you in there?"

I glanced at my watch and told myself that Sampson was obviously just out grabbing a before-the-moon-rose bite, but something—a tiny, niggling bit of doubt—inched at my periphery.

"No," I scolded myself. "He's innocent."

If I were a true private eye—one of those gun toting, leather wearing rebel chicks—I would have spun on my heel and jumped on to my Harley, then beaten some answers out of a low-life in a bar somewhere to locate Sampson and our unsub.

But I wasn't that girl.

I might have better aim now, but my wardrobe was full of synthetic materials and my head was a cavernous hollow in the "prove Sampson innocent" department. And motorcycle rides made my privates hurt.

Instead, I gave a dejected sigh, turned on my heel, and sunk my key into my own lock. I expected the usually loose-hinged door to pop open, but it stuck. I pushed it and it moved—slowly. I felt the small stirrings of panic starting in my limbs.

"Nina?" I called, imagining the non-look in her vacant eyes as her dead—dead for real this time—body sat slumped against our front door. "Nina!"

My heart clanged like a fire bell when the door was yanked open and Nina blinked at me, her face set in what I had come to know as her "what the hell is it now?" look.

"What?"

I fell into her, wrapping my arms around her, relishing the chill I felt as her skin touched mine. She shook me off her.

"I thought you were dead."

She cocked her head, a waist-length lock of glossy black hair tumbling over her collarbone. "That's sweet."

"I thought your body was crushed against the door, pinning it shut." I peered around the door. "What was crushed against the door, pinning it shut?"

Nina pulled me in by my wrist, her eyes lighting up with her grin. "Tah dah!" Her spokes-model arms were gesturing toward a tower of cardboard boxes.

I pointed. "What's that?"

Nina's grin didn't falter. "It's a hibachi. And a barbecue set. And a *Kiss the Cook* apron. We should have more barbecues."

"I don't cook and you don't eat. And aren't you afraid of fire?"

She shrugged, noncommittal. Her eyes focused on the stack and she plucked a smaller box from the tower. She gave it a curious sniff, then a shake, and finally ripped off a string of packing tape.

"Yes!" she hissed, dropping the box. "I've been waiting for this forever!" Nina slid off three sheets of bubble wrap and pointed some bizarre-looking electronic gun at me.

I ducked.

"What the hell is that?"

"It's a label maker, silly." She had the thing on now and was furiously tapping the tiny keyboard. She grinned when a glossy strip of white tape pooped out the muzzle end, the name SOPHIE LAWSON in heavy black ink. She slapped me with the tape.

"Thank you. I always wondered why we never wore name tags at home."

Nina continued her tapping on the keyboard. "This is going to make everything so handy. I figured as long as I'm stuck here at home, the least I can do is get organized. Getting organized has been my New Year's resolution every year since 1937."

"What happened in 1937?"

She rolled her eyes and slapped a CHACHA name tag on the dog. "Let's just say I know exactly where Amelia Earhart landed. She was such a troublemaker," she grunted.

"And on that incredibly awkward note, what is all this about?" I gestured toward the boxes.

"I told you, I'm getting organized."

I raised my eyebrows and Nina frowned, her lower lip popping out. "It's either this or sit in this apartment, staring at the walls and going bat-shit crazy. And don't tell me I can go out at night. You know what goes on at night? Nothing. Nothing! A woman can only slink through Poe's so many times before all the stupid brooding vamp-men start looking the same."

"And a rollicking good day to you, too," Vlad said, pushing through the front door with a laundry basket on his hip. He shimmied through the two-foot gap Nina's boxes allowed and I gaped at his threadbare T-shirt, at the baggy cargo shorts that exposed his marble-white legs.

Then I clapped a hand over my mouth and tried not to laugh.

"I didn't know the Vampire Empowerment Movement allowed shorts. Aren't they distinctly non-vampire?"

Vlad glared. "Bite me." He flopped down on the couch with his laundry basket and began plucking out socks. I didn't know what was more shocking: Vlad without his stupid ascot or Vlad doing laundry.

"Ooh!" Nina clapped her small hands and snatched up the label maker once again. "I'm going to go label my clothes by decade!"

She disappeared into her bedroom-slash-clothing showroom and I flopped onto the couch, upsetting Vlad's laundry basket and blowing out a long sigh.

He folded a pair of Christmas-print boxer shorts and cut his eyes to me. "Everything all right?"

"No," I moaned.

"Do you burst into flames when you go outside?"

"No." I picked at an errant piece of chocolate on my pants. "It's just that—it's just that I want to help Sampson, but I feel like such a failure. I tried to get information today and you know what I got?"

Vlad raised his brows while he rolled his socks.

"Squat. I got squat. I feel like I can't do anything right. My crime-fighting career is over before it started." I was trying to make light of the situation, but what I really want to say weighed in my gut like a fat black stone. What really concerned me is that I had begged Sampson to stay and in doing so, I'd practically signed his death warrant.

"Hey." Vlad chucked me on the shoulder, his cold fist feeling good against my hot skin. "Don't be so hard on yourself. Things are going to be okay. And your crime-fighting career isn't total crap. Remember? You caught the bad guy last time."

"After accusing you and the entire Vampire Empowerment Movement."

Vlad's gaze was surprisingly sympathetic. "But you caught the bad guy eventually."

"By shooting him in the ass."

"So you need a little weapons work."

I crossed my arms and shoved my bottom lip out. "I need a lot of work."

Vlad pushed his laundry basket aside. "You know what I hate? People who feel sorry for themselves. People who can leave the house on a sunny day and not toast up like a charcoal briquette. People who have all the resources they need right in front of them yet systematically refuse to take advantage of them." He crossed the living room and began rifling through the hall closet.

"What are you talking about?" I said, kicking off my shoes. "Oh my God!" I was on my feet the second Vlad turned around, brandishing the largest sword I'd ever seen. I threw my hands up. "Okay, okay, I'm sorry! I won't complain!" I felt myself stepping backward, then felt the back of my calves clunking against the couch. "Don't kill me!"

Vlad's expression was staid. "I'm not going to kill you, I'm going to help you."

I crawled up on the couch, eyes wide, heart so used to thunderous pounds I was certain it would never go back to normal. "What are you talking about?"

Vlad jumped into a prissy-looking fighting stance and brandished the sword. "I'm going to teach you how not to shoot an assailant in the ass."

I straightened up. "You're going to teach me to shoot with a sword? Even I know that's not going to work."

Vlad's sword dropped and he pushed out an exasperated sigh. "Do you want to learn or not?"

My eyes traveled the cool steel length of the sword. "Really?"

"Don't say I've never done anything for you."

I stepped up and met Vlad in the center of the room, reaching for the sword. He handed it to me, then went back to the coat closet and pulled one out for himself. I pointed with the sword. "Do we really keep these in there? Because it doesn't seem like such a good idea."

"I'll be sure to have Auntie Nina re-label the contents of the coat closet to include swords."

I glanced at the razor-thin edge of my sword. "And a warning."

I stepped up and shut the Vault, the came of the room...
reaching for the vessel. I handed it to her, then went back
to the cover-close and pulled the coat her arms it. I pointed
with the world. "Do we really keep them in there? because
it here? I knew they would...

"Well here to have made sign to her," he grumbled of
the coat-closet somehow over her.

I glanced at the patch in a edge of my sword, stand
a wound,"

Chapter Six

Vlad leaned up against me and the chilled wisp that came off his undead body gave me gooseflesh. "Hold it like this," he said, clamping his hands over mine.

I grinned and looked over my shoulder at Vlad. *This is what it must be like to have a brother*, I thought.

He narrowed his eyes, the top of his lip turning up into a snarl. "Stop looking at me like that. It's gross."

Yep, exactly like a brother.

Once Vlad approved my grip—something between holding a golf club and swinging a softball bat—he stepped away and plucked up his own sword.

I swooshed my sword swashbuckler style and tried out a few pirate "Walk the plank, mateys!" and "Arggghs!" for good measure. "This is fun!"

He just shrugged, ignoring me, feeling the weight of the sword he held, tossing the jeweled handle from hand to hand. "This'll do." He pushed himself up and smiled at me. A kindly, affectionate smile. "Let's spar," he said.

I felt my eyebrows rise and my bladder fill. "What?

Spar? In case you haven't noticed, Vlad, these are real weapons. Really *big* real weapons."

Vlad ran a pale finger up the length of his blade and I watched in horror as the sword sliced his skin neatly. What blood he did have—he had just sucked down two pints evidenced by the bags he was apparently incapable of throwing away—bubbled along the cut line. He licked it away and watched the wound close in on itself, the new skin regenerating immediately.

"I'm out," I said, dropping my sword. "I can't do that." I pointed at his now-perfect skin.

Vlad rolled his eyes. "I'm not going to stab you, Sophie. Or even gut you. I'm going to spar with you. How do you expect to ever learn if you won't wield a sword?"

"Accidents happen," I said, crossing my arms in front of my chest. "Accidents happen and limbs are lost and *not* regenerated."

"It takes a lot of blood for us to regenerate a limb." He jumped into fighting stance, sword standing royally in his grip. "I'll go super easy on you."

I raised an eyebrow.

"I promise not to cut anything off of you."

He swished the blade across our filled-with-crap coffee table and a single leaf—cleanly sliced from my plant—fluttered gently to the fake veneer. "Come on," he taunted.

"Promise not to cut anything off, or almost off, or slightly through? 'Cuz I'm a bleeder." Vlad's eyes flashed and I pointed at him. "And if you eat from my sliced-up bloody body, I will haunt the shit out of you until you stake yourself."

"Are we going to spar or what?"

I sucked in a breath and picked up my sword. "Okay. But I do the swishy stuff and you just stand there."

"No assailant with a sword is just going to stand there, Sophie."

"Okay." I mimicked his wide-legged, bent-knee stance and raised my blade. "Maybe just try blocking me."

"Okay. But no limbs."

"'Kay," I said, doing a twinkle-toes-style boxing dance. I waggled the blade in front of me, liking the weight of it in my hands. I thrust the sword toward Vlad. He did a *Matrix*-style back bend and avoided my blade. I lunged for his exposed left side. He sidestepped around me.

"You're pretty decent at this," he said, impressed.

I shifted my weight. "Maybe I've found my niche."

I tried a few more jabs and Vlad explained how he avoided them. "Okay," he said, "I want you to aim for my blade. Since swords tend to be the same length, your best bet is knocking your opponent's weapon from his hand, and then going in for the kill."

Usually talk of killing made my stomach roil, but now, with the sword in my hand, the idea of beating an opponent exhilarated me. I thrust and Vlad blocked me, our blades clanking together. I was starting to sweat, but Vlad's only indication of exertion was the flop of dark hair that had loosened from his usually manicured and shellacked hair helmet.

"Try it again," he said.

I did, and he did.

"See what I did there?" he said, indicating the way he angled his sword to block mine from nearing his body.

"Yeah," I said, my breath coming in short bursts. "Show me how you did that?"

Vlad grinned and raked a hand through his hair, pushing it back over his forehead. His grin was sweet and boyish, his black eyes reflecting a spark of life I hadn't seen before. It was heartwarming, even with the sharp angle of his fangs pressed over his bottom lip. He repositioned himself and swung his blade in a graceful arc.

"See? If I come at you like this"—he jabbed—"you block like this."

I mimicked his smooth arc, feeling my own smile press up my cheeks. "Like this?"

"Perfect."

"What are you two doing?" Nina stood in the doorway, her label gun at the ready.

"Vlad's teaching me to sword fight."

Nina pursed her lips together and nodded. "That's good. I always say when someone is horrible with a non-lethal weapon like you are with the Taser, you should give them a lethal one."

"Actually," Vlad said, "she's really got the hang of it. She's quite good."

As we continued sparring, Nina crossed the room and tore open another box, pulling out a mammoth wheel of glossy label stickers. "I'm halfway through 1910," she said by way of explanation. Then she put her hands on her hips and stared at us, her sour expression lightening to a small smile. "Wow, you are pretty good."

"Okay, now let's practice that blocking. I'll go after you, you block me."

My palms suddenly seemed sweaty on the grip. "Um, shouldn't I be wearing some sort of protective gear? Like a sword-proof vest or something?"

Vlad shrugged. "You didn't think I should when it was the other way around."

"Yeah, but you're way more immortal than I am."

Vlad grinned. "Then let's hope you were paying attention."

He jabbed, and I jumped. He thrust, and I blocked. On a lunge, our swords struck each other with so much fury that

ChaCha barked at the loud clang and yelped when a tiny spark crowned the clash. I was grinning, dancing wildly, growing confident in my ability.

I was *Sophie Lawson: Sword Fighter*. I finally really did have a chance to strut my stuff in those leather pants and tight bustiers, and people would no long throw a fit when they saw me toting a sword that never got mentioned again!

"En garde!" I growled with a deep French accent as I jumped onto the arm of the couch.

"En garde!" Vlad repeated, using one hand to twirl his imaginary moustache as he mounted the couch.

Our blades met again and Vlad lunged toward me. "Remember, it's not all about blocking. It's about being aware and moving your body, too."

Sophie Lawson: Sword Fighter was born to do this. It ran in her veins. Her fire-red hair trailed down her back like the blood of so many who had challenged her—and failed . . . is what I was thinking when I took that poorly calculated leap onto the coffee table.

Which broke.

I was so enamored by the sexy clang of metal on metal that the sound of pressboard furniture at decent prices splintering and cracking whooshed right by me. I lost my grip on the sword as I went down. I saw the edge of it fly past me, the blade catching on the light as it spun end over end.

"Knock, knock!"

"No!" Everything dropped into painstakingly slow motion. I lurched forward somehow thinking I could still catch the jeweled handle as it sailed over the chair. I drew my howl out as though the power of my voice alone could slow the weapon's trajectory as it raced toward Alex's head.

And then I heard the sickening sound of the blade stopping, lodging itself deep.

Nina clucked her tongue. "We are so never getting our security deposit back."

I chanced a look up, the tension in my body coiled to the point of physical pain. "Oh, thank God!"

The sword was stuck deep, all right—about a half inch up from the peephole on our front door. A full two inches of the blade poked out of the door's hall-side, and an inch from that? Alex's throat. He looked at me with wide eyes—their cornflower blue was clouded with a twinge of terror, and overcome with anger.

"I brought you a peace offering because I felt bad about today," he said between gritted teeth. "I guess I should have brought dessert, too."

Nina and I spread out Alex's Chinese spoils—Nina keeping her distance from the garlic pork, of course—while Vlad and Alex did their best to dislodge Excalibur from the door.

"On the plus side," Alex said, "you do have a hell of a throwing arm, Lawson."

I felt a burgeoning sense of pride.

Hey, it was *something*.

"I thought you were pretty clear on the 'don't throw your weapon' thing after the last incident, though."

My sense of pride was eaten by a flame of annoyance. "Oh. Did you mean I'm not supposed to throw any of my weapons? Silly me, I must have misunderstood. So hard to keep all these big, important rules in this pretty little head of mine."

I waggled my head and Nina hid a smile behind a cupped hand. Alex just shot me an unamused glare while Vlad gripped the sword handle, steadied a foot on the door, and gave a herculean yank. When the sword didn't budge,

Vlad skulked to the closet, fished around a bit, and finally emerged.

He hung a dusty Christmas wreath on the speared sword.

"Done and done," he said, wiping his hands on his pants.

We sat down at the table, Alex and me across from each other, Nina and Vlad working on their dinner blood bags at either end.

"So," Nina started, her cheeks going hollow as she sucked down her dinner, "are there any updates in the heinous murder case?"

I tried to flash Alex a look—saying what, I'm not entirely sure—but he was elbow deep in egg rolls and chow mein and avoided me.

"No, nothing new."

Nina shuddered. "Having some crazed killer on the loose like that just gives me the heebie-jeebies."

"And it's a total waste of ten pints."

I stabbed a hunk of sweet and sour pork and grimaced at Vlad. He gave me a tiny half-snarl that suggested he remembered the human empathy training I shoved down his throat and backpedaled. "And it's a huge tragedy for those chicks, too."

"So you guys are pretty convinced it's a murderer, then?" Alex asked, his eyes trailing from Nina to Vlad.

"As opposed to what?"

"A demon. Or you know"—Alex wiggled his fingers, offering the universal sign for oogedy-boogedies—"other stuff."

Vlad tossed his empty blood bag and leaned back in his chair with an ineffectual shrug. "Doubt it."

There was a beat of chow-mein-chewing silence until Nina poked me. "Anything interesting happening at UDA?"

I thought of my useless meeting with Feng. "Um, no, not

exactly," then crunched into an eggroll. "Oh, you know what? Dixon came in to see me."

Nina visibly brightened, her chest swelling. "Really?" she asked, a single eyebrow cocked seductively, her I-knew-it smile tacked in place. "Did he ask about me? It's nice that he worries, but he should know by now that he has absolutely no chance with me anymore. No way, that ship has sailed. But"—she brushed her glossy black hair over her shoulder—"I really can't blame him for carrying the proverbial torch." She flashed a bloodstained grin and my egg roll turned into a steel fist in the pit of my stomach.

"Actually, no, Neens, he didn't ask about you."

Her lip curled into a disgusted glower. "Whatever. So what did he want?"

"A vampire was murdered."

Everyone at the table—except me—sucked in a collective breath and I suddenly found myself very interested in my food.

"I can't believe you're just telling us this now, Sophie."

"Who was it?" Vlad wanted to know. "Did Dixon tell you what happened?"

I looked up and directly into Alex's eyes. They were fixed on me—not accusing, but not pleased, either. "Um, I forgot. Well, I didn't *forget* forget, it just kind of slipped my mind."

"So what happened?" Vlad repeated.

"Do you know Octavia?"

"Ugh. I hate her," Nina groaned. "She's all prim and proper and 'oh, I'm Victorian, you should be prop-ah' and crap. It's like seriously? Get an afterlife. In this century."

"It was Octavia who was killed."

Nina's coal-black eyes went wide and even darker than normal. "Oh. That's awful. That poor woman!"

"Uh, question?" Alex raised his chopsticks. "Aren't

vampires—you know, you guys"—he used his sticks to motion to Nina and Vlad—"immortal?"

"No one is truly immortal, Alex," I said on a sigh, stealing Dixon's quote.

He cocked his head. "Well, actually . . ."

"But you're dead. You're, like, super dead. Heavenly dead," I explained.

"So are they!" The chopsticks waggled between Nina and Vlad again, launching a hunk of combination fried rice across the table.

"What the hell is heavenly dead?" Vlad wanted to know.

Nina groaned. "Can we not argue who amongst us is dead or more dead or the absolute deadest or," she paused, scrunching her nose, "heavenly dead, whatever that is, and just get on with it? What happened to Octavia? How was she killed? Does Dixon know anything?"

I picked up a napkin, began peeling off strips and rolling them into little balls. "She . . . was beheaded."

"Beheaded?" Nina breathed.

"Holy crap, is that even possible?" Alex asked.

"It's one of the only ways to truly kill a vampire. Wooden stake through the heart." Vlad counted off on his fingers. "Fully engulfed in flames, or . . ." He swallowed, his Adam's apple bobbing. "Beheading. Do they know who did it?"

I shook my head.

Alex wiped his hands on a napkin and rested his elbows on the table. "Not to be insensitive, but isn't it pretty difficult to do? I mean, you've got extra strength, right?"

Vlad's tongue snaked over one of his fangs. "Yeah. It wouldn't be easy."

"Could a human do it?"

"It's unlikely."

Alex glanced at me. "Do you think this killing could have anything to do with the Sutro Point homicide?"

"Oh, I don't know. I mean, that was—you know, breathers, and this was—"

"A werewolf could kill a vampire," Nina said quietly.

"What was that?"

"A werewolf. Super strength. Chip on its shoulder. A werewolf could kill a vampire."

"And probably a Kishi demon, too," I added. "A Kishi demon could kill a vampire. Or a Wendigo, maybe."

Alex swung toward Nina. "Why would a werewolf kill a vampire?"

"They're unstable," Vlad said simply.

"Actually," Nina said, "it's pretty unlikely that a werewolf would go after a vampire—or vice versa."

"Despite what popular media would like you to believe." Vlad had to put in the VERM's two cents.

"So the whole vampires-hate-werewolves thing is made up."

"Not exactly," Nina said, blinking at Alex.

"It's just blown out of proportion. The majority of us have no problems with them. They're fine. They retrieve, roll over, fetch slippers. . . ." Vlad grinned and poked a fang into a second blood bag.

"What else did Dixon say about the murders?" Alex asked, dipping the stubby end of an egg roll into a dish of hot mustard.

I fidgeted, then stuffed my mouth with a mammoth bite of chow mein. "Um, not much," I said finally, trying my best to get my food down my rapidly closing throat.

"'Not much' like he doesn't know about it, or 'not much' like he had nothing to say about it?"

"Dixon has something to say about everything," Nina groaned.

Vlad's eyes flashed at his aunt. "Dixon Andrade is a very well-respected man."

"I didn't say he wasn't," Nina answered. "Well-respected men can be total windbags, too." She shot Vlad a sweet-as-pie grin—or at least it would have been sweet as pie if her fangs weren't tinged fresh-blood red.

I pushed the food around on my plate, my internal dialogue arm-wrestling over what I should and should not tell Alex. "Dixon thinks that the person responsible for the vampire death may have been a werewolf, too." The words came out in a solid chain before I had the chance to stop them. My admittance felt like a betrayal, a silver bullet in Sampson's heart, and silence blanketed the table.

"So, who's filling Octavia's position?" Nina asked slowly.

I looked up curiously. "I don't know. Blakely Grimshaw, I think."

It may have been the fresh pint of blood coursing through her frozen veins, but Nina's face seemed to go from every-day pale to fire engine red. Her nostrils flared and she fisted her hands, squeezing the remains of the blood bag merci-lessly until blood bubbled around the straw she had shoved into it. "That's just like a man. Blakely is, what? A hundred? A hundred and five? And she always wears those stupid little tank tops so she can show off those fake melons of hers."

Alex leaned down and lowered his voice. "Vampires can have fake boobs?"

I shrugged and wound a noodle into my mouth, relieved that the subject had been changed. "News to me."

"Ugh! I can't believe the nerve of that man! What even qualifies that little twit to take over for Octavia? Octavia was brilliant."

"I thought you hated her," Vlad mumbled.

"Did you want Octavia's position?" I asked Nina.

She rolled her glazed eyes. "No." She drew out the word.

"Of course not. I wouldn't be caught dead again doing that."
She flicked her hand distastefully.

"So?"

She plopped out her lower lip. "I would have liked to
have been asked."

"You're impossible," I groaned.

"It's what makes me lovable." She grinned.

"Okay," Alex said, eyes raking from Nina to me. "What
makes Dixon think that it was a werewolf who murdered
this victim?"

"The brutality," I said, my voice suddenly a hoarse
whisper.

"Like the Sutro Point murders."

"That bad?" Nina asked, apparently no longer pissed.

I nodded while the images of those women crept back
into my mind. I shifted in my seat, feeling suddenly sick,
suddenly bargaining with God, Buddha, or whoever else
was listening to help me keep my kung pao down—and
keep Sampson out of the picture.

"Well, if there was a great deal of brutality, the only other
race with the power to remove the head of a vampire is the
werewolf." Vlad cocked his head, a slight appreciative grin
playing on his bloody lips. "Although Buffy the Vampire
Slayer got in a few lucky chops."

"I can't believe you, of all people, watch that," Nina said.

One of Vlad's ink-black eyebrows quirked and all the
humor drained from his face. "It's official Vampire Empowerment and Restoration Movement research."

Nina rolled her eyes. "And I volunteer at the Red Cross
for the cookies and juice."

"They do have good cookies," I mumbled to my plate.

"So, other than—" Alex began.

"Kill theory," Vlad supplied.

"Other than kill theory, there is no other evidence that this woman was killed by a werewolf?" Alex said.

"I really don't see what else it could have been," Vlad said, crumbling his empty blood bag.

I knew Nina was staring at me; I could feel her eyes burning a hole through my temple. "That's not entirely true," I said to my chow mein.

"What's that?" Alex asked.

I glanced up. "Well, there are other demons that are powerful. And, it wouldn't really make sense for a werewolf to go after a vampire. Werewolves kill to feed, so they go after meat and blood. They hunt by smell. Vampires don't have a smell."

"You're welcome," Nina said with pride.

"But humans have a smell?" Alex asked with raised eyebrows.

"A powerful one." Vlad's eyes were hooded and dark, and his lips snaked up into a sly grin.

"You just ate," I warned him.

"So, basically, there's a good chance that the murders we're looking at—human and vampire—aren't connected."

"Right," I said, completely uncertain of what I was proving.

"No," Vlad said at the same time. "They're definitely connected."

"So, we're exactly nowhere closer to where we were pre-dinner," Alex said, raking a hand through his hair. "Hey, Lawson, can you come up after work tomorrow, and maybe we can get an angle on this thing?"

I nodded, not really hearing what Alex was saying due to the loud, uncomfortable buzzing in my head.

We all jumped when the Christmas wreath that was circling my sword finally flopped to the ground, the top cut cleanly by the blade.

* * *

Alex had just left and I was scrubbing errant grains of rice off the kitchen table when Nina came up beside me.

"Here," she said, handing me a package.

"What's this?"

"A ShamWow. Like a chamois, only . . . wowier. Whisks water away like nobody's business. I ordered it—"

"From QVC?"

"You'll thank me. It's a total life-saver. And the price was right."

"We really need to get you out of this apartment. Why don't you go down to Poe's or something?"

Nina slumped at the table. "No one's around. With heat like this, most of us took off or headed underground. I'm so insidiously bored. But try the ShamWow."

I unwrapped the thing and eyed her. "What did you do when this happened before?"

She shrugged. "I had a nest. There was a bunch of us. We'd just migrate somewhere gloomier. But I can't do that now."

"You can't?"

Nina used her fingernail to pick at a grain that my Sham-Wow missed. "Nope. This is home. This is where I have roots."

I couldn't help but feel a tender warmth growing in my belly. "That's sweet, Neens."

She narrowed her eyes, but her lips were quirked in a tight smile. "Don't get used to it."

"So, what happened to the people you used to nest with?"

Another shrug. "Some moved on, one got killed, some . . ." She waved at the air.

I sat across from her, my eyes wide. "What?"

"There's a huge suicide rate among vampires."

"Really? I had no idea."

"Eternity is a really, really long time."

I frowned, considering, and Nina let out a long sigh. "Think about it. Every minute you're alive is one moment closer to your demise. Every single moment, you're aging. Your body is breaking down, cells don't reproduce, everything is slowing down. Every day is one day closer to your death. Not me. Not us. Every day is . . . just another day. Every moment is just another moment. No closer to death, no closer to any kind of finality. You should be happy with your wrinkles, with your gray hair."

I felt my upper lip roll into a snarl. "What's the homicide rate among vampires? Big?"

Nina rolled her eyes. "You've got romance. You've got 'til death do us part.'" There was a distance in her eyes, a wistfulness that I don't think I've ever seen before. "It's romantic."

"Do you ever—" I kneaded my palm, looked away. "Do you ever think about it? Death, I mean? Suicide?"

Nina swallowed. "Eventually, we won't be friends anymore. You'll age and I'll look like this. Will will die, you'll die and . . . I've thought about it. It scares me, death. I don't know where I'd go."

"You mean like Heaven?"

Nina cracked a half smile that was mirthless.

"You're a good person, Neens. Of course you'd go to Heaven. You're the best person I've ever known. You're the best friend I've ever had."

"I damned my nephew, Sophie."

"But only because your sister begged you to! He would have died otherwise. He was sick. You had to save him. That was a good thing to do."

She stood up and headed toward her bedroom. "Was it? He's alone, like me. We're all alone."

My voice was small. "You'd go to Heaven. Your soul is good."

Nina's hand was on the doorknob, her back to me. "I don't have a soul."

She clicked the door shut behind her and I kneaded the ShamWow in my hands, good and evil flip-flopping in my mind. Was it really that easy? Did the good become bad— even if things were out of their control? Nina had been turned into a vampire—but she was good. And Sampson—turned into a werewolf. A good man turned into a bloodthirsty animal. If he did things—terrible, heinous things—while he was a werewolf, things that he didn't remember the morning after, in his human form, did that make him bad through and through?

I swallowed hard and stood up, pressing the cloth to the fake veneer table and scrubbing until my shoulder ached.

Because there was something else.

It nagged at the edge of my mind. A murmuring that I couldn't stand to hear—but couldn't seem to shut out.

My father.

The devil.

I tried to push the thought—the image—away, but it was etched in my mind. If a girl was born of evil, could she ever truly be good?

The next morning was hotter than the previous one and I dressed in gauzy layers. I poured myself a travel mug of coffee while assuring Nina, who stared up at me with the most pitiful puppy dog eyes in the underworld, that I would bring her a whole cache of celebrity trash magazines and let her color my hair once I got home.

It was surprising how a play-by-play of Kim Kardashian's

postdivorce woes and a box of Clairol Ravenous Red could bring a fanged smile to my roommate's pale face.

"What about me?" Vlad said with a monotone glower. "BloodLust Four?"

Vlad glanced down at his computer screen—currently flashing the blood-splashed graphics of BloodLust 3—and grinned. "Cool."

"Anything you want me to let Dixon know?" I asked Nina.

She pressed her lips together, then turned up her tiny ski-jump nose. "Not at all."

I stepped into the hallway and paused in front of Will's door. I took a few tentative steps, then pressed my ear to the door.

"You know, it works better if you hold a glass to it."

I whirled around, clutching my thundering heart while Mr. Sampson smiled at me from the hallway.

"I'm sorry, I uh—knocked," I lied, "but I didn't hear anything. Wanted to make sure you were okay."

Sampson held up a paper Starbucks cup. "Had to get out. Will's place is nice but full of tea. And did you know he keeps his cleats in the dishwasher?"

"The racks help stretch out the leather," I murmured. "So, you're getting some cabin fever cooped up in there, huh?"

"Not really," Sampson said, sinking Will's key into the lock. "I've been able to get out, get some information."

A little flower of hope bloomed in my gut. "Oh, really? Anything worthwhile?"

Sampson swung his head and my hope died. "Nothing panning out yet. But I'll keep you posted. Have a good day at the office." He flashed me a smile that was kind enough, but almost bordered on aloof. The slight chill stayed with me all the way through the workday.

* * *

I had successfully avoided Steve's unholy stink and Dixon's eyebrows-up stares when 5 PM rolled around. I wasn't particularly excited to study the minutiae of the Sutro Point crime scene—especially since my guts had been wound in a tight, angsty coil for the last eight hours—but I was ready to leave the office. But first I had to finger-walk through the Underworld Detection Agency files, snagging out any creature, demon, deathwalker, or dragon that could have the ability to kill a vampire—or at very least, had the ability to remind Alex that something other than a werewolf could be responsible. My stack wasn't huge, but it was a start, and I was able to escape the office without fanfare. I felt my tension rise as the elevator brought me closer to Alex and the crime scene photographs. I tried to convince myself that it was solely the details of the case that had my pulse racing, but every time I thought of Alex, of those ice-blue eyes pinning me with one of his steely gazes, it wasn't just my pulse that throbbed.

"Get yourself together, Lawson," I murmured to my reflection in the silvery wall. "Murder, mayhem, clearing a dear friend. Not sexy time." I glared down at my zipper. "Not sexy time."

I kept up my no-sex mantra all the way to the diner across the street, where I picked up a double bag of burgers and fries. By that time, I was so enamored with the smell of greasy fries and oozing cheeseburger that I had abandoned the idea of taking Alex into a dark corner, and instead fancied taking a cheeseburger there.

Yes, I am a fickle lover.

The police station was filled with the usual buzz—ringing phones, squawking shoulder radios, officers trying to calm down screaming clients. The smell of sweat and fear hung heavy in the air and was only offset by the cheery shafts of sunlight that made their way through the three inches of dust on the big bay windows. I wound through the maze of desks and people, keeping my eyes firmly focused in front of me and my hands on my shoulder bag, my thumb digging into the corner of one of the file folders. By the time I got to Alex's office I had worked the folder into a stinging paper cut, the pain a calming reminder that these demons were the only ones who caused pain, were the ones who could be truly bad.

I stopped in front of Alex's office door. He had moved offices since our last meeting and this new office—more permanent, I guessed—actually had his name stenciled on the door. It should have made me feel comfortable that Alex was rooted enough to his job, to San Francisco—*to me?*—that the police department had seen fit to paint his name on the door, but suddenly, nothing made sense anymore.

I rapped gently with the back of my hand. "Alex?"

I didn't wait for him to invite me in, even though I should have known better by now. Instead, I pushed open the door and my knees immediately went rubbery and weak and before I knew it I was staring at his coffee-stained carpet, knees hugging my ears, wildly sucking in huge gusts of stale air. Alex was crouched by me with a paper bag in one hand, his other hand resting gently on my knee. The heat from his palm seared my skin and helped to reground me.

"It's okay, Lawson. Just relax." His voice was soft and comforting. He patted my knee awkwardly and thrust the paper bag directly into my upside-down line of sight. "Do you need this?"

I slowly straightened up. "No, I'm okay."

"Do you want me to turn this around?" He was standing next to the huge white board that had made all the blood rush out of my body and strangled my heart. The entire board was covered in full-color photographs of the bodies from Sutro Point. And although I was *there,* had actually physically seen the bodies, they failed to have as much impact as they did here, photographed, laid out in graphic, static detail, mouths forever locked in silent screams, fingers constantly clawing for safety that would never come.

"It's okay." I turned my chair around so I wasn't staring directly at the unseeing eyes of one of the victims—a blond girl who, before that morning, was probably close to my age and carefree, judging her life by the day, by her exercise routine, by what she was going to have for lunch that afternoon. I stifled a shudder.

Alex set a paper cup of water on the arm of my chair and leaned back against his desk. He kicked out his long legs and crossed his ankles, crossed his arms in front of his broad chest. His eyes were wide and bright and had that uncanny—but comforting—way of seeing me so completely that I shrank back a little bit in my chair.

"Where's my culinary fee?" He shot me that cocky grin, but I couldn't appreciate it. I pulled the Fog City bag from my purse and pushed it toward him.

"You're not eating?"

I shook my head. "Not much of an appetite."

Alex looked startled. "Are you sick? What about a donut?" He reached into a pink pastry box sitting on a stack of procedural handbooks and waggled a sprinkled donut in front of my face. I felt my lip curl and my stomach acids churn.

"I don't see how you can eat with that"—I gestured to the white board—"and all of this going on."

Alex dropped the donut and grabbed his burger, splatting a packet of ketchup on it. "All of what going on?"

I took a short breath, feeling an anxious flutter go through my belly. "Everything."

Alex set his burger down, his eyes turning to a deep ocean blue. "It's a practiced skill."

I watched Alex eat for a few silent moments, stacking and restacking the UDA files on his desk. "Did you pull any files? You know, ex-cons, or unsolved cases with similar MOs?"

Alex smiled behind his burger. "Someone ought to get you a badge."

I cocked my head, my angst turning into slight annoyance. "I'm serious. Does the department have any leads about who might have done this? Gang retaliation, Satanic offering, or something?

"Do you know how many actual cases of Satanic offerings there have been in San Francisco County?"

I felt my brows raise, suddenly obsessed with knowing if any of my neighbors—past or present—had set out a little offering to dear old dad.

"How many?"

Alex shifted his burger to one hand and wrapped his free fingers into an O-shape.

"Zero?"

"Nada. None."

"That you've found," I clarified.

"That have panned out to be actual acts of true Satanic ritual or Satanism. Generally, it's stupid kids or your everyday socio-slash-psychopath."

"I don't know if that's supposed to make me feel better or worse."

Alex shrugged and stuffed a Sophie-worthy handful of fries in his mouth.

"So, you've got no leads."

Alex rubbed his palm over his forehead, raked his fingers through his dark curls. "That's the thing, Lawson. I looked—I really did—but nothing matched up to anything in the system. There were no prints, which means that our perp was careful or DNA-aware." Alex glanced up at me, the statement in his eyes.

"Or didn't have prints—or standard DNA."

He nodded, his mouth contorted in that false, "sorry to have to point it out" kind of way.

"I'm not entirely sure that whoever did this was normal." His eyes set on mine again and this time, the accusation seemed to burn into them. The weight of my secret—and my guilt—sucked all the air out of the room.

I needed to tear my eyes from Alex's, so I chanced a glance at the whiteboard, my stomach protesting with a nauseous wave when I did.

"Are there any pictures of your vic?"

I shook my head. "Of course not."

"Oh," Alex said, "right—because they turn to dust, right?"

"Uh, no, Buffy, they don't turn into dust. No film. Can't be seen on film whether or not they're dead or . . . dead again."

"That's a problem."

There was a beat of awkward silence. Alex popped the last of his burger into his mouth and downed a mouthful of fries. I pulled the files closer to me, cutting the stack in half and pushing those toward Alex. "We should probably get to work on this," I said. "We have a lot of files to go through."

Alex paused, his eyes going soft.

"What?"

"You're really tightly wound right now."

"Of course I am, Alex. There's a psycho killer on the loose ready to Filet-O-Fish his next vic."

"We're never going to make any headway with you in this state."

I gritted my teeth, anger surging through my already tightened muscles. "With me in this *state*?"

Alex held up his hands placatingly. "I'm sorry; I don't mean to offend you. I just think you need to relax a little bit. Do a little stress release before we get started."

I crossed my arms and leaned back in my chair, scrutinizing the hard set of Alex's jaw. "And I suppose you know exactly what I need to relax."

He cocked an eyebrow. "I have a few ideas."

I heard Alex's shirt rustle as he slipped out of it. It didn't take long for my eyes to adjust to the low lights, but once they did I felt my jaw clench and did my best to unlatch my eyes from the white T-shirt that clung to his every hard curve. It hugged his chest; the flimsy fabric pulled mercilessly over each stair-step abdominal muscle, straining over his biceps, just exposing the lickable feathers of his winged tattoo. I felt my mouth start to water again, felt my palms go from dry confidence to schoolgirl sweaty.

He said this would relax me, but suddenly my every muscle fiber was on high alert, every synapse firing to embrace every sound, the smell of heat and fire that clung to the air between us. I closed my eyes and breathed deeply, managing to channel a sense of calm—that flitted right out the window when I heard the snapping of his belt.

My eyes flew open and Alex's were intent on mine. "Are you sure you want to do this?"

I nodded, not trusting my own voice. Then, finally, "Stress release."

"As long as you're sure. I mean, this is what relaxes me. . . ."

I forced a smile that I hoped looked as calm and collected as I *didn't* feel. "Me, too."

Now it was his turn to smile and something about the relaxed, almost sleepy grin that he shot me made the tension start to loosen. "A girl like you?" he said, "I have a hard time believing that."

"You don't know everything about me, Alex Grace."

I liked the sexy, smoky tone of my voice and Alex seemed to, too. He came closer to me, extended a hand. "As long as you're sure."

I licked my paper-dry lips and stared at his hand, my stomach seizing. I took it, finally trusting, and laced my fingers through his. The immediate sense of comfort washed over me; that sweet feeling of home set in.

"Yeah," I whispered.

Alex pulled me close to him. He let my hand go and it fell limply to my side, the singe of his touch turning my hand suddenly icy cold. I felt his breath, moist and hot on my ear, as his lips trailed through my hair, his fingers tangling in it, brushing it aside. I leaned into him, and after all the gentle motion, his hands were suddenly firm on me, sure. He turned me quickly, with so much need that gooseflesh covered every inch of my skin, exposed and not, and I felt my breath rising, then catching in my throat. His chest pressed against me and my back immediately arched, my rump pressing against him, heat searing every inch of me. I knew my blush was evident and obvious and it made me want to hide—but the feel of his body against mine was magnetic and I feared I couldn't move, even if I really wanted to—which I didn't.

His heart beat in a steady, dizzying rhythm against my shoulder blade as his palms traced their way down my arms.

"As long as you're sure . . ." Alex whispered. His voice was so calm, yet so authoritative. The whole situation was overwhelming, the emotion buzzing all around me, the air electric. I started to tremble—a tiny, delicious tremor that

Alex must have taken as a sign because he pulled me even tighter against him until I could feel his belt buckle at the small of my back.

I nodded mutely. Then, "I'm sure."

I felt his hands move. I felt him take a step away from me—disappointing, even though the step was minuscule. The sudden air between us was cold. Then suddenly he was against me once more, one hand wrapping me against him, the other at my hip.

"Touch it," he said, his voice a heart-stopping rasp. "Hold it in your hand."

I tried to spin, to protest, but he held me firm so I couldn't look at him. "I—I don't think I can." I knew I sounded weak and immature and schoolgirl silly. I felt him nod behind me.

"You can."

All at once his hand was on mine, fingers interlacing, gently positioning me. I cupped my hand to receive him as sweet anxiety filled my every pore.

"It's bigger than I remember," I said, my voice a throaty whisper now.

I licked my lips again and Alex pressed forward, the soft stubble on his chin rubbing against my temple. I felt his lips press up into a satisfied smile. "That's good. That's right. Do you like it?"

I tried to nod, to give some indication that I was here, invested in the moment, but everything felt rooted to this one spot.

I was Sophie Lawson.

And as usual, I didn't know what the hell I was doing.

"I can hear your heartbeat," Alex murmured. "Don't be nervous. I know this isn't your first time." There was a hint of mischief in Alex's voice and I smiled. "It's okay, Lawson," he said.

I closed my eyes and let Alex's voice slip through me. I

let it warm me from tip to tail, let it give me strength. And then I used my hand to push his away, repositioning mine.

"Are you sure you're ready for that?" Alex rasped.

"Are you sure you are?" I drawled, looking over my shoulder.

Another sexy half smile. Another glinting tweak in those bedroomy, cobalt eyes. "You should be wearing safety goggles."

"Right." I masked my juvenile need to giggle uncontrollably. "Safety first."

I felt Alex gently push his leg in between mine and I widened my stance.

"Both hands," Alex said. "Arms up."

I did as I was told, snaking my other hand over Alex's piece. It felt heavy in my hands but alive, electric.

"I forgot how much I missed this. I was really scared the first time but now—"

"Shhh." Alex's hands trailed down my arms until his were outstretched, too, his hands clasped over mine. "You're a natural. Remember what we talked about. Slow . . ."

"No jerking."

"Right. Give it a gentle squeeze."

Alex must have sensed my anxiety because he squeezed my hands and whispered, "Gentle," in my ear. It sent shivers down my spine.

"Okay." I felt the weight in my hands. I felt his hands, warm, on mine. I squeezed—gently, slowly.

This was going to be okay.

I was going to be good at this.

It seemed to fire in waves. Molten sparks that shot through my body. There was moaning. There was screaming.

There was me, huddled on the ground, crying. "Aughhhh," I wailed. "I can't do this! I suck!"

Alex crouched down in front of me, his smile so wide it

pushed up to his earlobes. His body was shaking and his eyes were glassy, rimmed in moisture. "No, Lawson," he fought off a round of guffaws. "You're a bad shot now, but you'll get the hang of it. I promise."

"Go ahead!" I moaned. "Laugh at me. I know you want to."

I had barely finished my permissive sentence when Alex flopped onto his butt and howled like a country bear, smacking at the ground. I crossed my arms in front of my chest, anger creeping into my soul. "It wasn't that bad for a second time!"

Alex wiped his eye, sitting up and gasping for air.

"I bet I even hit the target this time. Maybe not on his body, but I'm sure I hit the paper." I sprang to my feet and fiddled with the lever that zipped the paper target toward me. I examined it with narrowed eyes.

"Well?" Alex asked, brushing off the seat of his pants and standing behind me.

I mashed the lever back. "It was there."

"Really?" He yanked on the lever from the target in the next booth over. "You sure it wasn't here?"

"Well, I said I knew I hit the target, right? I just didn't specify which target."

"Smooth." He raised his eyebrows. "Try it again?"

"Maybe firearms really aren't my forte."

Alex was already curling me into him. "All the more reason for you to go again. You can only get lucky with ass shots so often."

I turned, my face reddening. "You knew about that?"

That sexy half smile again. "A hot chick doesn't shoot a complete lunatic in the ass without the entire force hearing about it."

I felt oddly proud—both because my ass shot to Roland Townsend had made me a legend, and because as Alex curled me into him for the second time in ten minutes, I didn't pool into jelly. Completely.

I shot off a few more rounds and little by little—little by very little—my aim was improving. By the time I had cleared about a dozen, Alex was sitting on the cement bench behind me, popping peanut M&M's into his mouth. I turned and looked at him over my shoulder.

"Some teacher," I harrumphed.

"You're doing great. You went from hitting the ground to hitting the ceiling to hitting someone else's target to—" He stood up, squinted, and then nodded, impressed. "Hitting your own target."

"While you sit there eating chocolate."

"If you must know"—he popped a handful in his mouth—"I've been keeping an eye on your form."

The slant to his smile was nothing short of shameless and the heat that had zipped through my body now pooled low in my belly—and lower into my panties. "Well, how is it?"

Alex quirked an eyebrow. "How's what?"

I dropped the magazine from my gun, feeling its heat on my palm. Something about handling that thing made me feel bold, confident—dangerous. I looked at him through lowered lashes, snaked my tongue over my tooth sexily like I had seen Nina do a thousand times. "My form."

It was fleeting—but definite. Red shot across Alex's cheeks and his usual cool demeanor was challenged. He quickly regained control, put both booted feet on the floor, and strode toward me. "Let me help you with that."

"I can do it."

Alex stopped short of me, arms crossed in front of his chest, trademark half smile cutting up the left side of his cheek. "You sure?"

I was fumbling now but desperately trying to hold my cool. Sexy women who said lascivious things like "how's my form?" didn't look half as sexy trying to jam bullets into an empty magazine. "I can get it." As if on cue, the bullets popped out of the spring load and littered the cement floor.

Alex grinned but didn't say anything. He just stepped toward me, his hands going for the extra ammo on the counter behind me. My hands were at my sides, one holding the empty magazine, one holding the unloaded gun. Alex's arms caged me and now I stared at his chest, smelled the faint odor of singed gunpowder and perspiration. I didn't think about snaking my arms around his waist, sliding my weaponed hands up his muscled back and pressing my lips against his.

I just did it.

I heard the ping of the bullets as Alex brushed them aside, crushing my body up against his. He pulled me against him and I fought to get closer, to close every bit of space between us. His arms wrapped around me, fingers tangling in my hair. I was kissing him and he was kissing me back—hard, hungry kisses. I nibbled his bottom lip, felt his tongue moving into my mouth as he picked me up and set me back on the cement divider, spreading my legs and pressing himself closer. I locked my legs behind his back and pulled him toward me. When his lips left mine and started a trail down my bare neck, I felt the intensity break inside of me, my whole body tingling, trumpets blaring—

I pulled away. "What's that?"

Alex didn't bother answering and when his lips closed around mine again I didn't bother thinking about it—until I felt another zing, this one pressed up against my inner thigh, dangerously close to—"That's my phone," Alex groaned.

I was still panting, still feeling the verve of desire as it rocketed through my body when Alex yanked the phone from his pocket and gave it a cursory glance before tossing it aside. I dove for him. "Who was it?" I mumbled in between devouring those incredible lips and flicking my tongue over the salty curve of his neck.

"Station."

"Station?" I paused and he pulled me toward him, rhythm unbroken. "Is it serious?"

The discarded phone started blaring again, hopping along the sawdust floor as it vibrated wildly. I hated to tear my lips from Alex's, but I couldn't stop myself. "Maybe you should check that."

Alex stepped back and cocked an eyebrow. "Seriously?"

"It could be important."

He blew out a long sigh that seemed to crush his entire body. "You're right."

He turned his back and answered the phone while I wracked my brain trying to figure out the sexiest way to lounge against the cement cubicle we'd been making out in. Alex turned to me.

"So, is it serious?" I asked in my best imitation of a Grace Jones–sexy voice.

"Homicide always is."

I opened my mouth, but Alex held up a hand, then brushed a thumb over my kiss-puckered bottom lip. "Don't think we're not picking this up again," he said with a sexy grin.

My nipples hardened while everything else softened.

Inappropriate love lesson number thirty-five: Homicide shouldn't be an aphrodisiac.

Chapter Seven

Alex made a beeline for the parking lot, snapping his shoulder holster back on and barking into his cell phone. I hurried behind him, jamming my gun into my shoulder bag, then thinking better of it, and trying to jam it into the waist-band of my pants.

Not a lot of room in the back of my pants these days.

"You want me to drop you off on the way?" Alex asked as we crossed the lot.

I narrowed my eyes and he rolled his. "Of course not," he sighed.

Alex's SUV had a chic row of cop lights on the dash, which made screaming through intersections and his pole-position driving completely warranted. He loved it. I loved keeping my innards on the inside and not flying through windshields, so I was pressing myself into my seat as far as humanly possible, and praying to the God of Ford that they weren't cutting corners on seat belts. But with a murder in front of me and the city racing beside me, I didn't have much time to focus on my fear—or my squashed sex drive.

When we turned into the Pacific Heights neighborhood,

Alex slowed and I was able to dislodge my heart from my throat.

"Hey," I said, peering out the window. "Doesn't this area look familiar?"

"It's Pacific Heights, Lawson. You've been here a thousand times."

"No, I haven't been here a thousand times," I said, speaking slowly, eyes still swishing over the darkened sidewalks. "I've only been here . . ." I bit my bottom lip, considering, "Ummm . . ."

Then it hit me.

"There!" I pointed frantically across the cab, my arm just under Alex's nose. "Right there!"

"We're supposed to go to forty-nine California. That's thirty-six. It's not even the right side of the street."

"No, that's where we went when—" My stomach started to quiver. It had been a long time, and I had, unfortunately, seen my share of crime scenes in the years since. But, much like with riding a bike or sex, I guessed you never forget your first time.

Alex nodded. "The Collector case."

I nodded back. "Uh-huh."

It was the first crime scene I had ever been to, and I couldn't help but remember the pristine room, the high ceilings, and the tulips leaning so gracefully over the cut-glass lip of the vase. I also couldn't help but recall the woman who'd looked as though she had just fallen into a light and peaceful slumber, with her golden-blond hair splayed over the pillow, her pale pink lips pressed together. Under her satin blankets her chest was torn open, her heart removed.

It was an image I never bothered to strain from my mind, because I knew it was burned into my subconscious.

I rolled down the window and pressed my head out, gulping in a huge lungful of the slightly salt-tinged air. I leaned back into the car. "Did they tell you anything when headquarters called it in?"

Alex chewed his bottom lip and shook his head silently—a sure sign he knew more than he was letting on.

"Alex? I can handle it."

Silence.

"I have a gun, you know."

He gently let his foot off the gas but kept his gaze fixed on the street ahead. "Are you threatening me with an unloaded gun?"

I sucked a quick breath through my teeth. "Just tell me: is it as bad as last time?"

"Let's just say property values are about to plunge again."

"Huh?"

Alex nodded toward the house on the other side of the street, just a few houses past this one. Police lights were washing the sidewalk in rounds of red and blue as officers unfurled their yellow crime scene tape and held back curious onlookers. An ambulance was stationed with back doors open, but no one was inside, and no one seemed to be moving very quickly.

"I don't suppose it's worth asking if you want to stay in the car," Alex said.

But my eyes were glued to the house.

Yes, I'm a wimp. Yes, I turn into a quivering bowl of jelly when blood—that isn't nicely encased in a blood bag—is present. But this was something different. It wasn't a fear so much as a deep foreboding. An all-over sense that once I walked into that house, something would be set in motion and nothing that I knew would seem real anymore.

I licked my lips and put my hand on the car door. "No, it's not worth asking. Let's go."

Two ashen-faced pup officers ran out of the house as

we approached the walk. Both doubled over in the bushes rimming the house, but only one started to vomit. A chill started at the base of my neck and went down my spine. I hugged my elbows and hung close to Alex.

We stepped into the foyer of the residence—it was big and grand, as to be expected in the neighborhood, but it was empty, a collection of orb-eyed statues staring at no one. A murmured hum came from a room just to our left and I followed Alex as he headed straight for it, the heels of my boots click-clacking on the marble floors and bouncing off the mile-high ceilings.

The dim room was immediately ten degrees hotter than the deserted foyer and crammed with bodies in flak jackets and weapons belts. A bank of black-and-white televisions lined one wall nearly floor to ceiling, and a desk ran the entire length underneath, littered with wired telephones and a complicated-looking control panel.

"What is all this?" I whispered to Alex.

"Panic room, essentially," he muttered.

Officer Romero was one of the officers crammed in the room and he looked over his shoulder when he heard my voice. "State of the art." He waved his hand over the equipment. "I don't even think the CIA has this kind of shit yet. Grace, Lawson. Glad you're here."

"Who needs this kind of security?" I asked, trying my best to pick up the home owner's identity. "The president? Justin Bieber?"

"Tia Shively."

Alex and I looked at each other, blank faced.

"Very wealthy. Old money," Romero said.

"Silver-spoon-in-her-mouth kind of thing?" Alex asked.

"More like golden microchip. Married to Kidson Jobs."

"The concert promoter?"

"Actually"—Romero shut his notebook—"the former

barista. Apparently old Kidson made Tia's lattes with a little something extra because she married him six months later." Romero shrugged. "I don't know. Maybe he just had an enormous dipstick. She swoops in, marries Kidson—she's twenty-five, by the way. He's out of the country and something trips the house alarm out here."

Alex gestured toward the monitors. "So is this the crime scene?"

"No." Romero shook his head. "It's the crime."

Officer Romero barked out an order and a space opened up at the desk. Alex and I squeezed our way in so we had a better vantage point. "That one there is a camera facing over the back fence."

Alex nodded and I squinted at the grainy image. I could barely make out gray, oblong fuzzy patches; I assumed they were juniper bushes.

Romero tapped the screen. "This is a stone wall right here." He pointed to a short white block that peeked through the blobs of trees. "Roll it back a few minutes, will ya, fella?"

The screen dissolved into a series of skips and lines and returned to the same grainy picture. "This is the crime?" I asked.

"Just wait." Romero never took his eyes off the screen. "There!"

Another blob. This was so dark it was almost black and moving fast. It popped up over the fence and tore across the lawn. The juniper blobs seemed to tremble as it whipped by.

"What was that?" Alex wanted to know.

Romero moved to the next screen. "This is the living room. French doors open up from the backyard"—he motioned back to the first screen—"into this room."

"Okay . . ." Alex said.

"Oh my God!" My heart stopped when I saw it. It still wasn't completely clear.

But I knew exactly what it was.

I started swallowing hard, trying to quell the frenetic thump of my heart. *No,* I told myself, *it couldn't be.* But even before I could continue on my personal reassurance effort, Romero rewound the tape again. The black blob bounded backward out of the front doors and across the lawn, and threw itself over the fence. Romero pulled his sausage-y finger from the button and the grainy line shot across the screen once more, as did the blob. I looked down at my shoes.

Alex nudged my shoulder and I looked up, my eyes locking on to his.

"Then there's this," Romero continued, completely unaware of my and Alex's silent conversation. I held my breath, an anxious flutter rippling through my stomach.

The image on the next screen was a bit easier to make out. It was the living room, set up with a glowing fireplace, a coffee table as big as my bedroom, and two overstuffed couches that could sit an entire football team each. A woman was curled up on one end of the couch, barefoot, with a loose-knit afghan thrown around her torso. Her expression was blank and if it weren't for her dark eyes that caught the flickering reflection from the television screen and blinked occasionally, I would have thought she was already dead.

It was less than a minute before the woman snapped to attention, sitting up on the couch. Even on the silent, black-and-white tape, her terror was clearly evident from the ramrod straightness of her spine, from the way her eyes went from lifeless orbs to saucer-wide and frighteningly alive. The blob from the other screen broke through the French doors. The glass seemed to explode more than shatter, the shards of glass seeming to stop and float on the grainy film.

I licked my lips and implored myself to look away—I knew what was about to happen. But it was impossible. My eyes felt physically drawn to the picture and I narrowed my gaze, trying to hide my wince as the blob—now more clearly an animal, hunched on all fours with shaggy, dark fur that was dotted with glass shavings, leaves, and dirt—tore across the room and went directly for the woman on the couch.

She reared up, trying to push her small legs against the hulking cushions, but her speed was no match for the animal. It cleared the couch in a millisecond, was on her a second later, and before I could let out a breath—or a cry—the woman was his. She swatted once and he grabbed her arm in his massive paw, giving her a yank that shook her entire body; she flopped like a rag doll. Her head lolled, long hair flying in sad, luxurious waves around her, her eyes directly toward the camera as the animal's jaws snapped open, then quickly closed around her neck. I watched in terrified horror, my eyes locked on hers, as the life drained out of them. There was no reflection, no vision. Her eyes went immediately to cold, hard marbles that gazed, unseeing, into the eye that had caught her demise.

"It's a wolf." I'm not sure if I said it or if Alex did, but either way I felt both guilty and betrayed. Like I should have said something then, should have somehow apologized or stopped it, but I was still riveted to the screen.

The wolf dumped what remained of the woman's lifeless body—clawed and blood covered—and looked directly into the camera as if he knew we were watching him—as if he knew *I* was watching him. There was no remorse, no wild hunger, no rabid fire in his eyes. He simply blinked as a droplet of tar-colored blood—her blood—dripped from his razor teeth onto her rapidly paling forehead. He shifted then and she flopped from the couch onto the shag carpeting, discarded, destroyed.

The camera cut out then, the image of the staring wolf and the broken woman seared into my memory forever.

It seemed like an hour passed as we all stood in the room, staring at the bank of television screens. The temperature seemed to rise with every minute and I felt the sweat bead above my upper lip, begin to prick at my hairline. My clothes felt immediately sticky and damp, and Alex swung his head to look at me.

"You okay, Lawson?"

We had been partners—friends—long enough; I knew that he knew what I was thinking. But I still felt the overwhelming need to hide any indication of my suspicions.

I nodded and opened my mouth, but when I tried to talk, my throat felt stuffed with sand. Alex put a hand on my shoulder and squeezed gently.

"Is there somewhere we can grab a drink of water?" Alex asked Romero, but kept his eyes on me.

"Yeah, sure." Romero stepped back from us. "I can grab you guys something. You're going to want it before we take a look at the crime scene . . . and probably to wash your mouth out with after." Seemingly unaffected, Romero left the room and Alex and I were alone.

"So?" Alex's brows went up into his bangs.

I flopped into one of the big leather executive chairs set in front of the monitors and swiveled so my back was facing them. "So, what?"

Alex cocked his head, his lips pursed. "Wolf."

The way he said it, I wasn't sure if he was asking or telling me. I started at my thighs, drew a squirrely figure eight on my jeans with my fingernail. "Is that what you think?" I finally asked him.

I heard Alex sigh. "I thought it, you said it."

My ears burned.

"Did you recognize it—uh, him?"

I know the question wasn't meant to be inflammatory, but I was suddenly mad. "No, I don't know who that was," I hissed. "My—*our* werewolves adhere to strict bylaws. You know it's true, Alex. If not, this wouldn't be the first case like this you've ever seen."

Alex crossed his arms in front of his chest. "It isn't."

He turned and walked away leaving me sitting in the monitor room, the hum of the TVs mercifully drowning out any sound in my head.

Romero led us on a cursory walk of the crime scene. There wasn't much to see as the room was in shambles from the attack, but every gauge, every blood-soaked slash brought me back to the Sutro Point crime scene, to the vacant eyes of those two girls as their blood pooled in the dirt. The magnitude of the destruction, of the images on the tape should have prepared me for the body. I steeled myself as we closed in on it, our bootied feet sinking into the heavy pile carpet, the blood bubbling around my toes. I knew it would be bad. But until Romero peeled back a few inches of the blood-soaked cloth covering Tia Shively, I didn't know how bad.

I tried to suck in a breath. I tried to keep my knees from buckling, to keep my stomach from folding in on itself as what remained of Tia—what remained of her mangled body—looked up at me. Her face was so ravaged that I could only imagine what she must have looked like in real, non-grainy life. But even in death, her terror—her torture—was unmistakable.

"Oh God," I breathed.

Alex nodded curtly once, all the blood rushing from his face and leaving it a pasty, sallow yellow. Romero dropped the corner of the sheet back down. "I thought we'd never see anything worse than the last one." He laughed a barking, guttural laugh that had no joy in it and shook his head. "Guess I should have known better."

"You have any leads?"

Romero shrugged. "You saw the tape, Grace, same as I did."

"So what are you calling it?"

"Wild animal attack."

My mouth felt glued shut. My feet felt rooted to the floor, but I felt like I wasn't there, that I was watching the entire scene from above, ready to change the channel, to turn off the TV at any moment.

Romero jerked his head toward me. "Maybe you should get her out of here."

I knew I should be angry. I was tired of being meek, of being led away by the elbow or patted on the head with a patronizing smile, but Tia Shively was more than I could take. I felt Alex's fingers close around my arm; I felt for the floor with my toe as I tried to take a step, and suddenly I stopped.

"Are there any other cameras?" I managed.

Romero blinked. "Uh, no. I mean, she's got six cameras, and you saw—" He breathed heavily, the buttons straining on his uniform. "You saw what happened."

I shook Alex's hand from my arm. "You think what did this—you're sure it was an animal?"

Romero scratched his chin. "I don't want to face the media and tell them that there is a wild dog loose in San Francisco. A dog—or wolf, or fuck, a wooly mammoth— that's doing this kind of thing. People are going to think the police department has lost it. But you saw the same thing I did. That wasn't human."

I licked my lips. "What are you planning on doing?"

Romero swung his head toward the other officers and crime scene investigators in the room as they brushed for fingerprints and bagged evidence. He leaned in close and Alex and I leaned toward him. "I'm not a man who believes in any of this hoodoo or myths, but I saw what I saw. I'm getting my men silver bullets and I'm telling them to shoot to kill."

Alex and I were silent as he drove me back to my car. We had just pulled into the police station parking lot when he looked at me, his face partially obscured by the moonless night.

"You still think this murderer could be human?"

I swallowed heavily and felt exhaustion wash over me. I had held my face steady through the crime scene and spent the entire drive home digging my teeth into my bottom lip and blinking back tears. This couldn't be right.

Alex killed the engine and palmed the key. "Are you sure you don't have anything to tell me, Lawson?"

I shook my head silently. I didn't trust myself to open my mouth. *If I told Alex that Sampson was back, Alex would ask him questions and Sampson would tell the truth and once he was cleared, we'd able to find the real killers,* I reasoned. *Or,* I told myself, *I could tell Alex and Alex would interview Sampson and Sampson would tell the truth and Romero would shoot to kill.*

Sampson couldn't, I repeated silently. *He wouldn't.*

"Lawson?" The streetlight picked up the glinting blue in Alex's eyes and I felt more disconnected, more unsteady. There was Will, there was Alex. There were two heinous murder scenes that pointed to a werewolf—and I had one hiding out across the hall from me. I was normally a good girl. I was normally one-sided and easy and flat.

The old Sophie would hitch her chin and act indignant.

The old Sophie would fumble with her gun, go lobster red, and eat an entire sleeve of marshmallow pinwheels.

"I don't know what you want me to say to you, Alex."

When I was little, I told everyone that my father was a solider, off fighting in some foreign war. I had an image of him in my mind—he had my unruly, curly red hair and his lips set hard in that weird, straight-line way that mine did. My eyes were my mother's—though in my memory hers were more distinctly emerald—but everything else that was weird or off or laughable about me came from my father and all of it was admirable and distinctive and inherited from a man who was a hero. A man who saved people by the country-full, who put himself in danger every day because he knew, inherently, fundamentally, what was right.

He never faltered.

He would come back for me one day and I wouldn't have to wonder if it was him because he would know me by my looks, my mannerisms, because so much of me was so distinctly *him*.

I told myself this story over and over again before I fell asleep, so often that I believed that even if the details weren't exactly right it was mostly true—I was like my father and my father was a good man.

And then the whispers—hushed, murmured, caught on the wind—started. My father was bad. Was evil. Was the reason that people died, killed, murdered, tortured. I wasn't anything like him.

But as I drove away with Alex leaning against his car watching me go and three women murdered, destroyed, cooling in the morgue, I began to wonder if I was just a little bad, too.

If I didn't have faith in Sampson.

If I let these women die just because I wanted to be right. Or because I just didn't care.

I was standing in the hallway outside of my apartment, staring at Will's closed door. I extended my fist to knock and then dropped it down to my side again. *What am I supposed to say to Sampson?* I wondered as I gnawed on my bottom lip. *"Hey, Sampson, so glad to have you back. And I really am doing everything I can to get you reinstated as head of the UDA, but first things first: have you been ripping human beings apart limb by bloody limb? Just checking."*

My stomach had been a tight knot since we left the house in Pacific Heights. When Alex left me in the monitor room I steeled myself, and eventually followed him into the living room, where I was sure I would be able to easily explain away everything we had seen on the tape: the blob was a rightfully pissed-off gorilla who had escaped animal testing at the Mars factory. It was a steroid-infused Chihuahua left over from a Mexican drug lord. Perhaps a shaggy-legged holdover from the Manson family.

But the scene—and the body left behind—offered no such easy explanation.

The glass door was broken clean through, just as we had seen on the tape. Whatever had torn through the glass had done so with a thick tuft of fur protecting its skin because the majority of blood—so, *so* much blood—discovered at the scene belonged to the victim, Ms. Tia Shively.

The carpet was shredded. The once unblemished leather couch was torn into thin ribbons, with blood soaked clean through to the cotton and down that poked out from the cushions. There were bits of fur—five- to six-inch locks of dark downy hair—that I tried to examine. But when I reached down to poke at them with my gloved hand I almost couldn't stop the burn of the bile as it rose up my throat. The bits of fur were matted with rust-colored, congealing blood and—and this is where my esophagus betrayed me—chunks of Tia Shively's skin. Its edges were already curling as its moisture evaporated. A crosshatch pattern of wrinkles and scratches were already beginning to show.

I don't remember backing away, don't remember stepping away from the scene, but suddenly my burning skin was awash with the moist cool of the city night and I was in the backyard, doubled over, hands on hips, my boots making the leaves and twigs crunch underneath me. Alex's hand burned at the small of my back and he was murmuring something that was probably meant to be soothing, but all I could hear was the crash of blood as it pulsed through my ears, and all I could see were those emotionless eyes, caught on camera, daring me to catch the monster that did this.

"Tell me you have some sort of lead," I remembered saying to Alex. "Tell me some band of terrorists or drug dealers or gangbangers or geo-cachers have taken responsibility."

But when I looked up at Alex he wouldn't look at me. "Your guess is as good as mine is, Lawson."

His words came burning back into my mind now and my hand went limp at my side. I'd known Pete Sampson most of my life. He couldn't have done something like this.

He wouldn't have.

If he'd known.

I turned away from Will's door and went to my own, slamming it hard behind me and sinking down on the carpet. When I'd worked for Mr. Sampson, one of my most significant job responsibilities had been chaining him up at night. Not just on moonlit nights, but every night, because, according to Sampson, one could "never be too careful." I had considered him noble then and my responsibility simply part of the job. I never considered that there were things that Mr. Sampson might want to do, might need to do, might not be able to stop himself from doing if not for the chains. I looked mournfully over my shoulder, my heartbeat fluttering. Since he'd returned, Mr. Sampson had never asked me to chain him up. I swallowed down the lump that was growing in my throat.

"You know we have a couch, right?"

I blinked up at Nina, who had soundlessly appeared in front of me. She was barefoot and dressed in one of those adorable retro jumpers that showed off her pale, flawless thighs and proud shoulders. Her dark hair was clipped into two long, glossy pigtails and with her pursed, coral-pink lips she looked like any other twenty-something enjoying the sudden burst of San Francisco heat. If you didn't know, it was impossible to tell that should she step one perfectly pedicured foot out onto the sizzling sidewalk, she'd burst into flames.

And if you didn't know that Pete Sampson's wide, Crest-white *human* smile could turn into snapping jaws with the shade of the moon, you'd blindly trust him, even when the evidence to the contrary was staring you right in the face.

I pulled my knees up to my chest and rested my chin on them, then blinked up at Nina. "I think I may have made a huge mistake."

Just saying the words made my muscles twitch. I felt guilty—for doubting Sampson and for *not* doubting him.

Nina flopped down on the carpet across from me, folding her legs underneath her. "I was wondering when you were going to bring this up."

I swallowed. "You knew?"

Nina nodded. "It was impossible not to, Sophie." She reached out and brushed her fingers over my kneecap. Her fingertips were icy, but the gesture was warm. "Did you really think you were fooling anyone?"

I flopped my head back, letting my skull thunk against the door. "I guess I was fooling myself. And now"—I closed my eyes—"and now people are dead."

Nina blinked.

"People are dead?" she repeated, her lips moving slowly.

"Alex and I went to two crime scenes. The teens on the Sutro Point trail, and then one at a house in Pacific Heights tonight." I tried to suppress and involuntary shudder. "It was one of the most horrible things I've ever seen."

Nina looked genuinely stunned—and horrified. "How did that happen? I mean, it's been a long time for me—a very long time—but from what I remember, people don't usually die."

I frowned at Nina. "What are you talking about?"

She cocked her head and narrowed her eyes. "What are you talking about?"

"I'm talking about Sampson."

Nina's coral pink lips dropped into an astonished O; her coal-black eyes followed suit. "You slept with Sampson, too?"

"What? No!"

She splayed a hand across her chest. "Oh, thank God. I know I told you to loosen up a little bit, but I didn't mean that loose." She blinked. "Wait. What are we talking about again?"

I pushed myself off the floor and splayed my fingers over my chest. "I was talking about Sampson coming back and three people dying. Four, if you count Octavia."

"And I was talking about you having sex with Will."

I felt all the color drain from my face. "What?"

Nina shrugged, eyebrows raised in that *Yeah, so?* look.

"You know about me and Will?" I stumbled forward when I got goosed by the doorknob as the front door opened.

"Sorry, Soph," Vlad said in his unaffected grumble. "Didn't see you there. What about Will?"

Nina spun on her heel and went to the kitchen, yanking open the fridge. I heard glass tinkling and cellophane crinkling as she searched inside. "Sophie slept with him."

All the color that drained from my face must have gone out through my feet and rooted me the carpet. For a fleeting second I thought that perhaps if I stayed perfectly still, I could blend into the apartment landscape and everyone would forget that I was there—that I had ever been there.

"Way to go, Sophie." Vlad chucked me on the shoulder on his way to the dining table. He seemed to lose interest in me the second he sat down and booted up his laptop. "I don't like either of them, but I think Will might be the lesser of your two evils."

"No." Nina shook her head, straightening up and massaging a blood bag. "I was hoping she'd hold out for Alex again. I like the whole fallen angel thing." She hipped the refrigerator door closed and waggled her sculpted brows. "Doomed love. So romantic."

Humiliation crept up my neck. I wanted to interject something, to change the subject, but all I could come up with was what I was sure was a look of complete dumbstruck silence.

"But I still don't get how you sleeping with Will is making people die," Nina said, popping a straw into her snack.

"We are not talking about sex," I said finally, my teeth gritted. "Or Will." I looked from Nina to Vlad and back again. Nina was sucking her fresh-from-the-fridge bag of O Negative, her cheeks hollowed with the effort. Vlad gave me one of those blank teenage boy looks, then clicked on his game. I sighed, not entirely sure that I wanted to restart a conversation about other mistakes I may have made.

I grabbed my jacket from the peg by the door and my shoulder bag. "I'll see you guys later," I said, clicking the door shut behind me.

I stepped into the hallway and paused in front of Will's door yet again, then pressed my ear up against it. I could hear Mr. Sampson moving around inside, could hear the muffled sound of people on television making mundane conversation. I closed my eyes.

"Please, Mr. Sampson," I whispered to the closed door, "please don't be the one responsible for any of this."

The movement on the other side of the door stopped abruptly and I stiffened, then hurried down the hall. I snaked around the corner when Sampson yanked the door open and stepped into the hallway. He had a dish towel thrown over one shoulder and one of Will's aprons tied around his waist, Charles and Camilla smiling smugly from their spot just under his belt buckle.

"Sophie?" he said into the hall.

I straightened and took a tiny step from my hiding spot. "How'd you know it was me?"

He raised an eyebrow. "I fetch, I roll over, and I have incredible hearing. What are you doing lurking in the hallway?"

I blew out a defeated sigh. "I'm not sure."

"Come in."

I followed Sampson into Will's apartment and leaned my hip against the counter as he went to work poking at a steak crackling and caramelizing under the broiler.

"I didn't know you cooked."

"A man's got to eat. So what's going on with you?"

I closed my eyes and lobbed my head back against the microwave. "I want to help you, Mr. Sampson, I really do.

But I just don't know where to start. You've got to give me something to go on."

Mr. Sampson swung his head. "I told you, Sophie, you don't need to worry yourself about me right now. Not with what's going on over at Sutro Point. You have a job to do."

I swallowed, not feeling the least bit convinced.

"Like I said, I appreciate you wanting to help me, but you don't need to. I'm going to do what I can from here and if I can't find what I need, I'll move on."

"You mean you'll go back into hiding. To running."

Sampson shrugged and began scrubbing potatoes in the sink. "You should be helping Alex find this murderer."

I gave him a closed lipped smile. *How am I supposed to tell him that so far, tracking down this murderer had only brought me here?*

"Sampson." I worked the grout with the tip of my fingernail. "Look, I want to help Alex and I want to help you. I can do both. But I need your help. What do you know? Where do I go? How do I get my hands on this contract, or figure out who penned it? Right now, I'm not just looking for a needle in a haystack, I'm looking for the actual haystack."

Sampson smiled softly and popped two freshly scrubbed potatoes into the oven with the steak. The luscious smell of the meat wafted out and I felt my mouth water, despite my growing desire to shove my head in the oven beside it.

"So about finding the contract. Maybe Alex and I can do a little double-detective work."

Sampson whirled to face me. "You didn't tell Alex I was here, did you?"

"Of course not. Though—" I was going to say that Alex would be a bigger help than just me. I was going to say that Alex would have better ideas and together, we'd have a better chance of finding the holder of the contract. But I knew what Alex thought now. And I knew that if Alex knew that Sampson had been hiding out in San Francisco, Sampson would be suspect number one in the recent murders. Alex wouldn't want to accuse, wouldn't want to believe it, but Alex was a detective above anything else. And right now, all the evidence pointed in one direction.

Mr. Sampson eyed me. "You're not going to listen to me, are you?"

I looked away. "I said I was going to help you and I am. I can solve both."

Sampson smiled and shook his head. "I appreciate your faith, Sophie, I really do."

Give me something, I wanted to beg. *Give me something to go on.*

"Is there anything you can think of that will help? Anything that I"—I pushed my hand against my chest—"that I can do personally to help?"

I watched Sampson's chest rise as he sucked in and let out a long breath. "Well, you can get into the UDA."

I shrugged. "Of course. Wait—you don't think that someone at the Agency—"

Mr. Sampson held up a silencing hand. "It's just a theory I'm working on. I'll need you to get me some files."

I scanned the counter, yanking a sheet of paper out from Will's stack of takeout menus and expired delivery coupons. I glanced at the paper—some sort of handwritten litany—flipped it over, and sat poised with my pen at the ready. "Whose files do you need?"

"I need you to get the file of every werewolf that has gone through the Underworld. Past, present, and deceased."

I wrote the word "werewolves" on the paper and Sampson glanced down on it with a slight smile. "Really?"

I folded the paper and shoved it in my back pocket. "I like to be prepared. What else?"

Mr. Sampson paced, rubbing his chin with the palm of

his hand. "Well." He looked over his shoulder as if he was appraising me. "I think that's a good start."

I rounded the counter so that I was nearly nose-to-nose with him. "This is a start, but I'm going to need more than files to help you out of this mess."

"I can handle Feng and Xian, if that's what you're inferring."

It's not Feng and Xian I'm worried about.

"Please."

Sampson's eyes held mine for a beat before falling. "Well, there is one thing. A guy. He's—he's kind of in between the two worlds—Underworld and regular. He's a halfbreed. Mother was a demon, father was a regular guy."

A little flicker of community struck up in my belly. *There are others like me?*

"He's like me?"

Sampson looked at me, his eyes kind. "No, Sophie. Mort is nothing like you. His father killed his mother."

And yet, I wasn't totally convinced that Mort had a worse father figure than I did.

"He vowed to kill Mort, too, so Mort's pretty much gone into hiding, but he keeps tabs on everything in the Underworld."

"Why would he keep tabs on the Underworld if his dad was mortal? He was the one who killed. Shouldn't he be focusing his attentions elsewhere?"

"He does that, too. Mort's problem is slight paranoia and that he is a recognizable half-breed. There are people in the Underworld who don't like that very much." He sucked in a breath. "People who want to kill people like him."

"And like me."

"They think that half-breeds are sullying the demon gene pool."

I felt as though I had just been kicked in the stomach. I

had never belonged anywhere—my mother had killed herself, my father had left me, my high school life had been dominated by bullies and jeers. The Underworld Detection Agency—and Sampson—had taken me in and made me feel like I belonged. I knew people weren't crazy about my being human—but I never thought that I was in danger because of it.

"Why didn't I know that people wanted to kill half-breeds?"

Sampson clapped a gentle hand on my shoulder. "Because at the Underworld Detection Agency we're family, and we always protect our own. We keep tight tabs on that kind of people."

I should have felt bolstered by Sampson's protection, but I didn't.

"So, Mort. He makes a living pitting demons against each other. Not exactly a stand-up guy, but if there's any information out there, Mort's going to know about it."

"Okay," I said, feeling a twinge of angst. "How do I find this Mort guy?"

"We're not going to go find him, Soph. I'll go."

"You can't. If this guy is not very good and has a bone to pick with the Underworld—or with everyone for that matter, you're toast. I'm going."

"It's not safe," Sampson said, carefully enunciating every word. "You're not going alone. Period. End of story."

"So you're going to stay here and rot until Will comes back, then you're going to run away like a pup with his tail between his legs." I stopped, realizing what I'd said. I chanced a glance at Sampson and I could see the fire in his eyes, see the slight curl of his lip.

"Sorry, Sampson, but I'm going."

"You're not going alone."

I put my hands on my hips, ready to make a deal. "I have an idea."

Chapter Eight

"So, Dixon told you about this guy, huh?" Alex asked.

"Yeah," I lied, nodding, keeping my eyes focused on the freeway as it whizzed by. "Dixon said this guy might have some information that could be useful—um, for the case. He might know what Feng was looking for, or if there is a new demon we should be looking at." I had fabricated the story and repeated it numerous times to my reflection in the bathroom mirror, but I could still read suspicion in Alex's questions. I tried to play it as coolly as possible, but bat wings flapped in my stomach and my guilty conscience was working overtime.

I could feel Alex's icy blue eyes studying my profile, but I refused to look at him. "And you trust Dixon? I mean, we've been driving for almost an hour now. Are you sure he's not leading us into some crazy vampire den?"

I gulped. "What do you mean, do I trust Dixon? Of course I do. We got over our whole issue. Why? Don't you trust Dixon?"

Alex shrugged, his eyebrows rising with his shoulders, "Hey, I'm just the arm candy," he said, switching lanes. "Is this where we exit?"

I squinted down at the map Sampson had drawn out for me. "Yeah, this is it."

"Who is this guy again?"

"Dixon," I said his name carefully, "said this guy is kind of—like, he kind of works on both sides. Underworld and non-Underworld, I guess. He's—he's kind of like me. Half-breed."

Alex savored my last statement before replying. "Did Dixon tell you that, too?"

I wracked my brain for any additional crumb of information that Sampson may have offered that I could attribute to my fake conversation with Dixon. All I could answer was a piddly, "Yes."

"So this guy might have information on who—or whatever—tore these people apart?"

I took a tiny sip of the latte I was holding. "Yep."

"And you don't know anything else about him?"

"Nope. Just that he's, like, a super librarian. He knows something about everything."

"Isn't that called the Internet?"

I rolled my eyes and pointed. "There! Between the trees. That's the road."

Alex squinted. "It's unpaved."

"He warned me it was rural."

"How does this guy know anything living this far out from society?" Alex asked as branches flopped against the hood and windows of the SUV.

The dirt road wound another hundred feet through weeping trees and waist-high weeds, then opened onto a clearing. Or what would have been a clearing if it hadn't been packed with discarded car parts, pieces of old furniture, and the remains of a VW Bus.

"Are you sure this is it?"

I looked at Alex. "Do you see any other houses around here?"

"I'm not sure. There's so much crap out here. Maybe the other houses exploded."

I flashed an uncertain smile. "Vampire night clubs, bald-headed biker pixies, and now"—I waved toward the remarkable graveyard of crap—"this."

"Can't say it's never an adventure with you, Lawson."

I undid my seat belt. "You say that like it's a bad thing."

The car lurched to a stop between the remains of a bus and a selection of rusting movie theatre chairs. "Do you think the car will be okay here?"

"Not sure. That bus will either eat or mate with the SUV."

"Again, never a dull moment."

I pushed open the car door and looked at the house skeptically. There were piles of general crap all around it with weeds shooting out in the few bare spots in between. The roof was puckered in places and set at a weird angle, and stacks of shingles not yet tacked down were used to weight a cheery red checked tablecloth over what I surmised were holes. I was fairly certain the mounds of crap were holding the whole place up and as far as finding the secret to clearing Sampson here—well, let's just say I didn't have much hope.

We made our way through the maze of dead car parts and thistle weeds to a porch equally loaded with all manner of junk—most of it shoved into ancient Target bags and molding cardboard boxes—and knocked on the front door.

"Who's there?" came a gruff voice from the depths of the house.

"Um, my name is Sophie Lawson. Are you Mort Laney?"

"Who's asking?"

I looked at Alex, who hid his obnoxious half smile behind his palm. "Still Sophie Lawson."

"Who sent you?"

I paused, feeling heat in my cheeks while Alex studied me. "Underworld Detection Agency."

Silence.

"Mr. Laney?" I knocked again and the door creaked open a half-inch under my fist. I poked my head into the house, then recoiled. "Holy crap," I whispered to Alex.

Alex brushed up against me, his lips at my ear, his eyes wide as he stared over my shoulder into the house. "Now we know how he knows everything," he said. "He *has* everything."

"Laney, we're coming in."

The door only opened about twelve inches and I had to suck in my stomach and shimmy to get myself through it. When I did, I ended up at the bulbous end of a makeshift walkway, lined with eyebrow-high stacks of newspapers, a mountain of dusty *National Geographic*s, and a precarious stack of water-less fish tanks filled with lightbulbs and naked Barbie dolls.

I took a tentative step, my sneaker crashing down on an army of food wrappers. I leaned back against Alex and dropped my voice to a low whisper. "Are you packing?"

"Packing?"

"Your gun!" I hissed.

"Yes, Cagney, I'm packing. But what the hell good is it going to do in here? One shot'll ricochet off the tower of 1970s Tupperware and get me straight between the eyes. Or do you think his collection of Princess Diana commemorative plates will block a bullet?"

I thought back to my own apartment that was likely being swallowed by cardboard boxes, packing peanuts, and whatever was on the QVC Power Hour as we spoke. "You don't have to be so snarky."

Note to self: Cut up Nina's credit cards ASAP.

"Don't you touch my Princess Diana plates! You chip even one of them and I'm suing!" Laney yelled.

"Because the only thing better than a hoarder is a litigious hoarder," Alex whispered.

"Mr. Laney, we—we come in peace. We just want to ask you some questions," I said, doing my best to skirt a suitcase stuffed with dusty VHS tapes. "I'm from the Underworld Detection Agency. You know, in San Francisco? I was told you might have some information on Feng and Xian Du. Or on a murder." My shoulder brushed against what was either a wig or a dip-dyed possum. My skin started to crawl. I paused and tucked my hands into my pockets, feeling Mort Laney's National Park of Shit closing in on me. "A murderer."

Alex and I paused when we heard the slight shuffle of movement coming from the back end of the house. "What did you say your name was?"

I sighed. "Sophie Lawson."

More shuffling. More crinkling. Then a bad, white-blond comb-over appeared between twin towers of molding books.

Mort Laney.

He had the roundest head I'd ever seen, despite the oblong comb-over, and ears that stuck out like doorknobs on either side of his skull. I felt my hand slyly smooth my own hair, tug at my ears in an attempt to make certain I hadn't sprouted what could only be an unholy combination of demon and human. Mort pushed up a pair of heavy, black-rimmed Coke-bottle glasses that immediately slid right back down his bulbous red nose as he squinted at us. I saw his eyes flit to Alex, sweep over his mountain of junk, and then come to rest on me.

He licked paper-thin lips and stared at me for an uncomfortably long time.

"You look just like him," he whispered.

"Mr. Laney?" I asked.

"Mort. Please call me Mort." Mort pushed a liver-spotted hand through a fort of floral foam and pointed. "Come through there, please. And be careful! You break anything and I'm—"

"Suing, right," Alex finished.

I looked over my shoulder at Alex, who shrugged, then followed me along the narrow pathway that Mort pointed to.

I paused when Mort's wormhole of stuff opened up to a surprisingly pristine—and open—kitchen.

"Whoa," Alex whispered, peering over my shoulder, then back over his at the army of crap. "It's like we hoarded our way back in time."

Mort's pristine kitchen may have been free of additional matter, but it was firmly entrenched in 1973. I blinked at the avocado-colored appliances, at the chrome-and-Formica dining table where Mort sat, fingers laced together, glasses pushed up high on his nose.

"Hello, Mr.—Mort," I said, when I was finally able to see the man. "My name is Sophie and this is Alex."

Mort stood, stepped forward, and shook my hand, nodding. The smile on his face was serene, but his eyes were darting, carefully examining my face and hair. I felt the immediate need to check myself for boogers or broccoli teeth—or to hide my private bits behind the laundry basket filled with beheaded Cabbage Patch Kids.

"It's uncanny, really." Mort was still shaking my hand and I yanked it back, keeping my smile kind and fixed.

"Thanks so much for seeing us," I said, sitting down quickly.

"And you are?" Mort looked up at Alex as if seeing him for the first time.

"Just a friend," Alex said, casting a sly glance at me, and pulling out a chair for himself. "Just along for the ride."

Note to self: Dismantle Alex, leave parts strewn about in hoarder's graveyard, I thought as he licked his lips, enjoying Mort's ogling far too much.

"Ah, that's better, isn't it?" Mort said. "Please, sit. May I get you some tea?" He jumped up before we had a chance to answer and clinked around the kitchen, gathering mugs and tea bags, then finally sitting down again.

"Now, why did you say you came here? Not that I mind." Again the darting eyes, then the gaze that settled a bit too comfortably on me.

I cleared my throat. "Well, Mr.—Mort, I was wondering if you might have some information. Uh, Dixon—Dixon Andrade—said you knew about all sorts of things." I raised my eyebrows, drew out the word "things."

"Dixon?" Mort frowned, tapping one gnarled finger against his stubbled chin. "He's running the Underworld Detection Agency now, isn't he?"

"That's right."

"Look." Alex leaned back in his chair. "There have been some murders in San Francisco—a double homicide, and a single, two nights apart. It looks rather heinous and Ms. Lawson here"—he eyed me, and his cool-cop routine was giving me a migraine—"thought that maybe you'd have some information on the type of demon that could be responsible for the kind of destruction that we saw with this case."

Mort bobbed his head, seeming to consider. "You didn't have anything listed at the Agency?" he asked, slick little tongue pushing across his bottom lip.

I glanced at Alex. "We're working on some things."

"She also thought you might know if something new was in the area, or if the Du sisters had a new contract."

Mort's eyebrows went up. "The Du sisters? Feng and Xian?"

Alex glanced at me, a smug look of satisfaction in his cobalt eyes that shot a cold wave of nervousness through me.

"Something new in the area"—*Does Alex know about Sampson?*

The look on Alex's face—now one eyebrow cocked, lips pursed, just slightly upturned—told me everything.

He was playing me.

I shot him a silent death glare, then did my best to look at Mort, unaffected. "Right," I said simply.

"Now, why are you two together?" Mort asked.

I started. "Uh—excuse me?"

"You two." Mort pointed. "Why are you together?" He blinked at Alex. "You don't work at the Underworld." His eyes raked over Alex and I felt the urge to gloat now that Alex had been eyeball-raped by Mort. "You can't."

I watched as Mort straightened his glasses, leaning toward Alex. He licked his lips again and smiled. "I never seen one 'a you before."

"One of who?"

Mort's eyes slid between us, murky behind the thick lenses of his glasses. He drew a circle an inch above his head and pantomimed the imaginary halo falling to the table ground. "You know."

I felt my eyes widen. Usually, I was the one the nutters could pick out at fifty paces. They didn't often know that I was the Vessel, but beginning in the second grade with Nancy Nottingham's relentless taunts, people were always able to zero in on my different-ness. Not a single person—demon, dead, or dead again—had ever been able to pick up on Alex's angelic state, fallen or otherwise. It felt good to be the "other" for once.

Mort grinned again, this time showing a row of crooked, corn-yellow teeth. "Neat."

We were silent for a moment before Mort repeated, "So why you two?"

"Carpool lane," I said quickly, before Alex could shrug off the angel thing and scare Mort off with his police department badge. "There was traffic and I wanted to use the carpool lane so my friend Alex came along. So, you mentioned Feng and Xian?"

"You did," Mort said, resting his hands on the tabletop.

"Right. I was hoping you could tell me something about their current contracts. Or projects. Or"—I bit my lip—"conquests." I looked around again and scooched to the edge of my chair, unsure if Sampson's written-on-wolf-hide contract was lurking somewhere around here, somewhere between the crap and other crap. The idea grossed me out more than the naked Barbies did.

Mort continued grinning at me with his weird, serene smile. "Is that all you want to know about?"

My heart started to thud and I felt Alex's eyes on me, challenging me. "For starters."

A sliver of pink tongue darted out between Mort's pressed lips and he stood up, walking to the edge of the kitchen and poking into a particularly hairy-looking stack of books and paperwork. "I'm sure I have some information that may be of help to you around here somewhere. You know the Du family hunts werewolves, right?"

"Yeah," I said, pushing my chair back. "But who sets them up?"

Mort's fingers continued walking through the heap of papers. "Most of the charges they take on their own accord. Like vigilantes, I guess. Not supposed to, I know, but they do. But occasionally, if someone has a problem with a particular wolf, they will go to the Du family directly."

"Anyone can do that?" I asked.

Mort looked at me and shrugged. "Anyone, I suppose. I don't see exactly what I'm looking for here." His milky eyes flicked over me and set on Alex. "You look tall. Would you mind helping me for just a second? I fear the book I need might be tucked back here"—Mort gestured blindly over his shoulder—"and rather high."

I looked at Alex imploringly and he pasted on a genteel smile. "I'd be happy to help you, Mort," Alex said to him. And then, to me, "If I get tetanus out here, it's on your shoulders."

"Don't be so melodramatic," I hissed back. "You're immortal."

While Mort and Alex disappeared behind a wall of wrapping paper and eyeglass frames, I stood up and did my best to poke gently—and safely—around Mort's treasures. I could hear Alex and Mort crunching through the back hallway, could hear Mort shove items aside and instruct Alex where to walk. Knowing that Alex was probably wincing his way between a museum of Tab cans and plastic tubs of cat litter made me immensely happy.

I was eye to eye with a taxidermied owl when Mort stepped back into the kitchen.

"Where's Alex?" I asked.

"I'm afraid there are a few more books than I expected. Your friend is awfully nice, helping get down the ones we need." He smiled at me and again, did that longer-than-comfortable stare. "So you're Sophie Lawson."

"Uh-huh."

Mort took a small step closer to me and my hackles started to rise. I looked over his shoulder, cocking my head to listen for Alex, but all I could hear was the humming of Mort's teakettle and the shuffling of his feet as he took another small step toward me.

"Your glasses fell over," I said.

"What's that, hon?"

I pointed. "The eyeglasses and the wrapping paper. They must have fallen over."

Mort's smile didn't falter. "It's fine. You." He clucked his tongue and shook his head. "You, you, you."

"Mort?"

"I know all about you, Sophie Lawson." His eyes flashed and his grin went wider, pushing up his apple cheeks. "Half-breed. Kind of like me."

I took a tentative step back, leveling my foot on a pile of greeting cards. "Kind of."

"But so much more interesting."

"Alex?" Fear rose in my voice as sweat pricked out over my hairline.

Where is he?

"I don't know what you're talking about, Mort. I think you're just as interesting as I am. Half-breed. We're like family." I tried a friendly smile, tried my best to tamp down the anxiety that was clawing at my gut.

Everything shifted when Mort opened his mouth.

"*My* father's not the devil," he said.

The room started to spin when the teakettle hissed. I felt the weight of everything—Mort's statement, his ridiculous hoard—pressing against my chest and suddenly, I couldn't breathe.

I tried to answer Mort. I opened my mouth and heard the beginnings of a protest, but it curdled into a scream when Mort's arm went up and I saw the cool steel of the scissors he was clutching.

"He'll pay dearly. He'll pay so dearly for you."

I jerked and the scissors sliced down beside me, a hair-breadth from my ear.

"What the hell is wrong with you?" My quick sidestep

had dislodged a heap of magazines that put a good foot between Mort and me. I kicked and clawed at the garbage and he stabbed at me. "Alex!" I screamed, "Alex!"

In between the aching thud of my heart I heard Alex's muffled yell.

"He's checking out a book for you, sweetie," Mort said with unbridled glee. "My library is a bit unorganized, so he might be a while."

I lost my footing and tumbled forward; Mort grabbed me by my hair and I saw my own eyes reflected in the silver blade of the scissors as he raised them up again. Adrenaline raced through me, filling me with heat and fire, and I dove, feeling another cool slice as Mort's blade missed my face. His fingers lost their grip and slid through my hair, over my shoulder. His hand grasped desperately for me.

"Augh!" Mort slammed his fist down one more time and a pin prick of pain in my calf exploded into a thousand needles. I gaped at the scissors sticking straight out of my pant leg and a wave of nausea crashed over me as my jeans soaked up the blood.

My half-second pause gave Mort enough time to grab my leg with his other hand and pull me toward him. I could feel his fingertips digging through the heavy material of my jeans and I flopped desperately, trying to get a hold of something that would stop my slide. I discarded handfuls of yogurt cartons and showered him with mail as Mort kept pulling. I kicked at him but he barely flinched.

"What the hell are you?" I huffed, after landing a heel to his forehead.

"It's not what I am," Mort said, grabbing another fistful of my pant leg. "It's what *you* are."

I howled when he went for the scissors again, gripping the handle and wobbling the blade back and forth to get it out of my leg. The pain was phenomenal and I was hit with another wave of nausea, a crash of blinding pain.

"Lawson!" Alex's voice was closer now. "Where are you?"

"Kitchen!" I wailed

The crack of the gunshot was so surprising that Mort lost his bloody grip on the scissors and they flopped from the wound, disappearing in the sea of muck. My fingers found something heavy and solid and I gripped it, threw my entire weight into pulling it over my head and cracking it dead center on Mort's forehead as he lunged for me.

The stuffed owl made an impressive thud, its talons slicing from the top of Mort's head all the way through his eyebrow. Mort howled and clapped a hand over his forehead, the blood spattering between his fingers. He sputtered and stepped backward and I surged forward, clobbering him one more time with the bird, then throwing my entire body weight at him. He flopped onto his butt and I cleared him, gritting my teeth against the groaning ache in my calf.

"Alex!" I screamed again, kicking aside heaps of Mort's stuff. "Where are you?"

I swam my way toward the back of the house just as Alex was able to smash through what remained of a solid door and kick his leg through the fallen stash of eyeglasses. I yanked on his shoulders and Alex wriggled his way out.

"I was pinned in here by this crap?"

I tossed aside a soiled Care Bear and grabbed Alex's hand. "And don't think the entire police department isn't going to hear about it. Let's get out of here."

"Lawson, you're covered in blood."

"Let's go!"

The explosion of movement in the house caused every stacked item to stir and walls started sliding, giving up puffs of dust as magazines teetered and flopped from the tops of stacks, sailing to the floor. I heard Mort yelling as Alex and I took the obstacle course at record speed, finally stumbling through the cluttered foyer and over the front porch.

"Are you okay?" Alex said, slowing down.

"In the car!"

My heart was still thudding, adrenaline still racing through me. I had positioned myself in the front seat by the time Alex kicked the car in gear, was gripping the end of my seat belt when we flew in reverse, dust coughing up to the windows.

"What the hell happened to you?" I yelled the second our wheels hit paved road.

"Me, what the hell happened to you? That asshat shoved me in his 'library.'" Alex made air quotes around the word. "And kicked down three piles of shit to pin me in there. What about you, Vidal Sassoon?"

"What are you talking about?"

Alex jerked the car off the road with a squeal and pulled down the visor in front of me.

I gaped.

"That fuck!"

"You didn't notice that?"

I narrowed my eyes at Alex. "No, I was a little busy trying not to have him slice my head off." I glared at myself in the mirror. "I had no idea he sliced my hair off."

Though I've never been incredibly crazy about my mane of unruly red curls, I did have at least the minor pleasure of an even haircut.

Not so now, thanks to hoarder turned hairdresser, Mort Laney. His scissors of doom had lopped off a fist-sized chunk of hair just over my left eyebrow that left my scalp oddly naked all the way to my left ear. Baby sprigs of inch long hair shot up around my newly exposed scalp.

"He couldn't have just attacked my car like everyone else?"

I heard Alex stifling a laugh and I smacked the visor shut, then slumped back in my car seat. "I suppose you think this is hilarious."

"Hey, I was neck-deep in stuffed animals and wrapping paper. I'm not judging. But Lawson, I saw blood." He leaned over and awkwardly patted my new buzz cut. "Are you sure he didn't get you?"

I looked at my hands, then down at my blood-spattered jeans. "He stabbed me." It was matter-of-fact, and I waited for the surge of pain.

Nothing.

I moved my leg.

And there it was.

Another stab of nausea-inducing pain. "Shit! He stabbed me in the leg!" I touched the wound gently and recoiled.

"You were running on adrenaline." Alex leaned forward, his palm resting gently on my thigh as he fingered the tear in my jeans. "That's going to need stitches. Are you okay?"

"It hurts," I said miserably. "It hurts, I got a shitty hair-cut, and you got bombarded by an avalanche of crap, all for nothing." My eyes started to burn and my throat tightened. The tears started, burning hot tracks down my cheeks. I sniffed. "I'm sorry."

Alex pushed the car into drive again and pulled onto the road. "You really think I'd let a crazy-ass half-breed hoarder stab you for nothing?" He grinned at me with that cocky half smile, which seemed strangely comforting, and flopped a heavy sheaf of papers onto the console between us.

"What's this?"

Alex shrugged, maneuvering the car into traffic. "Honestly, it could be the answer to everything we're looking for or eight thousand expired Enfamil coupons. I just took what I could grab."

My newly naked scalp was cold. My leg throbbed and ached. But things were finally—if only a little bit—starting to look up and that felt good.

"Hey, where are you going? The city is that way."

"Yeah, but the hospital is this way."

"I don't need to go to the hospital," I said, hiding my wince. "A little Bactine, a couple of Band-Aids, and this baby will be fine." I was itching to get back to research, to saving Sampson—but the throb in my leg was starting to make me a little woozy. "And maybe just an aspirin or two."

"No offense, Lawson, but I'm less worried about a little pain than I am about you getting norovirus or mad cow from Mort's scissors. You have no idea where they've been. Actually, I'd be surprised if Mort has any idea where they've been."

I shot Alex a glance and he curled his upper lip into a disgusted scowl. "There were two boxes of plus-sized lingerie in the 'library.' I don't think Mort's picky about the shit that he hoards—or from whom he gets it."

I shuddered, suddenly certain that each throb of pain was delivering a whopping cocktail of bubonic plague, alopecia, and bird flu.

"Can you drive directly into the emergency room?"

It's one thing to have just survived a shearing-slash-stabbing at the hands of a psychotic hoarder. It's a whole different thing entirely to actually have people gape *at you* at the emergency room of San Francisco Memorial. The blood from my scissor wound had dried into an immovable hunk so I leaned on Alex, swinging my leg pirate peg-leg style when a stooped man who looked like he had gone man-o-a-machine-o with the business end of a weed whacker slid three plastic chairs away from us. I glanced up at Alex, my arm threaded through his.

"Does my hair really look that bad?" The whole ride down I had avoided the vanity mirror. Now I patted the little furry nubs that Mort had so kindly left on the left side of my head.

"No," Alex said. "You look fine. You look like one of those cutting-edge chicks with one of those edgy, funky new hairstyles."

I narrowed my eyes. "Look at me when you say that."

Alex pressed his lips together, still avoiding my gaze. "Don't make me look directly at it," he whispered.

By the time we got through the emergency room—with a very vague explanation as to how one gets a scissor to the calf and fifty percent of a horrible haircut—plus a dramatic request by yours truly to be pumped with every inoculation, antidote, and drop of hand sanitizer possible, I was discharged with a handful of painkillers and a pair of hospital scrubs.

I limped into the waiting room and glanced around at the selection of slightly injured, severely injured, and hypochondriacs, and gulped.

Had Alex left me?

I had gotten nothing from Mort but tetanus and a bad haircut, and now Alex had deserted me. Sampson could be a rabid murderer, Mort could be making redheaded Sophie Lawson voodoo dolls, and I would die here, while being stared at by a man with a fork mashed into his right ear.

So this is how it ends, I thought dejectedly. With a tombstone that said, *Sophie Lawson: Probably Should Have Listened.*

I sniffled.

Though the painkillers took the edge off the pain, I could

feel hot tears at the edges of my eyes, and the niggling flick of anger starting in my chest.

"Oh, hey, you're out already."

I whirled, then groaned, doubling over. "Not enough painkillers!" But I steeled myself and pushed my fists against my hips. "Why did you desert me? Where were you?"

Alex patted my shoulder, his palm a delicious, comforting weight against my skin. "If I deserted you, do you think I'd come back?" he asked.

I frowned. "I have bad hair. I'm a little sensitive."

"Here." He reached into a plastic SF Memorial bag and produced the ugliest—but sweetest—hat I'd ever seen. It was a navy-blue trucker number with the words *Somebunny at SF Memorial Loves Me* written in hot pink glitter. A pair of floppy, plush, pink bunny ears shot out either side.

My heart melted. It could have been the painkillers, or the fact that I'd bludgeoned a man with a taxidermied owl just hours before, but the gesture was enormous and touching. I took the hat in both hands, holding it delicately like the treasure that it was.

"It's beautiful," I whispered, as Alex blurred in front of me.

He took the hat and perched it on my head, pulling it low over my mangled scalp. "How does it feel?"

"Like the crown jewels," I said, stroking one of the shoulder-length bunny ears.

"How much pain medication did they give you?"

I was leaning on Alex as he led me through the double doors into my apartment building, and by the time we reached the third-floor landing, he was carrying me, my head was lolled back like a rag doll, and I thought I was flying.

"Did you—did you kill her?" I heard Nina ask.

I heard someone sniff heavily at the air. "No, she's definitely not dead. But she smells like she's on the verge."

I rolled my eyes to the back of my head and saw Vlad, upside down, hands on hips.

"Where's your cape?" I mumbled.

"She's been drugged," Alex explained. "Painkillers. I think I'll just put her to bed."

"No!" I sat up in Alex's arms and all the blood that had rushed to my head drained to my feet while my plush bunny ears flopped against my cheeks. I blinked at the symphony of electric spots that danced in the living room. "Shower first. Must remove layers of dusty crap from skin. Hey, Nina, when'd you get here?"

Alex positioned me on the couch and Nina held out a hand for me. "I can take it from here."

I don't know why—or how, exactly—but I lurched forward, throwing my arms around Alex's leg. "I can't let you go," I warbled into his kneecap. "I have to make things right."

"Sophie." I felt Nina's ice-cold fingertips on my shoulder, working to loosen my vise-like grip on Alex's leg. I wouldn't let him go.

"Don't leave," I said, pressing my cheek against his rock-solid thigh and trying to talk to him over his crotch. "Please."

I saw the alarm in Alex's eyes—but there was a twinge of sympathy in there, too. "I'll stay." He looked at Nina. "I feel partly responsible for this anyway. I should have been protecting her."

Nina pulled her hand out of mine and put her hands on hips. "Yeah, you should have. What happened? Where were you when—what the hell is on your hat?"

"Somebunny loves me," I cooed.

"It was the only hat in the place," Alex murmured.

"I love it so much," I said, stroking one of the ears, my eyes starting to mist again. "This man is a prince."

Nina furrowed her brow.

"He tried to save me, Neens, honest. But he was pinned by one-armed Care Bears and Cool Whip containers." I mimicked Mort's stack falling, pinning my hero Alex in the library. "And I saved us with an owl."

"How many painkillers did they give her?" Vlad asked.

Nina dragged me into the tub, where I blubbered into the water and tried to explain away my new haircut. I guess I wasn't making much sense because before long she plucked me from the bath, rolled me in a bathrobe, and dumped me on my bed. I think I heard her mumble, "She's all yours," to Alex as I wrestled myself into a pair of underwear and my Giants nightshirt.

Alex knocked on my open door frame. "Are you decent?"

I felt my grin spread to my earlobes. "You're so gentlemanly."

With his hands shoved into his pockets and his shoulder pressed up against the door frame, he looked like an Abercrombie model, or one of the headless guys from a romance novel cover.

My whole body was weighted with the far-reaching ooze of the painkillers, but my mind seemed clear enough and I was desperate not to be alone.

"Can you come in here, please?" With enormous effort, I snaked a single arm free from my blankets and patted the mattress next to me. "Sit with me."

Alex looked uncertain, but he came into the room and stood beside me.

"Sit." I patted the mattress again.

"I don't think—I mean, you and Will . . ."

I tried to sit up, tried to get my eyes to widen and focus on Alex's drawn face. "No me and Will," I finally said, though my lips felt like flapping bananas. "No me and Will."

Alex's sweet lips pushed up into a half smile and he sat. "You don't have any idea what you're saying, Lawson, do you?"

His voice was soothing and melodic, the tone making my eyelids heavy.

"I know what I'm saying," I mumbled. "Will, me . . . not serious. It was—it was . . ." My tongue felt immovable. "It was you."

I felt Alex's palm on my forehead. A shiver shot through me as he gently brushed my hair away, his fingers playing through the long strands. I closed my eyes, letting the feeling flow through me.

"It was always you," I said.

"Shh, Lawson. You don't know what you're saying."

"I do," I said, certain I was nodding my head emphatically. "It's not Will. Will is my Guardian. You're my angel. My angel Alex."

I pried an eye open to see Alex's eyes on me, the intense cobalt fixed, focused. He licked his lips, his smile soft. "I'll always be your angel, Lawson."

"My angel Alex," I mumbled again. "Stay with me. Stay with me here, tonight. Stay forever." I reached out and found his torso, then worked my fingers under his shirt. He sucked in a breath when my fingertips brushed over his bare skin. He ran his fingers through my hair; I rubbed my fingers over his navel, up his stair-step abs. "Please, Alex."

"Lawson . . ."

Suddenly, I didn't just want him—I *needed* him. Desire flowed through every inch of me and my body, heavy and leaden twenty minutes ago, was suddenly alive and on desperate fire. I sat up, clutched at him. I tangled my fingers in his hair and pulled him to me, pressing my lips against his, kissing him hungrily.

He kissed me back and something inside me exploded. I gripped at his chest, slid my other hand from his hair to his shoulder, yanking to remove his shirt. He grabbed my hand and when he pulled his lips from mine, their immediate absence felt so wrong it was painful.

"What?"

Alex's breath was ragged, labored. His skin was hot, but his eyes and his touch were gentle. "We can't do this, Lawson. You don't want this. You're drugged."

I swung my head. "No, no. I know what I want. I want you."

Alex gently pushed me away from him, using his other hand to cup my chin. "You're gorgeous."

Pain filled every inch of me and the edges of my lips pulled down. "You don't want me?"

He brushed a thumb over my bottom lip. "I want you more than anything, Lawson."

"Is it Heaven, then? You don't want to do anything to keep you out of Heaven again?"

His eyes suddenly went dark and bedroomy, his smile wry but slightly lascivious. "The things I want to do to you would keep me out of Heaven forever and it'd be worth it." He brushed a tender kiss over my forehead. "But not now. Not like this."

"But I—"

"Shh, sleep, sweetheart."

I tried to protest, but Alex's arms were strong around me and my body had gotten heavy again. He laid me down gently, pulling my covers up and tucking them around me. I was suddenly so incredibly tired.

"You're a good angel," I murmured.

I heard his soft chuckle as he straightened. "Go to sleep, okay?"

I nodded, pushing my head into the pillow. My eyes were

narrow slits now; I could just make out Alex's back as he turned to leave.

"I love you," I muttered.

I was groggy, but I saw him stiffen and pause. Then he pulled the door gently shut behind him.

Chapter Nine

The day after my run-in with Mort and the San Francisco Memorial emergency room was blissfully uneventful—as long as I kept my mind away from thinking about my romantic mumblings to Alex the night before. I wasn't one-hundred-percent clear about the exact goings-on of our conversation, but every time I even considered it, my mercury rose and my complexion went from day-glow white to midlife crisis Corvette red. I had a grand plan to slink out of the Underworld Detection Agency and finish my Sampson investigation myself, while contributing to Alex's homicide investigation via e-mail or possibly carrier pigeon.

However, I was unable to get one Payless Shoe Source faux-leather heel out the door before I came face to bloodless face with Dixon Andrade.

"Miss Lawson." His eyes coasted over me. "That's a lovely hat."

My hand flew up to the enormous *Titanic*-style headpiece I wore. After spending twenty minutes this morning trying to perfect a half-bald-head-hiding comb-over, Nina gave up and slapped the giant saucer on my head.

"Thanks. I was just on my way out."

"Certainly," Dixon said without stepping aside. "But first I was hoping to talk to you about our previous discussion. If you have the time, of course." His expression was kind enough, but his eyes were cold steel, letting me know that I'd damn well better have the time.

I took two tentative steps back into my office and slunk into one of my visitor's chairs while Dixon settled himself across from me.

"Have you and Alex been able to come up with anything?"

I thought of my fingers ambling all over Alex's bare chest the night before and shook my head, probably a little too emphatically. "No, nothing."

"But you two have been working together?"

"Yes, sir." I knew I should have been uber focused on Dixon and his werewolf hypothesis. It could be the one thing that could prove—or disprove—Sampson's innocence, but my mind and body only wanted to head back to the relative safety of my bed and my previous drug-addled state. "Have you found anything new?"

Dixon looked away and then back at me. "Can you take off that hat? It's a bit distracting."

I clamped my hand over it. "No. It's . . . crazy hat day. Here. At the office." I laced my fingers together. "Promotes employee bonding. New thing from HR. You must not have gotten the memo."

"Okay."

"So has anyone else spotted this wolf? Or been attacked?"

Dixon shook his head. "Not as of late."

I stood, my swinging shoulder bag a half inch from Dixon's forehead. "I am going to take that information upstairs right now to Alex, and we will throw ourselves headlong into this investigation." My eyes flashed. "Some more.

I mean, still." I shot him a bared-teeth smile. "I'll have a report for you tomorrow. How's that?"

Dixon rose slowly. "That would be nice."

"Okay, well." I waved frantically. "Gotta go."

I was so amped by the time the elevator doors opened that I didn't stop to consider how much I didn't want to run into Alex, and hurried directly through the police station vestibule and right out the front door.

My poly-cotton twinset began sticking to my back the second I stepped onto the baked concrete of the parking lot. The fog inching in at a snail's pace and the twilight pink-gray of the sky, coupled with the still-searing heat gave the entire town an eerie, zombie-apocalypse-type presence. I was pleasantly surprised that such an apocalypse hadn't yet begun and that my car still looked as miserably pieced together now as it had when I left it this morning. I probably should have at least sprung for a paint job, but I was honestly growing accustomed to my little vamp-mobile. And besides, this way I would never mistake my Honda Accord for anyone else's.

I slipped inside, blasted the air-conditioning, and backed out, screeching to a heart-wrenching stop when I saw Alex in my rearview mirror. He had his hands on his hips and he waited, nonplussed, while I threw my car into park and desperately swallowed my heart out of my throat.

"What the hell are you doing?" I screamed, wrestling my seat belt off and flying across the parking lot at him. "Did you not see my car? It's a car. You should have."

"It's not a big car," Alex said, cocking his head to the side.

"It's multicolored and has the word *VAMPIRE* spray painted on the hood."

"Yeah . . . are you planning to get that painted over anytime soon?"

I narrowed my eyes. "Yes. Right after they finish painting the house in Tuscany. Is there a reason for you standing behind my car or do you just hope to become a speed bump in your *next* next life?"

"Well, I guess someone's feeling better."

My heartbeat subsided long enough to remember that I had kind of professed my love to Alex the night before. I felt my mouth drop open. "Is that why you threw yourself behind my car? Because last night made you suicidal?"

"Suicidal?" Alex said, one eyebrow raised questioningly. "No. I'm not the one with the bad haircut."

I blew out an annoyed sigh. "What exactly was it that you wanted, Grace?"

Alex's grin was sly. "Thought you might like to grab a bite."

I am a lot of things: strong. Mouthy. Semi-independent. But I wasn't made of steel.

"What kind of bite?"

He shrugged. "Your call."

I arched a brow. "Your wallet?"

"All right."

Rather than try to wrestle my giant hat into the car I tossed it in the trunk and replaced it with a frayed ball cap that I pulled low over my eyes. When I got into the car Alex looked at me and crossed his arms in front of his chest.

"I'm a little insulted that you're not wearing the hat I got you."

"Some*bunny* found another hat."

Alex's cheeks bloomed a bashful pink. "Forgot about the lovely inscription."

I snapped the door shut and Alex and I were off, windows rolled down, air pulsing through the cab of the car.

"Feel like Italian?" I asked as I flipped on the turn signal.

"Always."

"North Beach it is."

"Hey, did you know there's supposed to be a maze of underground tunnels under North Beach?"

I grinned. "And here I thought I was the expert on the goings-on under the city."

We pulled up to a stoplight just off Union Avenue and I listened to the car idle, to the faint sounds of someone playing a saxophone on a distant corner. And then there was something else.

A wail—or a moan.

"Did you hear that?" Alex asked, ear cocked toward the open window.

I turned the stereo off and leaned out my own window, holding my breath for a silent beat. A lazy wisp of oregano-scented air wafted into the car, and on it, a chorus of low moans. They were desperate, insistent rumbles that cut through the city noise.

I furrowed my brow. "What is that?"

Now the moans and rumbles were joined by thumps, then a shallow scraping as though something—or someone—was being dragged.

Alex's eyebrows went up. "Lawson?" I saw his hand hover around his concealed gun.

I held up a silencing hand. "Wait, Alex. I think it might be—"

"Zombies?"

They engulfed the car before the word was out of his mouth, their fingers scraping against the paint, lifeless limbs thumping against the mangled exterior of my vamp-mobile. Alex's eyes were wide, distressed, his face ashen as their fingers came through the open window, clawing at him, touching his skin, ruffling his hair. Zombie fingers brushed at my face, too; a clammy hand landed on my arm, grabbed a fistful of my shirt.

I couldn't help myself. I started to giggle.

Alex, swatting at the grey, rotting arms that waved at him, looked at me incredulously. "You're laughing? This is funny to you?"

One of the zombies had curled his fingers under my neck and was actively tickling me now, giggling back at me as my laughter grew, his grin wide and goofy. I clamped my knees together and tried not to wet myself. "They're— they're—they're real!" I squeezed out, throwing the car into park and doubling over myself.

"Of course they're real!" Alex said. "How the hell do we kill them?"

"Double tap!" A zombie on Alex's side of the car yelled. "Cardio-oooo!"

"Beeeeeer," another one groaned, a rivulet of black-red blood dribbling out the side of his mouth. "Beeer!"

Alex wrinkled his brow. "Is that zombie asking for beer? Can they do that?"

I was laughing so hard now that tears were pulsing from my eyes and I started to cough. Finally, I got hold of myself. "They're real, Alex. They're real people."

Alex paused, his lip curling up into a snarl as another zombie wannabe poked her full torso through my window. "Graiiiiiins!" she moaned, stiff arms waving. "Graiiiins!"

"She's a vegetarian," I said by way of explanation.

"What the hell is going on here?" Alex wanted to know.

Veggie-Zombie bared a mouth full of grayish teeth, half smeared with a thick coat of shiny black greasepaint. "Zombie pub crawl," she informed. "We're only on our second pub." She craned her neck to look out the wind-shield. "Light's green." She wriggled out of the car and I inched forward, Veggie-Zombie's undead brood wailing and flailing in the street behind us.

"There's hundreds of them," Alex said, staring out the back window incredulously.

"Probably."

"You're not the slightest bit spooked by that?" Alex said.

"Why should I be? Those zombies are in way better spirits than the ones from the Underworld. And they can be satiated with beer. The ones at the office? Ugh. They're supposed to have eaten before they come in, but if you even look the slightest bit intelligent, they're salivating all over your desk. I had a guy suck the hair tie right off of my pony-tail once."

Alex shook his head in disbelief. "I'm hearing the words, but they don't make sense." He was silent for a beat and I glanced at him from the corner of my eye, his serious expression starting my giggles all over again. He gave me a dirty look. "Look, you've got to cut me some slack."

I shot him a devious smirk. "And why's that?"

"Come on. It's ninety degrees in San Francisco, we processed a murder scene that was right out of a Wes Craven film, you were shish-kebabed by a hoarder, and suddenly, the streets are overrun with the thirsty dead." He brushed the zombie-fist marks out of his shirt. "It's perfectly normal that a guy would get a little unnerved."

"Or that a guy could scream like a little girl."

"I didn't—"

"Geez, there's no parking around here," I said, letting Alex know in no uncertain terms that the case against his manly screaming was closed. "Did everyone in the city get a car?"

"Apparently, zombies don't like to carpool." He grinned.

"See? You're warming up to the faux undead already. Ooh, spot!" I cut hard on the wheel and screeched my little tin can of a car into a shaded spot at the edge of a residential street. It was dark and quiet, a half block full of row houses with lights off or curtains pulled tight, silver flashes from televisions creeping out the cracks. We walked back down to North Beach and found a restaurant with tables set up along the sidewalk. It was flanked by moaning zombies carrying pint glasses and iPhones, but with the heat still heavy on the night breeze, it was perfect. I broke a greasy, cheesy breadstick in half and took a gooey bite.

"Mmm . . ."

"So, I take it you're off the painkillers?"

I nodded, working to unstick the cheese that was sizzling on the roof of my mouth. "Yeah," I said, my hand going up to my hat. "The cut doesn't hurt much anymore. It's mostly the sting of the bad hair."

Alex smiled, the grin going all the way up to his eyes, making them seem to sparkle in the low light. I thought of the night before, of the gentle way he'd stroked my hair. and my stomach fluttered while my heart did a quick little double beat.

I may have had only half my hair and a scissor wound in my leg, but at that second, I felt like a very normal girl on a very normal date, with a good-looking man. No, an amazing-looking—and amazing in general—man. The way he smiled at me—the way his eyes burned right into me— made me feel like the only woman in the world, like a supermodel with a full head of hair. Suddenly, I didn't regret last night's drug-addled fog and romantic ramblings. Will was nice, but this was Alex.

And I loved him.

The realization shot through me from tip to tail, making me slightly dizzy and giddy at the same time. I *loved him*.

I, Sophie Lawson, loved him, Alex Grace.

My eyes started to water and my cheeks began to hurt from my love-struck grin.

"Someone looks like the cat who swallowed the canary," he said to me.

I let out a slow breath, my heart beginning to thunder wildly. For once in my life, my mind was littered with images of rose petals and cartoon hearts, rather than blood bags and bodies. When Alex rested his hand on the table, I pulled my own out of my lap and tentatively placed it over his.

It was a test.

He smiled, and pressed his thumb on the outside of my hand, then opened his fingers so mine could slip inside.

My whole body sung.

"This is nice."

Alex cocked his head. "What is?"

I shrugged. "This. Me, you, breadsticks. The city *out there.*"

"Don't tell me Sophie Lawson is getting the suburban itch."

"No, I love living in the city." I frowned. "Sometimes I just wish it weren't so . . . volatile."

Alex seemed to consider, then cocked his head at me, giving one of those *Father Knows Best* expressions. "Lawson, you know that wherever you go—"

"Stop," I said. "I don't want to hear it. Please indulge me in my non-demonic, non-everyone-wanting-to-kill-me fantasy of a suburban life, complete with white picket fences, kids' soccer games, and a big shaggy dog."

"No minivan?"

"Volvo. Two-point-five kids. Laughable mortgage. One of those plastic ducks out front that you dress with the seasons."

Alex grinned at me. "Seasonal duck dressing? Sheesh,

Lawson, I figured you might want a break, but I never pegged you for the Donna Reed type."

I narrowed my eyes, feeling indignant. "I can be the Donna Reed type. Why? Don't you think I could be the Donna Reed type?"

Alex crunched on a particularly cheesy breadstick and spoke with his mouth full. "That's right. Never question the homemaking prowess of a woman who can shoot a pot roast seventy-five feet." He grinned and I felt my cheeks redden.

"That was one time. And, if I recall correctly, I was—"

"Three sheets to the wind?"

"I was going to say imbibing excessively, but we'll go with yours, sure."

"Okay." Alex leaned back in his chair, wiping his greasy hands on a napkin. "So you're living in suburbia with your shaggy dog and your two and a half—"

"Two-point-five," I corrected.

"Two-point-five kids." He blinked out at the starlit city. "Is there a guy in all of this Norman Rockwell goodness?"

My heart did a little neurotic patter. Was he saying he wanted to be a part of my future? I turned to look at Alex, who continued to study the skyline. His profile was perfect— a thick head of run-your-fingers-through chocolate brown curls, dark brows that, when cocked, could make a girl lose her inhibitions—and possibly her panties. A strong, straight nose. Pronounced chin with just the right amount of stubble. I felt the flutter in my stomach but mustered my courage anyway. First I batted my eyelashes in that sexy way that Nina did so effortlessly. Then I prayed to God that the majority of the cheese and marinara sauce in my appetizer had made it into my mouth. Then I lowered my voice into what I hoped with a sexy octave.

"Why do you ask?"

Alex's head lolled toward me and he laughed. "Nice, Lawson."

I rolled my eyes but eyed him. "Do you ever dream of running away?"

"To the suburbs?" He shook his head. "No."

"Where would you go? You know, if you could?"

It was fleeting, and if I hadn't been looking at Alex so hard I would have missed it—the hint of sadness that darkened his eyes and flitted across his face. He pursed his lips and the muscle in his jaw jumped and I had to look away, feeling a lump growing in my own throat.

"Sorry."

The longer an earthbound angel walked the earth, the more he started to remember about his previous life. To us it would seem welcome, but to someone who will never again be able to touch a loved one or share a memory with a friend, it grew nothing short of hellish after hundreds of years. Alex had been earthbound for a while now, and I knew from the darkness that marred his handsome features now and again that the memories were pouring back, and they were strong, powerful—and hurtful.

I took a deep breath and squeezed Alex's hand. "So, about the other night . . ."

"Now, what can I get you two?" The perky blond waitress bounded between us and the spell was broken. Alex broke his hand away from mine to pick up his menu, and I took an enormous glug of water, my stomach knotting. I blinked at Alex as he spoke to the waitress and lost all my nerve. After she took our orders and left, Alex leaned toward me again. "What were you saying?"

I smiled and chewed on my bottom lip, scanning the restaurant. "Um . . . check out that guy, three p.m."

Alex looked to his right, his gaze blanketing the slow-moving traffic. "I don't see anyone."

"Your other three p.m.," I hissed, jutting my chin.

"Okay, my right is your left. And your three p.m. is roughly nine-twenty."

"Way to be precise. Do you see him?"

"Who? Nineteen-ninety-six?"

The man in question was clean cut, his bouffant at least three inches from his scalp and so stiff it moved in one giant mass in the light breeze. He was sitting by himself at one of the tiny patio tables, his rayon color-block shirt buttoned up to his neck. I felt my mouth drop open when he scooched back from the table and crossed his long legs.

"Shut up," I whispered.

"What now?"

"Z. Cavariccis."

Alex's expression was blank. "I'm sorry?"

"Z. Cavariccis. The pants? Don't tell me you don't know what Z. Cavariccis are."

Alex just shrugged and I gaped. "They're pants. Really ugly pants, but like, the quintessential ugly pants of the nineties."

"Oh," Alex said, his mouth full of cheesy garlic bread. "Forgive me for misplacing that little nugget of Americana."

I pointed at him with my own piece of bread. "You should know this shit if you don't want to be found out as, you know . . . angelic."

"Z. Cavariccis. Right." He tapped a finger to his head. "Locked away. Have you seen our waiter?"

"He has a girlfriend!"

The woman who took the seat across from Nineteen-ninety-six was petite and elegant, wearing a silky one-shouldered sundress straight out of Paris fashion week.

"How did Fashion Forward end up with Ninety-six?"

"Who had the penne?" our waitress asked.

Alex raised his hand and shot me a triumphant grin. "I guess we'll never know."

I buried my fork into five inches of pasta-cheese, cheese-pasta perfection, but I couldn't keep my eyes from wandering back to the fashion time machine going on behind Alex. There was something off about the couple.

I dipped my hand in my purse. "Can you excuse me for a minute?"

"Must be serious if you're leaving lasagna."

"I'll be right back."

I passed Fashion Forward and Ninety-Six with my cell phone pressed to my ear. Nina picked up on the second ring and I slipped behind a potted plant, where two pub-crawl zombies were groping each other lovingly. They scattered when they saw me.

"What's up, buttercup?" Nina asked.

"Fashion question."

"Ooh, my favorite kind. If I have to be cooped up in this hell hole, at least I can give fashion advice to make your world more beautiful."

"Color-blocked rayon shirt and Z. Cavariccis."

I could practically hear the horror etching into Nina's face across the phone line. "What did you say to me?" Nina whispered.

"You heard me. A color-blocked rayon shirt and Z. Cavariccis. And he's got one of those Jordan Knight bubbly bouffants."

"Does he have an earring?"

I chanced a glance around the palm and narrowed my eyes. "Yeah."

"Ah, just as I suspected. He's new."

"New?"

"Old."

"Old?"

"Stop repeating everything I say. He's dead, Soph, dead. No one steps out in rayon, Z. Cavariccis, and a single stud. It's the dead man's triumvirate. He's newly made, newly out, and he's probably on the prowl."

I rolled up on my tiptoes when a waiter blocked my view. Ninety-six laced his long, thin fingers through Fashion Forward's and she gazed into his eyes, batting her thick, over-mascarraed lashes. The adoration oozed off her.

"His nails are probably all broken from digging out of the coffin—check for dirt, too."

I squinted, and although I could see the shape of their linked fingers, I wasn't close enough to see the telltale graveyard dirt or broken nails.

"I can't tell if his hands are dirty. What else you got?"

"Well, once awakened, he'd be thirsty. Confused, but mostly thirsty. He'd be looking for easy prey."

I bit my thumbnail. "Would he take his prey to dinner?"

"No, he would eat his prey *for* dinner. What's going on out there?"

"That's what I'm trying to figure out. Thanks for the tips." I clicked my phone shut and arced around the potted palm, then nonchalantly brushed Ninety-six's outstretched arm as I went back to my table.

"Everything okay?" Alex asked, his plate of pasta half empty.

"He's warm."

Alex quirked an eyebrow. "I know I shouldn't be surprised, but seriously? Your lasagna's a he?"

I rolled my eyes. "Not my pasta. Ninety-six."

"What were you expecting?"

I scooted my chair closer to Alex's and dropped my voice. "If a guy walks out dressed like that"—I angled my brows—"then he likely doesn't know how far behind he is. You know, fashionably."

"And that means . . . ?"

"God, Alex, do I have to spell everything out for you?"

"Yes. Please."

"He's dead. At least I thought he was."

"But he's warm, so horror of all horrors, he's a live guy in twenty-year-old fashion? That never happens." He popped another bite of penne into his mouth.

I cut into my lasagna and chewed thoughtfully. "I don't buy it. In this town?"

Alex put down his fork and knife. "Now that's one thing I truly love about you, Lawson." He blinked at me, his eyes catching the sparkle of the twinkle lights strung in the trees, his loose curls lazily licking the tops of his ears. I knew I was supposed to be flummoxed and mercurial and angered about his and my recent string of romantic follies, but when his voice dropped into that spun-sugar sweetness and the cornflower blue of his eyes pulled me in, I was a kitten, purring. The sexy softness of his voice dripped through me and I put down my own knife and fork, knitted my hands in my lap, and waited.

"What do you love about me, Alex?" I drew out my words, each one hanging on the soft night air.

"I love that if there's a seemingly simple solution to an issue, say, a gentleman preps for a date by pulling out his best date duds—"

"Circa twenty years ago."

"Circa twenty years ago, he can't possibly just be a victim of fashion circumstance. He has to be newly risen from the dead."

I smiled sweetly. "The simplest solution is often the best solution."

"And rising from the dead is simple for you, eh?"

I picked up my wineglass and leaned back in my chair. "I call 'em as I see 'em. Hey, where'd he go?"

"Looks like his date didn't mind his fashion flaws as much as you did. They're leaving."

"We should follow them."

Alex blew out an exasperated sigh but threw down a few bills anyway. "Fine."

I reached for his arm, but when I turned around, I was eye-to-glassy-eye with a pub crawl zombie. He dropped open his mouth and gurgled, little bursts of beer-soaked air bubbling in my face. "Ew!" I tried to edge around Beer Zombie, but there was another behind him and two more behind her. Nineteen-ninety-six and Fashion Forward had disappeared among the stiff, moaning crowd.

"I guess we're not chasing bad pants tonight," Alex said with far too easy a smile.

A little nervous zeal wound through me. Was I sending a woman to her blood-sucking, badly fashioned doom?

"You're overreacting, Lawson. You work for a company that *detects* guys like that. Any new vamps?"

I bit my lip, considering. "No. But—"

"You're jumping to conclusions."

I scowled. "Well, he's Cabbage Patch-ing to them."

Alex cocked his head, silent, but challenging. I blew out a defeated sigh. "It is possible that I may have rushed to judgment as I have, on occasion—"

"Jumped to a conclusion or two?"

I cocked what I hoped was a menacing brow. "Not jumped. Hopped. Frolicked toward."

Alex swung his head. "You're impossible."

We edged our way between the beer-soaked zombies and beer-buying zombie sympathizers, and then zigzagged into a slip of a store selling gelato and delicate, hot-off-the-iron pizzelles. The fog had finally blanketed the hot evening and I shivered, rubbing my palms up my arms.

"Cold?" Alex asked once I had my gelato-slash-pizzelle spoils.

"A little."

He shimmied out of the button-down shirt he was wearing over his fitted tee, and I tried to convince myself that the my immediate salivation was due to the proximity of my dark chocolate pinot noir gelato, rather than the sweet hunk of ice creamy goodness flexing his muscles in front of me. Either way, I was engulfed in jaw-dropping, panty-melting pleasure with a spoonful of gelato in my mouth and Alex's gentle touch as he settled his shirt on my naked shoulders. His fingers trailed the tiniest bit across my collarbone, leaving a trail of electrical sparks that shot licks of fire directly to my belly. I clamped my legs together and pleaded with my intellect to remember that I was in the throes of a moral issue, caught between two men I really cared for. Then Alex gently cupped my chin and rubbed his thumb carefully over my bottom lip.

"You have a little bit of chocolate sauce there."

I couldn't take my eyes off his sly smile, the drip of chocolate on his thumb as he brought his hand to his mouth, parted those perfect lips, and licked.

The heat that roiled low in my belly starburst and was everywhere now; the angel on my shoulder reminding me of my morals had been solidly sucker punched by a red-leather-wearing demon who told me to pounce when ready.

I stopped and stepped in front of Alex. "About last night."

There was a sweet look of sympathy on Alex's face that cut right through me. "It's all right, Lawson. I know what that was all about."

I took a step back. "You—you know what *what* was all about?"

"This." Alex made circles with his arms. "All of this. The

nerves. The awkwardness. It's all right. You were drugged last night. You had no idea what you were saying. I know what you meant. You love me, we're friends."

"Oh," I said, stunned, nervous heat shooting through me. "No, that's not what I—that's not what I meant."

"You don't have to explain it. I know about it. You and Will, I mean. I'm not exactly happy about it, but you know." He shrugged and jammed his hands in his jeans pockets, starting to walk around me. "He can give you stuff that I can't," he said to the sidewalk. "He can give you a future."

Alex wouldn't look at me, but I saw his face tense up. He cleared his throat.

"Alex, Will and I . . ." I bit my bottom lip, started kneading my palm. "We—but we—and we're not."

Alex put a reassuring hand on my shoulder and gave me a practiced smile. "It's okay. You don't have to explain."

"There's nothing serious between Will and me, Alex."

"Like I said, you don't have to explain." He turned and I grabbed his arm.

"I might not have to explain, but you do. What do you mean Will can give me something that you can't? What can Will give me that you can't?"

Alex studied me hard, his eyes going so dark they were almost chrome colored. I watched his Adam's apple bob as he swallowed. "Will can give you a future, Lawson. That's something I could never do."

I felt like someone had punched me in the stomach. "What?"

Alex opened his mouth, looked like he was about to explain, when a howl sliced through the silent night. He straightened, his blue eyes going from sympathetic and human to seasoned-cop hard in less than a millisecond. "Did you hear that?"

"Unfortunately, yes."

A string of howls answered back, but these were short and yippy, and ended with the guffaws of drunken zombies and North Beach partygoers.

"Stupid kids," I muttered.

We stepped into the darkness, our moment gone, my gelato a syrupy, melted mess. I scanned for a garbage can to toss it, then stiffened.

Suddenly, there was a charge in the air. It was the same thing that made cats arch their backs and spine their tails; the same thing that put dogs on snarling alert. My hackles went up, adrenaline boiling my blood. I licked my lips, the saline taste of danger in my saliva.

I heard the growl, first.

It was a low, predatory rumble. Earthy and primitive, like nothing I've heard before.

Except I had heard it before. Once.

My feet were rooted to the ground, but I turned my head slowly. The rumble was low enough that I couldn't hear which direction it came from. But it called to me, and I *knew* where it was.

"Lawson." I heard Alex call behind me and I slowly held up a hand, silently willing him to understand, to stay put.

And when I turned again I saw it. A wolf, in the narrow, darkened corridor between two houses. I could make out nothing but his eyes and his teeth as the black rim of his lip curled up into a fearsome snarl.

The sclera glowed an eerie yellow-green, but it was the silky black of his pupils that drew me in. The edges were jagged and rimmed in a bloody red. Sampson once told me the black was the wolf eye; the red, where it tore through the man. I took a tentative step back and the wolf eye kept its focus on me. There was no flicker of recognition, no restraint in his eyes.

I wet my lips with my tongue. "Sampson?" I whispered.

A low growl. Not confirmation, not denial. Animalistic.
"Lawson!"

The wolf was over me before I knew it. I felt the slice of his claw over my shoulder, heard the thud of the powerful body hit the ground behind me, watched in horror as it crossed the street, scaled my car, and took off into the surrounding darkness.

Alex grabbed me before I fell.

"Lawson! Lawson!"

I blinked up at him, utterly dazed.

"What the hell? What the hell was that?"

"Werewolf," I said, my voice low and hoarse, the word itself like a betrayal.

"Who was it?"

I felt myself start to shake. "I really don't know."

And it was the truth.

After an uncomfortably quiet ride home, we pulled into the police station parking lot.

"First the Shively case, now this," Alex said.

I almost added the Sutro Point murders but thought better of it. "Yeah."

"And you didn't know anything about this."

"No."

"I'm sorry, but isn't that kind of what the Underworld Detection Agency does? I mean, don't you detect things that come out of the Underworld?"

A roiling heat went through my body, though I wasn't sure who I was mad at. "I told you, Alex," I started, enunciating every word carefully. "I don't know. Dixon thought that Octavia was killed by a werewolf."

"Which you very quickly ruled out."

I slammed the car into park. "I just didn't want anyone to jump to any conclusions."

"And now people are dead."

"Oh, no." I turned around in my seat so that Alex would get the full effect of my pissed-off glare. "Don't you try and pin this on me. You and the whole freaking San Francisco Police Department have done jack crap on this case. You'd still be looking up your own asses if it weren't for me and my information. And you still don't have any actual evidence that your murders and mine are connected." I was seething mad now, feeling thirty steps—or paw prints— behind this entire investigation. I wanted nothing more than to dump Alex out of my car and go confront Sampson.

"I really can't believe you, Lawson. You're so damn fixated on protecting the memory of your precious werewolf buddy that you refuse to look at the facts. You'd rather give up the Underworld than admit that someone you care about might not be what you think he is."

I was floored. "Are you talking about Sampson?"

Alex's eyes flashed hard. "You tell me," he said, before kicking the car door open and slamming it hard behind him.

I drove home in silence, letting the rumble of the engine thrum through my entire body and blinking back tears that I refused to let fall. I was angry at everyone—at Alex, for his outburst; at Sampson for not knowing—or not telling me that there was another wolf in town; and at myself for being so stupidly trusting. I refused to believe that I was responsible in any way for the murders, but I couldn't keep the guilt from welling up inside me. By the time I pulled into the apartment building parking lot, my throat was aching from the solid lump and my dry eyes were burning. I wanted nothing more than a jug of wine and a sleeve of chocolate marshmallow pinwheels, and for the world to stay sane for just one night.

I'd deal with the fate of San Francisco first thing in the morning.

I pushed my key into the lock and edged through the door, pausing and frowning before turning on the light. The apartment was a sour-smelling, stuffy, dim box thanks to the closed-tightly blackout curtains. Once my eyes—and nose—adjusted I looked around.

"Nina?"

She was stretched out on the couch, still in that adorable, silky jumper, but now the flouncy fabric at the bust line was limp. One of the straps had flopped down toward her elbow and her hair matched the jumper: limp, floppy. Neither had been washed. Vlad was stretched out on the floor in front of her, corpse style. His eyes were dull, and his bare, pallid chest shone eerily in the dim glow from the muted television. He was wearing nothing but boxers and his usually slicked back hair was disheveled. I blinked, unable to tear my eyes from Vlad's concave, white marble chest. He looked like a starved, felled statue of David.

"You guys look like you're dying," I said with a frown. And then, concerned, "You're not dying, are you?"

Nina rolled her eyes. "We might as well be. This is torture!"

"Fucking torture," Vlad echoed.

I chewed the inside of my lip. "Is there anything I can do?" I stepped forward, gingerly touching Nina's calf—still ice cold. "Do you need to be like, refrigerated?"

The sharp annoyance that flashed across Nina's face let me know that she was nowhere near dead, and the current situation wasn't as dire as she and Vlad portrayed it. "We don't need to be refrigerated. We're vampires, not sides of beef."

I held up my hands placatingly. "Hey, just trying to help.

I'm a born and bred San Franciscan. This heat thing is a little weird to me, too."

"We should go back to Seattle," Vlad moaned from his spot on the ground.

Nina's eyes rolled back once more. "Never again. Too close to all those sparklers."

I put down my purse and snuggled with ChaCha. The heat was apparently too much for her, too, as her usual spastic patter was more of a lazy lope tonight.

"Hey," I said, eyes flicking to the TV screen. "News."

Vlad shot the remote control at the TV, and the coifed newscaster roared into action. "We're at day three of the most severe heat wave the San Francisco Bay Area has ever seen. While most of you are out there enjoying the heat, some of you are left wondering, when is it going to end?" She flashed a set of dazzling, blue-white veneers, then shuffled her papers and flirted with the camera once more. "Usually, San Franciscans can depend on the offshore flow to beat the heat, but not tonight. We don't have a cold front in sight! And rain? What's rain?" The anchorwoman guffawed while Nina and Vlad groaned.

"That's it. We're going to die here."

The news cut from the in-studio view to a sweeping picture of Pacific Heights, zooming in on the yellow-taped house Alex and I had visited earlier. My stomach sunk and guilt weighed my shoulders down.

"How was your day?" Nina said without opening her eyes.

I thought of Dixon, of the zombies, of my blow-out with Alex. I thought of the way he'd told me that I was betraying the Underworld as my eyes shot over Nina and Vlad, looking so listless, so helpless. I swallowed hard. "Not over," I said softly.

Chapter Ten

I sucked in a sharp breath before knocking on Will's door. I heard Sampson moving about inside, then his gruff voice.

"Who is it?"

"It's me," I said. "Open up."

Sampson pulled the door open two inches and stared me down, as if trying to make sure it was really me. "Hi there, come on in."

I went straight for one of Will's lawn chairs and sat down prissily, kneading my palm in my hand.

"Everything okay, Sophie?"

I looked up, then swiped the hat from my head and watched Sampson's eyes bulge. "Oh. Did you—mean to do that?"

"Courtesy of Mort," I said.

Sampson clamped a hand over his mouth. "Oh, Sophie, I'm so sorry."

"But that's not why I'm here."

Sampson sat across from me. "Did you find something out? Did you hear something?"

"Oh, I heard something all right. Is there something you want to tell me, Sampson?"

The openness in Mr. Sampson's eyes struck me, and I wasn't sure if he was good at looking innocent, or I was bad at reading faces. "I don't know what you mean."

"Alex and I were in North Beach tonight."

Sampson's eyebrows went up. "Oh? Anything interesting?"

I narrowed my eyes and leaned in, trying again to read his expression. "There was a zombie pub crawl."

He smiled.

"And a werewolf."

All the color drained from Mr. Sampson's face. His mouth fell open just slightly, his eyes widening. "Excuse me?"

"A werewolf."

"Sophie, you—" He paused, seemed to regather his thoughts. "You don't think it was me, do you?"

"I don't know what to think anymore, Sampson."

He stood up. "I should go."

"No!" I jumped up so quickly my lawn chair flopped to the ground. "No. You shouldn't go. Every time something gets sticky, you try and leave. What you need to do is sit down and tell me the truth." I don't know where my sudden burst of bravado was coming from, but even as Sampson looked up at me, his dark eyes challenging, I couldn't consider backing down.

I wouldn't.

Sampson's expression softened and he looked at me as if considering. I watched his chest rise and fall as he sucked in a long breath and blew it out, one hand on his head, thumb massaging his temple. "I should have known this would happen."

"You should have known what would happen?"

He swallowed, and I saw the sympathy in his eyes. "I

didn't want to come here. And I never would have if there had been any other way."

"What are you talking about?"

He righted my chair, then gestured to it. "Sophie, sit down."

I did as I was told, clasping my hands on my knees. "You need to tell me everything. This wolf was in North Beach and there were hundreds of people around."

"I really thought I could end this." He raked a hand through his hair and looked away from me, the bright earnestness in his eyes gone, strangled out by something I knew far too well: secrets.

There was a mammoth silence; the kind of silence that speaks volumes and fills a room with so many ifs and maybes and what-ifs that they buzz like a swarm of bees, until the air goes electric, the pressure smothering.

"Why did you come here? Why now? You really could have cleared yourself at any time."

Another deep, shaky breath.

"I do want to stop running. I do want to face down the werewolf hunters and get my life back. But . . ."

"But?"

"But the timing isn't exactly my own. Remember when I told you about the den in Alaska?"

I nodded.

"When I got back, everyone I cared about was dead. It was horrible. I've seen a lot of things in my life, Sophie, in both of my lives, but nothing like this. The hate, the destruction that these people faced—it was overwhelming and it was all because of me."

"No, Sampson, it wasn't," I said, shaking my head. "You didn't do it. It was—"

"I know who it was, Sophie." Sampson's eyes flashed like raw steel. "And so does Nicco."

"Nicco? Who's—"

"He was part of the brood. Like a son to me." The sadness in his voice was compelling, and I thought I saw his eyes begin to mist.

"I'm sorry. Losing him must have been awful for you."

"I didn't lose him. He survived. He was gone when they attacked. This"—Sampson rubbed the tip of his index finger over the silvery scar that crossed his eyebrow—"was what he did when he found the bodies."

"He attacked you?"

"I was the only one alive. He saw me and he reacted."

"Oh my God."

"I was able to subdue him—finally—he's a lot younger and a lot stronger than I am, but once I did, I explained what happened. And who was responsible. Nicco was enraged. He wanted revenge." Sampson shrugged almost imperceptibly. "The young ones always think revenge is best—an eye for an eye, you know?"

I nodded. "So?"

"So, Nicco and I left Alaska. We traveled together until I could figure out what to do. When I did"—he smiled, but it was humorless—"Nicco wasn't too happy about it."

"What did you decide to do?"

"Hide deeper. Disappear all over again."

"I take it that wasn't what Nicco was thinking."

Sampson shook his head. "He wanted vengeance. Pure and simple. He wanted the werewolf hunters to suffer the way our den did. He called me weak and old; he called me a coward for not going after them. And maybe Nicco's right. Maybe I am a coward. Maybe I am weak. But Sophie, I never wanted this." He held out his palms and the desperation cracked his voice. "I never wanted any of this."

I remember Sampson telling me the story of his second birth. The way he'd been bitten, how he could feel the power racing through his veins and feel his whole body shaking, changing, absorbing the legend—the curse—of the were-wolf. He hadn't sought it. He hadn't wanted it. But it had taken hold inside him, it rooted, and there was no way to kill the beast without killing the man.

"So what did Nicco do?"

Mr. Sampson swallowed slowly as if the very effort hurt. He looked at me, his eyes suddenly clouded and dark. "I think you know."

I sucked in a heavy breath and licked my lips. "Then you have to help me. We have to stop him."

Sampson shook his head. "I've been trying to. I don't—I can't find him. It's like he's gone completely off the grid."

"That's why Feng and Xian can't find him. You're number one on their list, but they act like they don't even know he exists."

"I think so. So I guess I can take some solace in the fact that he's safe from them."

Anger roared through me. "If Nicco is responsible for all of this, he shouldn't be safe. Not from anyone."

Sampson looked as though he was going to challenge me, but seeing the fire glowing in my eyes, he thought better of it. "I didn't think he ever wanted to hurt anyone."

"Yeah, well, he did."

I trudged back to my apartment in a foggy daze. There was someone else. Sampson had lied to me. Sampson had known that this person, this Nicco, was responsible all along, and had kept it a secret. This time, I couldn't keep the tears from streaming over my cheeks. Whether they were from anger, disappointment, sadness, or exhaustion, I couldn't be sure, but I walked into my own apartment, cut through the living room without saying a thing to Nina or Vlad, and crawled into my bed. I tried to brush everything off and fall asleep. I tried to convince myself that I wasn't the catalyst for all this destruction.

After what seemed like hours I gave up trying to sleep and padded into the living room, where Nina was perched in front of the television, eerily illuminated by the silver glow, telephone pressed to her ear.

"What are you doing?" I whispered.

She held up a single finger. "But do I still get the free gift with purchase with that?" she was saying. "Because I called while there were still seventeen left. It's not my fault you didn't answer the phone. Operators were supposed to be standing by."

I edged around her and dug my cell phone out of my purse, then headed back to my bedroom, speed-dialing Alex as I walked. I sat in my bed, listening to his phone ring.

"One," I whispered in the darkness. "Two . . ."

"Grace?" His voice was gravelly and I could hear the mattress shift under his weight.

"Were you asleep?"

"What else would I be doing at four a.m.?"

"Sorry. I couldn't sleep."

"Take an Ambien."

I let his grouchiness roll off me, chalking it up to sleep deprivation. "I have some information about the case."

There was a beat of silence, and when Alex spoke again all the sleep had gone out of his voice. "What kind of information?"

I crossed the room and pushed my door shut, cutting off Nina who was now demanding free shipping in the living room. "There is another wolf in town."

"Another wolf?"

"A wolf. A werewolf."

"That's not news, Lawson. We saw the wolf, remember?"

"Yeah, but—" I stopped short, biting my words. I couldn't

tell Alex that Nicco was not Sampson. I couldn't mention Sampson at all until I could prove his innocence. "Um, Dixon confirmed it. He thought we should know."

"I appreciate the heads-up, Lawson."

"Sorry to have woken you."

I sat in the darkness, phone pressed to my ear, listening to the dial tone and feeling exceptionally confused and alone.

Vlad was sitting at the dining table when I woke up the following morning. His laptop was open in front of him, casting the usual silvery glow over his pale skin. He had his chin in one hand and an American Red Cross mug in the other. The blood inside his mug had stained his lips a heady red.

"Morning," I said as I plodded past.

"Hey. I made coffee."

I stopped. I lived with two vampires and was hiding a werewolf in my Guardian's apartment; few things stunned me in this life. Vlad, doing something for someone else—especially when that someone was little ol' mortal *me*—truly stunned me.

"You did? Why?"

He kept his eyes focused on his laptop. "Auntie Nina said you had a pretty rough night." He brought his mug to his lips, his eyes flicking up at me. They went round and saucer-wide. "Whoa."

My hand flew to the short, shooting strands on my left side and I felt my face fall. "I'm assuming that expression means coffee won't make this look any better."

"Maybe if I'd made waffles, too."

"Thanks, Vlad."

He turned around in his chair as I went to the kitchen and

poured myself my usual—half coffee, half sugar—and rooted around for a suitable breakfast.

"Hey, Soph?"

I swung around, coffee/sugar in one hand, Pop-Tart held between my teeth. "Huh?"

"Nina said you got stabbed the day before yesterday."

My heart swelled. *Vlad cares about me!*

"I did, but just in the leg." I pulled up my pajama pants to show off my neon-green bandage. "So it hurt, but I'm going to be fine. Totally not a big deal." I offered him my most motherly smile. "Sorry to have worried you."

"You didn't. I was going to say you got stabbed and"—he gestured toward my head—"that. I was just wondering why you care."

"Why I care?" I pulled out a paper towel, dropped my breakfast on it, and sat down next to Vlad. "What are you talking about?"

"These murders. A couple of people you don't even know. A vampire that you never even spoke to. I mean, why do you risk"—he pointed to my shorn side—"everything—your hair, your life—for people you don't know?"

I broke a piece off my Pop-Tart and nibbled around the frosted edge while I considered Vlad's question. His eyes were still on me, black as tar, deep as night.

"I guess I just feel like I have to."

"Like you're some sort of superhero, vanquishing evil in all its forms?" Vlad smiled, the pointed edge of his incisors standing out stark white against his bloodstained lips.

I smiled back, but felt no joy. I thought of Mort—a half-breed, like me, his demonic side clearly visible as he stabbed and sliced at me through his hoarded stash. I thought of Ophelia, my own *sister*, who was murderous evil incarnate. And I thought of my father. The devil. Did I fight evil to right what was wrong in the world?

Or did I fight it because I knew, deep down, that I was part of it?

I took a long sip of my coffee and shoved half my Pop-Tart in my mouth. "Yep," I told Vlad. "The superhero thing."

Vlad grinned. "Don't tell Nina. She'll order you a costume off QVC."

The bedroom door slammed open and there was Nina, black hair in fabulous, face-framing waves, her dark eyes narrowed. "Don't tell Nina what?"

"That it's Diamonique week on QVC," Vlad murmured, going back to his game.

"You think I don't know that?" Nina marched into the living room and swiped Vlad's mug, downing the contents in one sip. "What I don't know is when I can get out of this godforsaken house. Do you know what's on daytime television? Eight hours of Dr. Phil and a parade of women trooping in a bigger parade of men who may or may not be their baby-daddies. It's excruciating."

"What happened to your novel?" I asked.

"Nobody ever makes any money writing novels. I'd have to die or cut my ear off for anyone to pay any attention to me." She fingered her earlobe. "And I can't do that. I've got too many earrings."

"And it was Van Gogh who cut off his ear. Painter. Not an author."

She shot me a death glare before flopping down on the couch, pushing out her lower lip. " I'm going to die in this apartment. A recluse."

"Neens, I've said it a million times: go out at night." My stomach gurgled, the image of last night's snarling wolf flashing before my eyes. "Or maybe try the fire escape."

She turned her bitter stare on me. "Not helping." She brightened, resting her chin in her palms. "So, what's on the crime-fighting agenda today?"

I jammed the other Pop-Tart half in my mouth, feeling the crumbs tumble over my chin and sprinkle on my chest. "Walking the dog and grocery shopping. Not part of the crime fighting but very necessary." I grinned and ChaCha yipped her approval.

I let the sun drench my shoulders as I walked while ChaCha trotted proudly in front of me. I was doing my best to smash the last twenty-four hours out of my brain, and I was doing it with a sundress that covered my Mort-inflicted wound and a big floppy hat.

I was trying to negotiate an earth-friendly bag full of groceries—just the staples: marshmallow pinwheels and cantaloupe—and ChaCha, who felt the incessant need to greet every vertical object with a raise of the leg, when my cell phone chirped, upsetting my entire careful balance.

"What, Nina?" I groaned, while pulling ChaCha after an errant cantaloupe.

"Where are you?"

"I'm on my way back from the grocery store. What's wrong?" I stopped, letting the cantaloupe lob its way down Nob Hill. "Are you okay? Is Sampson okay?"

"Yes, Sophie, I'm fine and so is your friend *Howard*," she stressed the name, "But your other friends popped in to see you."

"Friends?" Something in the pit of my stomach hardened. Sans Nina, Alex, and Will, I didn't have friends. "What friends?"

I could hear Nina move around on the other end of the phone line. "Pete and Re-Pete," she hissed.

"Pete and Re-Pete?" I asked. Then, a shot of knowing. "You don't mean Feng and Xian?"

"Oh, but I do."

I stopped cold and ChaCha danced around me in what I can only assume was a yip-yapping attempt to corral my fruit. "They're there now?"

"Yes," Nina said loudly. And then, dropping her voice to a low, barely audible hiss, "And they're weird. Get home. Now."

My heart was throbbing in my throat and my dress was soaked clean through by the time I got back to my apartment. ChaCha was panting and slowing down, but true to her traitorous terrier nature, sprung back to yip-yapping life the second I opened the front door. She bolted for Feng and Xian, who stood stalwart, collective eyes narrowed at me. I dropped my groceries and lunged for my errant dog, semi-certain that Feng would level a revolver at the thing, and pop her with a silver bullet.

"That your dog?" Feng said.

"Oh!" Xian threw her arms open, the gathered puff of her baby pink sleeves hugging her ears. Today she was dressed as a trampy Strawberry Shortcake knock-off, complete with striped tights and stacked Mary Janes. "She's so cute!" She snatched ChaCha from the floor and nuzzled the tiny pup to her face, her high-pitched pixie laugh ringing through the apartment.

"Well, this is weird," Nina said from her perch on the couch.

"Feng, Xian! So nice to see you! Why don't you sit down?" I gestured to our slightly puckered and mostly threadbare Ikea couch, and noticed that Nina had set out a spread for our guests. "Why don't you help yourself to some . . ." I paused. "Oyster crackers. And since when did we have orange Crush?"

"We didn't come to visit," Feng said, her lips held in what I was beginning to believe was a permanent snarl. "Xian sensed something."

Nina, Feng, and I all swung our heads to Xian, who had buried hers in ChaCha's belly.

"Xian?"

Xian looked up and batted her giant eyelashes. Her candy-pink lips slid up into a coy smile. "I love puppies."

"If only," Nina muttered.

"Um, not that it's not great to have you drop in this way, but, um—"

"What the hell are you two doing here?" Nina asked.

I shot her a scathing look that she batted away, mumbling, "The heat makes me crazy."

"So, what are you two doing here?"

Xian went right on scratching and cooing at ChaCha as though I hadn't spoken, but Feng pinned me with her hard brown eyes.

"The wolf."

I swallowed hard. "Beg your pardon?"

She glared up at me. "The werewolf. Are you going to give him up or are we going to have to take him from you?"

I pointed to ChaCha. "That's a terrier."

"And she was a gift," Nina said indignantly. "And now a part of the family."

"We don't want your dog," Feng said, expression unchanged. "You know what we want. *The* dog."

I crossed my arms in front of my chest and shot my own hard stare back at Feng. "Then why did you come *here*?"

Feng cocked a challenging eyebrow. "Do I really have to say it?"

"I thought werewolf hunting was in your DNA and she"—I jutted my chin toward Xian, who blew a raspberry on ChaCha's dog belly—"was some amazing tracker. Isn't coming to me for help like cheating?"

Anger covered Feng's face like a veil, her features going

even more sharp and hard than usual. "I'm not asking you for help. I was giving you an opportunity."

I barked a ridiculous laugh. "Really? Well, I appreciate the gesture, but I'd appreciate it more if you'd get the hell out of my house."

Feng pressed her lips together so hard all the color drained from them. She stood for a beat, her almond-shaped eyes challenging mine, before she hissed over her shoulder, "Come, Xian."

Xian reluctantly set ChaCha right on her feet, then stood up, straightening her puffy pink skirt and trudging behind her sister.

"Your puppy is absolutely adorable," she whispered to me.

Feng's nostrils flared and her whole body stiffened as if she had just smelled something awful. She leaned into me so her nose was just a hairbreadth from mine. "When you find what is left of your friend after I tear him apart, just remember that I came here, offering you the opportunity to turn him in and give him a respectable, single-bullet death."

I blinked, working to absorb the weight of Feng's words. "Wha—?"

"Don't worry." She grinned, pushing aside a sliver of baggy T-shirt to show me the gun at her waist. "I'll be sure to tell him that Sophie Lawson said 'game on.'"

I stood, dumbstruck, watching Xian and Feng disappear down the hall when Nina snapped the door shut. "I don't like your new friends, Soph."

I glared at her.

"Sorry!" She pulled me close to her in an ice-cold embrace. "I know how hard this must be for you. I know how much you love Sampson, and it must be killing you to think about turning him in."

I struggled out of Nina's hug and pushed her back.

"You actually think Pete Sampson is guilty? You think he's capable of something like this?"

Nina shoved a lock of dark hair over her shoulder. "I just don't understand why you insist on putting yourself in danger all the time."

I felt my jaw drop open. "I don't insist. I'm helping a *friend*."

Nina looked back at me, quiet.

I shook my head. "You *always* think the worst of people."

Nina's expression didn't change; it remained soft, with the slightest bit of yearning sympathy in the eyes. "I've been around a long time, Sophie. I've had more experience than you have." She reached out and touched her hand to mine. "You know what I love about you breathers? No matter what happens, no matter how much evil and ugliness you see every day, most of you still hang on to this unyielding belief that people are basically good."

"And once you lose your soul you lose perspective?"

Nina licked her lips. "No. You gain it."

Nina turned on her heel and was gone in an instant, her weightless body not making a sound.

I sighed, and leaned against the closed door. ChaCha came trotting over and stood on her popsicle-stick hind legs, doing her the-world-is-a-happy-place dance. I swooped her up.

"People are good," I whispered into her fuzzy muzzle. "Right?"

I waited a good twenty minutes until I was sure that Feng and Xian had left the building—and the general vicinity— before changing out of my sundress and swapping my floppy hat for a Giants cap. I stuffed my shoulder bag with my bass knife, a Taser, a granola bar, and two packages of Juicy Fruit before I paused, my hand hovering over my gun.

I wasn't chasing demons this time.

I snatched the gun and the bullets, swung the bag over my shoulder, and closed my bedroom door.

"Geez, Nina, you scared the crap out of me."

She was standing dead in front of me, silent. She blinked at me. "You're going to need this." She opened her hand, a flashlight rolling in her palm. There was a glossy black and white SOPHIE LAWSON label stuck to it.

"Why do you think I'll need a flashlight?" I gestured toward the bright sliver of light that was peeking through the blackout curtains.

"Because I know that you're going to do whatever it takes to prove that Sampson is innocent, that I'm jaded, and that you can save the world." Her cherry-red lips quirked up into a knowing smile that showed off her sharp incisors. "I count on it."

This time the lump in the back of my throat wasn't accompanied by fervent terror or a weighted bladder. "I love you, Neens," I said, pulling her into a hug.

I poked my head into the stairwell in true sleuth fashion, craning my head to see if there were any traces of Xian and Feng still lurking in my building. I found a stack of discarded Thai menus and someone's left shoe but no Du sisters, so I tapped gently on Will's door.

"Sampson?" I stage whispered into the jamb. "Sampson, are you in there?"

I pressed my ear up against the door when I got no response and listened intently for any movement inside. Nothing.

If I was going to take Sampson out of the prime suspect spot, I was going to have to do it on my own.

I hiked up my shoulder bag and headed down to the underground parking, feeling the adrenaline begin to trickle through my body. By the final flight of stairs I was doing my own Shaft walk, my own personal soundtrack blaring "Eye of The Tiger" in my head.

I was less enthusiastic when I got to my car, unable to recall any awesome crime fighters or sleuths who drove dented in Hondas with the word VAMPIRE spray-painted across the hood.

So much for staying incognito.

I pushed my key into the ignition but didn't start the car. Instead, I stared at my cell phone, feeling the gnawing need to call Alex, to make things right.

But what would I say? I couldn't come clean about Sampson just yet. And I couldn't tell him that I'd never meant to hurt him when I was with Will.

I quashed down the guilt, the need, the unease that I felt. *I need to help Sampson,* I told myself. *I can make things right with Alex when this is through.*

It was late Saturday afternoon so cars clogging the city streets were mainly the out-of-state kind that slowed in front of every big building and changed lanes repeatedly. Two carloads of people in I HEART SF sweatshirts rolled down their windows to take cell phone pictures of my car, what they undoubtedly believed was one of those wacky SF artist's statements.

I was overwhelmingly happy to turn into the police station parking lot, where my car was quite at ease amongst the other criminal junkers. Once parked, I raced into the station, doing my best to keep my eyes on my shoes and look as unassuming as possible. I hopped into the elevator, typed in my weekend code—the Underworld Detection Agency is strictly a Monday through Friday gig—and gripped a lock of my hair, twisting it furiously over my finger. It was the one nervous tic I had yet to break.

The doors slid open at the Agency and I poked me head out. "Hello?" I asked. "Anyone here?"

When no one—and nothing—answered me, I took a tentative step out, doing my best to stay in the darkness. Deserted and bathed in yellow emergency lights, the office looked like any other office waiting room, but tonight there was something eerie about it, as though every creature, every feared legend and boogeyman, were lurking in the darkened corners, jaws at the ready, just waiting to attack. The silence was overwhelming, oppressive, and the heavy beating of my heart seemed to echo in the darkness, ricocheting off every dim wall.

I steeled myself against my nervous twitter and slipped down the main hallway, taking the stairs to the absolute bowels of the building—and possibly of the earth.

There was a file room down there—it was a spot where paper files went to die and where Vlad and Kale would make out when they thought no one would notice.

I pushed open the door and was greeted with the scent of mildew and general age. The room was enormous and impossibly black; it seemed to swallow up the meager sliver of yellow light from my flashlight. I stepped into the room, hearing the ground creak under my feet, a drip in an overhead pipe. I was acutely aware of my breathing and everything in my body was on high alert as I pushed the door closed behind me. I couldn't shut it all the way, feeling as though the click of the door and the shadowed depths of the room would swallow me whole.

Though—or possibly since—the UDA has been around in various iterations since the medieval times, our filing system was woefully behind and every bit of paranormal information ever produced seemed to be housed here. Also, no one was ever able to agree on how to create a copasetic filing system with the paper documents, stone tablets, and the occasional indenture carved into human bone. Hence, our file room was part business typical, part Halloween superstore.

The file area for werewolves was near the very back of the room and blanketed by two inches of dust. I set my flashlight on a nearby box, doing my best to angle the light in a useful direction. While there were entire walls dedicated to the documents and records for vampires and a growing catalog for newly turned zombies, the werewolf corner seemed woefully miniscule—nothing but two metal filing cabinets and a lopsided stack of books that looked garage-sale ready. I wrinkled my nose and very delicately yanked on the metal drawer pull of the first cabinet. Four feet of mashed-together manila folders sprung out and I finger walked through, looking for the most recent and the vilest.

I frowned as I pushed through the year-by-year dividers, my sadness growing as the number of files shrunk. By the two thousands, I was down to a mere handful, and for the past year, there were only two files. I pulled them out and scanned the name tags—SAMPSON, PETE and HARRIS, SERGIO—and put them aside, poking into some of the previous files.

I pulled one open at random, my fingers and eyes going over the glossy black-and-white photograph that was stapled to the side. It was of a handsome-looking man dressed in early fifties garb. He was clean cut with an easy smile and ears that stuck out over the top of his white sweater. The goofy smile and big ears made his age impossible to pinpoint, but I supposed he was young, my age at the oldest. I yanked at the picture stapled behind this one and sucked in a sharp breath at the beady eyes of the wolf that peered back at me. Because of my job and my familiarity with the way Agency files were kept, I knew that the wolf in the photo was the man in the previous photo, even though there was nothing left of the goofy-looking guy. The ears that were big and off centered in the first picture were sharply angled and alert in the second. The easy smile and soft eyes of the boy were lost in the jagged canine teeth, the menacing gaze of the beast. I flipped through a few more pages of the file, noting that this client had signed his Agency agreement faithfully on the same day each year—which meant that he was willing to abide by our rules and allow himself to be safely contained at night, would not hunt human flesh, and would not be a threat to any person or demon he ran across. And then I saw his death certificate.

Wolf, someone had written in under *Manifestation at death.* And, under that, *Slain.* There was a newspaper article clipped to the back of the death certificate. It was yellowed and written in grainy Chinese. I didn't need to translate to know that the article credited the Du family with this wolf's death.

I had read my way through the first half of the files in the drawer when I heard it. My entire body went on high alert and I cocked my head, holding my breath, listening. A rustle. The flutter of papers. The deep murmur of voices being kept low. I slipped my flashlight into my pocket and the records room dipped into immediate and overwhelming darkness—all except for a yellow sliver of light that poured through the two-inch crack of the open door. Someone had turned on the hallway lights.

I crab crawled toward the light, keeping one hand on my flashlight, the other pressed against my chest, doing my best to muffle the sound of my clanging heart. I heard footsteps then, and I stopped in mid-step, my whole body stooped, aching, protesting the awkward stance.

". . . could become quite a problem," I heard.

"Not something I'm entirely worried about," someone responded.

Dixon. I wet my lips. *But who is he talking to?*

I took a hesitant step, certain that my every motion would ring out like china crashing. Footsteps. Conversation moving closer. Then, silence.

I held my breath and clamped my eyes shut. Sweat beaded at the back of my neck and I knew the scent beckoned like a lighthouse strobe. There were a thousand scents in a deserted office—daily clients, cleaning solution, Post-It notes, toner . . . the metallic scent of human blood, heavy with adrenaline, pulsing through veins.

Dixon knew I was there.

The tiny sliver of yellow light grew as he pushed open the door to the records room. I slipped behind a file cabinet and crouched low, pressing my palms to my cheeks, trying my best to absorb the heat that I knew was wafting from me in waves. I did my best to slow my heartbeat, to make my breathing shallow, barely discernible. I knew from living with Nina that the attempt could be futile, so when Dixon stepped into the room I prepared myself to face him, every inch of my skin tightening, the excuses and explanations spasming through my head. I watched from my crouched spot as his dark eyes swept over the file cabinets and boxes in the room while one pale hand rested on the light switch.

I licked my lips, then bit down hard on the bottom one as Dixon's light flashed toward my imperfect hiding spot. I glanced at the stack of files I had shoved aside with my foot. They were low and scattered, decently hidden by the darkness and boxes.

Dixon didn't turn on the light.

He didn't come after me.

He simply stepped out of the room, clicking the door shut behind him.

I stayed hidden in the records room until my thighs screamed and I was certain that Dixon and whomever he was with had left the building. Then I jammed the files into my shoulder bag, clicked on my flashlight, and tried to straighten up. My legs and nerves betrayed me and my new, heavier shoulder bag threw me off. I felt myself falling, vaulting backward. I saw the boxes and the file cabinets going up as I went down, and before I could think better of it, my arms shot out, my hands grabbing for anything that would halt my fall.

I heard my flashlight crash to the ground as my fingers wrapped around the metal bars of a shelving unit and I tried to shift my weight *à la* Angelina Jolie in one of her kick-ass roles—the darkness and my surge of adrenaline must have covered up the fact that most of the things I do are *à la* Paula Deen—as in requiring butter—and are slightly less shiftable in the weight area. My failed kick-ass move just sped up my fall, and I slapped down hard on the industrial-grade carpet, pulling the entire bookshelf on top of me. Books and papers sailed off the shelves and flopped on me, around me, everywhere; I let out inelegant "oafs!" each time a hardcover nabbed me in the chest.

I was nearly covered by a mountain of books when a sheaf of papers fluttered down like graceful, gossamer winged doves, landing in a heap about my face. One of the loose pages blanketed my eyes and nose and though I couldn't make out the words at that distance, I was able to see the writing.

I felt my eyes grow.

I recognized the writing—the curl on the tails of the Y's, the curlicued question mark.

I knew it because it was mine.

"What the—?" I struggled to sit up, rolling my flashlight toward me and gathering up the papers. My mouth dropped open with each new sheet. All of them were mine, all of them oddly inane. A high school report card. A letter to my grandmother from sleepaway camp. A series of photocopied Post-It notes, personal bills, an e-mail I had written to Nina.

I pushed the bookshelf back up and shoved the books back into it, finding a stack of stapled papers mashed between *So You Think Your Partner's a Vampire* and an embarrassingly over-read copy of *Twilight*. I thumbed through the papers and recognized those as well. Not mine.

My father's.

Chapter Eleven

I shoved everything into my shoulder bag, did a quick once-over to make sure the room looked the same, and took off like a shot. The angst that I'd felt when I'd first come down the elevator was back, only this time it was squarely focused not on getting found out by Dixon, but on wondering what it was that Dixon was trying to find out about me. The pages were beyond any personnel file, and the stack that belonged to my father were photocopies from a book that Alex had stolen from the uber-evil Ophelia and I had only seen once: my father's journal.

How the hell had they found their way to the Underworld Detection Agency?

My cell phone chirped as I waited for the elevator, the jaunty tune so oddly terrifying that I clamped my legs shut and willed myself not to pee.

"Sampson?"

"Hey, Sophie, are you okay? Nina told me about Feng and Xian."

"I'm okay," I said slowly. "Where were you though? I thought you were hiding out."

Sampson paused for a beat. "I was following up on some leads. I thought it would be safe."

"And did you find anything out?"

"I found out that Alex and the rest of the police force are certain that a werewolf is responsible for these killings."

"So is Dixon," I mumbled.

Sampson let out a measured sigh.

"Do they know about Nicco?"

I wasn't sure if it was the lingering adrenaline, a book-induced head wound, or something more intuitive, but I thought I sensed a bit of defeat—or admittance—in Sampson's voice.

"No. Sampson, we need to find Nicco. We need to find him and stop him and let everyone know that he's responsible. Not you."

There was a slow pause and Sampson breathed in. Then out. "I can't do that. I can't give him up."

Because he doesn't exist? The thought flew through my head before I had the chance to grab it, to savor it. *No,* I thought. *I saw the other wolf. . . .* But it had been dark, and I didn't know where Sampson was that night, and moreover, I wasn't completely certain of what Sampson looked like in wolf form.

"Sophie?" Sampson asked.

The conversation felt wrong. The slight, nagging accusation was bitter and bothersome. *Sampson,* I reminded myself, *Sampson wouldn't do this.*

But the evidence was overwhelming.

"Find him," I said before clicking off the phone.

I had made my decision the moment the heavy steel doors slid open on the cheerily lit police station vestibule.

I was chicken.

I *could* ask Sampson straight out. I couldn't let him know that I suspected him, that my reservation and mistrust was growing. But I could confront him with the most damning evidence.

And I knew exactly where to find it.

I hitched up my file-filled shoulder bag and cut through the main police station, walking with purpose. I nodded to a few meandering file clerks and complimented the dispatcher on her Farrah hair while I blasted out my I-totally-belong-here vibe.

And then I slipped down the hall toward Alex's office.

The door was closed, but unlocked. I slipped in, shutting it behind me, and clicked on the lights, stifling a very un-I-totally-belong-here scream when the buzzing overhead lights illuminated the white board where eight-by-ten photos of both crime scenes were pinned up. Each time I saw the destruction, the spattered blood, the torturous fear that these women must have felt, my stomach dropped lower and I found it hard to breathe. I did my best to avoid the photos and went to work picking through Alex's things until I found what I needed: the evidence collection kit for the Pacific Heights murder.

I tossed aside Ziploc bags of blood-spattered clothing, a soaked swatch of carpet and sofa pillow, and finally landed on the videotapes. There were six of them, identical, unlabeled.

"What are you doing in here?"

I stood with a start. I had already shoved two of the tapes in my bag and I clutched the others to my chest, my heart hammering against the flimsy black plastic. I licked my lips and pressed my lips into the warmest, kindliest smile in my repertoire.

"Officer Romero! What are you doing here?"

Romero didn't smile back at me. He simply crossed his arms in front of his chest and quirked a questioning eyebrow.

"Me? Oh, I was, um . . ." I glanced down at the tapes in my arms. ". . . picking up something for Alex."

Romero took a step in. "Alex asked you to come down here and gather state's evidence?"

I pumped my head. "Yeah, he meant to do it himself but"—I twirled an index finger a half-inch from my head—"doy! He forgot when he left today."

Romero shifted his weight, the edge of his lips turning up a quarter-inch. "Why would Alex need the tapes from the crime scene?"

"From the crime scene? Oh!" I barked a completely overzealous laugh. "Now I get it. You said 'state's evidence.' Yeah, these aren't that." I hugged the videotapes. "They're personal."

"Personal?"

"Uh-huh."

"What kind of personal videotapes does Alex keep in his office?" Romero took a step into the office, moving closer to me, his hand reaching for the tapes.

I spun, gripping the tapes harder. "They're sex tapes."

Both of Romero's eyebrows shot up, were lost in his dark hair. "You and Alex made . . ." He paused, counted. ". . . four sex tapes?"

Heat shot through me, and I was certain I had gone from my normal day-glow pale to lobster red in three short seconds. "Yes."

"Alex?" Romero's eyes raked over me. "And you?"

I was humiliated, but oddly indignant. "I could make a sex tape. I'm saucy."

Romero paused for a beat, and I nearly thought I was home free. Then he pulled his cuffs from his belt, held out his hand, and said, "Sophie, I need you to bring me the tapes."

I shook my head. "No." My voice had more power than

I'd intended and I was surprised. I licked my lips. "Can't you just trust me on this? Or, give me twenty-four hours. That's it. I'll have them back to you in twenty-four hours. Please?"

"You know I can't do that. Look, I'll compromise. If you drop the tapes and leave right now, nothing has to happen." He shrugged. "I won't even tell Alex."

"How is that a compromise?"

He shook the cuffs. "Otherwise I'm going to have to cuff you. I'm going to have to file a report." Romero took a step toward me and I sidestepped, letting Alex's big oak desk block me.

"I'm not a criminal, Romero. You know that."

Romero looked at me reluctantly. "Don't make this harder than it has to be, please."

"I'm not. I told you: twenty-four hours. No one has to know."

Romero's eyes went toward the white-corked ceiling as if the answer were pinned up there. "Fine."

I felt the relief crash over me in a tight wave. Deep down I had always been certain Romero was on my side, but he was a good cop and a new cop—deciding to help a newish friend couldn't have been easy for him.

"Thank you."

I dumped the remaining tapes in my shoulder bag and it yanked down on my shoulder. I really had no intention of bringing the videotapes back and that little fact nagged at me as I stepped toward the boyish-faced Romero. "I really appreciate this."

He just nodded.

I reached up to turn the lights out, hearing the cuffs snap on me in the darkness.

"What the—?" I thrust my arm out into the buzzing fluorescent lights of the hallway and jiggled my wrist, hearing the clink, clink, clink of the steel cuff against itself. "I thought we had an understanding."

Romero said nothing, just gave the cuffs a gentle pull until we were back in Alex's office. He flicked on the lights and unceremoniously clicked the loose cuff to Alex's chair.

"I get it," I said between gritted teeth. "I've seen this before. You're a bad cop."

Romero had my shoulder bag now and was pulling out the videotapes one by one. "A good cop captures criminals. That's what I was doing."

"I am not a criminal! I'm a—a good girl!"

"You told me you were saucy enough to make a sex tape. And you stole state's evidence."

"No," I said, yanking the chair along with me. "I *attempted* to steal state's evidence. If I didn't actually leave the building with it, it can't be called stealing and thus, not a crime." I wrangled against the chair. "Now get this off me."

Romero shot me an exasperated look before dropping the tapes and coming around the desk. He put a hand on each of my shoulders and guided me down into a sitting position in the chair.

"I'm going to do you a favor. I'm not going to file a police report and I'm not going to put you in a holding cell."

I crossed my legs and used my free arm to rest my chin in my hand. "No big. I've been in a holding cell before."

"What happened to you being a good girl?"

I demonstrated my range of motion.

"I'll keep you in here while I call Alex and he can escort you out. That way no one has to know." Romero smiled, a dumb kindness in his eyes. Had I not been handcuffed to refurbished office furniture, I might have thought his smile was warm and his eyes, intelligent.

Not now.

"Wait." My head snapped up. "Did you say you were going to call Alex?"

"Yeah, he'll come down and get you, won't he?"

I opened my mouth and then shut it again, suddenly mute. I shrugged my shoulders. Romero turned to leave, but turned back to me in the doorway. He pointed a single finger at me. "Now don't you go anywhere," he said with a smile.

I rolled my eyes. "You really think this chair won't fit through that door? You're an idiot," I huffed under my breath.

I waited for Romero to disappear completely before I grabbed my shoulder bag—tapes repacked inside—and began my seated scoot toward the doorway. I lined myself up and crept closer, attempting to clear the entire door frame like some sort of bizarre Operation game.

It hadn't occurred to me what I would do once I got out of the office. Not a lot of things raised eyebrows in this city—I'd once carried a six-foot-tall piñata on the bus and no one had batted an eye—but a woman handcuffed to a metal office chair and scoot walking down the block just might.

Whatever.

I squared myself up and launched myself through the door with a massive amount of F-you glee. Or at least I would have, had an arm of the chair not caught the door frame. Instead my chair stopped and I slid right off the leather seat, sailing until the slack went out of the cuff and I was slammed to the ground, my arm at an odd angle above my head.

"Epic fail," I muttered.

I pressed myself back into the chair and tried to ignore the new throb in my shoulder. On a determined sigh, I repositioned myself and slid toward the door frame once again, this time gently. I did my best to keep an eye on the arms of the chair, as they narrowly rubbed against the door frame. I could feel the edges of my lips turning up. I could feel that F-you smile.

I was sure that somewhere in our house, Vlad had stashed some kind of medieval weaponry that would free me forever.

But I didn't count on being stuck. The arms of my chair squeaked against the door frame.

I gripped them and wriggled, trying to loosen it up. I pressed my feet to the floor and clenched every muscle in my body as my sneakers tried to gain traction while I pushed. I was searching through my shoulder bag, looking for lotion to slather myself and my chair with when I heard Alex clear his throat.

His T-shirt was disheveled, his jeans wrinkled, and his dark curls had the unequivocal look of bedhead. He didn't look happy to see me.

"I'm stuck," I said, looking up with my best puppy-dog eyes in an attempt to win him over.

Alex blinked at me. Then, without saying a word, he lifted one foot and used it to spread my legs. Images of hot prison sex or Fifty Shades of handcuff sex flashed in my mind. My heart began to pound and the throbbing of my shoulder had moved to the pit of my stomach, threatening to drop lower.

"Alex." My voice came out a sultry whisper as I stared at his foot nestled a half-inch from my crotch.

Again, Alex didn't answer. He simply flexed his foot and gave me a solid shove back into his office. The back of my chair gently thumped against his back wall and I stared while Alex shut his door, then angled himself on the edge of his desk.

"You have exactly two minutes to tell me what the hell you were thinking and one to tell me why I should take the cuffs off." There was no humor in his voice, no trace of the easy half smile that usually graced his lips. His eyes were a dark, slate grey. The accusation in them pinned me to my seat, regardless of the cuffs.

"I wasn't going to steal them." The words were out of my mouth before I had a chance to review them, to edit them. I was lying and we both knew it.

Alex let out an exhausted sigh and pinched the bridge of his nose. "Do you want to tell me what the hell is going on with you lately?"

"What is that supposed to mean?"

"You're hot, you're cold, you're on edge and"—Alex licked his bottom lip—"you're a liar."

"A liar?" I was truly—and inappropriately—stunned. "What the hell are you talking about?"

It was rare that I had seen the kind of anger that flashed across Alex's face. His lips were pressed together, his teeth gritted. He crossed his office and yanked open a top drawer, throwing a sheaf of papers on the desk.

"What's that?"

"You don't recognize it?"

I got a little closer and poked at the stack with a single finger. "No, I really don't." I looked him in the eye. "Honestly. I've never seen any of those papers before."

"They're from Mort's place."

"What?"

"I told you, I wasn't about to get pinned in his pile of crap and have nothing to show for it. I left them in my car after the emergency room. They slipped under the console; I didn't go through them until tonight."

"The expired Enfamil coupons."

Alex wasn't fazed. "I got lucky. A few of them were of use."

"Okay," I said with a shrug. "But I don't know what any

of these are. I don't recognize any of them. Should I? Are they mine or something?"

He immediately looked away from me and grabbed a few sheets, shoving them under my nose. "I thought these were kind of interesting."

I looked down at the gridded sheets. "What are they?"

"I'm assuming pages from Mort's calendar. See? Doctor appointment, shit delivery."

I reluctantly took the pages. "Okay . . ."

Alex looked at me, the rage radiating off him in waves.

"I don't see what you want me to—" I stopped, my chest suddenly tightening.

A few of the boxes were marred with Mort's messy scribbles, but only one box had writing on it that was legible and in color: a big red circle and the word *Sampson*. The calendar date was the exact day that Sampson appeared at my front door. "Oh my God."

"How come I had to find out from Hoarder Mort about Sampson, Lawson?"

"I—I—" The words were truly caught in my throat.

"I asked you point blank and you lied to my face. Multiple times. You've held up our investigation. Now another person is dead."

I looked up, narrowing my eyes. "Oh, no. Don't you put that on me. I didn't kill anyone. I was trying to *protect* someone."

"I wasn't accusing you. If you feel guilty for something, that's all you. I'm just trying to clarify what our relationship was."

"Was?"

"Are we just friends? Colleagues? Were you using me to let your pals at the UDA get one over on us?"

"Friends?" I said to my lap. "We're more than friends."

Alex tucked a finger under my chin and tilted my head up to face him. "Are we?"

He let the question hang between us and I could feel the tension in the air.

Alex pulled a tiny silver key from his pocket and held it up for me to see. Silently, he pushed it into the keyhole and the cuffs clicked open.

"I'm not using you, Alex. I wasn't trying to get one over on you."

"But you didn't feel like you could trust me enough to tell me about Sampson. Even when I asked."

I swallowed hard, the tears rimming my eyes mirrored in his hard ones. "Sampson asked me not to tell anyone."

"I asked you to tell me. We could have saved a lot of time."

"Time?" I straightened. "You mean because Sampson is responsible for all these murders."

Alex shrugged, noncommittal. "Look at the calendar, Lawson. The dates match up."

"But it's not true! And I have proof it's not. There's another werewolf. The one we saw in North Beach!"

"You know that for a fact?"

"You saw him, Alex."

"I saw a werewolf, Lawson. I have no idea if it was or wasn't Sampson."

"It wasn't," I said, my voice sounding small.

Alex's eyebrows rose. "Did he tell you that?"

I nodded, suddenly slightly less certain.

"Was it also Sampson who told you to go see Mort?"

I didn't answer and Alex hung his head. "I'm just looking at the evidence, Lawson."

"That's why I didn't tell you!" I stood up so fast my chair went sputtering back, bouncing off the wall a second time. "Because you'd rush to judgment."

Alex shook his head. "We'd treat Sampson like any other person of interest."

"Don't you mean 'suspect'? And you would not treat Sampson like anyone else because you know what he is."

"So do you."

I jabbed myself in the chest. "I also know *who* he is. He's being framed, Alex, I'm almost sure of it. Or another wolf is tailing him and he's the one responsible. It's not Sampson. It's not."

"Where is he, Lawson?"

"It doesn't matter," I said, teeth gritted. "I'm not turning him in."

Ice settled over Alex's face. "If you don't tell me, I can charge you with obstruction of justice."

I hardened my expression, too. "Do it."

Challenge.

Alex slid his hand in mine and pulled me near him. I felt the cool metal of the cuff as it slid onto my wrist once more, locking with a terminal-sounding click.

Accepted.

I kept my eyes fix on Alex's. The muscle at his jawline jumped. "You can still get out of this, Lawson."

He was right.

As he went for the second cuff I snatched my shoulder bag and bolted out of his office. I speed-walked through the work floor, keeping my cuffed arm inside my bag. I took a chance, thinking Alex wouldn't follow me.

I couldn't understand why, but by the time I busted out into the clear, ink-black night, hot tears were rolling down my cheeks.

I cried all the way back to my apartment, hiccuping and sniffling until I parked my car. I pulled down the lighted visor and blinked at myself in the reflection: what remained of my hair was a wild, fuzzy, humid mess; red-rimmed eyes; bright red cheeks crisscrossed by mascara-edged tears. I slapped the visor closed, smacking myself in the face with my one dangling cuff.

"This better be worth it," I mumbled, rubbing the reddening spot on my forehead.

I had my key in the door when it snapped open. Nina stood there, framed by brilliant yellow light. Her hair was in a greasy topknot and her eyes were hooded and sunken until she saw me.

"The hair was one thing, but . . ."

I pushed past her and dropped my shoulder bag on the couch, giving ChaCha a cursory snuggle. She licked my chin and then must have been nipped by the cuffs because she jumped out of my arms and went running down the hall.

"So much for an ever-faithful companion."

"Sophie, you're wearing a handcuff. Stabbed, bad hair, hand-cuff." Nina counted on her fingers. "I know I said the heat makes people do crazy things but, sweetie, I think you may be taking it to extremes."

Vlad's pale head popped up from the other end of the coffee table. He was still shirtless and his hair was still a disheveled mess, possibly rivaling mine. His eyebrows went up and he nodded his head, impressed. "Cuffs. Cool. What'd you break out of?"

I felt myself go sheepish. "Police station."

Nina raised an interested brow. "You and Alex getting into the harder stuff? I like. . . ."

Vlad gagged. "Old people sex. Oh my God!"

"Look at me! Do I look like this was part of a BDSM sexcapade? Officer Romero *arrested* me!"

"What'd you do?" Vlad asked.

"Nothing!"

I got a double shot of vampiric "I don't believe you" faces.

"I may have stolen some evidence. But it was nothing to cuff me over."

"So how did you get out? Sampson bake a file into a chocolate cake?"

I looked down sadly at my cuffed hand. "No. Alex came in and let me go."

"Seems like shoddy cop work if he left the cuff on."

"Long story. I have to go across the hall."

"Fine." Nina flopped down on a chair I had never seen before. I don't know how I would have missed it, as it was an enormous leather monstrosity with buttons all over the arms and our living room is the size of a bread box. "It's not like we're going anywhere." She nudged Vlad with her toe, flipped a switch, and started to vibrate.

I pointed. "When did we get that?"

"Today," Nina said, closing her eyes as a low hum filled the room.

"Just like that?"

"UPS brought it. I ordered it from QVC. It's Heaven." She cracked open an eye. "Or at least as close to Heaven as I'll ever get."

"Wha—" I was going to say something; I figured I should since our house had gone from Ikea chic to the showroom at the crap factory. Open boxes were scattered everywhere, strips of bubble wrap popping out. We had a massage chair and a hibachi, and our tasteful, minimalist tchotchkes were being strangled by an army of fat cherubs, pig-tailed milkmaids, and crystal(ish) animals with numbered certificates of authenticity.

But my shoulder ached, my scissor stab wound stung and
my eyes went to the videotapes stashed in my shoulder bag.

I could only tackle one crisis at a time.

My stomach and my heart fluttered as I stood outside
Will's door for what seemed like the umpteenth time. I
licked my lips and then rapped on his door, feeling the sweat
break out along my upper lip.

There was no answer.

I tried again, then paused, waited. Finally, I rolled up on
my tiptoes and felt along the top of the door frame. I felt no
pleasure when my fingers fumbled across the spare key that
even Will didn't know was still there.

There was nothing in Will's apartment that would signify
that Sampson was even there.

And tonight, it seemed, he wasn't.

Will's array of lawn furniture and video games was still
artfully arranged. The teal chintz curtains left over from the
last owner looked ridiculous and out of place in the half-
empty apartment, but oddly seemed to match the cross-
stitched *Home Sweet Home* pillow that warmed up the
plastic chaise longue.

The kitchen counters were bare and a single glass glit-
tered in the drying rack. Nothing to signify that Sampson
had stayed here at all—nothing to signify that anyone
had. I swallowed down a lump of fear and headed for the
bedroom, hoping that there would be something there—
something to prove to me that my trust wasn't misguided,
that Sampson was spending his evenings reading *Tues-
days with Morrie* rather than taking out his werewolf
urges on innocent San Franciscans.

"Come on, Sampson," I muttered to myself as I poked around the pristine room. "Prove me right."

"Soph?"

I spun and Sampson was behind me, dark hair dripping wet, bare chest exposed. He had a towel wrapped around his waist and I was all at once hit with the heavy scent of Will's soap—plus a heap of guilt, angst, and inappropriate naked-man attraction.

"Oh, Mr. Sampson." I looked at him, felt the hot blush wash my cheeks, and then looked at the floor. "Sorry to catch you . . . naked."

"You okay?"

"Can you put some pants on?"

I waited in the living room, doing my best to make myself comfortable in Will's lawn chair—it was one of those old-fashioned numbers that squeezed every bit of your thigh and butt fat through its plastic slats. I was relieved when Sampson walked out, fully dressed, fairly certain that five minutes more of squirming in that stupid chair and I would be cursed with permanent slat butt.

"Sorry about that," Sampson said, taking the chair across from me. "I didn't expect you."

"I knocked," I said in a feeble attempt to explain myself and the obvious. "You didn't answer so I let myself in."

Mr. Sampson's smile was easy, trusting—like a knife in my heart. "I'm sure you had good reason. What's going on?"

Good reason. Yes, I wanted to say. *My good reason is that suddenly, after all you've done for me, I don't trust you. I think you're lying.*

I cleared my throat, then looked at my hands in my lap. "Mr. Sampson—" I hadn't planned out a speech in my head. I hadn't planned anything out, but it didn't seem to matter anyway, because all the words I wanted to say were stuck behind my teeth.

Sampson chuckled and his eyes crinkled. He leaned back and crossed one leg over the other, and if he wasn't in a lawn chair, he wasn't a werewolf, and I wasn't about to accuse him of murder, he'd look like a very Norman Rockwell father, about to bite the end of a fat cigar.

I licked my lips and pushed the words out. "Do you know Tia Shively?"

"The woman who was murdered in Pacific Heights?"

He said it. He knew.

I felt all the color drain from my face. I felt my whole body congeal into a quivering mass of terror and despair. Pete Sampson. *My* Pete Sampson. A murderer.

"I read about her in the paper this morning." He plucked the folded paper from the floor and offered it to me. I recoiled as if he were offering me a snake.

"I need to show you something."

"What is it?"

I fished the tapes from my shoulder bag and approached Will's mammoth wall of electronics, feeding the tape into the dusty VCR.

"We're watching a movie?"

I didn't answer. Instead, I took the remote, aimed it toward the television and pushed play.

"Sophie, I—oh my God. Where did you get this?"

"It's security footage from the Pacific Heights crime scene." And then, slowly, "It is—was—Tia Shively."

I chewed on the inside of my cheek while I watched Sampson watching the videotape. He flinched when the "wolf" crashed through the door and his eyes widened when Tia Shively was snatched up. But other than two tiny reactions, there was nothing else; no indication that he was—or wasn't—familiar with what was going on. I couldn't watch the screen myself, but I could tell by the silvery flashes reflected back what was going on.

I pressed PAUSE.

"Did you know her?" I whispered. "Was that you—changed—in the videotape?"

Everything in the world stopped. The entire city held its breath, waiting, waiting for the answer, the explosion, the ultimate firefight. Had I cracked the case, or accused a man who had been nothing but good to me of a heinous crime?

I watched Sampson's Adam's apple bob as he swallowed slowly. He was silent, and I couldn't tell if he was considering his answer or my question. And I didn't know which one was worse.

"Sophie?"

I felt the heat of tears forming behind my eyes. I wasn't supposed to cry anymore, wasn't supposed to bop around like a teenage girl, but I couldn't help myself and the tears overwhelmed me, fell down my cheeks in a steady stream. I threw myself to my knees and grabbed Sampson's hands.

"Oh, please, please tell me you didn't. And if you did, I can help you. I can get you away from here. I know you didn't mean it. I know you couldn't control yourself. You're a *werewolf,* after all, and it's not your fault—"

I choked on my own words. I choked on the image of the woman—Tia Shively—of the terror, the confusion that was in her eyes for that split second before they went cold—before the life slipped out of her body. My chest felt tight and I struggled to breathe.

"I'll get you out of here," I whispered again.

A tremor started in Mr. Sampson's hands and he pulled them out of mine and then stood up quickly, brushing by me. He raked a hand through his still-wet hair, and when he

turned and looked at me his eyes were dark—clouded—
shielded with something I couldn't recognize. *Hate? Anger?*

When Mr. Sampson spoke, his voice was gravelly. "You
really think I could do something like that?"

I pushed myself up, the tears still falling, silently now. "I
know that you wouldn't have meant—"

"Really?" He whirled and faced me full-on and I could
see now that the look in his eyes was anger, disappointment,
tinged with disbelief. "You think that I could tear an innocent person to shreds like that? *Three* innocent people?"

The tension in the room ratcheted up the temperature
by ten degrees, and I was rooted to the carpet, my mind
ticking—do I run, do I protest, do I stay?

I chanced a glance up at Sampson and when I did his
eyes locked mine. What I saw ran through me so deeply it
cut to the bone.

His eyes were glassy.

Red rimmed.

He pressed his lips together, but I saw the twitch, the
power that it took for him to keep his cool. "I can't believe
you, of all people, would think that about me. I'm not a
monster, Sophie. I thought you knew that." His voice was
low, soft—but it hurt.

"I'm—"

"No. If you think—I don't want to make you wonder. If
I'm an animal in your eyes, you should chain me up."

"No!" I swung my head, feeling my hair flop against
my cheeks. "I didn't mean—I don't think—it's just that . . ."
I let my words trail. I didn't know what I thought or what
I meant.

"You should do it." Sampson's voice was even. "If you
can't trust me, you need to lock me up." He offered me his
wrists. "Right?"

I wanted to tell him no. I wanted to tell him of course not, that I trusted him implicitly, but something ate at me.

Sampson shook his hands. "If it'll make all your doubt go away, go ahead." He looked sad, but tried a smile. "I don't blame you if you do. I understand. Sometimes I can't believe what I am either—and I know what people like me are capable of."

Chapter Twelve

My heart slammed so hard against my ribs I was certain there would be a bruise. I licked my lips. My saliva was sour and the blood that coursed through my head was unbearably hot, loud.

I wanted to be the hero. I wanted to know I was doing the right thing, but this was all there was: Sampson, standing in front of me, arms outstretched. Three women dead. I felt my soul going ice cold, felt my body close in on itself.

"Okay." The voice that came out of my mouth, that punctured the silence, didn't sound like my own. "Just for tonight." I said it as a kind of buffer, but Sampson just nodded.

"Where?" he said without looking up at me.

I drew in a slow breath, hoping the surge of oxygen would give me strength. "Down in the basement. The chains that—that used to be in your office are down there."

"You've been waiting for this."

"No." I felt my eyes flash. "I've been waiting for you. Not like this—it was just—I wanted to keep something of yours. After you left . . ."

Sampson gave a humorless bark of laughter. "Ironic." He

jutted his chin toward my one hanging cuff. "Is that to cuff me for the walk downstairs?"

I shook my head silently and opened Will's door.

We walked the four flights down to the basement in chilly silence, stopping on the landing just in front of the battered metal door. It was rusted, graffitied, and slightly dented, its shabby appearance betraying its strength.

"Well?" Sampson asked.

I had come this far, but was suddenly feeling unable to take the next step. My feet were rooted to the cement underneath us. Then I felt Sampson's hand on my shoulder.

"It's okay, Sophie."

I let the warmth of his hand travel through me. I stepped forward and sunk my key into the lock. Sampson brushed by me and walked into the basement. "Anywhere in particular you'd like to lock me up?" His tone was jocular, but the glint in his eye was hard anger.

I pointed to a heavy steel pipe and Sampson went and stood there, legs akimbo, arms crossed in front of his chest. I dug the old chains from the cardboard file box labeled LAWSON/LASHAY, #351 and quietly brought them to Sampson, opening the shackles and closing them around his ankles, looping the rest around the pipe. Each click was like a dour stab to my heart, and my hands shook as he held out his final free wrist. I tried to avoid his eyes, but something drew me upward. The derisive look of just a few minutes ago was gone, replaced by a defeated one that made his usually clear, sharp eyes look pale and milky. His gaze was a final silent plea.

I clicked the last cuff on and turned my back.

I thought that final click was going to be the worst, but my angst only grew as I neared the door. I wanted to tell Sampson I was sorry, that I truly did believe in his innocence, but the words were lodged in my throat.

"I'll be back when the sun comes up," I mumbled to the floor.

I heard the clink of his chains and his long sigh before I pulled the heavy steel door closed and flicked the lock.

The single light in the apartment vestibule was buzzing, its garish yellow light flickering, casting weird shadows over the tiled entryway. I shivered and hugged my elbows, giving one last glance over my shoulder toward the hallway I had just come from. Guilt was a solid black weight deep in my stomach, weighing on my shoulders. I should have felt some sort of relief, or a surge of energy that pushed me to clear Sampson's name, but everything about me was raw. I was exhausted, spent, confused. I wanted to sleep. I wanted to lie down and bury myself into my mattress, pull the covers up over my head and wake up in another life.

I was drowning in miserable self-pity when I heard the glass exploding. Jagged pieces of marble-sized glass came rocketing toward me and something huge—and heavy—clocked me right between the shoulder blades. I lurched forward, steeling myself against the back wall and trying to categorize what had happened when I felt someone grab me by my hair, yanking my head back until I thought my spine would snap. I heard individual strands of my hair breaking, felt them popping from my scalp like an army of tiny pinpricks. I tried to breathe, tried to take stock of my situation, but all I could do was see that stupid bare lightbulb wagging above my head.

"What the hell—" I widened my stance and pulled back against my attacker, ignoring the searing ache of my scalp.

I scratched at the wall and tried to regain my footing, but my assailant was strong and had the upper hand. There was another tug and I crashed against the warm body. An arm slung around my neck, tightening against my throat and I felt moist breath, hot lips on my ear.

"I should have killed you when I had the goddamn chance."

I knew that voice: Feng. But it was bitterer, more tinged with poison than I had ever heard it.

"Feng?" My voice quavered. I was almost too astonished to be afraid. I wriggled. "Let go of me!"

Feng's pit bull grip loosened a hair, but before I could negotiate a step, she turned me and shoved me hard up against the wall, her hair-pulling hand now at my throat. My shoulders ached, grating against the tile.

Feng's eyes were liquid fire, her mouth turned into the most hateful grimace I had ever seen. "I'm going to rip your head off, Pippi."

It wasn't until I pulled my head back against the wall—doing my best to disappear into it—that I noticed the blood. It was on her hands, on her clothes in spatters and streaks, and now burning into my skin. And it was fresh.

"Whose blood is that?"

Flame in her eyes. "You know."

I felt Feng's fingers tightening around my throat, her thumb starting to dig into my windpipe. "No, I don't," I choked.

Feng didn't loosen her grip, but she seemed genuinely stunned, momentarily confused. I clamped my eyes shut and channeled Buffy, doing the best—and probably the only—scissor kick of my life.

I felt Feng's hard belly against the sole of my shoe. I felt her ribs licking against it, cracking, and I heard her breathless groan. Her fingers slipped from my throat, her nails raking across my skin as she stumbled backward, crumbling in on herself.

In one stunned millisecond, she regained her composure and lunged for me. I thought of Vlad's combat tutelage and angled my body, leaning into Feng with an elbow across her sternum.

It barely stopped her and she laid her entire body weight into me, both of us flying backward, landing with a painful thud on the tiled floor. Her fisted hand clocked me in the jaw and I felt my mouth instantly fill with thick, velvety blood. I clawed at her face, unable to get any swing back for a punch, and tried to remember something defensively effective.

I started to squirm.

We rolled and jockeyed for position, thighs clamping, fingers fisted then clawed. "Why the hell are you doing this?" I managed to huff.

Feng tightened the strongest thigh muscles I would ever know and rolled herself on top of me. Her cheeks were flushed with effort, and tiny white bubbles were forming at the corners of her mouth. "You killed her. You fucking killed her. You killed them all, you fucking bitch!"

"I didn't kill anyone," I howled. "I don't know what the hell you're talking about."

Feng's fist connected with a bone-crunching strike. My whole skeleton started to throb, my eyes started to water. "Your fucking wolf! Your fucking wolf tore my sister apart. He ripped the shit out of everyone at the restaurant. Fucking animal!"

Feng's militant struggle slowed insignificantly and a single tear cut through the blood on her cheek. By the time it drizzled to her chin, her eyes were flaming again, her jaw set.

"He didn't," I breathed. "He didn't. He's been chained up."

I knew that Sampson had been chained up for just a few minutes. My hands were still cold from clamping the metal around his wrists. I knew that werewolves possessed a lot of nonhuman abilities, but super speed wasn't one of them. He *could* have been responsible. There would have been time—plenty of time.

But I kept trying to convince myself otherwise.

But Feng's maniacal expression remained unchanged. She reached behind her back and my breath caught when I saw the knife.

Mother-of-pearl handle. Glistening, razor-sharp blade. No match for a bass knife, had I even had it. My arms instinctively mashed against the wall, the one handcuff still locked around my wrist banging against the ancient tiles, a battle cry for the end of my life. I curled into myself as the blade came down, nicking the shoulder of my flimsy tank top, making an easy, clean slice through my skin. I used Feng's technique and threw my entire body toward her, palms shoving at her chest, her face, whatever I could make contact with. The second she began to topple, I rolled.

"That . . . wasn't . . . him," I panted as I crawled toward the door.

The vestibule door swung open, raking across my knuckles, and I looked up.

"Alex?"

I saw him lean down, felt his arms dig under my shoulders and pull me to standing. He slammed the door hard before Feng could get to us and she pounded frantically, her hand shooting out the hole that she had made with the rock and going after the lock. I stared down at her flailing hand as it was shredded by the broken glass. Velvety blue-red blood bubbled up from her knuckles and trickled over her fingers. All I could think of when I saw her ruined hand was raw meat.

But Alex wasn't distracted. He grabbed her hand and yanked her hard enough to smack against the door, then clamped a cuff on her, fixing the other one to the opposite door handle. Feng struggled.

"That's only going to give us a few minutes."

"But Nina and Vlad—"

"Can have a fresh meal," Alex finished. He grabbed my arm and shoved me into his car, flipping the lights to "spastic" and pushing the gas to the floor once he got in.

"You came to save me?" I asked, brushing away a trickle of blood as it ran over my eyelid.

The muscle in Alex's jaw jumped and I saw his fists tighten on the steering wheel until his knuckles went white. "I was just coming by to tell you about the massacre at the Du place. You weren't answering your phone, which usually means you're in a pizza coma or a life-and-death situation." There was no humor in his voice and his expression remained hard, fixed.

"Are we going there? To the Du place, I mean."

Alex didn't answer me, but when he squealed the car on a right-hand turn, I knew.

I was chewing on my thumbnail the whole ride through the city, thinking about Feng chained at the front door—though knowing she had probably already broken out—and Mr. Sampson chained in the basement. I prayed that the rage and fury that were etched on Feng's face would mean that the second she had freed herself, she would come after us, rather than deciding to go snoop around my building.

"What are you so nervous about?" Alex asked, eyes still focused on the windshield.

"I just got attacked by a crazed werewolf hunter, Alex, and we're apparently headed to the scene of a bloodbath."

"So you're not concerned that the person responsible for said bloodbath is now running loose in the city?"

"Sampson didn't do this, Alex."

"And why should I believe that, Lawson? Suddenly you're telling me the truth?"

I pressed my eyes shut. "Please understand, Alex."

My plea hung on the uncomfortable silence in the car until we slowed at the mouth of Grant's Gate. "I know Sampson had nothing to do with this because he's chained up." I watched Alex's profile, his hard jaw and set, determined eyes. "I chained him up in the basement."

"When?"

"Just before—just before—" I sucked in a shaky breath. "Just before Feng got me."

"So, Sampson was chained up for what, the last hour? Maybe two?"

I nodded, overtly lying, but still trying to convince myself.

Sampson wouldn't do this, I reasoned. *He promised me . . .*

And he spent a whole year pretending he was dead. The realization hit me like a fist to the gut and I felt my lips part, felt the words pressing against my teeth.

But Alex was ignoring me, cell phone pressed to his ear.

I studied the explosion of police officers unrolling crime scene tape and trying to hold back curious onlookers. Squad cars were parked up on sidewalks, giving us a still-narrow street to maneuver down once the office on patrol waved us through.

"We got to the crime scene just over an hour ago."

I raised my eyebrows, feeling a sense of relief for the first time in weeks. "See?"

"I see that this massacre happened at least ten to twelve hours ago. Were you with Pete Sampson ten to twelve hours ago?"

I opened my mouth, my brain racking through the last several hours of my life: prowling through the UDA, prowling through Alex's office, running out of the police station wearing fifty percent of a pair of handcuffs . . . knocking on Will's door, Pete Sampson coming out of the shower.

Just a shower, I told myself.

"You don't seem to be jumping in with a defense," Alex noted.

"Why are you so hell-bent on crucifying Sampson?" I roared.

"Why are you so hell-bent on keeping your head in the sand?"

I had never seen that kind of rage from Alex before. It should have frightened me, but it only made me throw my shoulders back, narrowing my eyes in a hard challenge. I had to believe in Sampson—*I just had to.*

"Get out," Alex spat. "I want you to see something."

The sea of police officers parted as Alex flashed his badge and I hurried behind him. It was still unnaturally hot for San Francisco, but now there was something else hanging in the air—something that clawed at my chest and made it hard to breathe. I looked around cautiously, wondering if anyone else felt it, too. No one seemed to; all eyes were saucer-wide and glued to the taped-off door of the Du delicatessen, Chinese America Food Wi-Fi Bathroom for Customers Only.

The silence should have alerted me. At no time in my entire adult life had I known my city to be as eerily quiet as it was now. No one spoke. No birds chirped. No cars backfired, no church bells chimed, no planes whooshed overhead. There was nothing but an impenetrable, unholy silence.

Alex paused in front of a table set up along the sidewalk, blocking the entrance to the delicatessen. A police pop-up tent shaded it, and the table was heaped with all manner of crime scene preservation material. The man behind the table nodded solemnly when Alex showed him his badge, and pushed forward to stacks of hospital-looking garb.

"Put these on." Alex didn't look at me when he spoke to me, and I picked up my own stack of disposable crime scene cover-ups.

"These, too?" I asked, referring to the tie-back paper hats left on the table.

Alex nodded, the tension stiffening his body palatable.

"Yeah, it's that bad," the guy behind the table filled in, handing me a hat. I saw his eyes go to my cuffed wrist. "It's couture," I said hastily.

I tucked my mass of red curls up and nodded to Alex. "I'm ready."

He grabbed my elbow and steered me to the door. I sucked in a preparatory breath and steeled myself, stepping into the dim delicatessen.

"Holy shit." It was out of my mouth before I had a chance to think about it, and had I thought about it, I would have screamed. The stark white tiles and Formica tables that I had grown accustomed to in the store were still there, only now they were stained a heinous red. The little anime dolls wielding swords and arrows and daggers were drowning in sticky pools of it, and all around me bodies were scattered in various positions of desperate escape: a small woman's fingers still curled, clawing the floor as she'd tried to pull herself toward the door; a young boy I recognized from a recent visit was only partially visible as he must have attempted to sprint out the back, and Xian, her bubble-gum-pink baby-doll dress in angry shreds, each tear to the fabric puckered and blood soaked, as if her attacker had had claws—claws that recently drew enormous amounts of human blood.

She had been lain on the counter that she usually stood

behind, her body dumped—or positioned—in such a way as to leave no doubt that the woman no longer lived. Her head was cocked at an impossible angle, her arms stripped down to sinew and bone. Her legs were folded daintily, carefully underneath her but on closer inspection they were just that: placed carefully underneath her as they were no longer attached.

There was no warning to the bile that seared my throat and I turned to run, but slid on a pool of half-congealed blood. I flailed, but it was useless and the blood-soaked floor rose up to meet me, my cheek smacking sticky linoleum, my palms sliding against pooled fluids, and when I opened my eyes, the eyes that gazed into mine were the clouded, sightless eyes of the dead.

I felt my stomach seize again, but Alex grabbed me, snatched me up from the ground and held me against him. "No," I screamed, kicking out and pounding his chest. "Why did you do this to me? Why? I didn't do this! I'm not responsible for this! I fucking hate you! You insensitive piece of shit!" The tears were coursing down my cheeks, commingling with snot and blood that was not my own. My whole body hiccupped and my heart slammed against my ribs. I didn't want Alex to touch me; I wanted to scratch out my eyes, to beg God to allow me to unsee everything that I just had. I wanted to be somewhere else, be someone else—even one of the sightless beings ruined on the floor. My whole world was crashing down around me and suddenly everything I knew was false.

"Calm down, Lawson, calm down." Alex pressed me nearer to him each time I struggled. I could feel his rhythmic heartbeat thumping against my shoulder and suddenly, I was struggling to breathe.

"Why did you do this to me?" I croaked.

Alex scooped me up in his arms now. "I'm sorry," he

whispered into my hair. He carried me across the deli and when he pushed me out through the glass door, the clean smell of the outdoors couldn't penetrate the heavy stench of death, the metallic smell of blood and ruin that hung all around me, that clung to my nostrils.

Alex set me down gently but still held me close. He looked down at me, his cobalt eyes searing. "I needed you to see what we're dealing with. What Sampson has done."

The tremor started deep in my soul. I felt it there, then felt it break into my body, seeping into every muscle, every pore. It ached when it went into my bones and twisted every muscle. Soon my teeth were chattering, and the bitter, bile-laced saliva pooled in my mouth. I wretched.

I wiped the back of my hand across my lips and spat.

"I'm sorry, Lawson. I shouldn't have brought you here like that. I was just out of ideas. I—you wouldn't listen to reason."

"So that"—I jutted my chin—"is your idea of reason?" I held Alex's eyes until he looked away.

"You had to see."

"I've seen it." I turned, shrugging out of my crime-scene garb. "But I still don't see what Sampson has to do with it."

Alex grabbed my shoulder and spun me to face him. "Really, Lawson? Look at *that*." He pointed to the trail of blood that came from the deli. "Whoever did that was not human."

"And that's how I know it wasn't Sampson," I said.

Alex's nostrils flared and he let out a deep disbelieving sigh. "Then give me someone else."

"Nicco," I said slowly.

Alex pressed his fingers against the bridge of his nose, his whole body visibly slumping. "I'm sorry, Lawson. I am really, really sorry. I know this can't be easy for you and I should have been more sensitive. What do you know about this Nicco guy?"

I started to shake my head. "Not much, but Sampson says he's out for revenge. And it would make sense, especially if it—if the trail ends here."

"Remember when you told me that werewolves are very few and far between in this city?"

"Well yeah, because of Feng and Xian."

"Did you find any active werewolves in the UDA files?"

I swallowed hard. "No, but—"

"Sampson sent you to Mort's. It took us an hour to get there and he tried to kill you. Do you think that wasn't a coincidence? Do you think someone who really cared would put you in that kind of danger?"

Tears stung at the corner of my eyes and I blinked slowly, feeling the first tear fall.

"But the files," I said. "Sampson told me to get the files." I dug in my shoulder bag, a tiny of flicker of hope all but doused. I found the piece of paper that Sampson had given me. "See?" I held it up. "He told me to look up . . . werewolves."

Suddenly, my skin was too tight. Everything hurt and my head started to pound. The paper trembled in my fingertips. Alex took it from me and turned it around.

"What is this?"

"It's a page from a UDA file," I answered.

"Were you missing a page?"

I shook my head. "No. I was missing a file."

Alex looked down at the page and shook his head sadly. "Nicco Torres. Werewolf. Deceased, Anchorage, Alaska."

"No. He's good," I said, biting off my words, rage burning tears behind my eyes.

"The good don't always stay good," he said, his eyes clearly avoiding mine.

"Sampson told me Nicco was the only other one to survive." I sighed, dumbfounded, a tremble going clear through to my soul. "It wasn't Nicco who vowed revenge. It was Sampson."

Alex licked his lips. "What do we do now?"

I closed my eyes and saw the destruction burned into my eyelids. Saw the torn faces, the ruined bodies, the rivulets of blood. I saw the single tear cutting through the blood on Feng's face, but I couldn't pull up an image of Sampson.

"We bring him in," I said, my voice cracking.

Alex leaned into his car and pulled out his radio, thumb at the ready. "Where is he? I'll have a car there in two minutes."

I put my hand on Alex's arm. "No. Not the police."

"Lawson, you saw what he did."

I swallowed as the tears poured down my face in a steady flow. "So you know what he's capable of. Jail won't hold him. You're just going to lose your officers. He'll go with someone he trusts."

A cool breeze started to kick up then, and for the first time in days the fog blew in in thick gray blankets. I shivered and held my hands over my bare arms. "He trusts me."

"Lawson, are you sure?"

I wasn't, but I nodded anyway. "I need to call Dixon. I need to tell him." My breath hitched on a sob that wracked my entire body.

This couldn't be happening.

"I need to tell him to have a team ready for—for him." I couldn't say Sampson's name anymore. The person—the monster—responsible for all this carnage, for lying to me, wasn't the Pete Sampson that I had known.

That Pete Sampson was dead.

I pulled out my cell phone and dialed the Underworld

Detection Agency, each ring of the phone slicing deeper into my heart.

I was doing this.

I was leading Pete Sampson to his death.

Dixon's voice mail clicked on and I cleared my throat. "Dixon, this is Sophie Lawson. I—I have the werewolf who killed Octavia. It's—it's Pete Sampson. He's here in San Francisco." It physically hurt to say the words. "I'll bring him to you."

I hung up my phone, numbness spreading through my whole body. Alex slid his arm around my waist and nuzzled me to him, but I had never felt more alone, more separate, than I did at that moment.

"Is Sampson secure where you have him?" Alex asked.

"Yeah."

"Then let's get your shoulder fixed up first."

The ambulance was right behind us, and the same paramedic who tended to me at the Sutro Point crime scene went to work cleaning the wound on my shoulder. I recognized him from the Pacific Heights scene , where he'd been handing out paper cups of water to the pup cops after they hurled in the bushes.

"We have to stop meeting like this," I said, feeling the strange need to insert some bland normalcy in the day. "Torres, right?"

"You've got a good memory," he said without looking up.

"Guess so."

The paramedic just smiled at me, and silently brushed mercurochrome over the wound. I winced and was about to open my mouth, but was stopped by a bone-rattling scream.

"Medic! Medic!" I heard as people started to mobilize toward the scream.

"It's Feng," Alex said.

"We should get out of here."

"No," Alex said, with a hand on my good shoulder. "She'll be taken care of."

I craned my neck to see two more paramedics restraining a flailing, screaming Feng. I should have been frightened, but my heart just lurched. Feng wasn't looking for me. Her eyes were focused on the open door of the family restaurant, her cheeks blanketed in a wave of fresh tears, her whole body vibrating under her wails.

"Nick!" One of the paramedics holding Feng said, "We need you."

My paramedic—Nick, I now knew—looked over his shoulder and then glanced back at me. "You're almost done, but I've got to tend to her."

"Don't worry," Alex said. "I can slap a Band-Aid on her."

Nick nodded and snatched a fresh pair of gloves out of his medical box before running toward the group restraining Feng.

"I feel really bad for her," Alex said, watching Nick join the group. Squad cars were starting to leave now and the restaurant was blocked off so most of the curious onlookers had ambled away. Those who remained looked up at the darkening sky with worry-etched faces and moved toward storefronts and awnings.

My cell phone chirped and I nudged it toward Alex as I held one arm up, using the other to poke around Nick's abandoned medical box for a Band-Aid.

Alex answered the phone and mouthed, *Dixon*.

My chest tightened, my heart starting to thunder again. "I—I can't," I mumbled. Even after all that had happened, I couldn't be the one to say the words. I couldn't be the one to tell Dixon, couldn't be the one responsible for Dixon giving the kill command.

Alex nodded and stepped back, walking behind a squad car for privacy. I sucked in a shaky breath and tried to locate a Band-Aid.

When my hand ran across something furry, I retracted it, disgusted.

"Ugh!"

What kind of injury requires something fuzzy in a first aid kit?

I pushed my hand into the medical box again, my fingertips touching the soft material.

"Fur?"

Shorn pieces, pressed to the back of the kit.

Long, brown—the kind that had been collected at the Sutro Point crime scene. I pulled out the piece and unfurled it, horrified, my eyes scanning the blood, the words.

"Oh my God."

The paramedic was the contract holder? It didn't seem right.

I shut the plastic case, my saliva going sour. Carved into the nameplate was the name *N. Torres.* And everything suddenly became clear.

"Nicco Torres," I whispered.

Chapter Thirteen

I launched myself off the tailgate of the ambulance, cradling my wounded arm in the other. "Alex, Alex!"

He wasn't far, but the distance between us seemed expansive as I ran in molasses-slow motion. The heat in the air was unnatural, stifling; the entire city seemed to have gone from buzzing and vibrating to stalled, silent, and breathless in that one small second.

"You can't! Don't!" I screamed.

Alex stepped out from behind the squad car and I watched in horror as he hung up the phone. I opened my mouth to explain, but my words were lost when the sky thundered and a flash of lightning cracked. All the emotion on Alex's face was lit for a single split second before going dark again, before rain started to fall in heavy, hot sheets.

I turned and Alex's finger's caught my wrist, his touch burning my skin. His eyes were pained. "Sophie," he said, the words almost lost on the hiss of the rain.

I stiffened. It was so rare that he called me by my first name and suddenly it felt too intimate, too close.

"I know you don't want it to be true."

The rain sizzled and steamed as it hit the pavement. I

turned my face to the sky, feeling the rainwater on my forehead, on my cheeks.

"It's not."

Chaos ensued as the rain pounded the ground. I grabbed Alex. "The paramedic," I screamed, pointing. "The paramedic is Nicco."

A raindrop zipped down Alex's furrowed brow. "The dead werewolf?"

I spun, looking through the rain and the mass of people ducking and reveling in the fresh rain. "That's Nicco!"

But he wasn't there.

"Come on," I said, grabbing Alex's arm. "We have to go!"

The rain thundered against the hood of Alex's SUV as we tore out of Chinatown, police lights flashing.

"So, Nicco is alive?" Alex asked.

I nodded, gripping the dashboard. "He's the paramedic. His name was on the first aid kit. It was on his name badge." I slapped my forehead. "How could I not have noticed that? He was at every crime scene."

Alex glanced at me sideways. "I'm sorry, Lawson, but that doesn't really prove anything."

I unfurled the piece of hide and it shook in my trembling fingers. "This does." Suddenly anger raged through me and I gripped the hide. "If I destroy it, it's over."

Alex's hand clasped over mine—hard.

"What are you doing?" I shrieked, trying to shake him off me.

"What are *you* doing?" he roared back. "You can't destroy the contract. Not yet."

"Why not? It's what we've been trying to do the whole time."

"Not we," Alex said, taking a corner hard. "You."

I watched the rain splash over the windshield and the

tremble started again. But this time it wasn't out of fear—it was rage.

"Nicco and Sampson could be working together."

I gaped at Alex. "Or Nicco could be working against Sampson. Sampson said—"

"Sampson has screwed you up at every turn. He sent you to Mort's. He fed you the fake UDA files."

I swallowed, my mouth going dry. "He didn't feed me the files. Dixon did."

"God, it's like people can't drive when it rains."

"And the contract was in his medical box, but so were a bunch of loose strands of fur." I shook the contract, growing more and more disgusted. "This fur."

"So?" Alex said, eyes focused on the road ahead. "Shedding?"

"He was framing Sampson."

"What?"

"Nicco was framing Sampson! God, Alex, I left Sampson chained up in my basement. Nicco heard us talking about it. We have to get there before he does."

"Or before Dixon does."

Alex took another hard corner and I dialed Nina, commanding her to answer the phone: nothing. I tried Vlad and prayed to Count Chocula's ghost that he would answer. Nothing.

A car cut in front of us, causing every other car on the block to honk and stop short. "Let me out. I can get there faster from here."

"Lawson—"

"Don't!" I exploded.

Alex closed his mouth and slapped open the glove box, his pistol nestled there. "Go," he said. "I'll be there as soon as I can."

I snatched the gun from the glove box and went tearing

into the street. My lungs were burning by the time I reached my apartment building, my scissored leg screaming in protest. I snatched open the door, screaming and huffing.

"Sampson! Sampson! Can you hear me?"

There was no answer and I slid across the slick vestibule floor, clawing for the door to the stairwell.

"Oh, God."

The door was busted open, whatever hit it powerful enough to crush the steel and nearly fold the door in on itself. "Sampson?" I yelled.

I choked on a sob. The chains I had used to bind Sampson were destroyed, broken as if the heavy chain was nothing but string. Blood and hunks of fur littered the floor, and a steady stream of rainwater trickled in from the broken window near the ceiling.

"Lawson, come on!" Alex called from upstairs. "They got into a car in front of me. Let's go!"

I shoved Alex's gun into my waistband and ran outside, throwing myself into the car. "We're never going to find them," I said miserably.

"Yeah we are," Alex said, putting his hand on my knee. "If there's one thing you can count on on a rainy day, it's traffic. Sampson got in that car." He gestured with his chin to a Suburban with blacked-out windows just a few car lengths ahead of us.

"Oh my God—someone answered my prayers."

"Romero did. I called it in and he set up a roadblock."

"Remind me to thank him when this is over."

"Better not. He's still pissed that you took off with his cuffs."

I held up my arm, the open cuff flopping around. "I'm beginning to like the look. It's dangerous." I clawed the dashboard. "Look! They're moving."

The car that held Sampson edged its way through traffic,

side-swiping cars until two wheels were on the sidewalk. Then the driver must have pushed the gas pedal to the floor, because the car took off like a shot, disappearing around another apartment building.

"We have to stop them!"

Alex shrugged, slammed the gas down, and took the same route the Suburban did.

"No wonder our cities are going bankrupt," I said.

"Do you want to catch this guy or not?"

I grabbed the sides of my seat and held on for dear life. "Punch it, Chewy!"

Alex zipped around the city like a pro while I concentrated on keeping my lunch down and figuring out what to do next.

"Are you putting on makeup?" Alex asked incredulously when I began rifling through my purse.

"Do me a favor and hold the car steady for a half-sec, will ya?"

Alex groaned until I found what I was looking for: Feng's silver bullet. I slipped it into the chamber and glanced at Alex in profile. His eyes flashed over me.

"You sure?" he asked.

"I have to be."

"Lawson!" I heard Alex's voice at the same time I heard the screech of tires. The seat belt tightened around me, and I gasped, the gun sliding from my hands and slamming into the dashboard. I threw my arms up as my body lurched forward, slowing the trajectory of my skull and stopping just short of going through the windshield. Smoke rose from the car's crumbled hood and the back of the Suburban was wedged securely into the front of Alex's SUV. Alex was pinned behind his air bag, dust swirling in the air.

"Alex!" I tried to paw away the air bag. "Are you okay?"

Alex's head lolled toward me, his eyes still a brilliant

blue even as a rivulet of blood worked its way down his eyebrow. "I'll be fine," he whispered. "Go get Sampson."

I opened my mouth, torn, but Alex pushed me with a shaking hand. "Go," he said.

I grabbed the gun and ran toward the Suburban.

It was empty.

I stumbled backward, dumbfounded. Our chase had taken us through the city; our crash had left us in an industrial area at the edge of town. The battered ground was littered with shipping containers and rusted-out warehouses. "Sampson?" I yelled.

The buildings tossed my call back to me in an endless echo. I took a careful step, trying to make out any sound over the rush of rain.

Then I saw the flash.

The pop came next.

I took off running, my thighs pumping, vaulting me forward as the rain soaked my T-shirt, weighed down my jeans.

"Dixon!"

He spun, then grabbed my arm. "He's in here."

I followed Dixon into one of the buildings. He went to loosen his grip on me, but something happened, and my back was pressed up against his front, one arm clamped around my waist, the other around my throat.

"Dixon?"

"You're such a good friend, Sophie. But not a very good employee."

"What?"

I had barely blinked by the time Dixon wound my legs with duct tape and did the same with my arms. "You shouldn't go through company files, Ms. Lawson."

He gave me a hard shove and I flopped into a folding chair, struggling against the tape. My eyes swept the empty warehouse for a weapon. There was heap of broken pallets, a length of twine, and then I felt like I had been punched in the chest. "Mr. Sampson?"

He was chained to the wall across from me, face forward on the cement, blood pooling at the edge of his mouth. There was a bullet hole just above his waist. It was fresh, but the blood was already starting to congeal.

"Is he dead?"

"No! Not yet."

"Wh—where's Nicco?"

Dixon cocked an eyebrow. "Out getting me a snack."

As if on cue, the warehouse door shoved open and Nicco—still dressed in his paramedic garb—pushed in. He was gripping Alex in front of him, the cut above his eye now bleeding profusely. A piece of duct tape was covering Alex's mouth and his shoulder slumped forward at an impossible angle. His hands were wound with a length of tape.

"Oh, God. Alex, are you okay?"

"Go ahead, tell her, Alex," Dixon said, a wicked smile crossing his face. "Are you doing okay?"

Alex nodded slightly and I felt my heart speed up again.

"I don't understand," I said breathlessly. "I don't understand what's going on."

Dixon blinked, his eyes going wide and sympathetic. "Don't you? Your friend Sampson came back to San Francisco to get revenge on those pesky Du sisters. If he could just find out who it was who hired them, he could at least buy some time."

I licked my lips. "But it was you who hired them. It was you, wasn't it?"

Dixon nodded bashfully as if I had just accused him of a terrific performance.

"Guilty. But you know how werewolves are—volatile. You've seen the files."

"You doctored them," I said, finally understanding. "You wanted me to find them."

"And you didn't surprise me." Dixon produced a flashlight from his pocket, twirling it in his hands until the white sticker was visible, the name 'Sophie Lawson' printed on it. "Such a good girl."

He smiled, baring his teeth. His smile dropped. "Don't worry, Ms. Lawson. Even if you weren't so predictable—it wouldn't matter. People were dying because wolfy boy couldn't keep his jaws to himself."

"But Nicco's a wolf." My eyes cut to the accused. "You know that, right? Nicco was the one who wanted revenge."

"And why he couldn't kill Sampson in Alaska like I asked remains to be heard, doesn't it, Nicco?" Dixon's eyes flicked over Nicco, who stood tall, still with a heavy grip on Alex.

"You were working together?"

Nicco cocked an eyebrow, flashed a disgusting grin. "You were fun to play with, sweetie. Sorry about the dog park though."

Dixon rolled his eyes. "Hard to get these beasts to keep their hands to themselves."

Nicco let out a low growl, his eyes cutting to Dixon, who ignored him.

"Anyway"—Dixon grinned, his ultra-sharp fangs pressed against his bottom lip—"Nicco had something I wanted. I had something he wanted. So we made a deal."

"What could you want with him?" I asked Nicco.

"I wanted him." He jutted his chin toward Sampson. "Dead."

"What? How could you?"

"How could I want the man who domesticated our entire race dead? That's your question?"

I turned away from Nicco, from the raw hatred in his cold eyes. "And what did you want, Dixon?"

He shrugged. "I wanted Sampson dead, too. I wanted the UDA to be mine—to be run properly. Maybe a little mayhem in the interim. By the way, Ms. Lawson, there's really no need for you to come in on Monday. As of today, the Underworld Detection Agency runs on an all-vampire staff."

"But Sampson was gone. He wasn't a threat to you."

Dixon crossed over to Sampson. I could see his chest rise and fall gently, but other than that, there was no sign of life. "Well, he isn't a threat right now. Either way, it was a win-win for Nicco and I to do business together. He gets to chew a few breathers—no offense, Ms. Lawson—and plant a few hairs, and I get to watch the show."

"Octavia?" I asked.

Dixon shrugged. "A little funsie for me to throw you off the trail. She got on my nerves, anyway." He stuck a thumbnail between two teeth. "And she stuck in my teeth."

"So now what? You're just going to kill Mr. Sampson?"

Dixon cocked his head, his smile still huge. "No, Ms. Lawson." He took his precious time dipping into his pocket, then displayed a silver bullet between forefinger and thumb. "You are."

Dixon leaned forward and snatched me off the ground, standing me upright.

I shook my head. "You're crazy. I would never hurt Sampson. And I would never, *ever* do anything for you."

He looked genuinely hurt. "It's not like you won't get anything for it." Dixon's eyes were on me. They were hard and laser focused, and seemed to roll into me, to pool around me and suck me in. But magic doesn't affect me—not ever.

Only right now, I was drawn. I couldn't look away.

"What are you going to give me?" My voice was breathy and low, and I almost didn't recognize it as my own.

Dixon was so close now that I shivered at the icy chill that wafted from his body. He leaned into me, his lips brushing over my cheek, leaving a frozen trail.

"Eternal life," he whispered.

My heart throbbed, and the blood rushing through my veins sounded unnaturally loud. Dixon licked his lips, his eyes still on me, but hooded now, relaxed. He walked slowly around me, as if examining every inch of me.

"No." It was a weak croak, but the effort of pushing the tiny word out past my teeth was immense.

"Aw," he whispered, "don't be afraid."

I tried to shake my head, imagined myself spitting in his face. But I was rooted, and his words were so very melodic.

I felt Dixon's fingertips as they walked up my spine, the cold and pain biting to the bone as he gripped. "You know, Ms. Lawson," he said, his breath a throaty whisper, "I'm really going to miss having you around the office." Another sly grin. "Until you come back, of course."

He slid a long, slender hand from my forehead to the back of my head, smoothing my hair and putting gentle pressure at the base of my neck. I felt his grip as he slowly gathered my hair and pulled on it. I arched backward and he grinned, his eyes traveling up the length of my exposed throat. I felt my own heart race, could hear my own blood pulsing; my muscles tensed and my insides dropped to liquid as Dixon's eyes latched on to the vein throbbing in my neck.

"Don't," I managed.

Dixon smoothed an errant hair from the tight ponytail he was making, then used his fingertip to frame my face. The gesture was so intimate that it dirtied me down to my soul, and I knew that if I survived this, no amount of washing would ever make me feel clean again.

"You really are very lovely," he said, his dark eyes staring into mine.

I blinked up and saw the ink in them; saw a mesmerizing starburst of gold and copper. It spun and moved and riveted me.

The glamours . . .

My eyelids started to feel unusually heavy. The heat that was searing me was now a gentle warmth, and the blood that was pulsing was now a low, melodic hum . . . like a lullaby.

I watched a red triangle of Dixon's tongue poke out and moisten his lips. "I'm glad we get to have this final meal together." He twisted my hair and pulled me lower, then used his other hand to smooth the skin on my neck. The cool of his hand was nice and I licked my own lips, suddenly overcome with thirst.

"I need a drink."

It was my voice, but my lips didn't move. I didn't make them move, didn't feel them move. But I was still talking.

"A drink, please."

"We have to finish off your friends," he whispered.

I don't remember moving, but I saw the walls of the warehouse bob as I nodded my head. Dixon took a single fingernail and sliced at the duct tape that hugged my left arm. My arm swung free, the handcuff flopping against my thigh.

"Thirsty," I said again, trying desperately to wet my lips.

Dixon cocked an eyebrow, then opened his coat and pulled out a gun. From somewhere deep down, I know I should have been terrified. Something—someone—in my gut was urging me to fight, but I was so tired, and so thirsty. I just stared while Dixon popped that single silver bullet into the gun. "Hold it now," he said, pressing it into my hand.

I felt my hand, alien to me, tightening around the grip of the gun.

"Drink."

Dixon smiled and his tongue curled around one angled fang. It was razor sharp. He moved his tongue, pressing the edge of his fang against the bottom of his lip. I heard the pop of the skin. I heard the rush of the blood as it bubbled toward the fresh wound.

I needed it.

"Thirsty," I mumbled again.

More smiling. More swirling of the coppers and golds in his eyes. I remembered that my grandmother had a clock that would swirl like that. . . .

I heard his fang slide out from his flesh. Could smell the musty, metallic scent of his blood. It filled me. I wanted it.

Dixon pulled me closer as the blood bubbled on his lower lip. He brought his head down, his lips coming to meet mine. I wanted to help, to bring myself to him, but I couldn't; everything was heavy. I tried anyway and my arm flopped loose, listless, like a rag doll's. It swung behind me, the metal bracelet cuff clanking against the metal folding chair.

The sound was startling.

It stopped the warm rush of blood, wrenched open my heavy eyelids.

"What the hell are you doing?" I cringed as Dixon's blood dropped on my chin. I squirmed to get him to loosen his grip but he dug in, pressing his lips toward mine.

"Look at me," he growled.

"No!"

"Look at me!" The rumble came from his chest; it was so low, I felt it rush through my entire body.

The glamours . . .

I backhanded Dixon as hard as I could, the muzzle of the gun digging into his belly. It didn't hurt him, but he was startled enough to jostle backward and I was fast enough to yank the gun, steady it, and aim it directly at Alex.

Dixon grinned at me. "You're going to send your fallen angel back to hell?" He blinked, his eyes spinning once again. I felt my lips snake into a smile, then I cut my eyes to Alex, Dixon's gun leveled right between his eyes.

"Duck!" I screamed, squeezing the trigger.

Alex and Nicco peeled down, one a half second after the other. Alex tumbled forward, his head smacking hard against the concrete. Nicco was the late one, and Feng's silver bullet pierced cleanly through his heart. His lifeless body crumbled over Alex's.

I stifled a nervous sob while Dixon looked surprised and vaguely pleased. I tossed the empty gun, hearing it slide across the cement, then dove for the pallets, yanking off a strip of wood.

"I didn't know you had any kind of fight in you, Ms. Lawson," Dixon said, licking his lips excitedly. "I love it when breathers fight. Gets their blood pumping. Tastes delicious. Nice shot, too. Guess that target practice is really paying off."

I gripped the piece of wood and steadied myself. "I thought you weren't going to kill me."

"Be nice," he said slyly, "and the offer is back on the table. Immortality."

He rushed me and I used his momentum against him, planting a foot and sweeping his knees with the pallet piece. I grunted and swung with as much strength and anger and hate as I could muster. I saw the blank, gaping faces of the women on the trail, of Tia Shively, of the ruined patrons of the delicatessen.

"No one is truly immortal, Dixon."

I felt the wood piece make contact. It didn't slice the way Vlad's sword would have, but Dixon's feet went out from under him and I heard the thud of his full body weight smacking against the cement floor. Had he any air in his lungs, it would have oafed out.

"Get back here!"

I used the wood piece as Vlad had taught me and swatted at Dixon's arms, blocking his reach as he rolled onto his knees and lunged for me. He was fast, but I was smart and for the first time in my life, confident. I lurched backward and tossed the folding chair at him, hearing the clatter of the metal as it tumbled over him.

"I'm going to kill you slowly," Dixon roared.

I looked over my shoulder and Dixon was a hairbreadth away, his fingertips reaching out, just grazing my throat.

He pitched backward when Alex's arms circled his neck, his hands still bound by the duct tape. Dixon's fingers wrapped around Alex's wrists and I heard the sickening sound of bones cracking, of Alex howling. I scanned the warehouse, my eyes going over Nicco's crumpled form and Sampson, chained, unmoving on the warehouse floor.

I felt the heft of the wooden stake in my hand and Dixon's eyes flashed with obvious amusement.

His eyes narrowed as the stake came at him, my grip sure.

"Go to hell, Dixon."

Chapter Fourteen

I was sitting in the San Francisco Memorial emergency room, flanked by Nina and Vlad, both of them staring on incredulously as I finished telling them the events of the night.

"That's unbelievable." Nina said, shaking her head. Her hair was pulled back in a wet ponytail that was soaking through her T-shirt. Once the heat wave had broken and the sky opened up, the city streets became engorged with people celebrating the rain. They threw their arms up and stomped through puddles; to the casual observer it may have looked like a rain dance.

To the rest of us, it was a vampire-heavy group, celebrating the end of sunshine internment.

"So Sampson is okay," Nina asked.

"Yeah, thanks to that werewolf super-speed healing thing. But Nicco . . ."

"Through the heart? I'm impressed, Soph. The heart is a much smaller target than the ass."

"Um, thank you?" I bit my bottom lip. "But hey, I'm really sorry about—"

"You're sorry you had to kill our boss?"

I stiffened and Vlad bristled; the woman sitting next to Nina perked up, her eyes growing wide.

"Don't worry," Nina whispered to her. "He was evil. I knew it the whole time."

"Alex Grace?" A white-coated doctor stepped into the waiting room and I sprang up.

"I'm here for Alex."

The doctor looked me up and down. I had cleaned up as much as I could, but there wasn't much I could do to hide the bruises and the half of my skull that was as bald as a cantaloupe.

"Rough night?" the doctor asked.

I cocked my head. "Actually, it was okay. Through here?"

I pulled back the curtain and poked my head in on Alex, who was stretched out on a cot. He grinned when he saw me, his arm in an enormous cast, a bulbous bruise purpling above his eye.

"Wow," I breathed, "What happened to you?"

"Very funny."

I lingered at the end of the bed until Alex beckoned me with his free arm. "Come here."

I swallowed and stayed where I was. "Am I coming in to see my colleague or my friend?"

Alex sighed. "Lawson, you came this close"—he held his forefinger and thumb a millimeter apart—"to shooting me. We'd better be friends."

I felt my grin pushing up to my earlobes.

"How's Sampson doing?"

I nodded. "He's fine. He took quite a beating so he's not healing as quickly as normal, but he's doing good. And word is already spread through the Underworld about Dixon and about Sampson coming back."

"Wow. That was fast." Alex shifted in his bed, his sheets falling down, exposing his naked chest.

I sucked in a shaky breath, but got a jolt of adrenaline, and tickled my fingers up Alex's chest. "It's too bad we're just friends and you're in a cast. . . ."

Alex's eyes flashed, his lips kicking up into that cocky half smile. "Oh yeah, why's that?"

I reached under the bed. "Because somebunny at San Francisco Memorial loves you." I planted the bunny-eared hat on his head and grinned.

Please turn the page for an exciting sneak peek of
Hannah Jayne's next Sophie Lawson novel
UNDER A SPELL
coming in August 2013 from Kensington Publishing!

"You want me to do what?"

In all my years as the only breathing employee at the Underworld Detection Agency, I've been asked to do a lot of things—hobgoblin slobbery, life-or-death, blood-and-flesh kind of things. But this? This took the cake.

Pete Sampson leaned back in his leather chair, and though I usually beamed with pride when he did that—as I had been instrumental in getting him reinstated as head of the UDA—this time, I couldn't. My stomach was a firm, black knot and heat surged through every inch of my body as he looked up at me expectantly.

"I really thought you would be excited to visit your old stomping grounds."

My knees went Jell-O wobbly then and I thumped back into Sampson's visitor's chair. I yanked a strand of hair out of my already-messy ponytail—my hair had been butchered by a neurotic hoarder not too long ago and was just starting to reach ponytail status—and wrapped it around my finger until the tip turned white.

"Excited? To return to the source of my deepest angst,

my inner-turmoil—to the brick walls that can only be described as a fiery, brimstony hell?"

Sampson cocked an eyebrow. "It's just high school, Sophie."

"Exactly."

Most people would say that high school is the most traumatic time in their lives—myself included. And since in the last few years I'd been shot at, stabbed, hung by my ankles, almost eaten, and sexually harassed by an odoriferous troll, *most traumatic* took on a whole new significance.

"Isn't there anything else we can do? Anything I can do? And I'm talking human sacrifice, demon sacrifice, total surrender of my Baskin Robbins punch card."

"Sophie," Sampson started.

"Wait." I held up a hand. "Are we sure we have to go in at all? And why me, specifically? I mean"—I rifled through my purse and pulled out a wrinkled business card—"it's been a while since you've been back at the Agency, Sampson. See?" I slid the card across the desk to him. "It says right there: *Sophie Lawson, Fallen Angels Division.*" I stabbed at my name on the card as though that would somehow give my title more emphasis. "Does this case have anything to do with fallen angels? Because if not, I'm sure there are other UDA employees who would be excellent in this investigation. And then I would be able to really focus on my current position."

Granted, my position more often than not found me pinning a big baddie to a corkboard or locked in a public restroom sans clothes, but still.

Sampson stacked my business card on top of a manila file folder and pressed the whole package toward me.

"You should go in because you know the high school."

"I'll draw you a map." I narrowed my eyes, challenging.

"And because everyone else around here—" Sampson

gestured to the open office and I refused to look, knowing that I would be staring into the cold, flat eyes of the undead—and the occasional unhelpful centaur. "Well, everyone else would have trouble passing. Besides, it's not like you're going in alone."

"I'm not worried about that. And hey, I'm flattered, but there really is no way I'm going to pass as a student."

Though I'm only five-three (if I fudge it, stand on a phone book and stretch), often wear my fire-engine red hair in two sloppy braids, and have, much to my best friend's chagrin, been known to wear SpongeBob SquarePants pajama bottoms out to walk the dog, it had been a long time since anyone mistook me for anything more than a fashionably misguided adult.

"You're not going in as a student. You're going in as a teacher. A substitute."

I felt as though all the blood in my body had drained out onto the brand-new industrial grade carpet. Because the only thing worse than being a high school student is being a high school substitute teacher.

My left eye started to twitch. "A substitute teacher?"

My mind flooded with thumbtacks on desk chairs and Saran Wrap over the toilets in the teacher's lounge. Suddenly, I longed for my cozy Underworld Detection Agency job, where no one touched my wedged-between-two-blood-bags bologna sandwich and a bitchy band of ill-tempered pixies roamed the halls.

"A substitute teacher," I repeated, "who saves the world?"

Sampson's shrug was one of those "hey, pal, take one for the team" kind of shrugs and I felt anger simmering in my gut.

"You can 'teach'"—he made air quotes that made me nauseous—"any class you'd like. Provided it's in the approved curriculum. And not already assigned."

I felt my lip curl into an annoyed snarl when Sampson

shot me a sparkly-eyed smile as if being given the choice to teach freshman algebra or senior anatomy was a tremendous perk.

"If this high school isn't about to slide into the depths of hell or in the process of being overrun by an army of undead mean girls, I'm going to need a raise. A significant one," I said, my voice low. "And a vacation."

Sampson nodded, but didn't say anything.

"So," I said, my eyebrows raised.

"Do you remember last year when a body was found on the Mercy High campus?" Sampson asked.

My tongue went heavy in my mouth. Though I was well-used to the walking undead and the newly staked, the death of a young kid—a breather who would stay dead—made my skin prick painfully. I nodded.

"That's what this is about?

Sampson didn't answer me.

"Her name was Elizabeth Thompson, right?"

It had been all over the papers: a local student mysteriously vanishing from an exclusive—and, before that day, safe—high school campus. A week later, her body had been discovered dumped near Fort Cronkhite, an old military installation on the Marin side of the Golden Gate Bridge. Though the story was told and retold—in the *Chronicle*, the *Guardian*—and the Mercy High School campus was overrun with reporters for the better part of a semester, there weren't a lot of details in the case. Or at least not a lot were leaked to the press.

"That murder was never solved," Sampson said, as he slid the file folder over to me.

"Didn't someone confess? Some guy in jail? He was a tweaker; said something about trying to sacrifice her." The thought shot white-hot heat down my spine, but I tried my best to push past it. "I still don't have to see what this has to do with the high school. Or with me having to go into it. I followed the case pretty closely"—I was somewhat of a Court TV or pretty much anything-TV junkie—"and I don't remember any tie-back. I mean, the girl was found in Marin."

"She was dumped in one of the tunnels at Battery Townsley."

I shuddered. "People go through there all the time."

"Her killer obviously wasn't concerned about keeping Elizabeth secret."

I shook my head. "I still don't understand what this has to do with us—with the Underworld. Everything about it screams human."

Sampson gestured to the folders and I swallowed slowly, then looked down at them. Directly in front of me was a black-and-white photo of a smiling teenager—all perfect teeth and glossy hair—and it made my stomach roil even more. My high school picture was braces doing their darnedest to hold back a mouthful of Chiclet teeth and hair that shot straight out, prompting my classmates to announce that my styling tools were a fork and an electrical socket. I yanked my hand back when I realized I was subconsciously patting my semi-smoothed hair.

"What? The prom queen—" I stopped and sucked in a sharp breath when my eyes caught the headline plastered over the photo: MERCY HIGH STUDENT MISSING.

I scanned quickly.

Mercy High School student Alyssa Rand disappeared Monday afternoon. Erica Rand, Alyssa's mother, said that she last saw her daughter when she boarded the number 57 bus for Mercy as she always did; teachers confirmed that Alyssa attended her classes

through lunch period, but did not show up
for afternoon classes. Police are taking student
statements and a conservative approach, unsure
yet whether to classify Alyssa as a runaway
or an abductee.

I looked up, frowning. "I don't understand. I mean, it's
horrible, but we don't even know if she's really missing."

"She is, Sophie."

Sampson pressed his lips together and sighed, his
shoulders falling in that way that let me know that he wasn't
telling me everything. "There has been talk of a coven on
campus."

Relief washed over me and I sort of chuckled. "Sampson, every high school has a coven on campus! It's called
disgruntled teenage girls with black dye jobs and too much
angst-y time on their hands pretending to read tea leaves
and shoot you the evil eye." I waved the article in my hand.
"I don't see how one has to do with the other."

"When Elizabeth Thompson was found last year, she
was in the center of a chalked pentagram. Black candles at
the points."

I licked my suddenly dry lips. "They didn't mention that
in the paper or on the news." There was a beat of silence in
which Sampson held my eye; finally, I rolled mine with a
soft, snorting laugh. "Wait—they think it was witchcraft?
Have you seen *The Craft*? *Teen Witch*? That's Freak Out
Your Parents With Wicca 101."

"She had an incantation carved into her flesh."

I blinked. "Carved?"

"I consulted both Kale and Lorraine."

I sucked in a breath, willing Sampson to stop talking.
Kale and Lorraine are the Underworld Detection Agency's
resident witches. Kale was recently run over by a car but

spent her down time controlling the elements, and Lorraine was the most powerful Gestalt witch the Green Order had seen in decades. She was also a top Tupperware saleslady and if anyone knew a true incantation—or, for Lorraine, how to burp a lid—it was these ladies.

"They both confirmed that the incantation was legitimate. Elizabeth Thompson's killer was summoning a demon—and not a good one."

"Oh." The word came out small and hollow, dying in the cavernous room.

"As I mentioned, Elizabeth's body was found seven days after she went missing. It was obvious that her attacker wanted—or needed—her to be found on that day."

"I don't understand. How do you—why—how do they know that?"

"According to the police report, an anonymous call came in at 7:07 that morning."

"Seven-oh-seven on the seventh day?"

"Of the seventh month."

I frowned, resting my chin in my hands. "Maybe her killer is just OCD, did anyone explore that angle?"

I knew the significance of sevens—and I knew the demon Elizabeth's murderer was calling.

"Seven is divine. Seven-seven-seven is—"

"Satan." The word took up all the space in the room and I found it hard to breathe.

Everyone knows 6-6-6 as the devil's "call" sign—or they think they do. And while it does have true significance—mostly in movies, fiction, and speed metal songs—it is more like a pop-culture high-five to the Prince of Darkness. The trio of sevens is the summoner.

My heart was throbbing in my throat. I knew the answer, but still had to ask. "Do they think the other girl—"

"Alyssa."

"Alyssa, do they think she—that she may have been abducted by the same person?"

Sampson's hulking silence was answer enough.

Something tightened in my chest, and Sampson, his enormous cherrywood desk and his entire office seemed to spin, then fish-eye in front of me. I gripped the sides of my chair and steadied myself.

"We want you to go into Mercy and see what you can find out about this so-called coven."

"Are they even rela—"

Sampson held up a hand, effectively silencing me. "The girls in the coven were absent from class the day that Alyssa Rand went missing." He eyed me now and swallowed hard. "They were also absent the day Elizabeth Thompson's body was found. The PD's notes say that these girls were cited for bullying Elizabeth."

A memory wedged in my mind and I was fifteen again, awkward, terrorized, cornered in a Mercy High bathroom by a selection of mean girls with Aqua Net hair and slouchy socks.

"How long has Alyssa been missing?"

"Forty-eight hours," said Sampson.

"So we only have five days," I said, licking my lips. "We should get to work."

the corner of his eye. I knew what he was thinking and it made my stomach burn.

Once the chief had left, Alex came toward me. "Is she ready?"

N. Torres nodded and I bristled.

"*She* can speak for herself."

Alex went on, unaffected. "Great. Are you ready?"

"Let's go," I said, brushing off the back of my pants. We took a few steps. "So, what's the official thought on the attacker?"

"There isn't one yet. Once everything gets processed, we'll have a better idea."

"Okay," I tried, "what's the unofficial thought?"

Alex swung his head and blew out a long breath. "I thought that one of these days I'd walk into a crime scene that wouldn't surprise me. Guess today wasn't that day."

I sighed. "I'll say."

We walked the rest of the way up the bluff in silence. I fell behind and trailed Alex until we reached the crest. "Geez," he muttered. "Doesn't anyone work anymore?"

I followed his gaze to the looky-loos being herded back by the police and their ineffectual metal fencing. The crowd size had at least doubled while we'd been checking out the bodies, and a steady stream of cars was clogging the street and the mouth of the parking lot.

I opened my mouth to respond but froze dead when the girl at the very front of the crowd caught my eye. Her long, dark hair was impossibly straight and glossy, barely rustled by the wind. She stood still, her back ramrod straight, her knuckles white from her death grip on the metal top of the fence. Everything about her said she was ready to jump, to fight, that at the slightest provocation this woman would snap. Everything about her was on high alert.

"Feng," I whispered.

Feng turned as though she'd heard me and her razor-sharp gaze split me in half. There was fire in her eyes and a determined angle to her mouth.

"Did you say something, Lawson?"

"Uh—" I stumbled. "Nah. Nothing." I pulled open the car door and slid into the warm cab; Alex did the same. "I just think I know someone in the crowd."

Alex dipped his key in the ignition and the car roared to life. "Demon or breather?"

I raised my eyebrows. "Nice with the lingo. She's a breather." I gestured toward Feng with my chin. "Right there. Up front. She's Chinese with the long hair."

Alex shook his head appraisingly. "She's pretty."

I got a weird stab of jealously but shrugged it off. "She's an assassin."

Alex clicked the engine off and he turned in his seat. "An assassin?"

I nodded, my eyes still on Feng, who had lost interest in me and was staring back toward the crime scene. She looked incredibly calm and statuesque among the other onlookers; most were shuffling, moving, jockeying for a better view. But Feng stood still, her eyes focused as if she could see something no one else in the crowd could.

I swallowed and faced Alex. "She hunts werewolves. Her family makes silver bullets and is responsible for slaughtering pretty much every wolf in San Francisco."

"So she's like a werewolf slayer?"

"Not like, *is*," I said morbidly. Alex seemed supremely unaffected by the disgust I felt when talking about the Du family's "work." "They work out of a deli in Chinatown."

"I wonder what she's doing all the way out here. And, you know, *here*."

I shrugged and Alex went for the ignition again and then stopped. He looked at me and the flick of the muscle in his chin made my heart sink. I knew that flick. It was the "I'm not letting this go" flick. "Why do you think a werewolf hunter would come out to a crime scene?"

I crossed my arms in front of my chest, giving Alex a hard look. "I have no idea. Maybe she did it. Maybe she wanted something else to hunt since the family business is going through a bit of a dry spell."

"You mean because they killed all the werewolves in town?"

I didn't say anything, but Alex still didn't start the car, still didn't break his gaze. "Are there any new werewolves in town, Lawson?"

I shook my head. "Haven't processed any in I don't know how long."

I saw Alex's Adam's apple bob as he swallowed slowly. "How about a werewolf who isn't new in town?"

A wire of heat snaked up the back of my neck. I stared out the windshield and focused on the line of trees edging the scene in front of me. "What are you talking about? And can we get going? I have to get back to work." I checked my wrist bone, hoping Alex wouldn't notice that I wasn't wearing a watch. Or possibly hoping that he *would* notice and change the subject. Instead, I felt his hand on my shoulder, his fingers warm on my cool flesh. Unwillingly, I turned to face Alex, to look into those earnest cobalt eyes. Eyes that a girl could fall into.

He is an angel. . . .

"Is he back, Lawson? Is Pete Sampson back in San Francisco?"

I looked out the window, doing my best to focus on a crushed Starbuck's cup in the parking space next to ours. I knew Alex could read minds. I also knew that he rarely did it to me, likely because the few times he did, my mind was full of him, wearing nothing but coconut oil and a cocktail umbrella. But I couldn't afford for him to do it now.

"I'm not going to read your mind, Lawson."

I bristled in an attempt to hide my fear. "Then how did you know what I was thinking?"

"Because I know you."

My heart throbbed, caught between wanting to tell Alex everything and wanting to protect Sampson.

"And I guess I'm just supposed to trust your angelic promises," I said, arms crossed in front of my chest.

Alex looked away. "I couldn't even if I wanted to."

"What? What are you talking about? You did it before." Heat rose to my cheeks, remembering his slick grin after the coconut oil thing.

"Something's changed now. Something's different."

I was genuinely curious. "What's different?"

His shoulders rose. "I don't know." He sighed, turning to me, and the look in his eyes truly wounded me. "I wish I did."

I felt the need to confess to everything I've ever done that may have hurt him, but he went on. "I tried to reach you when I was gone, and all I got was static."

"You tried to reach me?" It was a mere whisper, the words sticking in my throat. Tears stung at my eyes. *He had reached out. He had tried . . .*

Sampson. Focus. I let a little niggle of anger boil up, reminding myself that Alex wasn't trying to reach me: he was trying to read my mind. And a telephone was readily available and a hell of a lot more reliable than the "loving" mind dip.

I broke his gaze, seeing the tip of his police badge winking on his belt. "No, Alex," I said, shaking my head. "Pete Sampson is not back in San Francisco."

Alex started the car and I tried to quash down the guilt that welled up inside me.